Also by Lynnette Austin

MAGNOLIA BRIDES

The Best Laid Wedding Plans

Every Bride Has Her Day

Picture Perfect Wedding

must
love
babies

LYNNETTE
AUSTIN

sourcebooks
casablanca

Published by Sourcebooks Casablanca, an imprint of Sourcebooks, Inc.
P.O. Box 4410, Naperville, Illinois 60567-4410
(630) 961-3900
Fax: (630) 961-2168
sourcebooks.com

Printed and bound in the United States of America.
OPM 10 9 8 7 6 5 4 3 2 1

Where there is great love,
there are always miracles.

—Willa Cather

Chapter 1

IF MOLLY STILES HAD BEEN A VINTAGE CAR, BRANT WYLDER would have known exactly what to do with her. She wasn't, and he didn't.

But a man could look.

"Hey, you still with us?" his elder brother, Tucker, asked.

"Yeah." Brant tugged at the annoying bow tie.

"Good, because we have a job to do, and so do you," Tucker said.

"Understood." Brant met his brother's gaze. "Chill. This isn't one of your Marine reconnaissance missions."

"No, it's not. Which means no sniper's waiting to take a potshot at you, so stop whining."

"I'm not whining," he groused. "This wedding's a waste of time. I'd rather go with you to pick up that car."

"We've got it covered." His younger brother, Gaven, slipped into the rental car. "You'll check out those places we spotted yesterday, right? See if one of them will work for us?"

"Absolutely." His answer was automatic, his attention on the petite bridesmaid he'd escorted down the aisle. The woman was so drop-dead gorgeous, she made his palms sweat.

"It's important," Tucker reminded him.

"Yep." Brant eyed his watch. "That plane's gonna leave with or without you two."

Gaven started the car's engine.

"Text me pictures of that Vette."

"Will do."

Riding shotgun, Tucker rested a tattooed arm on his open window. "Sure glad it's dark. Anybody sees us in this four-door, plain-vanilla, sorry excuse for a car, our reputation's shot."

Brant laughed. "Drive safe." He tapped the car's roof, then took several steps back as it headed down the winding, oak-lined drive.

The taillights disappeared, and he was alone.

Well, as alone as he could be with a hundred and some other people.

Brant turned back to the wedding reception. Because the temperature was in the balmy midsixties, unusual for January even here in Georgia's Low Country, Magnolia House's massive front door stood open. Light, conversation, and laughter spilled onto the restored antebellum home's front porch.

Resigned to another hour or so of playing nice, Brant moved back inside.

At the bar, he ordered a club soda with a twist of lime and, popping cashews, chatted with a friend of the groom. All the while, he kept the brunette front and center on his radar.

She threaded her way through the small clusters of guests, paused to speak to several, then plucked a grilled shrimp kebab and a napkin from a passing waiter's tray. Raising the appetizer to her Kewpie-doll lips, she headed outside. Alone.

Brant set his nearly untouched drink on the bar and nodded to his new pal. "Nice talking to you, Will. You decide you want us to do something with that '72 Chevy Chevelle, give me a call."

Casually, he crossed the room and stepped into the night. Molly had wandered to the edge of the large front yard and stood in a pool of moonlight. The two of them had bumped into each other twice now, and she stirred up feelings in him—feelings he had no time for, yet itched to explore.

For such a petite thing, the lady had curves. Shiny, coffee-colored hair curled halfway down her back, and his fingers practically begged to mess it up. She smelled sexy as sin on a dark night and all but made a guy drool. Her pale-pink, bee-stung lips cried out to be kissed... but instinct warned him Molly could be dangerous. Very dangerous.

Brant ran a finger under his bow tie again and swore beneath his breath.

He felt restless. The sleepy little Low Country town oozed Southern charm. Its brick sidewalks might be buckled in places, but pride showed in the well-maintained storefronts. The American flag flew high and proud over the big stone courthouse at the end of Main, and in warmer weather, ferns and colorful flowers hung from the streetlights and shops.

Last night, he'd driven through town a little after eight. It had been quiet, buttoned-down, and locked up tight. The carpet rolled up early in Misty Bottoms, Georgia. He could live with that.

Good thing, because if things worked out right, he'd be spending a lot more time here. But right now? Instead of hanging around Magnolia House in this monkey suit, he could be flying off to Texas with his brothers or at their garage in Tennessee in his old jeans, replacing a clutch in the '48 Chevy he and his brothers were restoring. Heck, for what the daddy of today's bride had shelled out, Brant figured he could rescue a whole fleet of cars.

Still, if a person was bound and determined to tie the knot, they could do a lot worse than Magnolia House. Jenni Beth Beaumont—make that Jenni Beth Bryson now—had done one heck of a job bringing the grand old lady back to life, turning her into Magnolia Brides, a popular wedding destination. Her friend Tansy, who ran Sweet Dreams, and Cricket, owner of the Enchanted Florist, took care of the cakes and flowers, respectively. And the brunette? She ran the new bridal boutique in town. The women had done themselves proud.

Music drifted on the soft night air and entwined with the scent of roses and jasmine. Muted voices rose and fell.

He slipped a hand into the pocket of his tux pants and, feet crossed, leaned against one of the massive columns. In the morning, he'd check out a couple of possibilities he and his brothers had earmarked for Wylder Rides's new location. Then he'd hit the road to Tennessee to put out a couple fires at their shop. Life had been bumpy lately, but at this moment, it was pretty darn good.

A full moon added its magic to the star-filled Southern sky. As he picked out several constellations, he imagined even the seated queen, Cassiopeia, danced tonight with Orion, the hunter. No doubt every single woman here had hearts, flowers, and wedding rings on the brain. It tended to make a single man nervous.

A feeling of déjà vu stole over him. Several months ago, he'd stood right here while his pal Troy bit the dust.

His friends were disappearing as fast as sweet tea on a hot summer's day into the matrimonial abyss. Marriage wasn't in the cards for Brant. He and his brothers had a lot riding on their business, and he needed to concentrate on that. But tonight, while his brothers headed to Texas to inspect a barn find '53 Corvette that Wylder Rides had been commissioned to restore, he'd see if he could sweet-talk himself into a dance or two with sexy-as-all-get-out Molly.

At his previous wedding here, she'd tried her darnedest to escape the rush of single women desperate to nab the bridal bouquet. When the flowers had literally hit her on the forehead, she'd tried to pawn the bouquet off to anyone close. Could she be the one female not in a hurry to marry? Now, though, she stood beneath a magnolia tree, her face tipped to catch the moonlight. The breath caught in his throat, and for one fanciful second, Brant imagined a mythical princess or fairy.

He shook his head. The woman was real, and he wanted a dance, wanted to hold her in his arms. A little flirting? Harmless.

Stepping out of the shadows, he made his way to her.

"Beautiful night, huh?"

"Perfect." Slowly, she turned, a smile on her face.

"How about a dance?" Holding out a hand, he tipped his head toward the temporary dance floor in the backyard. "What do you say?"

She hesitated.

"I'm not asking for a lifelong commitment, sugar. Just a single dance under the stars."

Still, she paused.

"Oh, come on. The night's made for dancing."

"It is, isn't it?"

He caught her hand in his, amazed at its softness against his work-roughened one. "Let's give it a whirl. In the interest of full disclosure, I'm not the world's greatest dancer, but you shouldn't lose any toes." He glanced at her sequined stilettos, showcased by her cocktail-length dress. "Don't know how you even walk in those, let alone put on the miles you do, but I have to say that all mankind is grateful."

Smiling, Molly peeked at her shoes. "They're awesome, aren't they?"

He nodded. "You can dance in them?"

"I could run a marathon in these."

"Okay, then." The moon shone through Spanish moss that dripped from the live oaks, forming a lacy pattern on the dewy grass.

Kelly Clarkson's "A Moment Like This" played over the sound system. Reaching the dance floor, Brant slid an arm around her waist and drew her in, breathed in her scent. He fingered the fabric of Molly's dress. "I'm surprised the bride let you wear this."

"Why?"

"Most brides don't want to be upstaged on their wedding day."

She made a dismissive sound.

"You look spectacular." Brant's brow furrowed. "Gotta say, though, purple's an unusual color for a bridesmaid's dress."

"Kathy wanted bold. And I'll have you know," she said, amusement in her voice, "this isn't purple. It's plum passion, and it's all the rage right now."

"Can't argue with the expert."

"Your brothers left already?"

"Yep, taking care of business." Brant swung her out and brought her back in one smooth motion, felt her quick laugh in the pit of his stomach. The music slowed when the band segued into John Legend's "All of Me," and he drew her close.

Molly fit perfectly in his arms. She lived in Georgia and he in Tennessee, and that made her safe. And if the plans he and his brothers were working on panned out? Still nothing to worry about, he decided, since she lived in Savannah. When she rested her head against his chest, he wondered if she could hear the rapid thump of his heart. Ms. Molly was hot, hot, hot.

His hand slid a little lower, and without missing a beat, she relocated it to her waist.

He threw her a devilish grin. "I half figured you'd make a run for it before the bouquet toss tonight."

A quick blush of embarrassment gave way to a twinkle in her eyes. "You, sir, are no gentleman."

"Nope, can't say that I am." He inhaled deeply. Molly smelled of a midnight garden with just a touch of naughty. His body responded, and he willed himself to think about something else. "How's the city?"

"Savannah?" She shrugged. "I live in Misty Bottoms now. I opened a bridal boutique. Today's bride was my first." She grinned, dimples creasing her cheeks. "Kathy already had a dress but she lost a lot of weight this past year and wanted something a little more figure flattering. So she came to me."

The dance ended, and he reluctantly released Molly. "I'm driving back to Tennessee tomorrow."

"Speaking of driving, thanks for taxiing the last of the

rehearsal dinner's partiers home last night. I heard they celebrated pretty hard at Duffy's."

"No problem."

"I need to stop at my car before I go back inside. I left the little silver heart I attach to the bridal gown's garment bag in my glove box."

Brant walked beside her in the soft night air, a hand at her elbow, while the band played Blake Shelton's "God Gave Me You."

"I'm good, Brant, if you need to leave."

"You sure? It's pretty dark. No telling what mystical creatures might be stirring." He lowered his head. "Before we call it a night, I'd love to see the rose garden our friend Cole salvaged."

"What a mess, but after a lot of hard work it's incredible again."

The scent of roses surrounding them, they strolled through the yard. In the silver light of the moon, the flowers glowed and took on an almost magical, fairy-tale illusion. The house shimmered and welcomed, like the true Southern lady she was. Interlacing his fingers with Molly's, peace enveloped Brant.

They wandered across the expanse of lawn and through the blooms in comfortable silence.

From the parking area, he heard the sound of engines starting, of tires crunching on the long drive. "Looks like it's about time for lights-out. We'd better head back so you can finish up."

A slight breeze caused Molly to shiver, and happy for the excuse, Brant wrapped an arm around her and pulled her a little closer, surprised when she didn't pull away.

Reaching her yellow-and-white Mini Countryman, he made to open her door, then changed his mind, leaned in and gave her a quick kiss, one that should have been impersonal. Friendly. Instead, fire shot through him.

He pulled back, unsure whether he should be relieved or horrified that the expression on her face mirrored his own stampeding feelings. Clearing his throat, he said, "I'm taking care of a few loose ends in the morning, then heading back to Tennessee. And I already said that, didn't I?"

"Yes, you did. The kiss was nice, thanks, but you don't need to worry. I won't show up naked at your hotel door."

His breath caught.

She grinned, and he understood she knew exactly the effect she was having on him.

"I—" His phone vibrated. "Whoops. Sorry, but I'd better take this. My brothers probably forgot something. Organization isn't their strong suit. If you'll excuse me."

"Sure."

"Hello? Dad?" As he spoke, he made his way to a gnarly old oak. His father's voice was gruff, almost as if he'd been crying. Panic grabbed Brant by the throat. "What's wrong? Is it Mom?"

"No, Son, it's your sister."

"Lainey?" An ominous silence settled in. He glanced toward Molly and lowered his voice. "Talk to me, Dad." He heard the sigh, all but felt his father's despair.

"Lainey's been in a car accident. A serious one."

"Where is she?"

"Savannah. You still in Misty Bottoms?"

"Yeah, but I'm heading to Savannah as we speak."

Brant sprinted across the lawn and slid behind the wheel of his car, switching the call to Bluetooth.

"Where are your brothers?"

"On a flight to Texas to pick up a car we're restoring." His headlights swept over Molly, but he couldn't stop. Couldn't think about her now. "How bad is Lainey hurt?"

"The cop I talked to didn't have many details. The doctor's supposed to call later, but I'd feel a hell of a lot better with you there."

"I couldn't agree more." Brant turned onto the main highway. "Was anyone else injured?"

After the slightest hesitation, his dad said, "No."

"Did somebody run into her? Force her off the road?"

Another tremulous sigh filled the line. "A drunk driver caused the accident."

"Saturday night." Brant slammed his hand against the steering wheel. "I should have known. I hope the SOB in the other car wasn't hurt too badly, because I want the pleasure of wringing his neck myself."

"Son, there was no other car involved. No other driver."

"But you said—" His stomach pitched and a sour taste filled his mouth.

"Lainey's blood-alcohol level was almost twice the legal limit."

Brant swore. His sister had derailed in high school and fallen into the bottle. "She's been sober for five years, Dad."

"She has. Or so we thought."

His father sounded wearier and older than he ever had, and Brant found himself cursing whatever had made Lainey take that first drink—the first tonight and the first all those years ago.

"Even if your mom could fly, Son, it'd be tomorrow before we could get there. Lainey needs someone now, and I can't leave your mother."

"No, you can't." Since his warm, fun-loving mother had had a stroke, Dad had his hands full as her caregiver.

His heart thundering, Brant gripped the steering wheel. "Where's Jax? Did Lainey have the baby with her?"

"No. She left him with a friend."

"Thank God!"

His dad cleared his throat again. "That's the rest of the problem, though. When the friend caught wind of what happened, she dropped Jax off at the hospital. Said she had to work, and he wasn't her responsibility."

"Nice friend."

"Yeah, and now somebody needs to get him."

"Get the baby?" Sweat trickled down Brant's spine as he signaled and passed a car moving slower than a bus full of tourists on Nashville's Music Row.

"A policewoman who worked the accident scene was still at the hospital when Lainey's friend showed up. She's with Jax now, but if somebody doesn't come for him, they'll place my grandson in temporary foster care."

"Foster care?" Brant's fingers tunneled through his hair. "Jax is only, what, eight or nine months old?"

"Seven."

Geez! Seven? Dread clawed through Brant's brain and worked its way to the tips of his toes.

"Brant, your mother's calling for me. I have to go. Keep in touch, will ya?"

"But—"

"Gotta go. You'll do fine, Son. We can always count on you."

A heavy weight settled over Brant. "Yeah."

"Drive carefully, you hear? Don't need both of you in the ER."

"I will, and I'll call as soon as I know anything. Give Mom a kiss for me."

He clicked off and glanced in the rearview mirror, flinching at the wild expression in his eyes. Hadn't he less than an hour ago tempted fate by thinking that, despite a few bumps, life right now was good? Had he jinxed them?

"Come on, Lainey," he whispered. "Be strong. Whatever's going on in your life, we'll sort it out."

His Camaro ate up the miles while questions piled up in his head. The full moon had been romantic back in the rose garden, but on this abandoned stretch of road, it decided to play hide-and-seek behind the cloud cover. The car's headlamps cut through the darkness, reminding him exactly how alone he was.

A rush of emotions filled him—anger, helplessness, frustration. And overlying everything? An aching layer of sadness.

When Chris Young came on the radio singing "I'm Comin' Over," a sliver of regret slipped in as Brant thought of the pretty brunette in the plum-passion dress. A second helping of those perfect lips would have been nice.

He hadn't said goodbye, hadn't even given her an explanation. Probably better that way. No expectations.

Fog rolled in, and he slowed a bit. With Misty Bottoms hugging the river, no doubt the people here dealt with it often. He ran his wipers to rid his windshield of the light mist.

Then his mind turned back to his sister. What would he find at the hospital?

Chapter 2

MOLLY STOOD BESIDE HER CAR LONG AFTER THE NIGHT swallowed Brant's taillights. Then, the silver charm clutched tightly in her fist, she made her way back inside, stopping to hug Tansy. "That cake was outstanding!"

"Thanks." Tansy tipped her head. "Everything okay?"

"Yeah." She rolled her eyes. "Tired. That's all."

It wasn't her place to say anything about Brant's call. At least not until she knew more—which would probably be never, since she doubted she'd see him again. She'd overheard enough to understand he had a problem and could only hope it wasn't too serious. Leaving the kitchen, she closed her eyes and whispered a little prayer that everything would be okay.

The tulle and lace dream-come-true creation hung in the bridal suite. Molly took one last look at the fairy-tale wedding dress, its crystals sparkling in the light from the chandelier. Gently, she swaddled the gown in the garment bag, readying it for the trip home with Kathy's mother. She added the charm, and her job was done.

Someday she'd have her own fairy tale. But not now.

Walking down the sweeping staircase, she slowed. No Brant Wylder waited at the bottom or lounged on the porch.

Her mind flashed back to the moment he'd answered his phone. Disbelief and horror, along with a sense of urgency, had radiated from him. Something had upset the balance in his world. Her first guess might have been that it was a business problem, but his expression spoke of something more personal. She'd checked her phone, but there were no reports of plane accidents, so his brothers should be okay.

The call had taken the magic out of the evening, and she'd been sorry when Brant disappeared into the night without so much as a goodbye. Almost any man looked good in a tux, but him? Geez Louise, the man was gorgeous. Totally, absolutely, blazing-inferno gorgeous. The stuff of dreams.

And she'd cut out her tongue before she shared that with Jenni Beth, Cricket, or Tansy, her friends who created these incredible weddings. The three of them were so gaga in love, they thought everyone else should be, too. If they caught so much as a whiff of the single shared kiss between her and Brant, they'd have her waltzing down the aisle with him.

True, his almost offhand kiss made every other one she'd ever experienced seem like amateur hour. If he put his heart into it? Complete meltdown. However, despite what her friends would say, that didn't hint at a wedding in her near future.

Yeah, weddings and romance were her business. Her *business*. She could not, would not, be distracted. That Little White Dress was her life right now; Brant wasn't. He was here today, gone tomorrow—or rather tonight— and she'd better darned well remember that. Besides, Wylder had already lied to her. Despite his disclaimer, the man definitely knew his way around the dance floor.

A big sigh escaped as she headed for the pantry, where she'd left her purse. She'd mapped out her life years ago and penciled in a wedding after her business had taken off. Of course, she still needed to find Mr. Right.

Others might waltz willy-nilly through their lives. Not her. She'd set a course and drawn a timetable. For the next three years, she'd concentrate on her business.

She'd stumbled off course once. Big mistake. Huge mistake! She'd met Keith and had fallen hard. Absolutely certain he loved her, she'd convinced herself they'd be together forever. But Keith had little by little grown distant. She'd found out why when he confessed to sleeping with the office worker in the cubicle next to his.

She'd cried herself to sleep that night…and the next. The following day, she packed up anything and everything in her apartment that reminded her of him and tossed the lot out with the garbage. Then she took a good, long, hot shower and hit Reset. Lesson learned—as if her mom and dad hadn't been enough.

"Jenni Beth, unless you need me, I'm out of here."

"We're good, Mol." Jenni Beth peeked around the corner, two candlesticks in hand. "Thanks for all your help. Go home and put up your feet. Or catch some sleep."

"I plan to do both."

"I saw you and the Wylder brother on the dance floor." Jenni Beth arched a brow. "You looked pretty cozy."

Molly wagged a finger at her. "No, you don't. Just because you're in love, you don't get to wish it on everybody else."

Jenni Beth wrapped an arm around her friend's waist. "Not all men are like Keith—or your dad."

"I know that. I really do. But I have a lot to take care of before I settle into a relationship."

Jenni Beth sighed. "Your list again? I wish you'd burn that."

"Not going to happen."

"Why'd Brant tear out of here like the hounds of hell were after him?"

"I don't know. He got a phone call and left."

"Hmm."

"Hmm is right. 'Night."

"Wait." Jenni Beth set the candlesticks on the buffet. "Are you okay?"

"Sure."

"Something's taken the sparkle out of your eyes. Did Brant do something? Say something to upset you? Is that why he left so quickly?"

"No!"

"You know what?" Jenni Beth looked toward the doorway where Cricket and Tansy stood. "We've worked our butts off today. What do you say we take a minute to celebrate?"

Tansy held up a bottle of champagne.

Cricket nabbed four glasses, and before Molly could say a word, she found herself seated at the big island in the Beaumonts' kitchen.

After a toast to Magnolia Brides and another to themselves, Jenni Beth reached out for Molly's hand. "So fess up, pal. What's wrong?"

Molly folded her hands. What could she say? That if Brant Wylder lived close, he could become a major distraction? Worse, that she *wished* he lived next door?

That wouldn't do.

"It's nothing. Really. It's just—well, let me preface this by saying I'm so happy for y'all. Jenni Beth, you and Cole had a rocky start, but now? Newlyweds. Tansy, you and Beck got your second chance, and I don't know that I've ever seen two people so right for each other." She sipped her bubbly.

"And then there's you, Cricket." Molly grinned at Beck's eccentric cousin. "You moved back to Misty Bottoms to start a flower shop and fell in love with Sam."

Tansy's Caribbean-blue eyes narrowed. "Your point?"

"You all found love when you least expected, and that's wonderful. But it's not for me. Not yet, anyway." She shrugged. "Today's wedding kicked off a bunch of foolish what-ifs. Like the twenty-four-hour flu, though, it'll be gone in the mornin'."

After accepting a boxed piece of leftover wedding cake and a round of cheek kisses, Molly escaped. Tomorrow, she and the girls would gear up for their next wedding. At the end of Magnolia House's long driveway, she sang along with Kelsea Ballerini as she turned toward home, her thoughts returning to Brant and the dance they'd shared. To that should-have-been-innocent kiss. To the smolder and heat and wanting it left behind.

———

The gravel crunched beneath Molly's tires as she pulled into her parking space behind her shop. She'd forgotten to turn on a light when she left that morning, and her upstairs apartment looked dark and lonely. The newly repainted door creaked as she opened it, and she hustled up the stairs, dropping her purse on a small table before snapping on the lamp.

Bubbles, her cat, skidded around the corner to weave between her legs.

"Hello, sweetie." She twirled. "This is the first of my once-worn dresses for girls who can't afford one for the prom. I know I can talk other bridesmaids into donating theirs." Kneeling, she rubbed the old cat's head. "Every girl deserves her special night, and we can help with that, can't we?"

The cat meowed.

"Glad you agree, sweetheart."

Molly slid out of her shoes, wiggled her toes, and groaned at the sheer pleasure of bare feet. As much as she loved shoes, she also loved shucking them at the end of the day.

Reaching around, she unzipped her bridesmaid's dress. The plum-colored chiffon pooled around her feet. She caught a glimpse of herself in the mirror over the sofa, dressed in nothing but the pale-lavender lingerie she'd bought especially for today. An unashamed girlie girl, she moved to the bedroom in her sexy new undies to hang up the dress.

Belting her favorite silk robe, her thoughts returned to Brant. She'd noticed him earlier, propped casually against a porch column, watching her. When he asked for a dance and took her hand, she'd felt his calluses and understood he wasn't some pretty boy who lived off his trust fund. Brant worked for a living, and she liked that.

Then she'd practically stopped thinking as he'd pulled her close on the outside dance floor. Right there, under the stars, she'd all but melted into one big puddle. Brant practically smoldered, and he smelled every bit as good as he looked.

And the kiss…

Oh yeah, she'd wanted that second one. When she'd

felt an honest-to-gosh vibration, she assumed it was her body wakening after nearly a year's hiatus from all things male. Then he drew away to answer his phone, and that carefree, devil-may-care expression had disappeared.

Since she had no way of contacting him, she'd have to keep wondering what had happened.

Bubbles threaded her way between Molly's legs again. Reaching down, she picked up the cat and cuddled her, stroking the soft, white fur. She'd call Jenni Beth in the morning. Maybe she'd know how to get in touch.

Yep, and the fact she even considered doing that proved she was right to be wary of Brant. Bad idea. If she called Jenni Beth, her friend would start matchmaking. Maybe she could call Russell, one of the other grooms-men. He'd know how to get in touch with Brant—and he'd still be awake.

Before she could stop herself, she set Bubbles on the floor and made the call. She'd been right about Russell being awake. A whole group had moved the party to Duffy's Pub. Grabbing a notepad, she scribbled Brant's number, thanked Russell, and hung up. The second she dropped the pencil onto her nightstand, she fell back-ward onto her bed, an arm over her eyes. She couldn't phone Brant. Crumpling the paper, she tossed it into the trash.

Time for a refresher course. She stepped into her closet, pulled a baby-blue box from the top shelf, and carried it to her bed. Bubbles jumped up, padding to the center before dropping like a deadweight. Eyes unblink-ing, the cat seemed to ask, "What? I want to see what you're doing."

Molly dropped onto the bed's edge and, with a deep

breath, opened the box. She plucked out a dog-eared sheet of paper, her gaze shifting to a picture that stuck out of the pile. How had it survived her purge? She worked the photo out, and Keith Adair smiled up at her with those movie-star good looks that had blinded her to what lay beneath.

The photo joined the phone number in her waste-basket.

"There's a time and place for everything," she reminded herself, rubbing her temples. "Now is not the time to get sidetracked by a guy. Not even a good-looking one who can dance. One who has the most beautiful, intense green eyes I've ever seen…"

With a meow, Bubbles stretched out one paw to tap Molly's leg.

"I'm glad you agree." After plumping a pillow beneath her head, she sprawled on the bed and read aloud from the yellowed paper.

My To-Do List
By Molly Shea Stiles—Age Thirteen

1. Age 15—Find a better job than cleaning stinky Mrs. T's house
2. Age 16—Driver's license!
3. Age 17.5—Acceptance from University of Georgia
4. Age 18—Walk across the stage for my high school diploma
5. Age 22—Graduate from college!!
6. Age 23—Land a great job and an apartment of my own

7. Age 25—Accumulate lots of money in my savings account
8. Age 27—Open my own business
9. Ages 28–30—Pour my soul into the business. It'll be the best!
10. Age 30—Meet my future husband and say I do!
11. Age 32—My first baby, a little boy
12. Age 34—Give my son an adorable baby sister, even if he doesn't want one
13. Ages 35–52—Raise my children and send them off to a good college
14. Age 56—Sell my thriving business and retire
15. Age 57—Enjoy a second honeymoon in Hawaii
16. Age 62—Rock my first grandbaby to sleep

So far, goals one through eight had been checked off—right on time.

Just one short month ago, her emotions ricocheting between throw-up nervous and jump-up-and-down happy, she'd ended her lease on her small apartment in Savannah and made the move to Misty Bottoms.

Jenni Beth, Cricket, and Tansy had welcomed her into their destination wedding business, and her bridal boutique was doing far better than she'd expected. Besides today's wedding, That Little White Dress had already sold another wedding dress and five more bridesmaid gowns. On top of that, she had two appointments this week with future Magnolia brides.

For the next few years, she'd pour everything she had, everything she was, into her business. That Little White Dress would be the best wedding shop this side of the Mississippi!

She'd work at giving others their perfect wedding day, the beginning of their happily-ever-after. How many would actually have that, though? So much of what little girls had programmed into them from an early age turned out to be fantasy.

Thoughts of her mom and dad crowded in. Did she want to wrap her world around a man? Trust he would stay with her forever?

She had a good life; she should be content.

She looked again at numbers ten through sixteen. Yeah, everyone around her was pairing off, and yes, she was in the business of selling dreams. But was this list simply another way of buying into a false dream? Planning her entire life around something that wouldn't last?

Brant Wylder sure wouldn't, so if she was smart—and she was—she wouldn't give him another thought.

Chapter 3

OFFERING SILENT BUT PROFOUND THANKS TO THE GENIUS who'd invented navigation apps, Brant swerved into the hospital's parking lot.

With his heart racing, he loped through the ER's automatic doors. Hard vinyl chairs filled with the sick and injured greeted him, but a quick scan found no Lainey. No Jax.

A nurse, who reminded him way too much of Nurse Ratched, sat behind a window.

When she finally deigned to look up from her computer, he said, "My sister, Lainey Wylder, was brought in tonight. Car accident. Can you tell me how she is? Where she is?"

She opened a new screen on her computer. "Your name?"

"Brant Wylder."

"I'll need to see some ID, sir."

Fingers shaking, he reached into the inside pocket of his tux and withdrew his wallet. Flipping it open, he handed it to her.

"License only, please. If you'd take it out for me…"

"Oh sure, sure." He passed his ID. "How's Lainey?"

Holding up a wait-one-minute finger, she studied the license, looked back up, and gave Brant a thorough scan. "You're dressed a little better than most of our visitors."

"I was at a wedding in Misty Bottoms when my dad called."

"Magnolia House?"

He nodded. "My sister?"

"She's in stable but guarded condition, Mr. Wylder. I believe they're prepping her for surgery."

"Surgery?" His stomach clenched. "Can I see her?"

A younger woman dressed in scrubs walked through a set of double doors.

"Judy," Nurse Ratched said, "could you take Mr. Wylder back to see his sister?"

Judy threw Brant a sympathetic smile. "Follow me."

"Thanks."

He swung through the doors behind her. They moved past several curtained cubicles before she stopped and drew aside a privacy curtain. His baby sister lay unmoving, her face the same pale hue as the thin white sheet. Her eyes were closed, and a tangle of wires tethered her to beeping machines. Brant's stomach dropped to his toes.

Was she breathing?

Was he?

He took a step closer and, realizing his legs had turned to mush, white-knuckled the bed rail. "Lainey?"

Her eyes flickered open, then closed again.

Instinctively, he reached out and gently squeezed her fingers. "It's Brant, honey," he whispered. "I'm here."

She didn't respond, and he couldn't tell if she'd heard him or not, but he kept talking. Whether for her or himself, he wasn't sure.

"You're going to be fine, sweetheart. Everything will be okay. And don't fret about Jax. I've got him covered."

He prayed he did, that Jax was, indeed, here and okay.

The curtain parted, and a doctor stepped in.

Brant held out a hand. "Brant Wylder, Lainey's brother."

The doctor took his hand in a firm shake. "I'm Dr. Willis, Lainey's surgeon. Your sister's suffered some internal injuries along with a broken left arm. We're taking her to surgery." He studied Brant. "You're aware of the circumstances of her accident?"

"Only what my dad told me over the phone."

"There are a couple police officers down the hall who'll need to speak with you."

Brant nodded, his mouth Sahara-dry. "Could we—" He tipped his head, indicating the curtain.

The doctor drew it back, and they stepped outside.

His voice low, Brant asked, "My nephew? Dad said he wasn't involved in the accident."

"No, he's fine."

"Thank God! Where is he?"

"It's my understanding he's with the officers." A pair of orderlies entered the small area, and the doctor rattled off instructions. "I'm sorry, Mr. Wylder, but you'll need to leave now so we can take care of your sister."

Brant swept the curtain aside, leaned over Lainey, and kissed her forehead. "Everything will be okay, sugar," he whispered. "I love you, Lain. We all do."

Staring at her battered and bruised face, knowing what lay ahead for her, he'd have given anything in the world to take her place. But he couldn't. He'd never felt so helpless.

As they wheeled her out, he rubbed his tired eyes. His first order of business was to track down his nephew and speak with the police. Once Lainey recovered—and she would—she'd face legal problems. Maybe he could help with that. Not that he wanted her to skate scot-free. Part of her recovery would be confronting what she'd done. Still…

If only he knew why she'd been drinking, what had set her off.

"I wish you were here, Mom," he mumbled. "You always know what to do."

―⁕―

Halfway to the ER waiting room, a uniformed officer waited in the corridor, bouncing a crying baby in her arms. Another officer, looking stern, lounged against the wall. Seeing Brant, he straightened.

The look in his eyes had Brant's gut churning. Then his gaze swung back to the baby—his nephew. The one somebody had to take care of.

The one *he* had to take care of.

A moment of absolute and utter panic followed, a moment during which he fought the urge to bolt through the doors at the end of the hall and make a run for it. But he couldn't. This was Lainey's baby. The next generation of Wylders.

When Mom and Dad found out she was pregnant, the crap had really hit the fan. But the second they laid eyes on Jax, they'd fallen in love. Like one enormous Band-Aid, he'd healed the hurt.

When he'd turned two months old, Lainey had moved in with their aunt Flo in Florida. Now, although the circumstances flat-out stank, Brant couldn't wait to get his hands on the kid again. How he'd cope full-time with a baby scared the bejesus out of him, though. He'd enjoyed Jax when Lainey and the baby stayed with his folks, but the second he needed to be fed or changed, Brant had passed him on. Now? Nobody was in the field to catch the pass.

"You Brant Wylder?"

He nodded.

"I'm Officer Douglas, and this is Officer Blackburn. There's a strong resemblance between you and your sister."

"That's what people say."

"Sarah said you'd gone back to check on your sister, so I figured we'd catch you here, where we had a little more privacy."

"Sarah?"

"The nurse at the admitting desk."

"Ah. I didn't get her name."

Hoisting the baby to her chest, Officer Blackburn started pacing back and forth, patting his back and whispering to him. Brant's gaze followed them.

"Could I see some ID, Mr. Wylder?" the patrolman asked. "Gotta follow procedure."

"Sure." Brant pulled out his wallet yet again, flipped it to his driver's license, and held it up for the cop.

"Thanks."

"Why's Jax crying?"

"My guess is he's hungry. Blackburn was on her way to track down a bottle and some food when we heard you'd arrived."

Brant nodded.

"You don't have kids of your own, Mr. Wylder?"

"Me?" He pointed at his chest. "No. No wife, no kids."

"Well, seems that's changed. Temporarily, at least."

"Guess so." Brant wet his lips. "I haven't had much experience with babies."

"You'll learn fast."

Brant exhaled a long breath. "I sure hope so."

"The emergency card in your sister's wallet listed your dad's number first," Douglas said. "Seems he can't make it. Apparently, your mother has some serious health problems."

"Yeah, she had a stroke."

"You're second on the card, so tag, you're it," Douglas said.

Brant pinched the bridge of his nose and winced when another wail rent the air. Sounded like the kid was working up a good mad.

"This baby needs to be fed," Blackburn said.

Brant held up a finger and walked through the doors to the check-in window. "Sarah?"

"Yes?"

"Do you think we might get something to feed my nephew?" He placed his hands palms down on his tux jacket. "No baby food or formula with me. Did they bring anything from Lainey's car?"

"Actually, I think the friend had a diaper bag with her." She picked up the phone, spoke into it, and hung up. "It's back with your sister's things."

Officer Douglas had followed him. "I'll get it." He disappeared behind the double doors.

Brant looked at the female cop who stood beside him, compassion on her face.

"Can I hold him?"

"Sure." She carefully transferred the angry baby to Brant.

Instinctively, he cuddled Jax against his chest and rocked back and forth. The baby let out a shuddering sigh and snuggled closer, one little hand resting on Brant's chin. "Do you remember me? Hmm? I'm Uncle Brant, your favorite. Uncle Tucker and Uncle Gaven? Not important. No, they're not." He kissed the palm of the soft, little hand. "You lucked out tonight, kid. You got the handsome uncle. The undisputed genius of the family. Yes, you did."

The baby stopped crying and stared up at him with solemn eyes, tears clinging to his lashes.

Brant took the chubby fingers in his and raised them to his lips to give them a noisy kiss. Jax sent him a watery grin. "What are we gonna do, champ? Huh? I'm an okay uncle, but not much in the daddy department."

Officer Blackburn's smile disappeared, and her tone took on the timbre of a stern teacher. "Mr. Wylder, if you honestly don't think you can handle him, we'll call in Child Welfare."

"Oh, I'll handle it." He met her eyes. "Jax is not going into the system. Are you, kid?"

In answer, Jax crammed half his fist into his mouth and sucked furiously.

Blackburn nodded slowly. "Handsome little guy, isn't he?"

"Yeah, he is." Brant traced a finger down the side of Jax's cheek. "And he's stopped crying."

The baby's face puckered up, and his chin trembled.

"Uh-oh. Said the wrong word, didn't I?" He swayed gently and rubbed the baby's back. "Your food's coming." He peered down the hall, hoping he'd see the other police officer heading their way.

No luck.

Slowly, he started down the hall, jiggling Jax, with Blackburn beside him. "Guess I'd better stop on the way home for formula and baby food."

"They sell everything you'll need in the grocery store's baby aisle."

"Okay. Good to know." He scratched his head with his free hand. "It's been a long time since I've fed a baby."

"It'll come back to you. I've got a niece about this one's age. Want me to feed him this time?"

"Please."

Blackburn took the baby as Officer Douglas hustled down the hallway, a pale-blue diaper bag in hand.

Douglas tossed the bag to Brant.

Reflexes kicked in, and he caught it.

"There're formula and diapers in there along with a couple jars of food."

"Does he have any teeth yet?"

Blackburn ran a finger over the baby's gums. "Nope."

Holding Jax, she sat on one of the hard, vinyl chairs. "Dig out a jar of food. Anything's fine. And a spoon. A bib would be good, too."

Brant found everything and opened the lid on the jar. Passing it to her, he said, "Next time you do a fundraiser, let me know." He whipped out a business card and handed it to her. "My way of saying thanks."

Before she could pocket the card, Douglas took it. "You the Wylder who restores vintage cars?"

"That would be me."

He cracked a grin. "Caught a couple of your shows on TV. You and your brothers do one heck of a job."

"Thanks."

"Loved that Corvette you did. The one the guy had in his shed for, what, thirty-five years?"

"That was fun. My brothers are on their way to Texas right now to pick up one a guy found in an old barn." The whole time they talked, he kept his eyes on Blackburn and Jax. The kid ate like a trouper. Every time the spoon got close to the baby's mouth, Brant opened his own.

Blackburn saw him and laughed. "It's a reflex thing. I do it, too."

"I can't tell you how much I appreciate what you've done tonight for my family." He pointed at the baby, who was chowing down on the brightest orange food Brant had ever seen. "This will get us on level footing—then, we'll be fine." He recognized the words for a lie, but he'd do or say whatever it took.

"A high chair would make feeding him a lot easier and a lot less messy."

"Okay." He pulled out his phone and made a note to find a high chair, food, and formula.

"Get some bibs while you're at it."

He added bibs. "Any special kind?"

She grinned. "The bigger, the better."

"Big bibs. Maybe the size of beach towels?"

Douglas laughed. "You think that's funny. Now."

Brant groaned.

Blackburn fixed a bottle. "I'll let you feed him this a little later. He should sleep for a while afterward."

"Right."

The handoff completed, Jax squealed happily. Now that his tummy was full, he sat on Brant's lap and plucked at his bow tie with busy little fingers.

Douglas held out one of his own cards. "In case you

need anything." The patrolman rested one hand on the gun at his hip. "And Mr. Wylder? You might want to see about getting a lawyer for your sister."

Brant's jaw clenched. "Lainey is undergoing surgery, and you're thinking about tossing her in jail?"

"Nothing about this makes me happy," Douglas shot back. "But she broke the law."

"Understood." And he did. "You're just doing your job."

Jax whimpered, and Brant's gaze swung to the baby. "What's wrong?"

"He senses your anxiety," Blackburn said.

"What if I screw this up?"

"You won't." She stared straight into his eyes. "You know why? Because you're all he's got right now."

And didn't that rank right up there with the crappiest luck ever.

Chapter 4

Nurse Sarah came up to him after the officers left. "Ready to feed him that bottle?"

Brant nodded.

"You'll be more comfortable in the surgery waiting room. It's a lot quieter and a lot more private."

"Thank you. I don't suppose there's anywhere I can grab some coffee?"

"There is." She threw him an actual smile. "Tough night, huh?"

"Boy, there's the understatement of the century."

She laid a hand on his arm. "Your sister's in good hands. Dr. Willis is one of our best."

"Again, thank you." He shifted the baby and tossed the diaper bag over his shoulder.

Sarah gave him directions to the cafeteria and the surgical waiting room. "I'll let them know where you are so they can find you when she comes out of surgery."

Guilt at having dubbed her Nurse Ratched gnawed at him. "Wait. If you have a minute—" He held up a hand. "You asked earlier about Magnolia House."

"I did." Sarah sighed. "Is the place as wonderful as I hear? My daughter's thinking about having her wedding there."

"If you're looking for a place to get hitched, it's first-rate." Brant pulled his phone out from an inside jacket pocket. "Pictures of today's wedding."

"Oh." Sarah took the baby while Brant scrolled through the photos. "Looks like Patti and I will be taking a trip to Misty Bottoms. The house and grounds are exquisite."

Molly, in her plum passion, popped into Brant's head. "Everything there is perfection."

"Well, I'd better get back to my desk before someone sends a search party for me." She handed the baby back to him. "Good luck, Mr. Wylder."

"Thank you."

Eyeing the bottle and noticing the way Jax kept bending his head toward it, mouth open, Brant figured he'd better feed the kid first. His coffee could wait.

Sarah's directions led him to a quiet, empty waiting room. Exhaling loudly, he plopped down in a chair. "And here we are."

Jax gurgled his agreement.

Setting the baby on his lap, Brant said, "Your mommy is out of commission for a bit, kid, so it's just you and me. You good with that?"

"Babamagoo."

"Exactly my thoughts."

The two quietly eyed each other, then Jax grinned. Brant smiled back for all of three seconds, the time it took him to register the sudden warmth on his trouser leg. He lifted the baby and grimaced at the wet spot on his tux pants.

"You peed on me, imp."

Jax's lower lip trembled.

"That's okay. No harm, no foul. Well, foul maybe, but the dry cleaner should be able to get it out, right?"

Jax smiled and kicked his tiny feet.

"Why do I sense this wasn't an accident?"

The babble that followed was either justification or denial. Brant couldn't decide which. Forget *his* wet pants. Far scarier, Jax's sodden diaper had to be changed. But he could handle that, couldn't he? How hard could it be?

Digging into the bag, he found diapers and a small blanket. He laid the baby on it and unsnapped Jax's little suit. "You are just wet, aren't you? You didn't, like, make a mess?"

More earnest but totally unintelligible jabber.

"I'm going in." With that, he pulled the tab and nearly wept with relief. *Wet. No little surprises*. Plucking at his own damp trouser leg, he whispered, "Thank you."

He destroyed two diapers but got the third one on— loosely. But as long as the kid wore another one-piece thing, it should hold everything in place, right? Getting him into a dry outfit proved to be a major undertaking. It was as if Jax had grown ten arms, but he finally got the job done.

Swiping the sweat from his brow, Brant picked up the kid, scooped up the dirty diaper along with the two he'd ruined, and headed toward the restroom. He dumped them in the trash and rinsed his hands one at a time, while the baby wiggled in the other arm.

"Hey, who's that?" He pointed at Jax's reflection in the mirror.

"Babagaga!" Laughing, Jax leaned forward and high-fived the baby staring back at him.

After Brant pulled a few faces and tickled the mirror baby, he headed for a chair. Sitting down, he picked up the bottle. "Want this?"

His feet kicking happily, Jax squealed and reached for

it. Though he tried, it took all of thirty seconds for Brant to understand Jax couldn't quite hold it himself yet.

With Jax tucked into the crook of his arm, Brant popped the nipple into the baby's mouth and watched as he drank hungrily and noisily.

Officer Blackburn had been right. The bottle pushed him over the edge. Jax's eyes fluttered shut, then flew open, only to close again. Milk dripped from his mouth and ran down his chin, and Brant swiped at it with a tissue.

Silence.

Blessed silence.

Even in sleep, Jax's perfect little mouth worked as if still eating. Maybe he was dreaming of pizza. Brant's chest grew tight. Whatever happened, whatever it took, somehow or another, he'd take care of this child.

Right now, though, he was seriously draggin' butt.

The institutional-looking clock over the door marked time, and Brant's stomach rumbled, reminding him he'd last eaten at the wedding reception eons ago.

Time to find something to eat. He glanced at the baby and prayed he'd stay asleep.

Following both Sarah's directions and his nose, he found the cafeteria. Here, at least, the smell of food blocked the pungent odor of antiseptic cleansers and God only knew what else.

Outside the windows, the night was dark, the only lights the ones scattered through the parking lot. There was not much traffic in the cafeteria this time of night, and Brant suspected the food in the warming trays had been fresh five or six hours ago.

A burger seemed his best bet, so he ordered one, along with black coffee.

The worker placed everything on a tray, and Brant wondered not for the first time how mothers did it. Cradling the baby in one arm and moving at snail speed, he managed to make it to the closest table without spilling a single drop of coffee. It was 1:58 in the morning, and he and Jax had the place to themselves.

It felt eerie.

There were no booths with bench seats, so what was he supposed to do with the kid? Lay him on the table? No, he might roll off, and then there'd be hell to pay.

Propping his sleeping nephew in his lap, the baby's head drooping against his arm, Brant devoured his burger. He was chewing the last bite when Jax's hand started flailing.

"Oh no. Go back to sleep, little one. Please."

In answer, Jax let out a series of quiet little whimpers. When he'd cried before, he was hungry. Should Brant feed him again?

He slid his chair back and sat the baby on his knee, facing him. Jax quieted and blinked those owlish green eyes.

Brant stuck out his tongue, withdrew it, stuck it out again. Sure enough, Jax's little tongue peeked between his lips. Brant did it again, and so did Jax.

"Good boy! That's my little man." Brant high-fived him.

The game lasted a couple of minutes before Jax let out a sighing sob.

An older woman with a tray stopped at their table. She reached out and tickled the baby beneath his chin and received a beatific smile. "Aren't you the cutie?"

She nodded at her tray. "I have to get this up to my husband. He hasn't had anything to eat since surgery yesterday, and he woke up hungry as a bear." Still, she remained, smiling at the baby. "My great-grandson is about his age. What's your name, sweetie?"

"Jax."

"Good, strong name. You did well."

"Not me. He's my sister's."

"How wonderful you're spending time with him."

"We'll see." But he was talking to her back. She'd shuffled off. The baby began to cry again, and Brant jiggled him. The wails grew louder.

"*Shhh*. No more crying allowed. You need to man up, son."

Jax blinked tear-filled eyes, his lower lip trembled, and he let out another howl, showing off his toothless gums.

"How can anything so tiny make so much noise?" Sweat trickled down Brant's back. No wonder his sister had turned to drink again.

A nurse in pink scrubs and carrying a coffee smiled at Brant. "That baby's hungry."

"He just ate."

"Babies are always hungry." She nodded toward the diaper bag slung over the chair back. "You have food in there?"

Exhausted, Brant asked, "How about I buy you dinner, a snack, an early breakfast? Whatever you want."

"A bribe for feeding this baby?"

"Exactly."

—◦◦◦—

When they returned from the cafeteria, the room was still empty. *Not many surgeries this time of the night*, he guessed. Only emergencies, including ones caused by drunk drivers. What had Lainey been thinking to risk her life like that? Obviously, she hadn't been thinking about her son, her responsibility to him.

Since they'd be here awhile, Brant figured he might as well get comfortable. He laid Jax on the sofa, sitting on the edge to keep him from rolling off.

He undid his bow tie and stuffed it in his coat pocket, then unbuttoned the top couple of shirt buttons. His jacket and cummerbund came off next. With a sigh of relief, he tossed them onto the chair next to him.

A glance at the ugly wall clock told him it was too soon to call his brothers. Considering airport wait time, they'd still be in the air. Hopefully, his mom and dad were asleep. He could only cross his fingers that the hot little bridesmaid he'd run out on was home sleeping, too—alone.

The shrill of his phone startled him. "Hello?"

"Brant? This is Molly Stiles."

He pulled the phone away from his ear and stared at it. Was this for real, or had his tired brain conjured it?

"Brant? Are you there? It's Molly…from the wedding."

No need for her to identify herself. He'd recognize that voice anywhere.

"Hey, Molly. Everything okay?"

"That's what I wanted to ask *you*. You seemed upset when you left."

"I apologize for that. I should have explained."

"No. You didn't owe me an explanation, and you still don't. I probably should have waited till morning to call, if ever. It's just…" Her voice softened. "Are you okay?"

"I am. Or will be, anyway." Her voice soothed him, made him feel better and far less alone. "Right now, I'm in a hospital waiting room in Savannah." He gave her a quick, abridged version of the evening, leaving out any mention of Jax, who was happily eating his own toes. Boy, to be that flexible. "How'd you get my number?"

"From Russell, but don't be mad at him. I browbeat it out of him."

Brant laughed. "Are you kidding? I need to thank him."

They talked for a few more minutes before Molly said, "You've got a lot going on, so I won't keep you. I hope everything works out well for your sister."

"Thanks, Molly. I appreciate it more than you can imagine. Sleep tight."

"I will. Good night, Brant."

He held the phone a long time after he clicked off. *What do you know?* Molly Stiles had called him. Maybe the two of them could get together again after all. Then he glanced at Jax and gave it up. There'd be no time to play in his foreseeable future.

Still, she'd called him. He did a little air pump, then watched the clock's second hand make its slow rotation. The minutes dragged by. How long would Lainey be in surgery?

Tired of being ignored, the baby gave a loud squeal.

Brant scooped him up, settled into the least uncomfortable looking chair, and sipped his second cup of coffee. Jax yawned and popped a thumb in his mouth. His eyes fluttered shut. A late-night infomercial played quietly on TV, and Brant watched a past-her-prime actress tout the virtues of a wrinkle reducer guaranteed to make anybody look ten years younger in mere days.

"Does anybody fall for that stuff?" he wondered out loud.

No answer from the peanut gallery.

Certain Jax was asleep, Brant set down the empty Styrofoam cup, kicked back in the chair, and settled the baby on his chest. He wrapped both arms around his nephew and drifted into an uneasy sleep.

A hand on his shoulder woke him. Soft morning light filtered through a window, and Brant looked up into a pair of tired blue eyes.

"I'm Dr. Willis. We met in the ER."

"Yes." Fully awake now, Brant cleared his throat. "How's Lainey?"

"She's doing well. She'll need some time to heal, but there shouldn't be any lasting physical effects." He explained the extent of Lainey's injuries and what they'd done during surgery.

The baby cradled in one arm, Brant stood and held out his free hand. "Thank you, from me and my entire family, Doctor."

"You're quite welcome." Willis paused, then said, "This isn't my area of expertise, but driving under the influence…"

Brant ran a hand over his face. "Look, I know you see and hear this all the time, but Lainey's a good person. She had—apparently still has—a drinking problem. Five years ago, she did a stint in rehab and, as far as any of us knew, hadn't had a drink since. I don't know what triggered this relapse, but I will find out, believe me. You're right. She's lucky to be alive this morning, and I mean to do everything humanly possible to keep her that way. If she's willing and we can arrange it, I'd like to transfer her directly to a rehab center when she's well enough."

Dr. Willis stuck his hands in his scrub pockets. "Understood."

"May I see her now?"

"She's in recovery and still groggy from the general anesthesia. Why don't you go home? Get some rest." His gaze shifted to the sleeping baby. "That little guy was tuckered out."

"Yeah, it's been quite the night."

Willis nodded toward Brant's tux. "Hope the wedding we interrupted wasn't yours."

"What? Oh! No, definitely not mine. I stood as groomsman for a fraternity brother at Magnolia House."

Dr. Willis smiled. "Jenni Beth Beaumont. She did our wedding at Chateau Rouge not long before she left Savannah. Incredible planner and a wonderful person."

"She is both."

"My guess is your vehicle's not equipped with a baby seat."

"No, it's not. Lainey hadn't expected her friend to need Jax's, so she left it in the car. It was destroyed in the accident." And didn't it turn his stomach imagining Jax in it. "To be perfectly honest, I hadn't even thought about how I'd get him home. Don't suppose I can just seat-belt him in?"

Dr. Willis laughed. "No, don't suppose you can."

"What do I do? I can't even take him to the store to buy a seat. Talk about a catch-22."

"We keep a few around here for new parents who can't afford one. Why don't you stay put, and I'll have an aide round one up for you."

"I'd appreciate that. Again, thanks—for everything."

The doctor laid a hand on Brant's shoulder. "We'll take good care of your sister while she's here. Once she leaves, it'll be up to you."

"Yes, sir. Understood."

When he walked out the door, Brant dropped back into the chair. Two green eyes flew open, and Brant held his breath. Jax sent him a toothless grin, and Brant's heart melted.

"Good morning, champ. Been one heck of a night, hasn't it?"

A soft coo was his answer.

They sat in the pale light of early morning, two guys thrown together by family ties and fate. Just when Brant decided the whole thing might not be so bad, the baby's chin quivered, and his forehead puckered. "No, no, no," Brant moaned. "We agreed. No more tears. I'll put a thousand dollars in a savings account for you if you don't cry." Like a madman, he rooted in the diaper bag until he found a pacifier.

He plugged the piece of silicone in Jax's mouth and made a quick call to his parents, cradling the phone between his ear and shoulder and jiggling Jax on his knee. He filled them in on what little he knew, ending with a promise to keep them up-to-date.

Hanging up, he carried Jax to the window. "Look at all the cars out there. Over in the far corner? That's a classic Mustang like Uncle Tuck drives. This one's pretty beat up, but with a little work it could be a beaut."

Jax pounded on the window in agreement.

Brant lifted him into the air and flew him around the room while Jax made excited sounds and flapped his arms. Drool dripped onto Brant's face, and he swiped it away. "We have one more call to make, so let's land the plane."

Settling back in the chair, he dialed his brother.

"This better be good, Bro," Tucker warned. "Take-off was delayed, so by the time we touched down on Texas soil, rounded up our luggage, and made it to the hotel, we've barely been in bed an hour."

"Then you've done better than me. I haven't seen my bed tonight."

"What's wrong? Mom?"

"No." He took a deep breath. Best to do it quickly. "Lainey was in a car accident tonight outside of Savannah. Last night, now, I guess."

"Son of a—Savannah? I thought she was in Florida."

"Me too."

Gaven spoke up. "Tuck put us on speaker. Are Sis and the baby okay?"

"Jax wasn't with her. He's fine."

Hearing his name, Jax grabbed for the phone, and Brant shifted it to the other ear. "Lainey left him with a friend. Right now, he's sprawled in my lap, contemplating the best way to steal my phone. Thieving little bugger."

Gaven grunted. "How's Lainey?"

"She spent the night in surgery. I spoke with her doctor a few minutes ago. She's gonna be okay, but it'll take a while." He passed on the information Willis had shared with him. "We've got another problem. Lainey was DUI."

"No way." Tucker's voice was hard as steel. "She hasn't touched a drop in years."

"Five," Gaven added.

"I know." Brant rubbed his forehead. "But she did last night. Fortunately, no one else was involved, but the cops were here when I arrived. Once I can talk to Lainey, I'll know more, but we need to consider another round of rehab. If nothing else, it might stop a downhill slide. Maybe a good lawyer can get them to swap rehab for jail time."

A chirpy-looking twentysomething woman in scrubs sailed into the room, a car seat and a bag of goodies in her hands.

"Hey, I've got to go, guys. An angel's bringing me a car seat."

"For your Camaro?"

"Yep."

"You're gonna let a baby ride in your car? What if he urps?"

Brant sighed. "What choice do I have, Gaven? It's that or tie him to the roof."

Halfway across the room, the young woman gasped.

"I'm not even considering that." He held up the phone. "My brothers."

She nodded.

Jax spit out the pacifier and, whimpering, held out his arms toward the stranger.

Brant's jaw dropped. "You little Benedict Arnold." He clicked off and slipped the phone into his shirt pocket.

The perky aide smiled at the baby. "Somebody's hungry. I'll bet your diaper needs changing, too, doesn't it?"

Another diaper change? So soon?

"Ma'am, I have absolutely no right to ask this, but could you keep an eye on him while I run into the men's room? It's right there." He pointed across the small waiting room.

"Sure. Take your time and freshen up." She reached for the baby, who stopped crying and shot her a sloppy grin. "Daddy will be right back, honey."

"I'm not—" He gave it up. No sense even going there.

Half-ashamed of himself, he took the offered break. Hands planted on the vanity, he closed his eyes and fought to clear his mind. Instead, all of Lainey's problems—physical, emotional, and legal—barreled through his mind.

Add a baby into the mix, and it became a quagmire of the first order.

Brant opened his eyes and splashed water on his face. He looked like red-eyed roadkill. Nothing to do about it; he needed to get back to Jax. By now, the aide had probably deserted her station and run away.

He listened. No crying. No sound at all.

Fear speared through him. What if Jax had been kidnapped? He'd left him with a stranger.

He cracked the door and peeked around it. There sat the cheerful aide, Jax snuggled against her. She talked quietly to him while he drank his formula, one fist waving in the air, the other clutched around the bottle.

"Hey, he's quiet."

"I fed him part of the jar of veggies and changed

him. He was soaking wet and had made quite a mess, so I slipped him into a clean outfit, too. This bottle should finish him off. There're more diapers and formula in that bag." She tilted her head toward the canvas tote she'd brought.

"You are a miracle worker."

She laughed. "I've got two little ones of my own. Babies are a real blessing, aren't they?"

"Um, yeah, they sure are." With two fingers, he picked up the offending dirty diaper and carried it into the men's room. "Nasty."

"You've probably smelled worse, Daddy."

"Uh, Jax is my nephew. My sister—"

"Last night's car accident."

"Yeah."

"I heard she's doing well."

"According to Dr. Willis, we got very lucky." He nodded at Jax. "For now, I'm pinch-hitting."

"You'll get used to it really fast. And this baby?" She rubbed a finger under Jax's chin and got a milky smile as her reward. "You're a sweetheart, aren't you?"

Jax gurgled.

"You could use a bath, though, couldn't you? Yes, you could."

She walked her fingers up the baby's round little tummy.

He giggled and drooled.

"A bath?" A supersized headache exploded behind Brant's eyes. How in the heck did he give a kid who could barely sit up by himself a bath?

Oh yeah. All this could easily have driven Lainey to drink.

Then the baby laughed, and Brant did, too.

But it was short-lived as reality rushed back. He had to take this tiny creature home with him. Alone.

"Babies should come with instruction manuals. Okay, so diaper changes, a bath, and food at regular intervals." He ticked them off on his fingers. "I'm a mechanic and restoration specialist. I ought to be able to figure it out, right?"

"Absolutely. Good luck."

Brant shot her a quick look but decided her comment hadn't been sarcastic.

She strapped Jax into his seat and planted a quick smooch on his cheek. A Wylder through and through, the baby ate it up. The kid had a way with the ladies already.

Brant thanked Little Miss Sunshine, then set off down the hall, two diaper bags slung over one shoulder and a baby dangling in a seat from his other hand.

A few minutes later, as he stared at all the belts and buckles, he cursed the inventor of the contraption Jax slouched in. Sliding his sunglasses to the top of his head, he leaned in for another go at it. And Jax? He was getting a kick out of the whole thing, bopping Brant on the head with his rattle every time he leaned close.

How had his life taken such a huge detour? And with no warning.

If Lainey did go into rehab…

Oh boy. He was in for it.

Chapter 5

Weary and more than a little desperate, Brant pulled into the B and B where he and his brothers had stayed. He'd planned to check out this morning, take a closer look at the two properties they were considering for their new shop, then head back to Tennessee.

Those plans had been flushed down the toilet. He couldn't head home and leave Lainey to face this alone—which meant he wouldn't be checking out. *If* Annabelle had a vacancy for the next few days.

Brant emptied the contents of the hospital's tote into Lainey's diaper bag. He draped his rumpled tux jacket over the bag, then slung it over his shoulder and eyed his nephew. "Ready for this, Jax?"

The baby grinned and gurgled.

"You like Uncle Brant's Camaro, don't you?"

Jax bounced up and down in his seat.

"You've got good taste, buddy. In a few years, we'll put you to work at Wylder Rides. Maybe make you a partner." He huffed out a breath. "In the meantime, we have to persuade Ms. Annabelle to let us hang around another night or two. Or three. We'll stay close in case your mama needs something."

He pointed a finger at the baby. "You, young man, need to be on your best behavior, you hear? No crying." Studying the baby, he winced. "And try to keep that drool down a little. We don't want to flood the place."

After a few minutes of fussing with all the harnesses and belts, he managed to free both baby and seat. Pleased with himself, Brant started up the walk, shocked again at how heavy the carrier was. Yet women lugged the darned things all over the place. Well, he never had considered them the weaker sex.

They sure were the prettier sex, though. He thought about Molly Stiles and sighed for last night's lost opportunity. Then he tucked it away to concentrate on his more immediate problem. Fingers crossed that he'd catch Annabelle's niece working the front desk rather than the owner, Brant swung through the old oak door with its leaded crystal window.

"Mr. Wylder." Annabelle greeted him, wearing an orange-and-blue housedress that had to be a survivor of the fifties, dashing his hopes for an easy go of extending his stay.

"How are you this morning, Ms. Annabelle?" Holding Jax and the seat low at his side, he let the diaper bag slip from his shoulder and placed it on the floor.

The innkeeper sniffed. "Better than you, I'd imagine, since you never made it back after last night's wedding." Her eyes narrowed. "You look like yesterday's rubbish."

Brant grimaced. Wrinkled clothes, disheveled hair, and bloodshot eyes. He ran a hand over his chin. Yep, he needed a shave, too. "Can't argue about that, ma'am. I could definitely use a shower and some fresh clothes."

"That would be a start. Your brothers left after the wedding?"

"Yes, ma'am."

"I assume you found somewhere more to your liking to spend the night."

"Actually, no, I didn't."

Jax chose that moment to let out a stream of babble.

Annabelle slid the glasses she wore on a chain into place and peered over the antique desk. "What do you have there?"

"A baby."

"I can tell he's a baby, you young fool."

"This is Jax. Jax, I'd like you to meet Ms. Annabelle."

The baby gurgled and waved his chubby arms.

Stepping closer to the desk, he set Jax's seat on the beautifully refinished pine floor. "I'd intended to leave town later today, but my plans have changed. It looks like I'll be in Misty Bottoms a little longer than originally expected."

"Have anything to do with that?" She pointed at Jax.

"In a roundabout way, yeah."

"You the baby's daddy?"

"What? No. Jax is my nephew."

"Where's his mother?"

Brant rubbed the bridge of his nose. "She—" Lack of sleep amped his emotions, and his voice cracked. "My sister was in a car accident last night. Lainey's in Savannah. In the hospital."

Annabelle's expression changed to concern. "Oh, I am so sorry, Mr. Wylder. Will she be all right?"

He expelled a long breath. "She spent most of the night in surgery, but when I left, she was in recovery. Her surgeon assured me, given time, she'll be fine. I should be able to see her later today."

"Was that poor little thing with her?"

"No. Thankfully, he was with a friend."

"There's a blessing."

"Yes." He took a deep breath. "Here's the thing, though. I'm gonna need a room for a few more days."

Sympathy forgotten, the finicky innkeeper came roaring back. "We don't generally have babies here."

"Then we have something in common, because I don't usually travel with a baby."

"Actually, I misspoke." She drew her ninety-pound self up to her full five feet. "What I should have said was that we don't *allow* children here. Our rooms are full of antiques, and I cannot take a chance that—"

"Ma'am, with all due respect, Jax isn't likely to break anything. He can't walk. He can't even crawl." Brant held out his hands, palms up. "What's he going to do? Gum a piece of Limoges? I promise I'll keep all the good bric-a-brac away from him. We'll play catch with his Nerf ball instead of the Fabergé eggs."

"Got a smart mouth, don't you?"

He scowled. "My mother's hinted at that a time or two."

"He'll keep the other guests awake with his crying."

"Seriously?" He waved a hand toward Jax. The baby's arms and legs moved a mile a minute as he smiled and gurgled. "This happy baby? He hardly ever cries." Brant glanced toward the window and waited for the lightning that would strike him down for lying. He held his breath, but outside the wavy, original glass, the sun continued to shine. No rumbles of thunder. No bolts of lightning.

Still, he stayed on guard.

"Well, you are at the back of the house." Annabelle sniffed. "I suppose it's far enough from the other rooms that we can give it a try. For tonight. If there are any complaints, any whatsoever, you'll have to find some-where else tomorrow."

"Fair enough." And he supposed it was. Right now, he was so tired, he could barely think. He needed sleep. Lots and lots of sleep.

"Heaven help me, I'll probably regret this."

"You won't. Thank you. Thank you very much." He leaned across the desk and kissed her leathery cheek.

She blushed like a schoolgirl and waved a hand at him dismissively. "Get out of here." Her gaze dropped to the baby. "Both of you."

He scooped up Jax, thankful they hadn't been dumped, homeless, onto the street.

"I need to get a couple things from my car. Can I leave the baby here for a sec?"

"If you promise to come back for him."

He smiled and sent her a sharp salute.

Jogging back to the house, he heard Jax giggling. Annabelle sat on a chair with the baby at her feet. Leaning over, she talked to him and tickled his belly.

Hearing the door squeak, she looked up, turning beet red, while the little traitor at her feet grinned at Brant.

Tucking his surprise in his back pocket, Brant asked, "Cute, isn't he?"

"Yes, he is."

"You never had children?"

Melancholy clouded the older woman's eyes. "My husband died in an industrial accident six months after we married. I never remarried. My choice." She glared at him as if defying him to challenge her. "But I had my niece, Willow."

Brant saw the innkeeper through fresh eyes. Those few sentences explained a lot.

She stood. "You'd better get that child upstairs. Both of you could stand some cleaning up."

"Yes, ma'am. Thank you. Again." Brant grabbed the carrier's handle and headed for the stairs.

One battle won, but the war had only begun.

Halfway to the back stairs, Willow stepped out of a side room. She leaned against the doorjamb, her shoulder-length blond hair curling around her face.

Brant figured her for eighteen, nineteen max. Breathtakingly beautiful, she was bound to give the Misty Bottoms boys a real run for their money.

"I heard you talking to Aunt Annabelle. I'm sorry about your sister. Want some breakfast?"

He looked at the baby. So far, so good, but he didn't know how long that would last. If he was lucky, he'd make it to the room before all hell broke loose again. Hanging with Jax was like carrying a live grenade in his pocket.

"Nah. I think I'll head up to my room. I need to get cleaned up and catch some sleep."

"How about I deliver a tray to you?"

He was famished—and too tired to do anything about it himself. The kid had eaten all night, while he'd survived on god-awful hospital coffee and a quick burger.

Willow tipped her head. "Yes?"

"That would be great."

"Give me ten minutes."

"You bet."

Once in his room, he placed the car seat on the floor and fell onto the bed.

Jax whimpered, and Brant sat up quickly. "What's wrong?"

The instant the baby saw him, he grinned.

"Ah, you couldn't see me, so you thought I'd left. Though why you'd find me comforting, I haven't a clue. You do understand I don't have the faintest idea what to do with you?" He reached down and hauled the seat up beside him. "You did good, kid. Way to keep it together in front of the dragon lady."

He raised the baby's arms in a cheer.

Jax kicked his feet in glee, and Brant pulled off his tiny socks. "How's that feel? Bare feet." Then he toed off his own shiny black dress shoes. "If I ever see those things again, it'll be too soon."

He tossed them in the direction of his suitcase as a knock sounded on the door.

Opening it, he grinned. Willow stood there, tray in hand. The mouth-watering smells of bacon and maple syrup drifted to him.

"If that tastes even half as good as it smells, I'm in your debt forever." He took several steps back as she entered.

She set the tray on a small table by the window. With a dramatic flair, she removed the cover from the plate. "French toast with a pitcher of real New Hampshire maple syrup. My aunt's cousin sends it every year. I added an extra serving of bacon, some fresh-sliced Georgia peaches, and a pot of coffee. Strong and black, exactly the way you like it."

"Sweetheart, you are a life saver."

"Anything else I can do for you?"

"Nope, I'm good here." He waved a hand toward

Jax. "We're both good. Thanks again. I'll carry the tray down to the kitchen when I'm finished."

"That's okay. Just set it in the hallway." She pulled the door shut behind her without another word.

Brant pointed his fork at Jax, but before he could say anything, there was another knock on the door. He opened it.

Annabelle stood there, a small bowl and spoon in hand. "Seems only right Jax should eat, too." She set a small bowl of porridge beside his tray, then laid the spoon next to it.

"That was my baby spoon." She caught his gaze. "Yes, that makes it a true antique."

"I didn't say that."

"Didn't have to."

"But—"

"It's a gift. Time to pass it on." She moved to the bed and ran a finger down the baby's cheek. "Tell your uncle to stop being a grump."

Brant's eyebrows shot nearly to the ceiling.

Then the real Annabelle returned. "Doesn't mean I won't kick you out if the baby bothers the rest of my guests." She gave Jax a quick peck on the cheek and shuffled out, closing the door behind her.

"What just happened, Jax?" Brant scratched his head.

The baby explained everything, babbling a mile a minute.

"That's what I thought. Small town, great people— even if they try to hide behind a mask of crankiness." Brant turned the spoon over in his hand. "Shall we eat?"

He took a bite of the French toast, his eyes closing. Annabelle might be crotchety, but the woman could cook. He poured the rest of the warm maple syrup over the golden slices. "Oh yeah, this is superb."

They settled into a rhythm. He took a bite of French toast, then fed a spoonful of porridge to Jax. Or tried to. As often as not, the baby turned his head at the last second and the cereal splatted on his cheek.

Halfway through the second piece of toast, Brant slowed his pace. He watched as Jax followed the fork from his plate to his mouth and back again. The baby's mouth worked as if he, too, were eating more than porridge.

"Want a little taste of heaven? Hmm?" Brant swiped a finger through the maple syrup and laid it on the baby's lips. "Here you go."

Jax sucked on Brant's finger, bouncing for joy. Quiet, happy noises erupted from him. Brant dipped his finger in the syrup again and gave Jax another taste. "I doubt this is on your meal plan, but what the heck. Life's not worth living if you can't have a treat once in a while, right?"

Instantly, his mind again veered toward Molly, a treat for all the senses. That long, dark hair and those incredible eyes. Her scent alone could drive a man crazy...and her skin. So soft. How the woman could look so innocent yet so hot blew his mind. Ms. Molly Stiles had the look of an angel. He grinned. One of Victoria's Secret's angels.

Jax made an impatient sound, and Brant fed him another spoon of porridge.

If he and his brothers actually moved their business to Misty Bottoms, could he hope for a little more time with Molly? He feared, though, that like Icarus, he might get burned if he soared too close to the heavens.

Munching on a piece of crisp bacon, Brant pulled another bottle from the diaper bag. It was the last of the premade ones and gave him the feeling of having three laps to go in a big race with only enough fuel for two. He ate the rest of his breakfast one-handed while balancing Jax's bottle with the other.

When they'd both finished, Brant couldn't fight it any longer. "What do you say, kid? Want to catch a nap?"

Jax bounced up and down, fists waving in the air. He made soft gurgling noises and blew bubbles.

"Yeah?" Brant unzipped his dress pants and let them drop to the floor. He eyed the pee stain. "I don't know if those are salvageable, big guy. Guess only time and the dry cleaner will tell." After he removed his cuff links, the shirt followed.

In boxer shorts and a white T-shirt, he padded into the bathroom. When he came out, Jax let go with a stream of gibberish.

"What?" With a grin, he leaned toward the baby, then pulled back. "Oh, you stink!"

Jax whimpered.

"Sorry, sorry." He quickly held out a finger for the baby to grab. Jax popped it into his mouth and gummed it, while Brant tried not to breathe.

Okay, he'd managed a wet diaper, but this? Way above and beyond his pay grade.

Since this wouldn't be the last messy diaper Jax offered him, he'd better figure out how to deal with it. If he could turn a rusted-out skeleton of a car into a thing of beauty, he could certainly change a dirty diaper.

Jax grew more agitated; he probably couldn't stand the smell, either.

Keeping up a running dialogue, Brant spread out everything he figured he'd need. "Okay, kid, we've got a diaper and a spare, a pack of baby wipes, ointment, and a toy to keep you occupied." He shook the rattle.

Hustling into the bathroom, he grabbed a big fluffy towel and spread it over Annabelle's rug. The problem? A motor stayed still while he worked on it. Jax? A squirming wiggler. "Geez, kid, am I gonna have to calf-rope you to keep you still?"

Finally, he managed to unsnap the outfit's legs and crotch. Then he undid the tabs on Jax's diaper and peeled it away.

"Holy moly." He gagged. "This stuff is toxic!"

He fanned the air with a clean diaper. "We're gonna need to fumigate this room."

Freed, Jax kicked happily until Brant grabbed his tiny feet. "No, you don't, buster." He made a mental note to send his mom a huge bouquet of flowers.

He pulled the wastebasket close and grabbed a baby wipe. The baby stared at him solemnly.

When he yanked too hard on the first diaper, the sticky tab broke loose.

He worked the second diaper under the baby, who by now was like a wind-up doll gone haywire.

Brant grasped a corner of the diaper, but before he could pull it up and over, Jax started to pee. The stream shot straight up like an oil gusher. After one shocked laugh, Brant covered him with the now-damp diaper.

"Oh, my little man, you need to learn to control that thing."

Since the horse was already out of the barn, so to speak, Brant let Jax enjoy his nakedness for a few more minutes while he peeled off his own sodden T-shirt and tossed it in the direction of his ruined pants.

Finally the job was complete. Jax was safely and securely covered. The meager stack of diapers had taken a hit, and only one jar of food remained, along with a few scoops of formula.

The formula, at least, came with directions, but he'd need a couple more bottles. There had only been three in his diaper bag, and Jax didn't care for the hospital's bottles—the nipples were different.

"Okay, so let's see what the internet has to say about nipples, huh?" He leaned into the pillows and propped Jax up between his legs. The two of them started their web search. The touch screen jumped around when tiny fingers made contact. Brant slid it a fraction farther away. A bevy of links popped up, and Brant clicked on one. A video demonstrating breast feeding came to life.

"Whoops, not the kind of nipples I had in mind." He covered the baby's eyes and closed the site. Removing his hand, he looked down at Jax, who stared back at him. "How about we make a run to the store later and see what we find?"

He palmed the bottle his nephew had emptied earlier. "We'll take this along so we know what we're looking for. What do you think?"

A beaming smile was his answer.

The complete trust in those eyes awed Brant and left him more than a little thunderstruck at the responsibility.

"Let me dash off a quick email to your uncles." He had three words typed when Jax's little hand made contact with the keyboard. Laughing, Brant asked, "Something you want to tell them?"

"Gaa-daa." Drool dripped from his chin, and Brant swiped at it with a tissue.

"Bibs. Gotta get bibs."

Busily typing, Jax grinned up at him.

"You didn't say anything bad about me, did you?"

Jax's head bobbled from side to side.

"I'll take that as a negative." Brant spaced to the bottom of Jax's garbled mess and typed, "Love, Jax." He hit Send. *Let Tucker and Gaven figure that one out.*

He closed the laptop and set it on the nightstand.

"Time for some shut-eye." He shifted to his side and pulled the baby close, his head on Brant's shoulder. This would be okay.

His eyes drifted shut, and both Wylder men fell sound asleep.

The alarm clock on the nightstand read 11:15, and sun blazed through the blinds. He'd slept for almost an hour.

Brant's thoughts turned to Lainey. Guilt sucked at him. Instead of being here in bed, he should have stayed at the hospital. But they'd promised to call if anything changed, hadn't they? He closed his eyes, physically sick at the memory of his sister's bruised and battered face.

He needed to call, and now would be the time to do it, since Jax was still zonked out. An inch at a time, barely breathing, Brant slid away from the baby.

He punched in the hospital ICU's number, and a nurse told him Lainey was doing better than expected and was awake and aware, but fretting about her son. Relief swept through him.

Next he called his parents. "After I grab a shower and some lunch, I'll drive back to Savannah. I'll call when I get there, and if she's able, you can talk to Lainey."

"You aren't staying in Savannah?"

"No. I left from the wedding, so all my stuff was still at the inn. I'd promised Tucker and Gaven I'd check out a couple locations for the shop here, too. Savannah's close enough, I can be there in a jiff, if Sis needs me."

They talked for a while longer, then he hung up to phone his brothers. He filled them in on their sister's progress and asked, "How's that Vette?"

"Oh, she's one in a million," Tucker said. "I can't wait to make her pretty again."

"I doubt I'll have a chance to look at either of those properties today."

"Understood." Tucker hesitated. "Think we should take another shot at talking to the Lake Delores city council about approving our expansion plan?"

"No," Gaven said. "We've tried and tried, and they throw up one roadblock after another. Their minds are made up."

"We need more space," Brant said. "The only way we'll get it is to buy the piece of land next to our shop. Period. Without it, we're stuck."

"That's never gonna happen. Henry Roper and Jimmy Boone own that parcel and want to build an apartment building on it," Gaven said. "Since they're on the council…"

"We don't have a chance in hell," Tucker finished. "Well, Misty Bottoms is a great location."

"Yeah, it is. Did you get Jax's message?"

"The one where he said you were being mean and begged me to rescue him?" Gaven asked.

Brant laughed. "That's the one."

They were talking engines when Jax woke up crying.

"What's wrong with the kid?" Tucker asked.

"My guess? He either wants a clean diaper or food. Or both. He's a cutie, but he's a lot of work," Brant muttered. "And if I don't quiet him down, Annabelle will toss us both out on the street."

"She can't do that," Tucker said.

"Actually, she can. She has a no-children policy."

"But this is an emergency," Gaven said.

"Not to her. If you two feel like saying a few prayers for Lainey, send up a couple for me, would you? Right now? I've got to go."

"Hey, can you change a diaper?" Tucker asked.

"If the Force is with me." Brant let out a frustrated sigh, then admitted, "The last change took me three diapers before I got the job done." Jax wailed louder. "Later, guys."

After hanging up, Brant mixed up the last of the formula.

He draped a burp cloth over his arm and held the bottle in front of the baby. "Your drink is prepared, monsieur. But before your liquid refreshment, you must eat." He squinted at the jar with the happy baby on the label and wrinkled his nose. "Looks like your only option is the rest of your spinach, zucchini, and peas, *mon ami*. What do you think? Shall we give it a try?"

Jax's lip trembled, and he started to cry again.

"Yeah, don't blame you. I'd probably cry too, if I had to eat this. Pop a couple of teeth, and I'll give you some real food. In the meantime, this is all we've got."

He looked around for the best spot to feed Jax and settled on the tiled bathroom floor—not the most hygienic, but definitely the easiest to clean up. Or was it? He eyed the shower stall. Whatever they spilled, he could just hose off.

Fifteen minutes later, the baby leaning against one of Brant's legs and held in place by his other, Brant scraped the last of the veggies from the jar. "Here we go." He brought the plane in for a landing, sound effects and all, and managed to hit Jax's mouth.

"Yum. Wasn't that great?"

The baby smiled lopsidedly.

Some of the baby food had splattered on the tile, but Brant figured it would wash down the drain when he showered. A high chair moved up the ladder of necessities, although he should probably stop at the hardware store for a drop cloth to put under it.

Brant squinted at his nephew. Jax had pureed veggies in his hair, on his face and hands, and all over his outfit. Yep, and between his toes.

Worse, the kid had messed his diaper again. The foul smell wafted to Brant.

Another diaper change and then a clean outfit. The one he had on didn't look or smell so good. Brant closed his eyes and prayed for strength.

A bath would have to wait.

Or would it? Brant desperately needed a shower himself. Why not take Jax in with him? He'd skimmed a couple of YouTube videos on bathing a baby. Neither had touted showering with an infant as an option, but nothing ventured…

Chapter 6

Bundled up for the cool weather, Molly sat at the small table on her sunny upstairs balcony, one of the best features of her four-room apartment. She played with her orange-cranberry muffin, crumbling it into tiny pieces.

Instead of eating, she sipped at her coffee and called herself every kind of fool. What had she been thinking when she dug the crumpled paper out of her waste basket and called Brant last night? But darn, he'd looked so upset when he left Magnolia House.

No wonder. His baby sister had been hurt.

She yawned and traced her fingers over Bubbles's head and along her back. The cat purred and arched into her hand. Molly hadn't slept well after that call. Most of her restlessness she chalked up to concern—for him, his sister, and the rest of his family. Grudgingly, she admitted the tiniest part was Brant himself. The man was too handsome by far. Too sexy. Too…everything.

She touched a finger to her lips. The kiss, as fleeting as it had been, had stayed with her.

Brant had not; he was gone.

He'd no doubt stay in Savannah till his sister was out of the woods, then head home.

A few cars drove slowly by on the street below, fellow Misty Bottomers heading to church or breakfast. High in one of the oaks, a Savannah sparrow serenaded her, and winter jasmine scented the air.

Time to quit daydreaming and get something done.

Picking up her crumb-covered plate and empty cup, Molly walked back inside, a slow smile curving her lips. She loved her new home. While her Savannah apartment had been a little on the dark side, this place had windows galore and practically begged for a light, feminine touch—which she'd been more than happy to provide. Done in pale blues and white, the rooms over her boutique felt both fresh and relaxing. The old oak floors had refinished beautifully, and the kitchen cabinets had needed only a coat of white paint to bring them back to life. Jenni Beth's husband, Cole, had found her some incredible chandeliers through his architectural salvage company.

One peek inside her pantry and she shook her head. She could give Old Mother Hubbard a run for her money. Past time to restock.

Molly glanced at her worn leggings and seen-better-days sweatshirt. She should change.

In her shop, she wore black so as not to compete with the brides, which meant nearly half of her closet was filled with dresses, skirts, slacks, and tops in the non-color. To add flair to her outfits, she accessorized with jewelry and shoes, scarves, and hair accessories.

But that was for work. Off duty, she craved comfort and color. Sometimes she wondered if there weren't two of her, and she simply morphed from one skin to another.

Today? She didn't need to answer to anybody.

Today she was Molly. Just Molly. Tomorrow she'd once again be the professional wedding-boutique owner.

Besides, she'd dash into BiLo's grocery and pick up a few essentials. In and out in a flash.

Who'd see her?

At the bottom of the stairs, she couldn't resist sticking her head inside her shop. Barely a month old, her boutique enticed Molly as powerfully as Sleeping Beauty's spinning wheel had her, but hopefully without the dire results. Stepping into That Little White Dress was like being sucked into the pages of a fairy tale, one she never wanted to escape.

She'd stuck with her signature blue and white down here, too, both inside and out. The combination reminded her of seersucker, of whimsical summer afternoons and tea parties. Fresh, cool, and feminine.

A white wicker basket squatted by the front door, full of blinged-out flip-flops, great gifts for wedding guests. When it came time to dance, the ladies could kick off their blister-inducing, toe-pinching heels and slip into them.

In the far corner stood a papier-mâché live oak, resplendent in white lights and ornate bird cages and dripping with wisteria. Vintage cabinets displayed accessories, and a wall of gorgeous, once-in-a-lifetime dresses threatened to take her breath away every time she walked in. Because the gowns were so heavy, she'd ordered special heavy-duty hangers—in pale blue. Mirrors and a raised dais along with blue silk Louis XIV–style chairs completed the display room.

Number eight on her life's to-do list? Check.

Never mind that her mother had begged her to lose the list and just live life. Forget Jenni Beth had suggested a bonfire to burn the list.

Molly couldn't. She prided herself on keeping her dreams front and center, on remembering who she was and where she was going. What she wanted in life…and what she didn't.

Every once in a while, she caught that special look passing between her friends and their husbands or fiancés and couldn't help but feel a bit wistful. A bit lonely. But she'd have someone to share her life. Eventually.

On her way to the store, Molly drove past Annabelle's. Slowly. No Brant. No black Camaro. She told herself she wasn't disappointed, that the feeling in the pit of her stomach was relief.

As she walked into the grocer's, she admitted Brant was a temptation she'd find hard to resist. And speaking of temptations, Molly tossed a package of Oreos into her grocery cart. Her favorite midnight snack. Rounding the corner, still working to convince herself she was glad Brant was gone, she almost ran over him.

He hadn't left town! Yes!

No! She was mortified, and her hand instinctively flew to her hair. Why hadn't she taken time to do more than run a brush through it? Or to change into something other than purple leggings and her favorite faded blue sweatshirt?

Brant, on the other hand? Seeing him last night in that black tux, a girl could have melted simply catching sight of him. Today in worn jeans that hugged his hips and butt, and a forest-green, long-sleeved T-shirt, he looked rugged, badass, and every bit as delicious. Tux or jeans? How did a girl decide?

A high-pitched squeal caught her attention, and her eyes darted to the grinning baby.

Molly's shocked gaze flicked to Brant and met his incredible eyes, the color of grass after a summer rain and fringed with the long, thick eyelashes women are never lucky enough to be born with. The baby in his cart shared both.

Her forehead creased in a frown, then her stomach hit the floor as dread filled her.

His sister. Was the baby hers? Did Brant have the baby because she'd—deep breath—because she'd died?

No!

"Brant?"

"Molly."

"Your sister. Is she okay?"

He nodded, and her world righted itself. She'd never met Lainey, yet her heart raced from the fear that had careened through her.

"Molly, meet my nephew, the unpredictable, unrivaled champion sucker of the pacifier, Jax Wylder."

"Lainey's son?"

"Yep."

"Was Jax in the accident, too?"

"No. Thankfully, she'd left him with a friend."

"Is she doing better this morning?"

"She made it through surgery. Now she has to heal. In the meantime, Jax and I are spending some quality time together, aren't we, kid?"

Jax's grin widened.

"Don't let that smile fool you. The little bugger's a tyrant," Brant warned before he shifted his attention back to the baby food section. "Look at this." He stuffed his hands in his jeans pockets. "How can there be so many things to feed a toothless kid? Shouldn't they just drink milk from a bottle…or from their mama?"

A whimper erupted from the baby, and Molly watched as Brant spun, wild-eyed, to his nephew.

"Oh no, champ, not now. You don't want to look like a wuss in front of this beautiful lady. Remember what Frankie Valli said. Walk like a man."

Molly watched, mesmerized, as the five-o'clock-shadowed male picked up the small baby. When he held him close, swaying and patting his back, singing the Four Seasons song, she went all tingly.

Jax quieted, his tiny fingers finding the pocket on Brant's T-shirt.

Over the baby's head, Brant shot Molly a look. "Frightening that somebody would trust me with this little guy, isn't it?"

"Looks like you're doing fine."

"Looks can be very deceiving. I'm flying by the seat of my pants—and YouTube videos. Aren't I, Jax?" He disentangled the baby's fingers from his pocket and kissed each one.

Molly sighed.

"What's wrong?"

"Nothing." She blushed. "Nothing at all."

Brant kissed the top of his nephew's head. "Right here?" He pointed. "The consequence of sex."

"Sex?" Her mind blew a fuse.

"Makes a guy think."

It was making *her* think, too. And they weren't thoughts she should be having.

He raised a hand and rubbed his temple. "Here's the deal, Molly. I'm basically running on no sleep. Jax and I hung out at the hospital until Lainey was out of surgery and I talked to her doctor. Even after driving back from

Savannah, I couldn't crawl into bed, because this small mass of humanity wouldn't allow it. The kid's running me ragged. He eats, then he messes his diaper, and it's time to eat again. He's like one of those perpetual-motion machines, you know, or that scene where Lucy and Ethel work in that candy factory and the stuff just keeps comin' at them. I had no idea."

"What can I do?"

Brant leaned against his grocery cart. "I honestly don't know. Have you read about those sinkholes? The ones that open up and swallow everything? Right now, I feel like I've pitched headfirst into one."

"It's temporary, though, right?"

"I sure hope so."

"How old is Jax?"

"Seven months."

"What are you doing now? Today?" Molly asked him.

"After I restock diapers, formula, and baby food—" He shook his head. "Honestly, how much crap can a baby need? Anyway, after I get all the essentials...or the ones I know I need...Jax and I are making a run to Savannah. Lainey was out of it last night, then went straight to recovery after surgery, so I haven't had a chance to talk to her. I need to see her, to let her know I'm here, that the whole family has her back."

Last night, she'd figured Brant for a bad-boy bachelor. Maybe she'd misjudged him. Without thought, she slipped her free hand into Brant's and squeezed it. "She's lucky to have y'all." She hesitated. "Will they let you take Jax in to see her?"

When the baby reached for her, she looked toward

Brant. "Mind if I pick him up?" Without waiting for an answer, she plucked Jax from the cart. "Hey, cutie."

Brant blinked. "I don't know if he'll be allowed in or not. I honestly hadn't even considered that. See? That's what I mean. Everything is so complicated." His hand plowed through his dark hair, standing bits of it on end. "If not, maybe they've got like, I don't know, a day care or nursery or something."

"Want some company?"

"Excuse me?"

"If you don't mind, I'll ride to Savannah with you." She jiggled Jax on her hip, then swiped at the drool on his chin. "While you visit your sister, Jax and I can hang out."

"You'd do that?"

"Sure. Why not?"

He tipped his head. "I can think of a thousand other things you could do on your day off. I think, Molly Stiles, that in addition to being drop-dead gorgeous, you've got a big heart."

Molly blushed, then glanced at her clothes. "Gorgeous? I'm a mess. If I'm going to Savannah, I need to run home, put away my groceries, and change." She held the baby out in front of her. "Look at you. So sweet, and Uncle Brant's bad-mouthing you."

Jax cooed and babbled, then blinked one eye.

"Are you winking at me?"

He threw her a sloppy grin.

"Is it okay if I go with you while Uncle Brant visits Mommy? Hmm?"

The baby waved his arms, then made a beeline for her necklace.

Laughing, she covered it with one hand. "I do have a price, though." Her gaze slid from the baby to his uncle.

Brant's expression turned wary.

She smiled. "After you visit your sister, take Jax and me to my favorite Savannah lunch spot."

"Is it babyproof?"

"Very."

Jax let out a high-pitched squeal and thumped his feet against Molly's hip.

"See? Even Jax is excited about it." Molly kissed the baby's cheek.

"The kid's excited about anything he can put in his mouth."

Molly laid her hand on Brant's arm and felt the sizzle. Brant must have, too, because he pulled away, brows raised.

Steady. Stay steady. "It'll be okay," she said.

"Says you."

"Yes, says me. I'll pick up the last few things I need. Then I'm yours for the day."

"Mine for the day?" His tone held a touch of naughtiness.

She tossed him a saucy grin.

"You know," he said, his voice gruff, "a grin like that about cuts a man off at the knees."

Still smiling, she handed him the baby.

But when she pushed her cart in the opposite direction, he stopped her. "Whoa. Wait a minute, sugar. You can't leave me alone with all this." He swept a hand, indicating the mile-long aisle of baby foods and supplies. "Help me. Please."

"What does he like?"

"No idea. I haven't seen him since he was two months old, and Lainey took him to Florida."

Molly bit her tongue. Not a good time to ask about Jax's father.

"He's a beast now, but Jax was a preemie. So for the couple months he was here, he was way too tiny for me. Too breakable. And since Lainey was breastfeeding..." He shrugged.

Palming a jar of food, he gave it the evil eye. "Look at this. The label says number two is for a six-month-old. Jax is seven. Do I still buy him a two? Or do I bump up to a three?"

"Brant, I don't know any more about this than you do."

"Isn't it genetic or something? Part of a woman's DNA?"

She smiled ruefully. "No. I don't have younger siblings, no nieces or nephews. And before you ask, I never babysat. I have no experience whatsoever."

"But you must love babies. I mean, who doesn't?"

Jax let out a loud burp.

She laughed. "I do. Even burping male ones."

Despite herself, she gave in and helped him pick out enough food for a small army.

"What if I feed him something he's allergic to?"

"I don't think that'll be a problem. What have you fed him so far?"

"The stuff in his diaper bag."

"Feed him that till you talk to Lainey. Ask her today."

"Good idea, but boring."

"Well, then, try something different."

He palmed a jar of food. "Quinoa and kale? Seriously? That's like sending the kid off to some sissy spa. Real men don't eat this stuff." Shaking his head, he dropped it into the shopping cart along with a bag of organic pears and spinach mix and "strong veggies" in some kind of a squeeze bag with a Smart Flow spout, whatever the heck that was.

"Think I'll cut the kid a break." He tossed in a container of vanilla pudding mixed with bananas. "That should be good, right?"

"I'd like it…I think," Molly said.

"You know what, though? Tucker always breaks out in a rash when he eats bananas. Do you think Jax will?"

"He might."

With a sigh, Brant returned the pudding to the shelf. "It shouldn't be this hard to buy groceries for a baby."

They moved to the diaper section, and Brant groaned. "So does Jax need supersoft swaddlers or sensitive swaddlers?" He moved on to the next box. "Or maybe this twelve-hour protection that promises to keep him snug and dry for that long? That would cut down on the diaper changes."

He glanced at Jax, who had found a piece of lint on his blanket that fascinated him. "I don't think so. These must be for older kids with more bladder control."

"Actually," Molly said, looking more closely at the boxes, "I think they're sized by weight."

"Okay, that makes it easier."

"Do you know how much he weighs?"

"A little less than a car tire, so I'd say about seventeen, eighteen pounds."

"Seriously? That's how you figure weight?"

"Hey, I'm a car man. It's what I do." His shoulders slouched. "Give me a rusted-out car, and I can make the thing sing. Yet standing here in the baby aisle, I'm practically paralyzed for fear of screwing up." He tipped his head and scanned the ceiling. "If somebody's watching this on camera, you have my permission to laugh your butt off."

Behind him, an elderly lady, one hand cupped behind her ear, said, "What's that? Couldn't hear you."

He rubbed his tired eyes and, refusing to meet Molly's, swallowed a laugh. "I said I need some butter."

"You're in the wrong aisle, honey."

"I sure am. You have a good day."

"You too." She laid a wrinkled, age-spotted hand on Jax's cheek. "Your daddy's a good-lookin' guy, isn't he? So are you." After a little pat, she wheeled her cart away.

Brant watched her go. "I've always heard grocery stores and babies were women magnets, but that sweet, hard-of-hearing octogenarian isn't quite what I had in mind."

Then he smiled and turned to her. "You still willing to go to Savannah and spend your day off with us?"

"I am—but don't forget, you owe me lunch." She eyed the shelves of formula. "Do you know which of these he drinks?"

Brant whipped out his phone and brought up the picture he'd taken of the empty container.

They added it, along with baby wipes, no-tears shampoo, and a couple new bottles to the jumble around Jax.

Molly handed him a bottle brush. "Don't forget to wash those bottles before you use them."

"I won't. Maybe I can take them in the shower, too."

"What?" Her brow furrowed.

"Never mind."

"I need to stop at the deli," Molly said. What she really needed was some space between herself and Brant Wylder for a few minutes. He was—spectacular. He was so…so male.

He tagged along behind her. Swinging around, she asked, "What are you doing?"

"Going to the deli."

"Why?"

"Because I need lunch meat." He waved a hand at his cart. "All this is for Jax. I need food, too."

"Fine," she grumbled.

"Hey, Molly." A tall, older woman stood behind the counter, her white hair tucked under a net cap.

"How are you today, Ms. Ella?"

"Ah, my darned lumbago's acting up, but other than that, I ain't got nothin' to complain about. What can I do for you?"

"I'd like a quarter pound of chipped ham, please."

Behind Molly, Jax started fussing. Brant patted his back, whispering to him, and the baby practically burrowed into his chest.

She heard a huge sigh. Ella leaned on the counter, staring moon-eyed at Brant.

"Is there anything sexier than a big, strong man holding a baby?"

"No." Molly let out a sigh of her own. "Unfortunately there's not."

After they separated, Molly made quick work of her shopping. When Brant finished his, he met her at the front of the store.

"Want to follow me home?" she asked.

"Yeah, I do."

His low-timbered voice set off warning bells in Molly, and she knew he knew exactly what he was doing. The man was walking testosterone, and that slow grin? Whew. In a pair of jeans and a T-shirt that fit exactly right, dark glasses, and a backward ball cap, Brant Wylder pushed every single one of her buttons.

Then she glanced at Jax and laughed out loud. "Where did he get that?"

"The magazine aisle. I thought we could both use one."

The baby, now wearing a bright-red ball cap with the brim to the side, giggled.

"The kid's got NASCAR in his blood. I'd rather have an A. J. Allmendinger hat, but no luck."

"He's the driver you follow?"

"Yep. All the way. You a racing fan?" he asked.

"Me? No, but my dad is. He was a huge Rusty Wallace fan and practically went into mourning when Rusty retired. I'm not sure who he roots for now."

"How can you not know that?"

She chewed her bottom lip. "I don't see him often."

"Okay." Curiosity, quickly banked, had flared in his eyes. "Bristol's my favorite race. My brothers and I never miss it. In fact, we already have our tickets for next year. I'll get the kid an A. J. hat there if I don't find one before." He jiggled his keys, then quickly hid them behind his back when Jax reached for them. "Can't have those for a few more years, bud."

"Are you wearing jeans to the hospital?"

"Yep. I know you're used to seeing me in a tux, but

that's not me. This is. The Wylder brothers? Rugged. Manly."

"I know."

He cocked a brow. "How?"

"Your hands are working hands." She took one, turned it in hers, and ran a finger along it.

Catching an edge of unease in his eyes, she pressed her palm over his much larger one. "I like them. This is the hand of a man who protects, who fixes."

He folded his fingers over hers.

"You know where I live in case we get separated?"

"No."

"I live above my shop. That Little White Dress."

"Across from the wine and cheese shop?"

"Right."

"Short commute."

"I like it."

"Think I'll stop by the inn and drop off the stuff I won't need. Fortunately, Annabelle put minifridges in the rooms."

"Okay. See you in a few." She left him cramming the pile of supplies into his trunk.

Molly hit the house debating on whether to change clothes before or after she put away her groceries. Vanity won. She dumped her bags on the table and flew into her bedroom. What to wear? Her ruthlessly organized closet held work clothes on one side and casual wear on the other. Today called for something in between.

She stripped off her sweats and slid into a pair of black jeans. The faded sweatshirt went into the hamper.

Riffling through her choices, she considered several tops before deciding on a supersoft, lightweight sweater in pale blue. The longer sleeves might feel good in the hospital. Since the top had a scoop neck, she added a gold double-chain necklace with several dangly stars, then thought better of it and removed this magnet for little fingers.

While she swiped fresh mascara over her lashes—since she didn't have fabulous ones like Brant and Jax—the doorbell rang. Her heart nearly jumped out of her chest.

"What am I doing, Bubbles? Did I offer to go with him because he needs help or because I find him fascinating? And isn't that scary?"

The cat made a low, purring sound and twisted around her ankle.

The bell rang again.

Too late to question why now.

———

Brant watched as Molly, with a huge white cat trailing in her wake, took her own sweet time walking down the stairs toward them. The black jeans and soft-looking sweater she'd changed into practically had him drooling.

"Hey, Brant."

The second she opened the door, the cat whirled and sprinted up the stairs.

She grimaced. "That was Bubbles, who is by now cowering under the bed." She leaned in and gave the baby a kiss. "Hello, sweetie. I'm almost ready. Why don't you come up while I finish? I've got a few perishables to put away, then I'm good to go."

The baby in his arms, Brant followed her upstairs to an apartment filled with light. "Blue is a great color for you."

She blushed. "Thanks. I have a thing for it."

"Yeah, I see that." He had a nearly overwhelming urge to drop a quick kiss on her pert nose.

Her apartment, simple yet comfortable, seemed so...Molly, with old pine floors, big windows, the feminine touches. "My mother would go bonkers over this place."

With Jax balanced on his hip, Brant followed her into the eat-in kitchen—again, light and airy. A huge set of doors with transom windows above took up an entire wall and led to a stunning deck. A girlie-to-the-max crystal chandelier hung over the table. Everything except the pink flowers on the table was either blue or white. The space fit her perfectly, yet strangely enough, he didn't feel out of place in the middle of it all.

He nodded toward the living room. "Will your cat bother the baby if I put him down on a blanket?"

"No. She won't come out till you're gone. Then she'll slink around the room's edges until she's satisfied the enemy has left."

"Good to know." He plunked Jax down in the center of a spread baby blanket. Kneeling, Brant walked his fingers from the baby's belly to his chin and grinned at the giggle. Handing him a rattle, he said, "Here you go. Chew on this."

Returning to the kitchen, he watched as she dispatched the groceries into a spartan pantry and fridge. Food didn't appear to be high on Molly's priority list. Everything in them, though, had a very precise and exact spot, including the Oreos, which were a surprise. Maybe one of these nights they could share a couple along with ice-cold glasses of milk.

He peeked around the corner to check on Jax, who'd kept up a constant stream of gibberish. The kid was happy. The cat was nowhere in sight.

Gazing back at Molly, he watched a big bunch of broccoli disappear into her crisper. That, he decided, she could eat by herself. She kept her home the way he kept his shop. His house, though? A little more relaxed.

Before she closed the fridge door, she asked, "Want something cold to drink?"

"You have water?"

"I do." She handed him a bottle and took another for herself. Then she hefted her purse to her shoulder. "Ready if you are."

"Let's do it, then."

Two steps into the living room, he stopped so quickly, she bumped into him.

"Whoops, sorry," she said.

"Would you look at that?"

Molly peered around his shoulder.

Jax was on all fours. A little wobbly, he crawled a couple of inches before collapsing.

"Wait till I tell Lainey."

The baby rose again, an ear-to-ear grin on his face, and Brant grabbed his phone from a back pocket and videoed him as he moved toward them. He turned his head to show Molly, and they nearly grazed lips.

If he leaned in, would she spook and shy away, or would she meet him?

He didn't get to find out, as she stepped back.

"I think he's got that pretty well down pat. You do know what that means? Nothing will be safe, and you're really going to have to keep an eye on him. No more finding him where you leave him."

"Yeah." His stomach churned. So much to think about, to remember.

———

In no time, they were on the road to Savannah. Jax, true to form, fell fast asleep the minute the car wheels started to turn.

"See?" Brant jerked his chin toward the rearview mirror. "I swear, if I could drive him around all night, he'd put in a full eight hours of sleep."

"Hire a chauffeur."

He snorted.

"Or not. You need one of those plug-in swings. If it's the motion that puts him to sleep, that might work the same as a car."

"Not a bad idea. Or maybe I can get my hands on one of Ford's concept cribs. They've got it all figured out. You get the sound of the engine, the motion of the car, and LEDs to simulate nighttime city lights."

"You're pulling my leg."

"Nope." He picked up his smartphone. "And it's all controlled by an app on this."

"I want one," Molly said. "Might be good for insomniac nights."

Brant waggled his brows. "I can help with that."

She grinned. "I'll just bet you can."

Because the day had turned beautiful, they cracked their windows a couple of inches. It felt good, almost too good, considering the reason for the trip. Guilt nagged at Brant.

He felt her watching him. "What?"

"What happened to your sister wasn't your fault."

"I know that."

"Then why are you scowling?"

"I'm not."

"Seriously? I'm sitting here beside you, and believe me, that expression would have intimidated even Genghis Khan."

"Molly—"

She shook her head and held up a hand. "Not my business." Then she drew in a deep breath. "I know *this* isn't any of my business, either, but I can't help but wonder. Where's Jax's daddy?"

"Jason? Who knows?" Brant rested his right hand on the gearshift knob. "When Lainey got pregnant, my folks pitched a fit and demanded she and Dimwit get married." He sighed. "I never did think that was a good idea, but in the end it didn't matter. The night before the wedding, Jason bolted. Lainey was devastated, and my mom and dad were heartbroken for her. He never even showed up when Jax was born, has never laid eyes on his son. What kind of man behaves like that?"

"A real jerk. Unfortunately, there are a lot of them out there." Molly thought of her own father. He'd hung around longer than Jax's daddy, but he'd walked just the same.

Brant threw her a sideways glance. "There's more." He spilled it all: Lainey's teenage drinking problem, her rehab and five years of sobriety, and the DUI that caused her accident. "So we've got a lot on our plate."

"Kemper Dobson in Misty Bottoms is a great lawyer if you need, you know, legal help."

"I'll keep him in mind. Thanks."

"Even though I've never met Lainey, I'm so sorry for her. She's way too young to have so much history."

"You're a nice person, Molly."

"I have my moments." She twisted a small gold ring on her pinky. "What was she doing here, in Georgia? Your home's in Tennessee, right?"

"Yep. Lake Delores, just south of Nashville." He switched lanes, passed a car, and considered telling her about his possible plan to move to Misty Bottoms. Not yet. Still too many ifs. "I don't have a clue why Lainey's here. That's one of the things we need to talk about."

Molly glanced into the back. Spying Jax's limp arm dangling over the side of his car seat, she assumed he was still asleep. No matter what kind of tantrum he threw, her instincts told her she'd be far better off with him than in the room with Brant and his sister.

Chapter 7

"LAINEY?" BRANT STUCK HIS HEAD INTO HIS SISTER'S room, telling himself this first visit would be the hardest, that it would get easier.

"Brant!" Her voice sounded weak, her words slurred. "What are you doing here?"

"I came to see you, sugar." His fingers tightened on the doorjamb.

Two black eyes marred his sister's face, and her right cheek was swollen and discolored. Her chin sported a Steri-Strip over stitches, a cast protected her left arm, and he could only guess what the sheets hid.

Machines beside her bed beeped.

"Oh, honey." Stepping inside, he wrapped his hands around the bed rails, afraid to touch her, afraid he might hurt her. An IV ran into her right hand.

"Is Jax okay?"

"He's fine."

"Can I see him?"

"Maybe tomorrow."

Tears dripped from her eyes and ran down her bruised cheeks. "I miss him."

"Sure you do, but please don't cry. I..." He spread his hands, then grabbed a tissue from the box on her nightstand and gently dabbed at her tears.

She sniffled and, refusing to meet his eyes, turned her head to stare at the wall. "I screwed up. Again."

"Look at me, Lain. Whatever happened, whatever's wrong, we can fix it."

"No! No, you can't!" Her gaze, angry now, clashed with his. "You can't fix it, Brant. Don't you understand? You can't fix everything!"

Her words stung, and he stepped back.

"You think you, and you alone, are responsible for the whole family. After Tucker left for the Marines, you shouldered it all. You're not God, Brant! It's not your job to look after us."

"I don't do that."

"Yes, you do. And what's worse is, we let you. You make it so easy for all of us to sit back while you take care of us."

"I won't apologize for that."

"No. You wouldn't."

Molly's words from that morning in the grocery store rushed back to him. *This is the hand of a man who protects, who fixes.* She'd nailed him right from the get-go.

Lainey studied him. "You look tired."

He shrugged.

"Did you get any sleep?"

"Enough."

"Bull. One of the nurses said you stayed all night, waiting till I was out of surgery. You and Jax."

"I napped. So did Jax. Then we caught another hour or so at the inn."

She averted her eyes again, and Brant said nothing, simply waited. Outside her room, carts rattled past, nurses and visitors chatted, and a call button in the next room beeped. Someone in the room across the hall was watching an old *I Love Lucy* rerun.

"How's it going with Jax?"

He groaned. "That baby's a heck of a lot of work."

She nodded.

"That first messy diaper?" Brant made a gagging sound and got a hint of a smile for his trouble.

"Where is he now?"

"In the waiting room with—a friend."

That set off the waterworks again.

Brant felt useless. Since he didn't have a clue what else to do, he handed her another tissue and walked to the window. Hands jammed in his pockets, he watched people scurry along the sidewalk below and wished Molly were with him. She'd know what to say.

Then he remembered Molly's mile-wide grin, when Jax had crawled his first couple of inches.

"I have something to show you." As if it were a lifeline, he slid the phone from his shirt pocket. "Come on, Lainey, dry those tears so you can watch."

He pulled up the video and leaned down, holding the phone close to her. As the clip played, his sister smiled and patted at her tears.

"He's never done that before!"

"I didn't think so."

"And I missed it." She started to cry again.

Oh boy! He pinched the bridge of his nose.

"I'm a terrible mother!"

"No, I don't buy that. Jax is too perfect, too healthy, too happy. You're doing a great job, Sis."

She wiped her eyes and nose. "I have no right, but can I ask a favor?"

"Anything."

"Could you bring me a phone? I'd like to be able to call out. Long distance."

"I'll have one for you tomorrow."

"One more thing?"

"Sure."

"Would you load that video of Jax on it?"

His throat tightened again, and he battled his own damp eyes. "Yeah, I'll do that. I'll take a picture of him in his new hat, too. NASCAR."

She rolled her eyes, and he breathed easier.

"Hey, cars are the family business. A boy's never too young to start." He rounded back to their earlier conversation. "If you resented my help and didn't want me poking in your business, why'd you let me?"

"Because then I could blame you for my screwups. I didn't have to accept ownership when things went wrong." She studied the cast on her arm.

"Has it helped?" he asked quietly.

"No," she whispered.

After a century-long minute, Brant cleared his throat. "Dad and Mom want to be here, but…" He trailed off.

"Mom can't come, and Dad won't leave her."

He nodded. "Tucker and Gaven flew to Texas last night to pick up a '53 Vette. They'll trailer it back to Tennessee."

"I know. They called a little while ago."

"They did?"

"They told me they loved me…and that you'd take care of me." Lainey picked at a loose thread on her sheet. "Once again, you're left holding the bag."

"I wouldn't say that."

Her gaze met his, unwavering this time. "I would."

Spotting a chair in the corner, Brant pulled it alongside the bed and dropped into it. "So let's talk about you. How are you feeling?"

"Pretty sucky." She sent him a sidelong glance. "How mad are you?"

He hesitated, but decided to give it to her straight. "I've gotta be honest, Lain. I'm pretty pissed."

"I don't remember the accident."

"Because you were drunk."

She nodded.

"And that makes it worse, doesn't it?"

"Yeah." She sank into her pillow and closed her eyes. "They told me nobody else was involved."

"You were lucky. Someone else could be in here fighting for his or her life—or worse."

"I know," she whispered.

Oh, he hated this, hated everything about it. She looked so young, so hurt. So sorry. He wanted to bundle her up and hide her away from the world, but that wouldn't help. During the family part of her therapy last time, they'd stressed her need to confront her actions.

"Why are you in Savannah?" His voice sounded raw even to his own ears. "It's okay, I guess, if you don't want to tell me, but..."

"A friend of Jason's told me he'd moved here."

"Jason? You were chasing Jason?"

She swiped at her nose again. "I wanted him to see our son, Brant, to understand what a beautiful child we'd made. He had a job tending bar on River Street, near the Cotton Exchange, but I was too late." Her gaze lowered to her clenched hands. "He'd already quit his job and left with one of the waitresses."

Brant swore a blue streak. "I swear, I'll kill the SOB, if I ever get my hands on him."

"He's Jax's father."

"I don't care. That doesn't change the fact he's a miserable excuse for a human being. Your son has three uncles who adore him. He's better off without Jason in the picture."

Then he caught the expression on his sister's face, and his brow furrowed. "Tell me you don't still love him."

"I don't know." She winced and moved restlessly in bed.

"You hurting?"

"Only every inch."

"You need a nurse? Something to take the edge off the pain?"

"In a bit." She plucked at her sheet. "The bartender told me about Jason and his new girlfriend. That's when I had the first drink. I had Jax with me, so Ralph refused to serve me a second."

"Good for him."

Her face fell. "I miss Jason."

"Forget him, Lainey. He's not worth your tears."

"I tell myself that, and most of the time I even believe it."

Was he asking the impossible? Could his sister ever forget the man who'd fathered her child? The man she'd loved? He thought about Molly, out in the waiting room. If he fell in love with her and she left, would it be so easy to put her out of his mind? To set aside that smile, the joy that spilled from her?

Don't even go there. Not the same as Lainey's situation. He'd known Molly for less than two days, and they had no history.

"When I took Jax to Trisha's and asked her to watch him for a few hours, I didn't have any plan. I stopped at a convenience store for gas, saw the beer display, and bought a six-pack." She pulled the sheet over her head. "Dumb, dumb, dumb."

He laid a hand over hers. "We all make mistakes, Sis."

"Not that kind. It's not like I forgot to turn in my library book or added too much creamer to my coffee. Those are mistakes. Driving drunk? That's criminal, and I could have killed someone."

"Yeah, you could have. I'm not gonna lie, nor am I ready to bury you."

She gasped.

"I'm telling it like it is, Sis. No do-overs and no soft-pedaling this time." With a single finger, he drew down the sheet and carefully tipped her chin up so their eyes met. "I'm also telling you, though, that we'll get through this. Together."

"Don't you ever get tired of being the adult?"

He sighed, thought of Jax in the waiting room with Molly…and didn't answer.

For a few minutes, quiet crept into the room as both thought their own thoughts, danced with their own devils.

"Sis, I hate to do this, but I have one more question."

"I'm tired. I don't want to talk anymore." Her voice sounded small and unsteady.

He breathed in deeply, let it out. "The drink at Jason's workplace. Was that your first since rehab?"

No answer.

"I need to know, Lain. Are you drinking again?"

Her quiet tears answered his question.

———

When Brant stepped out of her room, he took a few minutes. Drained, he leaned against the wall, head back, eyes closed. A dull ache lurked behind his eyes, and he swore somebody had tightened a tourniquet around his forehead. Even his neck and shoulders felt tight. Stress. He needed aspirin, but that would have to wait. Figuring he'd put Molly through enough hell, he went to rescue her from Jax.

He needn't have worried. The second he turned the corner, he heard her talking to the baby in that soft, slow Georgia drawl that ensured every word had at least three syllables.

It reminded him of his mom, before her stroke. She'd grown up right here in Savannah. His mother's drawl was soothing, but Molly's churned up entirely different feelings in his gut, in his lower regions. And he'd better keep that under control. This wasn't the time for sexual fantasies.

"Ready to break out of this joint?"

Molly looked up from the baby, her eyes assessing. "How is she?"

He huffed out a sigh. "A mess. Physically and emotionally."

"But she'll be okay?"

"Yeah." He knelt beside her and started collecting the baby's things, stuffing them randomly in the diaper bag.

"Here." She handed him an aspirin bottle and the rest of her lukewarm soda. "You look like you could use these."

"Saint Molly."

Outside, the early January afternoon held a real nip, and Molly pulled Jax's blanket a little higher.

Brant's gaze traveled over her, in her sweater and jeans. Formal or casual, she made his heart beat just that little bit faster. Time to think about something else. He patted his stomach. "Are you as hungry as I am?"

"Starving."

"Does that favorite restaurant of yours sell any real food?"

"They do. It's the perfect spot for an easy—" She glanced at the baby who, happy two minutes ago, had started to whimper. "Easy and informal meal."

Brant scrounged in the diaper bag for the pacifier, and Jax sucked away, happy again for the moment.

As they crossed the hospital parking lot, Brant held up a finger and veered in the opposite direction. Molly followed.

He stopped in front of a restored '56 Chevy Bel Air and ran his eye over its fender and along its curves the way most men would over a woman. Tenting his hands over his eyes, he peeked inside.

"Nice," Molly said from behind him.

"Yeah, it is. Too bad they used the wrong paint."

"Excuse me?"

"This is a '56. It would have been Matador Red. Paint code 697." He shook his head. "Somebody used Rio Red, a '58 Chevy color."

"Does it matter?"

Mouth open, he rounded on her. "Does it *matter*?"

She shrugged. "Maybe they liked Rio Red better. Is it that big a deal?"

Rolling his eyes, he said, "Yes. Believe me, honey, it is." He reached for the baby. "I'll carry him. He's heavy." His nose wrinkled. "Take a look at that face. I think I know why he's fussing."

"Messing his diaper?"

"Oh yeah. I'll run him back inside. The men's rooms actually have changing stations."

"I'll let you, since I changed the last one."

He grimaced, then jerked a thumb at the Chevy. "When you're restoring a car like this, every detail matters. That attention to the small things is what separates Wylder Rides, the business my brothers and I own, from the rest. It's the reason we're so busy."

As they crossed back to the hospital, she asked, "What's happening with your business while you're here and your brothers are in Texas?"

"We've got four great guys who work for us. The shop's closed today, but I gave Rudy a call this morning and explained the situation. He'll open tomorrow, and they'll work on the projects we've got underway. They'll do fine till Gaven and Tucker get back."

Jax decided it was playtime the second Brant laid him on the changing table. He wanted to show off his crawling technique and flipped onto his stomach, then rose to his hands and knees.

"Not a good move, when you're three feet in the air." Brant grabbed him around the waist. "You have no fear, do you?"

"Ga-ga-ga-ga."

"Time to toss the diaper, big guy. We can't take a lady to lunch in this one."

It was touch and go for a bit, but eventually the job was completed, and he and a much sweeter-smelling Jax joined Molly in the waiting room.

They stepped into the cool air a second time and strolled to Brant's car.

"So where's this lunch mecca of yours?" he asked.

"Leopold's Ice Cream on East Broughton Street. You'll love it."

"Good. I'm starved."

She gave him directions to Abercorn Street and around Oglethorpe Square to East Broughton.

"Leopold's is one of a kind. The original store opened in 1919, right after the First World War. When it closed, his son had the good sense to store some of the furnishings, including a black marble fountain and an old wooden phone booth. He went to Hollywood and did some directing, I think. When he decided to reopen the store, one of the Hollywood set designers recreated his dad's shop. Walking into Leopold's is like stepping back in time."

"You're sure the baby won't be a problem?"

"Not even."

~~~

Half an hour later, Brant's headache was gone. He scanned the old-fashioned ice cream parlor and admitted that Molly had nailed the late-lunch choice perfectly. She'd made the entire day easier.

When he'd first laid eyes on her, his initial reaction

had been purely physical. The more time he spent with her, though, the more he liked her, really liked her. He could let that be a problem, or he could choose simply to enjoy their time together. For now, he'd go with the latter.

When their waiter showed up, Molly greeted him. "Hey, Dan, how's everything today?"

"Pretty good, Mol. Haven't seen you around for a while." His eyes moved to Brant, then to the baby playing pat-a-cake with the table top. "Somethin' I should know? You been keepin' secrets?"

"No." She grinned. "Dan, this is Brant Wylder and his nephew Jax. We've been visiting a relative of his at the hospital."

Dan's forehead creased. "Aren't you the dude that fixes up old cars and motorcycles?"

"I am," Brant admitted.

"Thought so. I've caught you on TV a few times." He shook his head regretfully. "Sure wish I could afford a '31 Indian Scout 101 like the one you restored for that rapper."

"That was the last year they made those."

"Sure was pretty." Dan pulled a pencil from behind his ear. "Know what you want?"

"We do." Brant tipped his head toward Molly. "Ladies first."

"She's gonna have a cream cheese and olive sandwich on white, right?"

"You've got it," she said. "And a glass of water, please."

"A scoop of tutti-frutti afterward?"

"Absolutely."

Brant's brows drew together. "You always get the same thing?"

"Here, yes." She handed her menu to Dan. "I love that sandwich, and not many places serve it."

"Cream cheese and olives?" Brant pulled a face. "I'd hope not."

"Oh, you so don't know what you're missing."

"I think I'll leave it that way. The roast beef with horseradish for me."

"Anything to drink?"

"A chocolate malt."

"Anything for the kid?"

"No, he'd better stick with his gruel." Brant stood the baby on his lap. "On second thought, when you bring Molly's ice cream, bring us a child's scoop of vanilla. Jax and I will share it."

"You got it."

"Do you have high chairs?"

"We do. I'll drop off your order, then be back with one." Dan hustled off.

"I guess you were a regular here." Brant steadied Jax as he tried out his wobbly little legs.

"I had to be on East Broad every Thursday for a meeting, so I'd stop here for lunch."

They ate, they talked, they laughed. Brant felt better than he had since before his dad's call.

While he fed Jax, now strapped into his own seat, Molly shared her dreams for her new shop, and he told her about Wylder Rides.

"Gaven and I started it. Tucker signed up for a stint with the Marines after his third year of college. The man's hell on wheels when it comes to working on anything with a motor. Even better, he's got a head for business, so when he decided not to re-up this last time, it was a good fit all around for him to join us." He took too big a pull on his shake and rubbed at his forehead. *Brain freeze.* "Right now, we have some serious growing pains, so we're scouting for a new shop location."

Yet another opening to mention that Misty Bottoms was their first choice, but again he held back.

"Good luck with that. Jenni Beth and the girls took me under their wings and smoothed out a lot of bumps."

"Friends will do that for you."

"They will."

"Thanks for being my friend today, Molly. I'd dreaded this trip."

Her dimples deepened with the smile she sent him. "More than glad to help, friend."

Dan brought their sandwiches, and they tucked into them. Brant ate one-handed and fed Jax his bottle with the other hand. He was getting the hang of this.

"Can I ask you something, Molly?"

"Sure—and maybe I'll answer."

He smiled. "Fair enough. You don't really know me, but you came with me today."

"Cole and Beck know you, and if they call you friend, you're a good person."

"Wow. Okay. So what should I know about you, Molly?"

"I'll share one thing. Then it's your turn."

"Okay."

"I like an open window when I sleep."

"Me? I sleep in the buff."

A quick laugh escaped. "Good to know—I guess. I

can't top that, so I'll go with my favorite candy bar. A Peppermint Patty, with Three Musketeers only a step behind."

"You can do better than that."

"No, I can't." She pulled a face. "Okay, how's this? I had a major crush on my eleventh-grade language arts teacher."

"All those dangling participles?"

She swatted him. "Your turn."

The sharing didn't go deep. Still, it was a start.

"Your turn, Jax. Tell Ms. Molly who your favorite uncle is."

Turning on his megawatt smile, Jax babbled.

"Come on," Brant urged. "Uncle…"

The baby made a sound.

"Brant."

Molly laughed. "Eat your sandwich, goofball."

He did. Molly made quick work of hers, too. Then their ice cream came, and they settled down to enjoy it, with Brant stealing a few bites of Molly's tutti-frutti.

He smacked his lips. "Much better than plain vanilla."

"Vanilla is very overrated."

She sat across from him, her incredible dark hair framing that stunning face and those dancing eyes. "Yes, it is," he agreed.

When they finished, Molly swooped Jax up for another diaper change before they hit the road. "My turn."

"Far be it from me to argue with a lady."

"Right."

Afterward, following her out the door, Brant's libido couldn't help but wish for a little more than friendship. Watching Molly and listening to her musical laugh and slow, sexy drawl did things to him...made him want things he'd put on the back burner.

Not that he was a monk. He'd dated and even had a couple of semiserious flings. But Molly? He didn't see her as fling material.

Ten miles outside of town, his phone rang. "Hey, Tuck. What's up?"

"That's what I want to know. How's Lainey?"

In the back seat, Jax waved his hands and jabbered loudly.

Brant laughed. "You get all that, Bro?"

"I got the part about you being incompetent, but I didn't catch the rest."

"Hah, hah. Lainey told me you and Gaven called."

"Yeah, it was short and bittersweet. She's really down on herself."

"She is—and rightly so. I know it's been tough for her, but she should have asked for help instead of running away. That never works." Brant filled his brother in on his visit. Halfway through, Molly laid her hand over his.

Thank you, he mouthed.

"Why don't you find some good-lookin' gal to keep you and the kid company? You can let her—"

"Before you go any further, big brother, you need to know you're on speaker and that Molly Stiles is with me."

The silence was so complete, Brant thought his brother had hung up.

"Molly, you really there?" Tucker asked.

With a Cheshire-cat grin, she answered, "Yes, I am, Tuck. How are you today?"

"I'll let you know just as soon as I remove my left foot from my mouth. I apologize."

She laughed. "There's nothing to apologize for, but I'll keep my eyes open for a good-looking gal for your brother. One I assume will take over baby duty."

Tucker's groan was more than audible.

"Actually, Molly did sit with Jax today while I visited Lainey. Her first ever babysitting job."

They talked another few minutes. Tucker apologized again, and Brant clicked off.

"And that was my older brother. Believe it or not, he doesn't usually talk much."

"That might not be so bad, all things considered."

They locked gazes, and both laughed.

When they reached her apartment, Brant hopped out, surprised at how much the temperature had dropped. "Brr. It must be close to forty." He walked around the front of the car and opened the passenger door. "You should have worn a jacket."

"I'll be fine. I don't have far to go."

He took her hand to help her out and marveled again at how delicate she was, how good she smelled.

She leaned into the back to give the sleeping baby a light kiss on the cheek. "'Bye, sweetie."

"Thanks again, Molly."

She turned. "No prob—"

He kissed her, his hands on either side of her face. The night warmed up, and for that brief moment, nothing existed but him and this woman. He changed the angle, took the kiss a beat deeper, traced her pouty lower lip with the tip of his tongue.

Disoriented, he lifted his head. "Sorry. That probably shouldn't have happened."

Her dusky eyes met his. "Probably not."

But she didn't move. Didn't step back.

After a heartbeat, his hands settled on her hips, held her there so close, the soft cotton of her sweater brushed his arm.

"I'd like to see you again."

"Why?"

Her blunt question disconcerted him. "I think you're—" *Sexy? Drop-dead gorgeous? Hot?* "Interesting," he said on a sigh.

"Uh-huh." She hesitated. "Brant, I'm glad I could help today, and despite the situation, I enjoyed myself. You and Jax are great company, but we both know there's no future here."

"Does there need to be?"

A perplexed expression flickered across her face, in her eyes. Her tongue peeked out between those glorious lips, and he nearly groaned.

"No, there doesn't. But you and me? We both have responsibilities we can't set aside because of—whatever this is."

"You're right." Reluctantly, he removed his hands. "Good night, Molly."

When she opened her mouth to respond, his lips covered hers again, hot and demanding, cutting off her words.

"What—?"

"That's the question I'm asking myself."

She frowned.

"I've been watching those lips drop kisses on Jax all day. I wanted one taste, but one wasn't enough. Neither was two." He drew her to him, his eyes on hers. Slowly, ever so slowly, he leaned in till their lips were a breath away.

"I want you, Molly. You feel it, too."

"I'm not a one-night stand, Brant."

"No. You wouldn't be."

"You won't be here long enough for us even to have this conversation."

He held out his hand, rocked it back and forth in a we'll-see-about-that motion. Then he got into the car and drove away.

What had he been thinking?

Molly stood in front of her store, the twilight deepening around her. What had just happened? Brant was—whew! Where to start? Smart, sexy, funny, a good conversationalist, sexy, a fantastic kisser, loyal to his family, and had she mentioned sexy?

And oh my gosh. Jax! What a sweetie! Those chubby little cheeks and incredible green eyes. When he giggled, she swore her womb started singing.

But to stand out here on the street, where any Misty Bottomer could drive by, and allow Brant to practically swallow her whole? Allow, heck. She'd participated. His car was long out of sight, but her heart still raced fast enough to catch up to him.

This couldn't happen again. Once? Impulse. A fluke. Twice? Impossible. She'd be ready if she ran into him and that sweet baby again.

"Okay, enough, Molly!" She unlocked the door, then leaned against the jamb, studying her quiet shop, a streetlight filtering through the big front window. "Here's your dream. The rest, both men and babies, has to wait."

But oh, today when Brant had passed Jax to her, she'd been totally unprepared for the emotions that swirled through her. She found herself leaning into him, breathing in his baby scent. Baby shampoo and lotion... and baby cuteness. Yes, that had an addictive smell, too.

His silky, fly-away hair had tickled her nose, and she'd found herself wishing he was hers. The longing for a baby to cuddle, to spoil, to love had flooded through her. She wanted to watch her own baby crawl for the first time, wanted to laugh and go all tingly while Daddy filmed it.

And she would.

But what if...what if...she waited too long? What if she didn't find that someone special when the time came? What if she missed the one meant for her? What if someone like Brant—

She laid a hand over her heart. What was so magical about thirty? Did she really have to wait for an arbitrary number?

It was stupid to ask when she knew the answer. It wasn't just the number. It was this shop. Her independence. Security.

Her father.

Keith.

This afternoon, playing pat-a-cake with Lainey's little boy, none of those had seemed important, but they were.

She refused to give up her dreams.

After hurrying upstairs to her apartment, she flicked on the overhead lights and hit the Power button on her stereo. A purring Bubbles emerged from the shadows to rub against her legs.

"We're good, aren't we, sweetheart? You and me."
She petted the cat.

She put on a light jacket. Grabbing her list and a
cup of coffee, she slipped out of her espadrilles and
into warm slippers and headed outside, Bubbles at
her heels.

Her gaze dropped to the aged paper with its faded
black-and-white print. Reason number nine. *Ages 28–
30. Pour my soul into my business. It'll be the best!*
That's what she'd been doing and needed to continue.
Only then could she move on to number ten. *Meet my
future husband and say I do!*

And yeah, the timetable with the age and all might
seem a bit silly, but it had worked for her so far. Goal
setting was important and having a plan to reach them
even more critical. Her eyes strayed to number eleven.
My first baby, a little boy.

Brant's nephew felt so right in her arms. Would her
son be anything like him?

If she was very, very lucky, he would.

She sipped her rapidly cooling coffee and, centering
herself, stared out into the quiet.

Sunday evening, and not a creature was stirring. All
of Misty Bottoms was in for the night, getting ready
for the new work week. By now, the kids had either
finished their homework or were fighting with their parents about it. Dinner dishes had been cleared, showers
taken, and pj's on in time for that favorite wind-down
TV show.

Molly missed her mother, missed the chaos of her
coworkers in Savannah. But she liked setting her own
pace, too. She liked not worrying about what somebody

else preferred, what someone else wanted to do. Living on her own was freeing.

And just a little bit lonely.

And, yes, she was just that little bit hungry for another taste of Wylder lips.

Chapter 8

AFTER STOPPING AT TOMMY'S TEXACO FOR GAS AND A JUST-in-case emergency midnight snack, Brant unlocked his door and carted Jax inside. By sneaking up the back stairs, he'd managed to avoid any of Annabelle's other guests.

Moonlight drifted through the windows. It was six o'clock and already dark outside. He was ready for summer, with its longer days. Flopping on the bed, he muttered, "Give me two seconds here, kiddo, and we'll see about your dinner."

The words had barely passed his lips when Jax started to cry. Brant's chin dropped, and he rolled off the bed, barely resisting the urge to cry himself. Tears. They might mean Jax was hungry or wet. Lonely or mad. All or any or none of those.

With a resigned sigh, he unstrapped Jax and brought him up to his shoulder. "Oh, phew!" Extending his arms, he held the baby away from him. "You stink again."

The baby let out a couple of hiccuping cries.

"Yeah, yeah, I know. Let's get you changed."

Tossing a towel on the bedroom carpet, he placed Jax in the center of it. With the wipes, wastebasket, and diapers within easy reach, he settled down to business. Concentrating, tongue between his teeth like a three-year-old with crayons, Brant barely resisted throwing his arms in the air in victory when he managed the change with more finesse than ever.

"Suppose you want to eat now, don't you?"

Happy again, Jax shook a drool-covered rattle.

"Tell you what. How about we work on that crawl before dinner?"

Jax rolled onto his stomach and got his knees under him.

"Well, I'll be darned. You understood, didn't you?"

Jax jabbered, moved three inches, and toppled. Like the Wylder warrior he was, he raised up again.

Brant kicked off his shoes, pulled off a sock, and tossed it a few inches in front of the baby. Jax immediately scrambled for it. Picking it up, he sat down on his newly diapered butt, waving the sock like a checkered flag.

Brant snatched it from him and threw it again, a little farther away.

Jax was off again.

Brant laughed. "Who needs a dog to play fetch?"

After a few more practices, Jax stuck his fist in his mouth and sucked on it.

"Message received. Hunger strikes." He eyed their choices. "Since we stocked up earlier, zee chef has a wide selection of veritable treats for the palate." He held up a jar of beets, and Jax stuck out his tongue.

"Okay, how about this?" Brant palmed a jar of pureed pork.

"Bababa!"

"Actually, bababa would be lamb, Einstein, but close enough. Pork it is."

Spoonful by painful spoonful, Brant fed him. He made swooshing sounds. "Here comes the race car in for repair. Open the garage door wide."

Jax joined in the game, but when he spit out two

mouthfuls in a row, Brant set aside Annabelle's spoon and bowl. "Okay, we're done here." He swiped the worst of the pork out of the baby's ears and off his forehead and cheeks.

Using a tissue to capture a glob on Jax's toe, he said, "I'll swear under oath I have no idea how that got there, small stuff." He rocked back on his heels. "I need a shower to wash away the hospital stench. Wanna join me?"

The clean diaper came off, and Brant hauled the naked little boy into the shower. Jax slapped at the water, giggling and jabbering—until he tipped his head back and got a nose full. Playtime over.

And Brant had yet to lather up.

After a couple of sneezes, Jax cleared the downed water and stopped crying. He snuggled quietly, curled against Brant's bare chest.

If there had been a hidden camera in this room, somebody somewhere would have been laughing his ass off. At the same time, Brant was astounded at the peace he felt, the belief that all would be well.

But he really did need to wash. After the quickest and least satisfying one-handed shower of his life, he wrapped Jax in a towel and used another to dry himself. Holding the baby in front of the mirror, Brant used a face towel to wipe away the shower haze.

He leaned close and stuck out his tongue.

Jax giggled and opened his mouth. His little tongue moved, but he couldn't quite pull off the trick.

Brant slowly stuck out his tongue again.

Jax managed to imitate him by the third time.

"You're a future Mensa member, kid."

The baby laughed, and Brant high-fived him.

Then Jax's face turned red.

"Oh no," Brant groaned. "Wait, wait, wait!" Holding him over the toilet, he whipped away the towel—just in time. "Not bad, kid."

After some struggling, Brant managed to get both the diaper and clean pajamas on Jax. "We need better sleeping arrangements, champ. Even when you nod off, you keep me awake. I'm afraid I'll roll over and crush you."

His gaze fell on Annabelle's antique cherry dresser. "Aha!" Pulling out the bottom drawer, he grabbed another fluffy bath towel and used it as a liner.

Both Wylder men would sleep in their own beds tonight.

He grabbed the new thriller he'd packed in his duffel and settled down in bed with the baby beside him, sucking on his pacifier. Fourteen pages in, Jax started rubbing his eyes. Within minutes, he surrendered to the sandman. Nearly floored with relief and fatigue, Brant tucked the baby into his makeshift crib, then crawled into his own bed.

The second he closed his eyes, he fell asleep.

Unfortunately, Jax chose that exact moment to wake, and the pattern was set.

Jax slept fitfully, waking every couple of hours. Brant paced the floor with him, worried something might be seriously wrong. Should he call a doctor? Wake Annabelle and ask her?

How in the heck did anybody survive this?

Standing in front of the window, Brant kissed the top of Jax's head. The baby gripped his T-shirt and tipped his head back to stare up at him. This innocent child trusted him. *Him!* Of all people.

Karma could be a sly, twisted little devil. A week ago, if anybody had so much as hinted that he'd be walking the floor with a baby in the middle of the night, he'd have suggested a good shrink. Yet here he was.

Finally, dawn peeked through the windows, and Jax sighed loudly and fell asleep. Brant felt like the walking dead and wanted nothing more than to curl up and sleep for twenty-four hours solid. *Yeah, like that's going to happen.*

How had Lainey coped? She hadn't, and none of them had realized it in time. Had Aunt Flo noticed? If so, why hadn't she given them a heads-up?

He kept walking, patting Jax's back, for another five minutes. When he stayed asleep, Brant carefully eased himself onto the bed, snuggling the baby up beside him this time. Within seconds, he tumbled into his own dreams.

Disoriented and sleep foggy, Brant slowly became aware of insistent pounding. Raising up on one elbow, he glanced around the room.

"You checking out today?" Annabelle shouted through the door.

Jax started awake and whimpered.

"No!" Brant answered. "Go away."

"You didn't buy this room, you know. I've got people coming who expect to stay here."

"Yeah, yeah, yeah. I'll take care of it." The second the words passed his lips, he remembered what Lainey had said yesterday. Had she been right? Did he try to handle everything?

Whatever. In this case he had no choice. "Any chance I can extend my stay?"

Silence.

"Annabelle?"

"I'm checking." Another half minute passed. "I can put tonight and tomorrow night in the end room. Two nights, that's it. I'm full up after that."

"Thank you."

"Yep."

Afraid to move, he heard the innkeeper shuffle down the hall in those too-big purple Converse sneakers she wore.

"Goodbye, Annabelle," he mumbled. Scooping the baby close, he sang what he could remember of a lullaby song, adding a lot of la-la-las for missing words. Jax quieted and, sucking his thumb, fell back asleep.

Brant joined his nephew in a little more shut-eye.

***

Molly had been up for hours. Since yesterday hadn't gone quite the way she'd planned, she set her alarm a little earlier and used the extra time to catch up. The girls would be here soon.

While she tidied her already immaculate office, her mind wandered. She'd woken this morning thinking about Brant and, strangely enough, about her parents. About the way her father had abandoned her and her mom. She'd brought it up a couple of times, and her mother had assured her it had nothing to do with her but that someday she'd understand. Molly had quit asking, afraid it really had been her fault, that her dad left them because of something she had or hadn't done.

Maybe—

The ringing phone jerked her out of her reverie.

"Good morning. That Little White Dress. How can I help you?"

"By giving me some information about my sister."

Straightening, Molly drew her phone away to read caller ID. She didn't recognize the number or the low rumbling voice, although it sounded familiar.

"Excuse me?"

"Is this Molly Stiles?"

"Yes, it is."

"Tucker Wylder, Brant's brother. We talked—sort of—yesterday."

"I remember. I'm afraid, Tucker, I haven't found a good-looking gal to help out with Jax yet."

"I'm sorry about that. I didn't know—"

"That I was in the car."

"Yeah, but that's not why I called. You went with Brant when he visited Lainey."

Since it was a statement rather than a question, Molly wasn't quite sure what he expected her to say.

"Here's the deal," Tucker said. "Brant tends to put a good twist on things, then works his butt off to make them come out that way. What's your take on Sis?"

"My take?"

"Yeah. How is she? Honestly?"

"I didn't see or talk to your sister. Brant was the only visitor allowed. I hung out with Jax in the waiting room."

A sound of pure male frustration came over the line.

Molly took pity on him. "I won't lie. Brant's worried

about her, but he insists she's getting great care and with time she'll be good as new. I believe him."

"You do?"

"Yes, I do."

"All right. Sometimes he pretties things up so the rest of us won't worry. How's he doing?"

A chuckle escaped despite her best efforts. "He's, uh, struggling with the whole baby thing."

Tucker laughed. "I'll bet. Wish I was there to see it."

"He wishes you were here to help."

"I will be. As soon as possible." He paused. "Thanks, Molly. I appreciate what you're doing for my family— and Brant, especially."

"My pleasure." Nice to know Brant had someone who worried about him.

While she was on the phone, Jenni Beth, Tansy, and Cricket had straggled in.

"Come on back," she called.

She'd walled off a corner of the showroom and turned the small space into a cozy haven. The pale-blue walls, white carpet, and crystal lamps conjured a feeling of peace. The outer wall slanted, adding, in her opinion, to the sense of intimacy. Black-and-white photos of brides covered the wall behind her glass-topped desk.

The three wandered in, chatting a mile a minute, and Cricket placed a vase of fresh flowers on the desk. The scent of blue hydrangeas and delphiniums, blush roses, and white Asiatic lilies added to the undeniable femininity of the room.

"I can't believe we're wrapping up the details for my wedding!" Cricket, wearing baggy cotton pants and a gauzy yellow top, dropped into a chair, her short crop of hair even wilder than usual. "It's finally my turn. Sam just kind of found me when I wasn't even looking!"

She grinned. "I'm a florist, so my wedding has to revolve around flowers, right? I want my bouquet to look like I picked the flowers from my own garden that morning." Cricket sighed. "Friday night, after rehearsal, we'll have a big old bonfire in the backyard. With champagne. Lots and lots of champagne."

"Until then—" The ever-organized Tansy held up two thermoses of mocha coffee and pulled four mugs from a tote. "Kitty's tending the bakery." Settling into one of the plush chairs, she slid off her shoes and opened a baker's box. "A sampler of goodies I'm testing for Valentine's Day. They'll hit my shelves at week's end, so if they need tweaking, tell me now. And be honest!"

Cricket groaned. "You do remember I have to fit into that utterly gorgeous dress Molly found for me, don't you?" She sighed. "I can't wait for Sam to get a load of that corset top and tulle skirt."

She sighed again and eyed Tansy's goodie tray. "The enemy. If I gain even an ounce, Molly will have to let out the seams."

"Seriously?" Jenni Beth, her blond hair pulled back in a long ponytail, scrutinized her friend. "You've lost weight."

"Nerves."

"So feed them." Tansy, in a slim pencil skirt and olive-green top that set off her auburn curls, nudged the tray closer to Cricket. "Try the red-velvet crepe. It's filled with mascarpone cream."

Jenni Beth tapped a finger on her chin and picked up a raspberry-buttercream-covered brownie. "This looks absolutely decadent." Her lips turned up in a mischievous grin. "Speaking of decadent, what's this I'm hearing about my roommate and one devilishly handsome Tennessean?"

"What?" Looking for all the world like a kid caught with her hand in the cookie jar, Molly swiped a cookie crumb from her lower lip.

"Did you or did you not go to Savannah with Brant Wylder yesterday?"

"He needed help," she answered slowly. "I played Good Samaritan."

"He is so hot," Tansy breathed.

"You can say that again," Cricket agreed.

Jenni Beth's gaze stayed on Molly.

"Geez!" Still holding her cookie, she held out her hands, palms up. "It's not like we had a smoking-hot date. Even if I were interested in him—which I'm not— we had a baby with us. A seven-month-old baby."

"Glen, over at the wine shop?" Jenni Beth licked raspberry frosting from her finger. "He put in a few hours yesterday."

"It was Sunday." Molly frowned. "They're closed Sundays."

"Which is exactly why he figured it would be a good time to stock shelves."

Molly went still.

"He stayed later than he'd planned."

"What a shame to spend his day off at work," Molly said quietly.

Her friend shrugged. "He saw... How should I put this? Some serious PDA occurring across the street." Managing to look innocent, she asked, "Did you see anything? Maybe outside your window? You know, when you were checking the weather or watching the sunset?"

"Nope, not a thing." Molly felt the hot blush and picked up her notebook. "Now, what still needs to be done for Cricket's wedding?"

The others shared a knowing glance.

Her fault. Small town. She should have known better.

Jenni Beth put an arm around her and whispered, "Don't shut yourself off, Mol. Stay open."

"I am."

"No, you're not. You're afraid you'll let yourself feel, then Brant will do exactly what your dad did."

Molly had no answer.

Wednesday morning finally rolled around. Bone weary, Brant yawned.

Incredibly, he and Jax had survived three entire days—and nights. Seventy-two hours that felt like three months. Sleep like a baby. Ha! Whoever had coined that term had some sick sense of humor. Babies didn't sleep. They napped only long enough to make you think *you* could sleep. The minute you shut your eyes? All hell broke loose.

Even before Annabelle's Monday-morning visit, he understood he and Jax couldn't stay at the B and B indefinitely. Heck, he was surprised she'd put up with them this long, and even more baffled one of the other guests hadn't complained or run them out of town.

Every day, he and Jax showered, ate, then burned up the road between Misty Bottoms and Savannah. More than once, he'd stopped for an emergency diaper change or a quick cuddle. The kid liked to be touched, but then, who didn't? He thought about those kisses he and Molly had stolen outside her shop. She was hot.

And she was busy. Fortunately, the hospital had a day care where he could leave Jax during his visits with Lainey. Physically, she was making progress, but Brant didn't kid himself. The hardest part lay ahead of them.

He'd kept the family up-to-date, and yesterday he'd tried to talk his sister into some Facetime with their parents. She'd flat-out refused, finally pulling the sheet over her head.

After a full half hour of silence, he'd kissed her forehead through the cotton. "I'll be back tomorrow, Lainey. Love you."

She didn't answer, and he'd left with a heavy heart.

On the way home, he and Jax had detoured to check out the first spot he and his brothers had tapped as a possible relocation site. He wasn't impressed. It lacked both the building space and the land they needed, so he'd ruled it out.

He'd wait till he was in a better frame of mind to scope out the second location.

But that was yesterday. More than Jax kept him awake last night. Somewhere around two, his thoughts wandered from his sister's mess to Molly. While he and Jax paced the floor, he remembered the feel of her in his arms. Her quick laugh and bottomless eyes. The scent that was uniquely hers, hot and sexy, feminine and innocent. Somehow she'd crawled into his head.

Massaging the back of his neck, he dragged himself out of bed. Six forty-five a.m., and he was exhausted.

Something had to change. He felt like one of those gerbils running on a wheel and getting absolutely nowhere.

Bleary-eyed, he punched the Keurig button and inhaled as the rich aroma of coffee filled the room. He took his first hit and scalded his tongue.

"Hot!" He took a second, more cautious sip and smiled. "Good."

Despite the caffeine, Brant dragged butt. He needed a shower, a shave, and some slightly less rumpled clothes. Jax, however, disagreed and demanded the morning be about him. A bottle didn't work. He spit out the peaches Brant tried to feed him. He even refused his pacifier.

Brant's number-one priority shifted from a shower to keeping the kid from waking their neighbors. He and Jax hustled down the back stairs and headed to the Texaco station.

Tommy, a Braves cap clamped over his wild head of copper hair, met him at the pump. "How ya doin' this mornin'?"

"Tired."

"A baby'll do that to ya." Nozzle in hand, Tommy said, "Hot coffee inside, if you wanna grab a cup. I'll keep an eye on the kid here while I fill your tank."

"Thanks. Think I will."

"Ham biscuits, too, if you're interested," Tommy called after him. "Wife made them not more than half an hour ago."

The biscuits smelled like heaven, but Brant decided to stick with caffeine.

A few minutes later, with fresh coffee in hand and a full tank of gas, Brant pulled onto the two-lane. They were running tests on Lainey today, so the doctor had asked him to stay away. That meant he and Jax had a whole day to kill here in Misty Bottoms. What the heck would they do? It wasn't as if he and his nephew could toss a football or fly a kite. Anxiety settled in. How did you keep a seven-month-old entertained?

He drove along the river with his heater on and his window cracked, enjoying the fresh country smells. Earlier, the fog had been heavy, but as the rest of the world woke, it too rose.

Brant glanced into the back seat and shook his head. As usual, the turning wheels had done the trick. The kid was out like a light, his left arm dangling limply at his side. Brant had a few quiet minutes to tussle with some important decisions.

First, though, he'd check out the second location on their list.

Pulling up to it, he remembered what they'd liked about it. This place had plenty of room. It needed some work, but that didn't scare him. What did scare him, though, was the back of the building.

There'd been a fire. A major one. And that meant the basic structure had probably been compromised. Once they stripped the remaining walls, who knew what they'd find.

This one was a definite no-go. It needed a total rebuild.

Frustrated, he crawled back in the car, shutting his door quietly, then peeking in the rearview mirror. He loved the kid, he really did. But he'd had no idea how much work and attention a baby needed. Dealing with twins or triplets must feel like being swept away by a tsunami.

After executing a U-turn, he'd started back toward the center of town when his phone rang. "Hello?" Fearful of waking Jax, he kept his voice low.

"Hey, Bro. It's Gaven."

"Where are you?"

"Lake Delores. We got in late last night."

A tiny fissure of hope cracked open.

"I can barely hear you, BT."

"Don't want to wake Jax."

"Gotcha."

They talked about Lainey and the Vette Gaven and Tucker had picked up.

"Neither of the places we tagged are gonna work for a shop." Brant gave his brother a rundown on each. "I'll keep my eyes open, though."

"Good enough. As soon as we take care of a few things here, Tucker and I'll head to Misty Bottoms. You still at the inn?"

"Yeah, but we've outstayed our welcome. Annabelle needs the room." He scratched his head. "I might have to book one in Savannah."

"Let us know. Tucker's telling me to wind it up. Talk to you later."

He hung up, and Brant was alone again.

Driving slowly along random streets, he was shocked at how many of the townspeople he'd come to know. He passed the huge lavender-and-green house at the end of Main. Tansy's Sweet Dreams. She and Beck, whose family owned Elliot's Lumber Yard, had tied the knot not long ago.

Speaking of Beck, Brant wondered, not for the first time, what it would take to get his hands on that guy's '65

Chevy short-bed stepside pickup. The thing was in perfect condition, except for one small dent in a back fender.
Since it hadn't been fixed, Brant smelled a story there.

Turning onto Old Church Street, he spied the peri-
winkle railroad car that housed Cricket O'Malley's
Enchanted Florist. Like so many small Southern towns,
Misty Bottoms had been headed down the tubes—in the
fast lane. When Jenni Beth transformed her family's
falling-down antebellum home into a destination wedding spot, the entire town had blossomed.

A lot of new stores had opened, and limping-along
ones now thrived. Cursing as the uneven brick street
gave his Camaro's suspension a workout, he shot a
quick glance at the rearview mirror. Jax hadn't stirred.

And then the day got a whole lot better. There they
were. Both That Little White Dress and its owner. Since
the street was nearly empty this early, he pulled in a
couple of car lengths behind her Mini. Molly stood on
a stepladder, struggling to replace a bulb. A gentleman
would've gotten out to help. Brant stayed put.

This morning she wore the very definition of the little
black dress. Whatever it was made of hugged her body
in all the right places.

He nearly swallowed his tongue as she stretched that
last little bit. The dress inched up, revealing more of
legs that would make any grown man salivate…and he
proved no exception. On her feet? Another pair of those
killer heels.

In a heartbeat, the temperature morphed from a cool
winter morning to a midsummer scorcher.

Off-limits, off-limits, off-limits, he chanted. *A looker
like her? Out of your league.*

He rested an arm on his open car window. Curiosity had him checking to see who caught this show on a regular basis. Across the street, the wine and cheese shop's windows would afford one heck of a view. So would the insurance company's. Anybody driving by would undoubtedly slow to take advantage of it, too. Heck, maybe he'd have to drive by Molly's shop more often—just in case.

Brant opened his door and slid from the car. Afraid to make even the slightest noise, he left his door unlatched.

He tapped Molly on the arm, heard her quick squeak of surprise, and set his hands at her waist as she swiveled. His eyes nearly popped from their sockets. The little black dress took on a whole new attitude, viewed from the front. A deep V neckline kicked *conservative* all to hell and back.

She flipped out earbuds, her full, strawberry-wine lips breaking into a smile. "Good morning. You're up and around early."

"So are you."

She grimaced. "Lots to do."

"The kid and I are riding around, checking out the town. Actually, he's in the car sawing logs while I drive him. We didn't sleep much last night."

"He's out of his routine."

"He's not alone. Why don't you let me finish that?" Without batting an eye, he lifted her from the short ladder and set her down on those incredible shoes. In five seconds flat, he had both the new bulb and the cover in place. "Anything else?"

He folded the stepladder.

"Just a box that needs to go inside." Stopping beside

his car, she bent and studied the sleeping baby. "He's so sweet. You just want to pick him up and cover him in kisses, don't you?"

He crowded her, stood way too close—and liked it. "Yeah, he looks like a little angel. One of those cherubs on greeting cards."

She nodded.

"Problem is, any minute now he'll wake up and start to cry or mess his diaper or insist on being fed or held or…" He shook his head. "And God help me, I thought it was so great he'd learned to crawl. I take it back. Nothing is safe, including him. If there's trouble, the kid heads right to it. No fear. In him. Me? Permanent stress overload."

"You'll get through this." She laid her hand over his, then moved to her Mini and slid a box from the back seat.

"What's in there?"

"Some new belts and accessories. I can't wait to see them."

"A little like Christmas?"

She grinned. "With every single shipment."

He studied her storefront, its name in a fancy font on the large front window: *That Little White Dress*. Beneath it, *Happily Ever After Starts Here* was written in a smaller font.

"A Cinderella store."

"Excuse me?" She hoisted the box a little higher and pulled a set of keys from her pocket.

"You know. Cinderella. Her fairy godmother did all that bibbidi-bobbidi-booing, and everything Cinderella wanted was right there in front of her. Your boutique is a place where grown-up little girls make their dreams come true. That's a good thing." Arms out, he stepped toward her. "Let me take that."

"I can manage."

"You aren't actually planning to make me look bad, are you, carrying it yourself while I stand here empty-handed?"

"Will Jax be okay?"

"Unless you plan on making me haul it a couple miles down the road. My window's cracked, so I'll hear him if he needs me." He took the box in one arm and yawned. "Sorry."

With narrowed eyes, he studied her. "I know you didn't jump on it the other day, but I'm still open to giving you some time with an absolutely adorable baby. I'll even forgo the rental fees."

She laughed. "Fantastic offer, but I'll pass. Wouldn't want to deny you that bonding time."

Red eyed from lack of sleep, Brant glared at her.

"Ooh, scary. But the answer's still no. I have a business to run, Brant."

"So do I."

"Yes, you do. But you also have brothers to pick up the slack. Here, I'm it. A business of one." She bit her lower lip. "Although that has to change. I need a seamstress for alterations. My dream is to find a wizard with a needle and thread who can also watch the shop in a pinch. If wishes were fishes…"

"Amen to that. This shop's a big undertaking. Must take a lot of capital to get something like this up and running, with the stock and all."

Her expression went flat, and Brant sensed he'd stepped on forbidden ground. "That would come under the heading of none of my business."

"No, it's okay." She bounced her keys in one hand. "My dad fronted the money—big mistake. I should have gone to a bank."

"Why?"

"He's...difficult, and our relationship is..." She flipped her hand back and forth. "Tenuous."

He raised a brow.

"And now you want the whole story." She glanced down the street.

"Only if you want to get it off your chest." Resolutely, he kept his eyes on her brown ones, refusing to let them drift lower to the very fine chest showcased by her little black dress.

She rearranged a couple of totes in the back of her car.

"Want those inside, too?"

She shook her head. "My father expects perfection. He's my dad, and I love him, but I've always felt the need to prove myself. I shouldn't, because he certainly screwed up."

"Was he abusive?"

"Not physically, no. He never laid a hand on me. Nor on my mother. His problem was more apathy, I suppose. But he's a big part of the reason I need to stay focused and do whatever it takes to make a go of this." Steady and determined, her gaze met his. "Why I can't get involved with anyone."

"Message received."

"Look." Her tongue peeked out between her lips. "I like you, okay? But right now I don't want or have time for anything serious."

"Good, because I don't want that, either. I'm not even sure I like you."

"What?"

He almost laughed at the shock on her face. Good. He'd surprised her. Finally, he felt a little more in control.

He shrugged. "You can be awfully pushy."

"Pushy?"

"And you're stringently organized."

"That's a bad thing?"

Saying nothing, he simply shrugged again.

Glowering, she glanced at her watch. "So glad we've had this little chat, but I have a bride coming in an hour to try on her dress. I have a lot to do before she gets here." Snatching the box from him, she disappeared inside.

He stood on the sidewalk, his hands stuffed in the pockets of the worn-almost-white jeans he'd thrown on. Good. He'd riled her. She'd think about him now.

His stomach rumbled; he was hungry. Like a window shopper, he stared into her store. Molly knelt, unpacking her box, a wedding-gowned mannequin beside her. The shop was a blend of vintage and modern, whimsy and business. A reflection of Molly, though he doubted she'd admit it.

Catching sight of his own reflection, he almost laughed. Molly had decided her business was her life, with no time for anything else. Maybe the two of them had been cut from the same cloth. Business first. Although he was fast learning other variables sometimes came into play. He glanced over his shoulder at Jax.

Other than the business thing, though? He and Molly couldn't be more different. She was whimsy and fairy tale. Cute little dresses and sexy stilettos. Him? Grease, jeans, and T-shirts.

Curiosity begged him to peek inside, but he didn't dare, with Jax asleep in the car. This baby thing was like being on a short leash.

His gaze moved back to the petite brunette in that body-hugging black dress, and he admitted a hunger for far more than food.

Right now, though, a couple of fried eggs would have to do.

Chapter 9

Brant strolled back to his car. If he'd ended up staying in Tennessee, he'd have missed running into the cute little shop owner.

Speaking of Tennessee, he'd give his brothers some time to get their feet under them, then give them a call, find out how things had gone at the shop while they'd all been gone. That would, undoubtedly, give him a quick reality check.

They'd expect a report on sites he'd scouted, and he had no good news there.

Through the open window, he snagged his dark glasses from the passenger seat and slid them in place. No sense advertising his red-rimmed, sleep-deprived eyes. Striding to a vending machine, he dug for some coins and bought a copy of the *Savannah Morning News*. He tucked it beneath his arm, then retrieved the still-sleeping kid in his car seat and headed for the cozy red-and-white diner down the street.

A couple of passersby stared as though they thought they should know him. That happened more and more often since their Wylder Rides projects were featured on the car and bike restoration shows the TV crowd enjoyed.

Even though it gave him an itch in the middle of his back, he normally smiled and said hello. Today he ignored them and plowed into the small café, aiming for a back booth. He hoisted the bulky baby carrier onto one seat, then slid into the opposite one, facing the wall. For good measure, he kept his dark glasses on. If he couldn't see anybody, they couldn't see him, right?

The middle-aged woman who came bearing coffee wore a name tag that read Dee-Ann. Since that matched the name over the door, Brant assumed she must be the owner.

"What can I do for you today, sugar?"

"How about a cup of that coffee? Hot and black." His stomach growled again, a reminder he hadn't hung around the inn for breakfast, hell-bent as he'd been on a quick getaway. He should have grabbed one of Tommy's ham biscuits.

She filled his mug. "Baby keep you up last night?"

He made a frustrated sound. "I think the kid's got a sleeping disorder."

"Doesn't look like it now."

"That's because he knows I can't catch a nap here."

Dee-Ann chuckled. "He'll get past that."

"That's what everybody tells me." Brant stretched and decided against the fried eggs. "Got any apple pie?"

"I do. Made it myself earlier this mornin'."

"Great! I'll have a piece of that with a big scoop of vanilla ice cream."

"For breakfast?" Her pencil hovered an inch above her order pad.

"You bet. Apple pie's not really all that different from a piece of coffee cake or a scone, is it, Dee-Ann?"

"Guess not."

"And the ice cream's my glass of milk in its frozen state."

"Point taken. Comin' right up." Her forehead creased. "Do I know you?"

Brant skirted the issue. "You might have seen me around. I was here for a wedding at Magnolia House a few months back and for another this past weekend."

"Okay, that explains it. Thought I recognized you."

When she left to place his order, he unfolded his newspaper. Halfway through the sports page, his food arrived.

"Thanks, Dee-Ann."

"You're more than welcome…" She hesitated, and he gave in.

"Brant. Brant Wylder."

"Ah. Of course." Recognition shone in her eyes as she warmed his coffee. "You fix up old cars."

He almost choked at the simple understatement. "Yeah. My brothers and I."

"Well, you let me know if you need anything else, honey."

"Will do." When he scooped up a forkful of her pie and brought it to his lips, he thought he might have died and gone to Heaven. "This is some of the best I've ever eaten," he mumbled around his second bite.

The bell over the door jingled, and despite himself, Brant glanced over his shoulder.

"Cole, how the heck are you?"

"Thought you were leaving right after the wedding, Wylder."

"You know what they say about those best-laid plans." He sipped his coffee. "Your wife puts on one heck of a wedding."

"She does, doesn't she?" Cole fairly swelled with

pride. "When she first got it in her head to turn Magnolia House into a wedding destination, I had my doubts. But Jenni Beth doesn't know the meaning of *can't*." He spread his hands. "So here we are."

"Knee-deep in weddings," Brant finished.

"Yep." Cole pointed at the sleeping baby. "What's this?"

Brant laughed. "It's a baby."

"Whose?"

"My sister's. Long story."

Jax picked that moment to wake with one long wail, his fists clenched. Brant groaned.

"I've got it. Finish your breakfast." Cole eyed the pie, then slid in beside the baby and hoisted him to his shoulder, patting and rocking. Jax's wail tapered to a few whimpers, then silence as his thumb popped in his mouth. He sucked contentedly.

"Thank you." Brant signaled for Dee-Ann to bring another coffee.

"Anything else this morning, Cole?" Dee-Ann set his drink in front of him and topped off Brant's.

"Nope." Cole raised his mug. "This is what I came for."

Brant gave Cole the abridged version of how he'd become a temporary daddy, including Lainey's upcoming rehab and legal issues. "I could go home, but I'd kind of like to stick close just in case. And that's my sad tale."

"Sounds like you've got a heaped plate."

"Yeah. Believe me, I'd rather be up to my waist in oil and engine sludge than stinky diapers."

Cole smiled. "Where are you staying?"

"That's another problem. A big one. I'm still at Annabelle's, but she has new guests coming who've reserved my room."

"Not very kid-friendly, is it?"

"No. Believe it or not, Annabelle actually bent her rules for me. She has a strict no-kids policy."

"She's a feisty thing and a little eccentric—"

"A little?" Brant arched a brow. "Have you seen those purple, size-eleven sneakers she wears? On that less-than-five-foot frame? And those fifties housedresses?"

"Okay, okay." Cole laughed. "A lot eccentric. But she's got a heart of gold." He winced. "It's just buried a little deeper than most."

"Tell me about it. The sun was barely up Monday when she came beating on my door to remind me I didn't own the room."

Cole grunted. "I know of a house for rent, if you're interested."

"I'm here short-term," Brant reminded him. Guilt stabbed for not sharing his plans for a possible relocation. Still, if they couldn't find the right site…

"Doesn't matter. This place is sitting empty. Lem Gilmore owns it. Since it's more of a tax write-off than anything else, there's a chance he won't charge you anything. But then, we are talking Tightwad Lem, so it's hard to tell." Cole made a face. "He's not one for throwing money around, so it hasn't had much upkeep."

"I don't need anything fancy. A bed and a shower where I don't have to worry about the kid bothering anybody else will do it for me."

"Then this definitely qualifies. It's far enough out of

the way that the cicadas are about the only things that will hear him."

Jax, wide-awake now, eyed Brant's breakfast.

"Want some of this?" He held up a spoonful of ice cream.

Cole laughed as Jax's mouth worked. He strapped the baby in his seat, then took the spoon and fed Jax.

"You're pretty good at that."

Cole shrugged. "I don't know that I'm ready for a 24/7 thing yet, but I like babies." He leaned across the table and refilled the spoon from Brant's plate. "You want to take a ride and look at the house? If you don't like it, just say the word. No skin off my back."

"You bet."

Brant and Jax followed Cole on a narrow two-lane road to the middle of nowhere. Jax, having had a long nap, jabbered the whole way. Every once in a while, Brant would wave over his shoulder and Jax would giggle.

"We're on our way to look at a house, Jax. No more Annabelle. What do you think about that, huh?"

"Ba-ba-ba-ba."

"Couldn't agree more. Blah, blah, blah, blah."

Jax cooed and blew some bubbles.

Cole pulled into a gravel drive beside the small house on Claggett Mill Road, and Brant followed with more than a few misgivings. If the yard was any indication of what the inside looked like, they were in trouble. If they did move in, the first order of business had to be getting somebody out here to mow the foot-high grass and weeds.

Jax slapped his hands on the car window.

"I know, I know. You want out." Grabbing the carrier, Brant followed Cole down the sidewalk, worried this might turn out to be a wild-goose chase. He wouldn't move the baby into a rat's nest.

"You have a key?"

"Nah. Lem lost it a long time ago and never bothered to get another. Guess you could call a locksmith, but it would be cheaper to grab a new lockset at Beck's."

Cole leaned against the porch railing. "If you decide to do that, don't toss the old one. A lot of people come into my architectural salvage place looking for doorknobs like this. I'll talk to Lem about it."

"Speaking of Lem, does he know I'm looking at the house?"

"I called him on the way."

A minute later, Brant stood in the center of a boxy living room and missed his own house in Lake Delores. His own life. Jax burbled, and Brant stared down at him, feeling as though his life had been torn away from him. This wasn't his kid, wasn't his life. He was in a holding pattern, and he didn't like it. Worse, he didn't see any way out.

And that made him feel like a louse, lower than low.

Cole cleared his throat. "Not much, I know. You're in a tough spot, aren't you?"

Brant grunted.

"For what it's worth, I couldn't do what you're doing."

"Sure you could."

"Nope." He waved a hand. "What do you think?"

Quietly, Brant wandered through the rest of the house: two bedrooms, one bath, a small living room, and an eat-in kitchen. The decor could only be described as minimalist. It was surprisingly clean, though.

Leaning against the kitchen counter, his feet crossed in front of him, Cole said, "Lem's wife comes by once every week or so and hits the surface. As long as it's theirs, she insists it's clean."

Brant set Jax and his seat on the worn maroon sofa.

Not wanting to be left alone, Jax started whining.

"Okay, okay." Picking him up, Brant again wandered from room to room. "You know what? This'll work."

"Good. One problem checked off."

"I'll collect my gear from Annabelle's today, if that's okay with Lem."

"He said to consider it yours for as long as you need it. No cost."

Brant ran the palm of his hand along a jaw that definitely needed a date with his razor. "This is the strangest town."

"Why do you say that?"

"Everybody I've met—including the temperamental Annabelle—has gone out of the way to help."

"Misty Bottoms is a small town, pal. We take care of each other."

"Guess so. But I'm not—"

"While you're here, you are." Cole moved to the door. "I've got an appointment in Savannah, so I need to take off. You good here? Anything else I can do for you?"

"Don't think so. I really appreciate this, Cole."

"No problem. Welcome to your new home." With a mock salute, he walked away, leaving Brant a little bit more impressed with Misty Bottoms.

—∿—

Heading to Annabelle's, he stopped in a small park and fed Jax, then changed him head to toe. It sure would cut down on the laundry if he got more food into his nephew and less on his clothes.

"Let's take a minute, kid, and relax." Pulling a blanket from the car, he spread it and freed Jax from the carrier. "There you go."

The second Jax's butt hit the blanket, he rolled onto his knees and took off. When he hit the grass, he stopped and looked up at Brant.

"Different, isn't it?"

"Da-da."

Brant sucked in a breath and reminded himself it was simply baby talk, exercising those vocal cords. The *da-da* had no meaning to Jax. He rubbed his chest and plucked a piece of grass. Sitting down, he held it in front of the baby. "Grass."

"Ga-ga."

"Good start."

Jax pushed up and sat, bending over, his uncoordinated thumb and forefinger working hard to capture a single blade of grass. When he failed the fourth time, he started to cry.

"That, champ, is a mad cry. Got it." He tossed his own piece. "I'd give you one, but it would go right in your mouth. Since you're not a cow, that's probably not a good idea." He scooped up the baby and raised him high.

Jax's tears turned to giggles.

"You like that?"

They played the game a few minutes, Jax giggling

harder and harder. Finally, Brant said, "Enough. I don't want you upchucking on me." He snatched up the blanket and headed to the car.

On the outskirts of town, he spied Beck's lumberyard. "Might as well pick up a lock."

Jax gurgled his approval.

Stepping inside, he was impressed. Elliot's wasn't some small mom-and-pop, thrown-together store, but a thriving, well-organized business. He nabbed an empty cart. "Your chariot, Sir Jax."

He lowered the baby seat inside and headed off to the hardware department.

Beck found him there with a lock in each hand. "The one in your right is plenty, unless you're locking up Fort Knox."

"It's for Lem Gilmore's place out on Claggett Mill Road."

"You're putting a lock on his house because—?"

"Jax and I are moving in. Temporarily. It's past time to leave Annabelle's."

Beck cracked a grin. "I'll bet it is. Back when I was a kid, I, uh, had some trouble with a tree branch in her yard. It didn't quite hold my weight, and I spent an entire Saturday cleaning out her basement."

"Ouch," Brant said. "Speaking of trees, you don't happen to know anybody who does yard work, do you? Lem's needs some serious mowing."

Beck crooked a finger, and Brant followed him to a huge corkboard. After searching it for a few seconds, Beck removed a business card. "Bubba's your best bet. He does good work, and he's reasonable. You ought to send Lem the bill."

Brant shook his head. "It's the least I can do, since he's not charging me rent."

Beck's mouth dropped open. "That cheapskate never misses a chance to make money."

"Seems he has this time."

"We'll see."

As Beck walked away, Brant couldn't help but wonder what he'd gotten himself into. A baby and a house…and, it would seem, a debt to Lem Gilmore.

The bubble that felt a whole lot like panic ballooned in his chest again.

Chapter 10

SINCE JAX WAS FED, CHANGED, AND HAPPILY OCCUPIED trying to eat his toes, Brant decided to take some time to explore Misty Bottoms. The surrounding countryside was wild and untamed. When he came to some bottomland, he stopped on the side of the road and stepped out of the car.

"Toto, we're not in Lake Delores anymore."

Jax chattered at him from the back seat, and Brant leaned in. "Want to take a peek?"

Holding the baby and bouncing him, Brant looked out over the sea of marsh grass. He gave a low whistle and Jax startled, eyes wide.

"Did I scare you? Sorry." He whistled more quietly while Jax watched. Then again. The baby's fingers brushed over Brant's lips before he pursed his own, to give it a try. No sound came out. "It'll come, short stuff. Give it time."

Jax grinned.

Brant wished he had his boots, but they hadn't come with him for the wedding. He breathed in the distinctive odor of the gooey pluff mud left behind when the tide receded. One thumb tucked in his pocket, the other arm around Jax, he simply stood, taking it all in. Georgia's Low Country was night and day from his native Tennessee, but he liked it. Very much.

A breeze blew, and over the earthy odors, Brant

caught a whiff of another very distinctive one. Jax had messed his diaper. Again.

"Good trick, Superman. Your bottomland's stinky, too."

Brant hung his head in resignation. It had taken him weeks to track down the leather for his seats. Covering the passenger side with two blankets, he draped an arm over the squirming baby to hold him in place and executed the fastest one-handed diaper change on record.

"Dang, I'm getting pretty good at this."

Jax agreed.

On the way back to town, he turned onto Old Coffee Road. A mile or so past a beat-up mailbox, he hit the brakes and backed up, a grin spreading over his face.

"Would you look at that?"

There sat the sweetest old service station he'd ever seen—wearing a For Sale sign. Feeling like he'd just taken the checkered flag, he pulled up to the outdated pumps. The terra-cotta-colored metal canopy was flaked and peeling, but the building itself looked sturdy. Old metal signs covered its front. A huge red Mobil flying horse hung over the door. The place had the look of a museum or one of those sets at Disneyland. Frank and Mike, from *American Pickers*, would go crazy here.

Opening his car door, Brant walked to the center of the road and looked both ways. Not a neighbor in sight. How much land went with the building? Enough for the Wylder brothers to set up shop?

Excitement rippled through him. What better place to restore vintage cars and motorcycles than in a vintage building? He jotted down the number on the For Sale sign. Quinlyn Deveraux. He'd seen her real-estate office in town.

When he unstrapped Jax, the baby curled into him and smiled. Not his baby, but that no longer mattered. As panicked as he'd been when Officer Blackburn handed Jax to him, as much sleep as he'd lost, Brant couldn't imagine not having this time with his nephew. And that was a step, wasn't it?

If he could only get him housebroken.

With the baby tucked against his chest, Brant stepped up to the grimy windows. He picked up a stick and knocked away some of the cobwebs. Shading his eyes with his free hand, he peeked inside. "What do you think, kid? This front room would make a good office, wouldn't it?"

Jax slapped at the dirty window, and Brant grimaced. "Don't put that hand in your mouth till I get it wiped, okay?"

"Dadagama!"

"Right."

Walking around the outside of the building, Brant saw both what was there and what could be. It needed a lot of work, but he and his brothers could handle that. In addition to his automotive skills, Brant was pretty darned handy with a hammer. The summer he turned eight, Tucker had been wrapped up in Little League baseball, and their mom, pregnant with Lainey, had dragged Gaven kicking and screaming to swimming lessons. While they did that, Brant and his dad had built an incredible tree house, complete with a front porch. They'd added a high railing at his mother's insistence. No girls, including Lainey, had ever stepped foot in it. It was their guys' hangout clear through high school.

This old station would be a challenge, one he looked forward to.

From down the road, he heard a car coming. Molly and her little Countryman zipped into view. Slowing, she pulled behind his car.

Leaning out the window, she smiled. "Imagine meeting you out here, Brant Wylder."

"Hey, Molly Stiles. What are you up to?"

"I delivered a couple bridesmaid's dresses to Jenni Beth. Then, since I had a latte from Tansy's and it was such a beautiful afternoon, I decided I might as well put the windows down and go for a ride. I'm still finding my way around, you know?"

"I do. Lake Delores isn't a big place, but it's not Misty Bottoms."

"What are you two doing out here in the wilds?"

"Actually, we were out for a ride, too, and…" He cocked his head. "Would you mind holding Jax for a couple minutes?"

"Not unless you intend on making a break and leaving him with me."

He laughed. "Nah. The kid and I are doing okay today."

She slid out of the car, and Brant groaned. "Mol, you're killing me slowly."

A questioning frown creased her forehead.

Instead of answering, he let his gaze drift from her mass of curls, over her vivacious face, then slowly down her body, encased today in a black knit dress that showcased every inch, every curve, and on to model-perfect legs that ended in a strappy pair of black and silver pumps.

He cleared his throat. "Need I say more?"

A slow smile curled her lips. She reached for the baby, who went into a paroxysm of joy at seeing her. He kicked his little legs and laughed, and Brant watched her expression soften as she lost herself in the feel of him, the smell of him, the joy of him. He sure hoped Molly planned to have a couple of kids someday, because it was plain as that little snub nose on Jax's face that she loved babies.

Catching a strand of her long hair, the baby wrapped it around his fist and took it straight to his mouth. Grimacing, Molly bent her head to give herself a little more slack.

"Ouch." Brant stepped toward her and freed her hair, then found himself leaning closer, breathing in her fresh, feminine scent.

She took a step back. "What are you doing?"

"You smell so good."

"Are you sniffing my hair?"

A goofy grin on his face, he said, "Yeah, I am."

"You are so weird."

The grin stayed in place. "Yeah, I am."

She shook her head. "What are we going to do with your uncle, Jax? He's cuckoo." Molly made a circling motion around her ear with her finger.

"Hate to add fuel to the fire, but I think I'm gonna buy this place."

A laugh bubbled out of her. "You're kidding, right?"

"Nope."

"It's falling down."

"Actually, the building appears sound. Mostly, it needs some cosmetic fixes."

"If you say so, but why would you want it?"

The sticky part. Confession time. Might as well dive right in. "My brothers and I are considering moving our business here."

She went flat-faced. "As in permanently?"

"Yes."

"But that—" Her tongue darted out to wet her lips.

"Changes things, yes."

"Can I ask one question?"

He figured he knew what that question would be. "Sure."

"How long have you known?"

"We've been talking about it since before Kathy's wedding."

"And you didn't say anything?"

"No. Our plans were…are…very tentative."

She nodded, but said nothing.

In for a dime, in for a dollar, he decided. "Jax and I found a new place to live today. Well, not a new place, but new for us. We're waving goodbye to Annabelle's, aren't we, pal?" He waved at Jax, who flapped his own hand. "Cole scored it for us, and we're moving in today."

He could practically hear her mind working, trying to digest his news.

"Furnished?" she asked.

"Badly." He chuckled. "But we can live with it for now. It'll make life with the kid here a whole lot easier. If you can keep the Jaxster entertained for a few minutes, I'd like to walk around the place and make a video for my brothers."

"Give me a sec." She handed the baby back to him, whipped a band out of her pocket, and secured her caramel-streaked brown hair. Then she held out her arms for Jax. "It's safe from little hands now."

"Smart lady." Brant pulled out his phone, then traipsed around the perimeter of the building, shooting it and the surrounding area from all angles. Molly had taken his news better than he'd expected—maybe. When he glanced over his shoulder, she sat in the grass, that mind-blowing dress tucked beneath her. Jax, held out in front of her, tried out his pudgy legs. The wobbly baby looked for all the world like a drunken sailor. Brant started a new video, one that held his interest far more than the potential business site.

Looking up, she caught him. "Stop." She hid her face behind the baby.

"I'm, uh, taking it for Lainey."

"You are not." She plopped the baby down in front of her.

He clicked a still shot.

She laughed. "Quit!"

"Okay, okay. I'm done." Grinning, he dropped to the grass beside her and sprawled out, resting on one side to face her. "Thanks. Easier to do that without a baby riding my hip."

"Are you sending the video to Tuck and Gaven?"

"Yep."

"Do it now. We're good."

And they were, he realized. With the sun shining overhead, a cool breeze surrounding them, and soft grass beneath, he felt better right here, right now, with Molly and Jax than he'd felt in a long time. Even before he came to Misty Bottoms for the wedding, he'd been out of sorts.

Something about this woman restored his equilibrium. At the same time, something about her sent him skittering out of control, and that didn't make any sense at all.

He wanted to touch her, taste her, spend time with her. Dangerous.

"Want to share dinner?" Molly asked. "Nothing fancy. During a lull at the shop, I ran upstairs and threw some beef stew in the Crock-Pot. One of the advantages of living where you work."

A quick smile flitted across his face. Dinner with Molly? At her place? Oh yeah.

Then he remembered Jax and dialed down his expectations for the evening. There'd be no hanky-panky. How did anyone have brothers and sisters? Between the time issues and operating on little or no sleep, how did parents manage a sex life? Maybe that explained why he and his brothers had been shipped to his grandparents' house almost every Friday night…and it was best he didn't think about that too much.

He concentrated instead on Molly. Their first kiss had been kind of an accident. The next few? Impulse, but pure dynamite. He needed a chance to taste her again.

"What do you think, bud?" he asked Jax, forcing himself to take it slow.

When Jax babbled, he tipped his head up to meet Molly's gaze. "He said yes."

"I'm glad."

"Me too. Can we bring anything?"

"Formula and diapers."

Dinner with Molly. A big high-five. On top of that, he had a house, had found—he hoped—the new location for Wylder Rides, and had shared his plans with Molly. No more secrets. Could the day get any better? He grinned. Oh yeah, if he was really, really lucky.

He headed over to Annabelle's with Jax and packed up their stuff. At the front office, he settled his bill and thanked her for putting up with them. Certain she'd break into a happy dance when they left, he refused to look back, not wanting that visual seared into his brain.

The car loaded, Brant and a fussy Jax drove to their new, very temporary home. He pulled up to the house, grabbed the diaper bag and baby, and performed what he expected to be the first of many diaper changes there. Handing Jax a biscuit to slobber on, he carried in his single duffel bag, then made several trips to haul in the baby's stuff. Next time he ran into Cole at Duffy's Pub, he owed the man a beer.

Standing in the middle of the living room, he scrutinized the area. What did he need to place higher, out of reach of Jax's curiosity? Were the floors okay for a crawler?

Leaving Jax strapped in his seat, Brant went in search of a broom and mop. Even though Lem's wife had cleaned, he intended to give the floors a quick going-over before turning the baby loose on them.

By the time he finished, he was sweaty and Jax was angry. He wanted out of his seat, wanted to explore and burn off some energy. Between his bout of housework and tramping around in the dirt and grass earlier, a shower was at the top of Brant's priority list. Fat chance he'd get lucky tonight, but stranger things had happened. Besides, his mother would smack him upside the head if she found out he'd been invited to dinner and hadn't taken the time to wash up.

He shook out his last clean outfit, picked up Jax and the ever-present baby seat, and headed for the shower, praying the plumbing worked.

He plopped a pacifier in Jax's mouth and stuck a rattle in his hand, then stripped and stepped under the water, grimacing at the tepid spray. As soon as he finished, he'd crank up the heater and hopefully score some hotter water.

Speaking of scoring, he'd spotted a washer and dryer in the hallway closet. On his way home from Molly's, he'd pick up laundry detergent, cereal and milk, and more formula. The kid plowed through the stuff like a pig through slop. If he continued to eat at this rate, he'd be a stand-in for the Pillsbury Doughboy by the time he turned one. Maybe Brant should consider investing in a baby-formula company.

Eyes closed, lukewarm water drizzling down on him, he got real with himself. He might not want marriage or a family, but he did want Molly. Thoughts of her stalked him day and night.

His chances of having her?

About zilch, and that sucked. Totally.

—⁓—

Molly hadn't planned to fuss. A simple dinner offered to a man with no family to help him. That's all tonight was.

Baloney.

She might feed that to someone else, but she knew better. She'd invited Brant to dinner because she wanted to spend more time with him and that beautiful little boy—which was exactly what she'd promised she wouldn't do!

As she stirred the stew, she chastised herself. Hadn't she warned herself over and over that Brant was dangerous to her plans? That it wouldn't take much for him to derail her? Hand curled around her old wooden spoon, Molly replayed the afternoon, saw again the delight on Brant's face as he poked around the outside of that old service station. He looked a whole lot like a kid with an exciting new toy.

What if he actually bought it? Mixed emotions ran through her. Would he stay in Misty Bottoms? Live here? She let out a long breath. She'd prepared herself to resist the temporary temptation that was Brant Wylder. Could she handle permanent?

And Jax. That baby turned her inside out.

Brant had pulled the rug out from under her today, and she supposed she should be angry with him. But it was business, and she understood that. He needed to do what worked for him and his brothers. This sure changed the playing field, though.

She transferred the soft, still-warm rolls she'd picked up at Tansy's into a basket. Maybe she'd manage to get through the evening without touching Brant, without picking up Jax or inhaling that sweet baby scent. Without kissing those chubby cheeks or his uncle's stubbled chin.

If she could do that, she wouldn't ache for a baby of her own to cuddle, for a man who'd love her, only her.

A man who would stay with her forever, who wouldn't pack up and leave with no warning.

A man she could trust.

At the core of her problem, at the heart of her list, lay the need for that trust. The stability it would provide. She needed the constancy her mother had lost when Dad left, and she couldn't imagine having that with Brant. He was as married to his business as she was to hers. And he hadn't trusted her with his plans. Had instead kept them from her. Would he have fessed up if she hadn't run into them at the station?

Still, he loved and fretted over his family...but would he always? Hadn't her dad loved her and her mother, worried about them?

Right up until he left.

And wasn't she a mass of conflict and contradictions?

She was cutting lemons for their water when the doorbell rang.

Trouble had come to her home—at her invitation.

Chapter 11

BRANT ARRIVED RIGHT ON TIME, ONE HAND WRAPPED AROUND a baby-seat handle and the other holding white gerbera daisies. A diaper bag hung off one shoulder. Never had he, in his wildest imagination, considered showing up at a woman's house for a dinner date quite like this. But then, it wasn't a date. It was simply dinner, a dinner Molly was good enough to share with him and Jax.

When she opened the door, all thoughts of food abandoned him. Glad he'd changed into a button-down shirt and khakis instead of his usual jeans and T-shirt, he still wore his kick-around tennis shoes. It was them or those darned pinch-your-toes dress shoes, and he'd sworn they'd never go on his feet again. He'd donate them to the Humane Society and let somebody else spend a miserable evening in them—although that didn't sound very humane.

Molly? She'd scooped all that phenomenal hair into a sexy, curly mass on top of her head and wore a soft gray skirt that stopped midway between her knees and ankles. A black-and-white patterned scarf set off the layered white tank and gray sweater. Short black boots and black tights finished the look. He liked it. Casual and easy, with a touch of sass.

He held out the flowers.

"For me?" Her eyes twinkled.

"From the new guy in town and his nephew." He

tipped his head toward the baby. "Jax lobbied for a dozen red roses, but I told him it was too soon for that."

She grinned and opened the door wider. "Good call. I love daisies. Come on in. Everything's ready, so I hope you're hungry."

"Famished would be more accurate." He breathed deeply. "If it tastes even half as good as it smells, I might have to marry you."

"That's what they all say."

He caught sight of the fluffy white cat peeking around the banister at the top of the stairs.

Bubbles took one look at him and the wiggling baby and made a mad dash for the bedroom, slipping and sliding around the corner.

"Will our visits cause permanent mental damage to that cat?"

"No, she'll be fine." Molly led him into the kitchen, where he dumped the diaper bag on a chair.

She laid the flowers on the counter. Hands on her hips, she said, "You'll need to help me with this. I borrowed it from Darlene at Quilty Pleasures." She grabbed a wooden contraption from the corner.

"What is it?"

"It's a doggy gate. She uses it to keep Moonshine and Mint Julep out of her kitchen." She tipped her chin toward the top of the stairs. "With Jax crawling, I thought we should block the stairs."

"Molly, you're brilliant. I never even considered that." Understanding he was taking advantage, he dropped a light, easy kiss on her lips. "Thank you."

"Mmm. You're very welcome."

The two of them managed to secure the gate. Brant

wiggled it and was satisfied it would stay in place if an energetic baby rattled against it. Freeing Jax, he watched the baby scoot off to check things out.

"You're sure you're okay with this?" he asked.

"Absolutely."

When she moved into the kitchen, Brant stood halfway between it and the living room so he could talk to her but keep an eye on Jax.

"I'm afraid I have no appetizers and no wine. Although since you're driving, you probably don't want a drink, do you?"

He shook his head, then sprinted into the living room. "No, Jax."

Molly headed in behind him. Jax was busily pulling books off her shelves.

"He's a human wrecking machine. At Annabelle's, I tried babyproofing our room, but I swear, if there's anything he shouldn't get into, he sniffs it out. I'm exhausted just trying to keep him alive. I honestly think I'm too tired for sex."

Molly leaned in, fisted her hands in his shirt, and kissed him.

He kissed her back. "I was wrong. I'm not too tired."

He felt a tug on his pants and looked down to see Jax scaling his leg.

"Why don't we eat?"

"First things first." He picked up Jax and rested him on a hip. "One more taste." He took the kiss deep, with Jax jabbering away. When he pulled back, he suggested they move any breakables up higher.

Within minutes, the surfaces in the room were nearly bare, and the top shelves of her bookcase bulged.

"I'll help you put it back before we go."

"Don't worry about it."

While Brant fed Jax, Molly slid open the door to the patio. "It's a little chilly tonight. Otherwise we could eat out here."

"Why don't we give it a try?" he suggested. "If we get cold, we'll cuddle or come back in."

"What about Jax?"

"He's fed, and he's changed. My guess? He'll take a nap now so he won't be ready for bed when I am."

"Tough, huh?"

"You have no idea." He set the baby and his car seat in the kitchen and tucked a blanket around him. Spotting a small counter television, he asked, "Do you mind if I turn this on?"

"My TV?"

"Yeah. Jax likes to watch the Barrett-Jackson auction."

A laugh bubbled out of her. "You're joking, right?"

"No. Before we left the house, he was checking out a '59 Studebaker Scotsman pickup. Pretty green-and-white thing."

"I have no idea what that is, but you do remember Jax is only a baby, right?"

"Doesn't matter. The kid's a Wylder. We already have a handshake agreement that he's gonna work with us when he's older."

"Really?"

"Yep." Brant grinned. "And just so you know, the Scotsman's a stripped-down model. It came stock with only one taillight, one wiper, and one visor. No armrests. Scottish frugality."

"Is that legal?"

"I doubt it would fly today, but then?" He shrugged. "Guess so."

She watched the baby, now totally engrossed in the cars and the fast-paced auctioneer.

"Told you."

When she stepped outside, he followed her onto the deck. "He'll be good for a few minutes."

When she moved to the rail, he slid behind her, crowding her a little, enjoying the feel of her body against his. The town sprawled below them, the street lights marching in their sentry-straight rows.

He rested a hand on either side of her. "You smell good, Mol."

"I might say the same about you."

They were so close, he felt her deep breath.

She pointed to her right. "See the little park over there? The area with all the lights? It might be a good place to take Jax. I think he'd like the baby swings."

"Mmm-hmm."

She turned, and her lips were inches from his.

"Brant?"

"Molly?"

"What are you doing?"

"I'm thinking how much I'd like to kiss you again."

"That's probably—"

The kiss gave him a kick in the belly like none ever had. He sent up a small prayer of thanks when, instead of pulling away, she leaned into him and deepened the kiss.

When he finally gathered enough sense to draw away, she sighed. "Brant, I—"

Over the auctioneer, music from her stereo drifted to

them, and Bob Seger's "We've Got Tonight" played.
"Dance with me."

"Here?"

"Right here, under the stars."

Bubbles slinked out onto the deck and curled up in
a chair. Her tail flicked as her unblinking eyes stayed
on Brant.

"Does she bite?"

"No, you're safe."

He glanced over her shoulder at Jax, who was totally
wrapped up in the TV show, then took Molly's hand
and drew her to him. They moved together, and the rest
of the world disappeared. She rested her head on his
shoulder, and he closed his eyes. She felt so small. So
delicate. So powerful.

"Listen to the words," he whispered. "They say it all."

She nodded. "They do."

When the song ended, he spun her out, then back in.
"Thank you."

She laid a hand on the side of his face. "You're dangerous, Brant, and I should have my head examined for
admitting that."

He cocked a brow. "You're right. Don't give me so
much as an inch, Molly, 'cause, believe me, I *will* take
that mile."

"I'll consider myself warned. Come on." She took his
hand. "Dinnertime."

At the door they both stopped. While they danced,
Bubbles had sneaked back inside and was curled beside
Jax's car seat, sound asleep with one leg stretched out,
her paw resting on the baby's leg.

"It looks like Jax has a new friend."

Molly nodded. "Bubbles doesn't seem quite as enthralled by the auction, though."

After she arranged the daisies in an antique milk bottle, she gave them center stage, surrounded by three fat candles. They ate at her old farmhouse table with its mix of blue-and-white-striped chairs and high-backed white ones with their blue-and-white-plaid cushions. Jax, still in his carrier, sat on one of the chairs, playing with a whirling toy Brant had hung off the handle. The cozy room smelled of good food, cinnamon candles, and Molly.

It had been a long time since he felt this content.

After dinner, Molly put on some coffee. While it brewed, he changed Jax, then fed him a bottle. Halfway through, the baby's eyes drooped, and he fell asleep.

"Since he didn't sleep through his TV show, I figured this would happen."

"Does this mean he won't sleep tonight?" Molly stood in the doorway, holding two slices of apple pie à la mode.

"Who knows? There doesn't seem to be any rhyme or reason to that."

They ate in companionable silence.

Finally, Molly set her empty plate on the table and picked up her cup. "We talked earlier about the fact that neither of us wanted or was looking for anything from—" She hesitated, at a loss for words.

"From us? This thing between us?" he supplied.

"Yes." Her eyes darkened.

"But?" He encouraged her, almost afraid of what he might hear. Right now, some shared kisses, a dinner, and a dance or two were all good. But more than that? He didn't think he had it in him.

Still, the second she finished outlining the reasons *she* couldn't give *him* more, he wanted it. Human nature could be sadistic.

"Today's bombshell changed things, but regardless, the timing's off for anything serious." Her hand flew up. "Not that I'm saying I feel, you know, serious about you. I—"

"Molly, it's okay. I'm a big boy. I understand. Do I want you? Like my next breath. But that doesn't mean I expect it's gonna happen."

"Oh." She started to stand. "More coffee?"

"No. Sit."

Playing with a fold in her skirt, she said, "A long time ago, my life took an unexpected detour. I won't go into all that right now, but because of it, I set down a plan for myself. A very specific one. I'm on track, and I mean to stay there."

"I can appreciate that. I have a plan, too. Mine's probably not as rigid as yours, but my family and business, in that order, are top priorities. Things do crop up." Brant nodded toward Jax. "Case in point."

He stood and picked up his empty coffee cup. "Done?"

She nodded, and he carried their cups into the kitchen.

When he returned, he leaned against the doorjamb. "What you're saying is that you're not interested in starting anything with me."

"Or with anyone else right now."

"Right now," he repeated. "When will you be?"

"When I'm thirty."

"You have an actual timetable?"

"Why not?"

"Why not?" he repeated. "Because, honey, love is

something that happens when it happens. It doesn't check the calendar or count birthday candles."

She shrugged. "Real goals need deadlines."

"There's a difference between a deadline and a time-table."

"I think—"

Jax picked that moment to wake from his catnap.

Pushing away from the door, Brant said, "Time I get this guy home." He leaned down and kissed Molly's cheek. "Thanks for dinner. You have no idea how great a home-cooked meal tasted."

"I'm glad you came." She stood when he picked up the diaper bag.

"Maybe once I get settled, you can have dinner with Jax and me. If it fits your timeline."

She blushed, and he held up a hand. "That was a joke. A bad one. Truth is, I'd like to invite you to dinner. Or maybe to a movie night."

"Invite me, and I'll come." She bent and kissed Jax. "You be good tonight. Uncle Brant's had a long day."

"Dadada!"

"Yeah." Hiking the diaper bag onto his shoulder, Brant grabbed the baby and his seat, settled for another peck on Molly's cheek, and navigated the stairs.

Molly followed, watching as he loaded up and drove away. Then she turned the dead bolt and walked upstairs and out the back door.

On her deck, arms wrapped tightly around herself, she stared into the ebony sky. Thousands of stars twinkled, and a wide crescent moon danced in and out of the few clouds overhead. The night was romantic. Made for sharing. For dancing.

Yet she'd sent Brant home.

Because she wanted too much.

Because he made her heart race with only a look, a touch.

Because her dad had told her he loved her, right before he left.

She'd never heard him and her mom argue, never had reason to believe he hadn't told the truth when he said he loved them.

Yet one morning, she woke to find his bags packed and waiting beside the front door. Panicked, she'd run to the sofa where he sat with his coffee. Snuggling up beside him, she asked, "Do you have a business trip, Daddy?"

Slowly, he shook his head. "I'm leaving, honey." He kissed her cheek. "I love you. Remember that."

And then he'd walked away, leaving her and her mother in a tomblike house that was no longer a home. All the fun, all the laughter, left with him. He'd taken it, along with her trust.

She'd gone to bed that night and the next and the next wondering whether, if she'd kept her room cleaner or got better grades or played baseball, her father would have stayed?

Her thinking self knew he wouldn't have. But the little girl buried deep down inside still wondered.

Brant inserted his key into the new lock he'd installed and walked into a hollow-sounding house. Standing two steps inside the door, he surveyed his new lodging.

"Well, bud," he said to the baby, "another chapter in this wacky world of ours."

Jax gurgled in answer.

There was nothing familiar except the couple of arm-loads of his and Jax's things. He'd squeezed in a trip to the grocer's so they wouldn't starve and taken the time earlier to stop by the local cable provider. Technology ruled the world, and he needed internet. Without it, he'd be lost. Annabelle had furnished it at the inn, though that was probably Willow's doing. Now he had his own again, both for business and to catch some sports and news.

He prowled the house, too wired to sleep. After he tossed a load of laundry into the washer, he played peekaboo with Jax for a bit, then watched, laughing, as he crawled across the newly mopped floor. Unlike the bunny whose batteries never ran out, Jax finally wore down. Brant changed his diaper and slid him into a clean onesie. Sprawled on the ratty maroon sofa, he tucked his nephew close and fed him a bottle. Halfway through, Jax's eyes grew heavy and formula dripped off his chin. It was time to put him down for the night.

Yet even after Jax was sound asleep in his new dresser drawer, Brant roamed the house restlessly. He hadn't closed the drapes, and the moon shone in, illuminating the small front room. The unfamiliar sounds of the house settling in for the night kept him on edge.

Stepping onto the front porch, he rested his hands on the banister and stared into the darkness. Other than the moon and a couple of stars, he couldn't see another light. It was just him, Jax, and nature. The tension of the last few weeks slid away.

He rubbed grit-filled eyes. He needed some shut-eye desperately.

Wandering back inside, he did a quick check on the

baby. Still sound asleep. It didn't seem right to leave him all alone, though. Jax was so small. What if he woke and Brant didn't hear him?

Wasn't this what he'd wanted, though? A room of his own. Sleep.

Yeah, and he wouldn't get any, worrying about Jax.

Throwing in the towel, he picked up the baby, dresser drawer and all, and carried him into the master bedroom. What a misnomer. There was absolutely nothing masterful about the small space. In a real-estate ad, they'd call it cozy. He'd call it claustrophobic.

He set the makeshift crib down carefully, then plucked the worn paperback from his duffel. By the faint light of the bedside lamp, he read a couple of chapters before his own eyes grew heavy. Tossing the book aside, he closed his eyes and slept.

In his dreams, he stood on a raised dais as the gorgeous shop owner brought him dress after dress to try on. Even while he argued with her, insisting the bride should try them on, she added to the pile waiting for him.

A man's work was never done.

Chapter 12

THE DAY STARTED EARLY. JAX ACTUALLY SLEPT THROUGH the night, so by six o'clock he was raring to go. The kid was better than a rooster.

Brant's dream nagged at him. Seriously? Him in wedding gowns? Even under threat of death, that nightmare wouldn't be shared with a single soul. He tugged at his ear and wondered when his brothers would get here; he needed some guy time.

After he shook out the wrinkled clothes he'd forgotten in the washer last night and threw them into the dryer, he made a call to the hospital. He actually caught Lainey's doctor at the nurse's station. Halfway through their chat, Jax demanded food. One-handed, Brant opened a jar of fruit and fed him.

If he'd learned anything from all this, it was that a baby put an end to hopping out of bed and going. Spontaneity? The word had all but disappeared from his vocabulary. Satisfied that all was as good as could be expected, he ended the call and he and Jax finished breakfast, cleaned up, then drove into town.

Brant pulled into a parking space, and they headed to That Little White Dress. Even though the shop wasn't open, Molly was hard at work, fussing with a display of belts. Despite their bling, the lady held center stage.

He knocked on the window.

"Brant." Unlocking the door, she studied him, concern clouding her perfect face. "Everything okay?"

"It is. I spoke with Lainey's doctor this morning, and he gave me permission to take Jax in to see his mama."

Molly lifted the baby from his seat and gave him a big smooch. "Your mommy will be so happy to see you, won't she, sweetheart? Yes, she will."

Brant frowned. Why did women do that? Where did they learn baby talk?

Why did they do so many things that dumbfounded him?

He shook it off. "You're closed today?"

"I am. Thursday's are slow, so I spend them taking care of things I don't get to otherwise."

"You're busy, then?"

"Nothing that can't wait. Why?"

"Would you consider another trip to Savannah?" Quickly, he held up a hand. "Not as a babysitter. It's… I thought Lainey might need to talk. To a woman. It's asking a lot but…"

He read the indecision on her face, along with something else. "What's wrong?"

"Nothing. I didn't expect to see you again."

"Want me to leave?"

"No, and I'll be glad to talk to Lainey if *she* wants to. It has to be her decision."

He nodded.

"Are you leaving for there now?"

"Yes. Short notice, isn't it?"

"I need to run upstairs. Take care of a couple of things. I won't be more than a minute or two."

"Sure." While she sprinted to her apartment, Brant

carried Jax outside and strapped him and his seat into the Camaro. Then he held up a hand. "High five, baby boy. Molly's going with us."

He lifted one of Jax's tiny hands and tapped his bigger one to it. Jax happily kicked his feet and squealed.

The trip was bound to be emotional, but he no longer dreaded it quite as much.

When Molly got back downstairs, Brant and Jax were already waiting in the car. Opening her door, she handed Brant a bottle of water, then slid a second one into the console cup holder. "Thought we might want something cold."

"Thanks, I appreciate that. I passed my daily caffeine intake a couple of hours ago."

"Been up a while?"

"Since six a.m. But—" He held up a finger. "Jax slept through the night. Gold star to him."

"Having your own rooms probably helped."

Brant rubbed the back of his neck.

"He slept in your room, didn't he?"

"He's so little."

"Brant, babies can sleep in their own rooms. In fact, there's actually a name for that room. It's called a nursery."

"Yeah, yeah, I know."

"But you got a good night's sleep?"

He gave her a sidelong glance, reminding himself he'd take the whole wedding gown dream to his grave. "Yeah, I did. I read a little Lee Child till my eyes crossed and I couldn't focus on the words. Took me all of two minutes to fall asleep after I turned out the light."

"I'm glad. Fill me in on what the doctor said." She

shook her head. "Never mind. I—" She raised a hand, palm up. "Being a buttinsky. Sorry."

Shooting her a quick look, he said, "You're busy, yet you're taking another day to help. That's a long way from butting in."

She shrugged.

"Physically, Lainey's made great strides. She'll transfer to a rehab center this weekend." He tapped the steering wheel. "No contact with the outside world for the first week. Strictly enforced. That's gonna be tough for her and Jax."

"And for you."

He grinned derisively. "Yeah. There is that. After that week, though, she'll have morning phone privileges. No laptop."

"That makes sense, really. She needs to concentrate on herself. How about legally? I know you've worried about that."

"I followed your advice, Mol, and stopped by for a chat with Kemper Dobson." Brant passed an old truck towing a fishing boat. "I've gotta admit that when I first saw him, I had serious doubts."

Molly arched a brow. "He's experienced."

"Yeah, and a long-time member of AARP." He held up his hand. "And that's okay. You're right. A lot of experience comes with that gray hair. Anyway, he made a few calls for me. If there's a bright spot in all this, it's that since Lainey didn't hurt anyone else, didn't destroy anyone's property, and since this is her first DUI, the rehab and a hefty fine will cover it. Of course, she won't have her license for a while, but she shouldn't. She broke the law and endangered herself and others."

Brant met Molly's eyes. "It's still up in the air on whether or not her hospital bill will be covered. Insurance companies define DUI as intentional conduct. You drink, then hop in a car and drive. Pretty tough to argue that point. Her hospital and rehab tab will be considerable, though, so I'm hoping Dobson can work out something there. My brothers and I can take care of the damage to her car."

"You've covered a lot of ground."

"Unfortunately, we've been down this road before. Not the drinking and driving, although maybe she just never got caught. I honestly don't know. But this will be her second go at rehab."

He shot her a sideways glance. "I don't get it. Yeah, she had another bump with Jason, but that's been ongoing for a year, year and a half. So why now? After five sober years, why did she fall off the wagon? She needs the answer to that."

"The counselors will figure it out. That's what they do. And they'll help her find a better way to cope with whatever caused it."

She laid a hand on his arm, and he placed his free hand over it, glad to have her beside him.

"Did you leave anyone special in Savannah?" he asked.

"Other than my family?"

"Yeah. Guess that was my not so clever way of asking if you'd been dating anyone. Somebody who might still be on your mind."

"No. There was someone a few years ago, but right now? Like I said last night, not the time for relationship tangles, past or present."

With one hand draped casually over the wheel, Brant

sent her another glance. "You intend to work your butt off giving all these brides their dream-come-true weddings, but you don't want one."

"I didn't say that." She brushed at her hair. "I *do* want one. Eventually."

"When you're thirty. What's so magical about three years?"

"You wouldn't understand."

He took the hospital exit. "Try me."

"How's the bid on that shop coming?"

He slid his sunglasses low on his nose and looked at her. "Okay. Message received. We'll sideline that discussion—for now. On the business front, after watching the video, my brothers green-lighted the place. I hope I'm not screwing up, but it feels right, you know?"

"I do."

"Since they'll be here day after tomorrow, I'll wait to make the deal final."

"Smart. That'll take a lot of pressure off you."

"Yeah. This way, it's a joint decision." He glanced in the rearview mirror. "He's sleeping, isn't he?"

Molly twisted in her seat and nodded.

He shook his head. "The guys will fly into Savannah, then catch a cab to the hospital. After they visit Lainey, we'll head back to Misty Bottoms and they can check out the place. With its proximity to both Atlanta and Savannah, the location's prime. Add in the new life you ladies breathed into the town, and it's a winner in my book."

"I didn't do anything. I'm riding on the coattails of the other three."

"Not the way I see it. The four of you? One cohesive whole."

~~~

Halfway to Lainey's room, Jax got fussy.

Brant freed him from his seat and held him, patting his back.

A big burp erupted.

Brant lifted the baby to eye level. "Good job. Welcome to the guys' club, little man."

Molly smacked his arm. "Stop that!"

"What? You fed him before we came in. The kid's gonna burp. Baby 101."

"You're the expert now?"

"Kind of."

She made a face, and Jax laughed.

"Can't stay mad, can you?"

"Just cut out all that boys' club stuff."

"*Guys'* club. There's a difference." The baby in one arm and the seat in his other hand, Brant started down the hall.

"Now that Jax has his own room—not that he sleeps in it—did you get him a crib?"

"He sleeps in a dresser drawer."

Her eyes went wide. "What?"

"I took it out of the dresser! Geez, I don't put him away like a pair of socks at night!"

"You need a crib."

"Yeah, well, I don't have one. I don't have lots of things I need." His voice grew husky as he met her gaze.

She licked her lips. "Brant..."

"Yeah, I know. No fooling around till you're thirty."

He continued to look at her through half-mast eyes. "I'll come visit you in three years. How's that sound?"

"Now you're making fun of me."

"Believe me, darlin', nothing about this is funny."

When they reached Lainey's room, her bed was empty.

Brant ducked into the hall, where he spotted a nurse. "Excuse me. Do you know where Lainey Wylder is?"

She sent him a wide smile. "Since it's such a nice day, we bundled her into a wheelchair and took her out to the gardens."

"Thank you." Brant returned her smile. "Can you tell me how to get there?"

Molly stepped from the room and stole his breath. She looked so right standing there with a baby on her hip that, for a moment, Brant totally forgot the nurse.

When she cleared her throat, he whipped back around to her. "Sorry."

"They make quite a sight, don't they?"

"Yes, ma'am, they sure do."

She gave him directions, then said, "Someone else came to visit your sister, too. I believe he's still with her."

"Another guy?"

"Yes. I didn't get his name." She gave a quick description.

"Jason." Brant's face turned hard. "If he's upset her…"

The nurse laid a hand on his arm. "Did we make a mistake? Do we need security?"

"No." He shook his head. "I'll handle this myself."

"Brant." Molly took a step toward him.

"Stay here with the baby."

"No way. I don't get set on some shelf. That's not my style." She followed him down the hall. "Is it Jax's father?"

"Sperm donor," Brant snapped.

She winced.

"Sorry. Go back to Lainey's room, Mol."

"Save your breath." Molly practically ran to keep up with him, the baby jabbering loudly, no doubt picking up on the tension. "Don't do anything you'll regret. Lainey needs you. Jax needs you. It won't help anyone if you land in jail."

He stopped, his jaw set stubbornly. "I won't let Jason mess with my family anymore. He's already caused enough trouble."

"Understood. But think how this will shake down. Chances are you'll need Kemper Dobson's help with Jason. What if he brings charges against you for physical violence? Hmm? Who will a jury side with? Award custody to? The father or a hot-tempered uncle?"

He scrubbed both hands down his face and exhaled loudly. "You're right. I'll talk to him. That's all. Promise."

When they reached the door, Jason was looming over Lainey.

"I need some money. Your brothers have plenty, and they'll do anything for their little princess."

"How did you find me?" Lainey's voice shook.

"Still had a check comin' from the bar. When I stopped to pick it up, Ralph said you'd been lookin' for me, and that, according to your friend Trisha, you'd had an accident that landed you in the hospital. Didn't take more than a couple of calls to find you."

"I wanted you to see our son."

"Why would I want to do that?"

"Because he's yours."

"Maybe."

Brant let out a feral growl, and Molly gripped his arm. "Wait."

"Get out of here." Lainey blinked back tears.

"Ralph told me you had a drink. We both know you can't stop at one. That's how you ended up in here, isn't it? The court's gonna find you unfit." He pointed a finger at her. "You haven't seen the last of me, Lainey."

Then he smiled, an evil smile. "On the other hand, maybe you have. The last of both me and the kid."

Brant practically tore the door off its hinges. Lainey sat in the wheelchair, pale as parchment. Jason glowered at her, his hands fisted.

Brant's gaze dropped to Jason's hands. "Whatever you're thinking, I'd think again." His quiet voice dripped ice.

Jason, tall and even skinnier than he'd been the last time Brant saw him, sneered. "Why don't you go play with your cars? This is between your sister and me. It doesn't concern you."

"See, that's where you're wrong, Jason. It does concern me. This is my family you're messing with, and it stops now."

"Oh yeah?" Jason smirked at him, then turned his gaze on Molly, on the baby in her arms. Every molecule of air seemed to have been sucked out of the garden area. Even the birds ceased their singing.

Brant's stomach hit the ground. He felt helpless. Molly was right. If he so much as laid a hand on the worthless scum, he'd be the one spending the night in jail. He couldn't let that happen. Too many people counted on him.

"That my kid?"

No one answered.

He started toward Molly. "Guess I got myself a son."

"Jason," Lainey begged. "I'll—"

"You'll nothing," he spat. He turned his attention back to Molly. "I'll take the kid off your hands, and y'all will never see him again, 'cause unlike his mother, I ain't headed to no rehab for drunk driving."

"Jason, please."

"That kid's as much mine as yours. My name's on his birth certificate."

"You think contributing sperm makes you a father?" Brant asked. "You couldn't be bothered to marry your son's mother or even show up for his birth. You've never held him or walked with him at two in the morning when he couldn't sleep. You're a poor excuse for a father."

Lainey gave a small cry when Jason took another couple of steps toward Molly.

Molly pivoted on her heel, the baby on her far side out of Jason's reach, her expression fierce. "We've never met, but don't you dare come any closer."

Jason stopped, his smirk sliding away.

"You've made a huge mistake. I came with Brant today to see his sister. But this baby? He's *my* baby, and you *will not* lay a hand on him. Not unless you want to grow old behind bars for attempted kidnapping."

Lainey jumped in. "She's right. *My* baby is safe and being well taken care of, for which I'll be eternally grateful." Her eyes met Brant's, then Molly's, in turn.

Brant stepped forward. "It's time you leave, Jason. If not, I'll have one of the nurses call security."

"You haven't heard the end of this or seen the last of me." The door slammed behind him.

Molly sank onto a chair, shaking so badly, she didn't think her legs would hold her.

Brant took Jax and handed him to a crying Lainey.

When the baby started to cry, too, Brant said, "Lainey, pull yourself together. You're upsetting Jax."

Lainey swiped at her face and apologized for her behavior, for Jason, and for the responsibility she'd dumped on Brant.

"It's okay, honey," Brant assured her. "The important thing is for you to get well again."

"I will."

He looked from one woman to the other. "I haven't introduced you two, have I? I'm sorry. Sis, I'd like you to meet Molly Stiles. Molly, my sister, Lainey."

Lainey's eyes glistened with tears as they met Molly's. "I'm so glad to meet you, and I can't thank you enough for today."

"No thanks needed. I'm not sure Jason believed me, but there was enough doubt that he stopped. How about I find some cold drinks for us?"

Deep, dark sadness crawled through Molly as she left, giving brother and sister privacy. On her way to the cafeteria, she reminded herself this whole mess was the result of operating without a plan.

She stayed away for an hour, wanting to give Brant, Lainey, and Jax a good visit. Molly figured her chat with Lainey could wait till the next trip.

―᷍―

Neither she nor Brant had much to say as they left the hospital, and the ride home was very quiet.

When they pulled to the curb, Brant started to get out.

Molly laid a hand on his arm. "Stay. I'm good. It's time you and this baby get home."

"Mol, thanks again for today. Talk about thinking fast on your feet. I'm sorry we put you in that position."

"There's absolutely nothing for you to be sorry about. You've been left to mop up a mess you didn't make." She leaned across the console and dropped a kiss on his lips, one that lasted longer than she'd meant. "Later."

Let him think about that tonight.

Chapter 13

MOLLY STARED AT THE CEILING, IGNORING THE WEAK morning light. She hated conflict, and yesterday's was like a slap in the face, reminding her of the fights and turmoil between her and Keith. Movies and romance books painted love with a brush full of sunshine and promises of a happily-ever-after. In real life? Relationships were more like a game of Russian roulette.

When Brant asked for an explanation for the whole thirty-years-old thing, she hadn't given him one—because she didn't have one. It had all seemed so simple, had made so much sense. Now? She didn't know.

Everything had become a jumble.

Bubbles, sensing her human was awake, hopped onto the bed, purring and rubbing against her.

"Enough with the self-pity, right? I'm officially declaring a be-good-to-Molly day, and it starts now." She nuzzled her cat, stroked a hand down her back, and smiled when Bubbles arched into it. "First on the agenda? Tansy's Sweet Dreams for a truly decadent breakfast treat. Want some food before I go?"

Food. The magic word. Bubbles leaped to the floor and made a mad dash to the kitchen. Molly fed her, took a quick shower, and dressed for work in a black knee-length wool skirt, a cowl-necked sweater, and leather flats. No heels. Today was all about comfort.

Hopping into her Mini, she headed to Tansy's for

a fresh-out-of-the-oven croissant and her favorite tea steeped and served in one of her friend's beautiful teapots. Maybe she'd ask for the one covered in tiny violets.

"Good Morning Beautiful" came over the radio, and she sighed. What would it be like to wake beside Brant? To open her eyes to him after sharing the night? She patted her heart. Whew.

Yes, she was the one applying the brakes, but only because he wanted a fling, something temporary.

Wait. That's what she wanted, wasn't it?

No. She didn't even have time for that right now.

Confused, she rubbed her forehead.

She needed caffeine. Food. Because she definitely felt light-headed. Like that clichéd moth, she was drawn to something beautiful that would only bring hurt.

Pulling up to the curb in front of the pale-lavender and green Victorian, Molly simply sat, enjoying the view. With its manicured lawn and gardens, the wide veranda with the come-sit-awhile rockers, and the homey feeling, Sweet Dreams was exactly that. The perfect spot to relax and dream sweet dreams.

Tansy had lived upstairs for a while, but after she and Beck married in a small ceremony in the sweeping backyard, she and her young daughter had moved into his house. They'd talked about renting out the apartment, but Molly doubted that would ever happen.

Stepping inside the bakery, Molly found herself immersed in friends and neighbors. Heavenly smells of fresh coffee, cinnamon, and orange wafted to her. Since the morning was cool, the original fireplace, now converted to gas, added to the warm ambience. The tablecloths and centerpieces shouted Valentine's Day.

It was a little early, but Tansy argued that the more her customers had romance on the brain, the more business Magnolia Brides would garner. She'd filled glass snifters with red jelly beans, then arranged happy red silk tulips in them.

Exactly what Molly didn't need, a reminder she'd have no one to spend the special day with. Brant, with his smoldering kisses and touches that set her aflame, roared into mind.

Okay. Enough, Molly.

She wasn't anyone's valentine—her choice. And she'd come here to spoil herself, not to wallow. With that in mind, she greeted Jimmy Don with a huge smile. "Sheriff, how are you?"

"Doin' fine, Molly. You sure got lots of tongues waggin' about that new window display." He shot her a thumbs-up. "I like it. So does the missus."

"Thanks." Several others stopped her on the way to the counter where Tansy chatted and smiled while handing out specialty coffees and fabulous baked goods.

Her face lit up when she spotted Molly. "What brings you here?"

"I'm indulging myself."

"Well, you came to the right spot. Tea?"

"Yes, please, in your little violet pot, and I'll have a chocolate croissant."

"Find a seat, and I'll bring it to you." She frowned. "You look tired. Sleep okay?"

"Yesterday was…" She trailed off. Not her place to air Brant's problems. "No, not really."

She found an empty table by the big stone fireplace and smiled her thanks when Tansy delivered her goodies. Yesterday's fiasco replayed over and over in a loop. The day had started so well, the trip to Savannah almost fun. Even Jax had been in a good mood.

But the ride home? Grim.

The only reason Jason hadn't argued with her was because, when it came right down to it, the jerk couldn't identify his own child, and how sad was that? He didn't deserve Jax, and Jax certainly didn't deserve the father he'd been stuck with.

While Molly toyed with her croissant, Tansy, having no new customers, slid into the chair across from her.

"Something wrong with that?" Tansy nodded toward the flaky pastry.

"What? Oh, no. I've got a lot on my mind." Not really a lie.

She jumped to a safe topic. "Brant found a house for himself and the baby. Cole set him up in Lem Gilmore's empty rental."

"I heard. I didn't think Brant intended to stay long enough to want an actual house."

"Me, either, but he wants to stay close till he sees what all his sister might need." She didn't mention that Brant might buy property in Misty Bottoms. Again, not her story to tell. Still, guilt nagged at her for holding back from her friend.

Tansy raised a finger in a wait-one-minute and made the rounds with her coffeepot, topping off customers' cups. Slipping back into her chair, she said, "If he needs help with the baby, he should call Lucinda's day care. My Gracie Bella loves it there."

"Good idea." Molly stirred her tea absently. "In the meantime, Brant has this house, but nothing, absolutely nothing, for the baby. Jax is sleeping in a dresser drawer."

Tansy rolled her eyes. "Leave it to a man to think of that." She tapped her fingertips on the table. "You know, Darlene over at Quilty Pleasures might be able to help. Her niece had twins, and if I'm not wrong, she kept some of their things." She plucked a phone from her apron pocket.

After she dialed, she handed it to Molly.

"I don't know her very well," Molly whispered, holding the phone away from her.

"She's really nice. Honest. She lent you that—"

"Hello, Darlene?" She scowled at a smiling Tansy. "It's Molly from That Little White Dress. I'm at Tansy's, and we were talking. Um, I have a question. Actually, it's a favor. For Brant Wylder."

Darlene's dogs, Moonshine and Mint Julep, barked in the background.

"Hush, you two," Darlene admonished. "They want a doggie biscuit. But you've already had one this morning, haven't you?" she asked the Cairn terriers, reverting to baby talk. "Do I know Brant?"

"Probably not. He's been in a couple of weddings at Magnolia House, including last weekend's. He and Cole were fraternity brothers." Without going into detail, Molly explained Brant's sister had had an accident. "While she's in the hospital, he's caring for her seven-month-old son. Annabelle's isn't very baby friendly, so they've moved to Lem Gilmore's rental."

"That old place?"

"It's just short-term, and Brant seems to think it'll work." She glanced at Tansy, who urged her on. "He doesn't have anything for the baby, though, other than a few clothes and bottles. No crib."

"What's the little thing sleeping in?"

"A dresser drawer."

"Oh, for… Does he have a high chair?"

"No."

"A playpen?"

"No."

"Let me call my niece. I imagine we can take care of this, but we'll need a truck."

Tansy, who'd put the phone on speaker before passing it to Molly, said, "I'll call Sam, Darlene. Seems only fitting the old truck he bought from Lem delivers the baby things to his house."

An hour and a half later, Molly phoned Brant. "You still home?"

"I am. You said to stay put, so I did. Although I still have no idea why."

"Give me fifteen minutes, and you will." She clicked off. "Thanks, Sam. I appreciate this."

Sam, Cricket's fiancé and former NYC detective turned small-town deputy, said, "It's okay. You know, when I moved here from the city, I figured this place for the armpit of the world. Now? You couldn't pry me out with a crowbar. Misty Bottoms is a good place to live. You'll be happy here."

"I already am."

Hobo, sitting between her and Sam in the old truck, let out a sharp bark and placed his graying paw on Molly's leg. For a fleeting instant, she thought of the dog hair she'd have to pick off her black skirt and about the fact she hadn't opened her shop on time.

The heck with it. She rubbed the old dog between his ears and settled into the leisurely pace of the day. After all, this was what "Southern" was all about. If a person wanted to hurry, he should have been born north of the Mason-Dixon Line.

When they parked in Brant's drive, Darlene pulled in behind them. She'd left her sister to cover her shop, insisting it was time she met this newcomer.

Darlene's dogs, freed from her car, pranced daintily through the tall grass in their little blue outfits. Hobo hopped from Sam's truck and ran up to them. Before they bumped noses, though, the old dog hit his brakes, head tipped, and studied the Cairn terriers as if not quite sure what to make of them.

Darlene patted his head. "Look, Moonshine, a new friend." To Hobo, she said, "Maybe I should make you a sweater, sweetie. Would you like that?"

Hobo let out a yap and ran lickety-split back to the truck, practically melting into Sam's leg.

"What's wrong with you, boy? You afraid of those little things?"

Molly leaned close and whispered, "I think he's scared Darlene might actually make him a sweater."

Sam laughed. "There is that. Hobo's not much of a fashion plate."

His hair disheveled, Brant opened the door with Jax straddling his hip.

"Consider us the welcoming committee." Darlene marched up to the porch and stuck out her hand. "I'm Darlene Dixon. This is Moonshine and Mint Julep."

She chucked Jax beneath his chin. "And who are you, sweetie?"

"This is Jax."

The baby gurgled and handed Darlene his spit-covered rattle.

"Aren't you just the cutest little thing?" Her attention returned to Brant. "Rumor has it you don't have much for this baby, so we've come to take care of that."

Making little cooing noises, she plucked the baby from him.

"Since you've got two free hands now," Sam called out, "why don't you put them to good use, Brant? Get over here and help."

Looking slightly flummoxed, Brant did exactly that.

In no time, they had the crib, high chair, and play-pen inside, along with a well-used rocker. Darlene had thrown in an almost-new sofa cover and some towels.

"I don't know how to thank you," Brant said.

"It's what we do here in Misty Bottoms," Darlene said. "We help one another. I understand you fix cars."

He winced. "Sort of."

"That's a little like calling Michelangelo a house painter," Sam said.

"I don't understand." Darlene's forehead creased.

"It's okay." Brant sent Sam a wink. "You ever need work done on your car, you let me know."

Molly held up a finger. "We have one more thing." She popped Darlene's trunk, and Sam lifted out a large box. "I guarantee this will be your favorite."

Brant looked at the picture on the side and smiled. A baby swing. "Oh yeah, now you're talking."

"Tansy chipped in with us. It's kind of a shower gift," Molly said.

"A shower gift?" He shot a look at Sam. "Don't you dare breathe a word about this to the guys."

Sam grinned but drew his fingers across his lips, sealing them.

"Yeah."

Darlene ignored their shenanigans. "The twins' swings saw more action than a can of hair spray at Frenchie's salon, so we tossed them."

Brant wrapped her in a hug. "I can't tell you how much I appreciate this."

Sam shook his head. "We'll see if you still feel that way once you start putting it together."

"You're gonna help, aren't you?"

Sam puffed out his cheeks, then nodded. "Against my better judgment."

Jax tried out his new playpen while Darlene and Molly fought with the sofa cover and the guys tackled the swing.

Brant stared at the pieces strewn across the floor.

"Come on," Darlene said. "You put engines together. How hard can this be?"

"Foreign territory."

Darlene handed him the instruction sheet.

He laughed. "Did you look at this?"

"No." She peered around his shoulder and chuckled. "It's in Chinese."

Sam snagged the paper from Brant. "It has pictures."

Twenty minutes later, the women took the baby outside and sat on the shaded porch.

Darlene looked at Molly. "Suppose he's got any soap in there?"

Molly frowned. "Probably. Why?"

"Both those boys could stand to have their mouths washed out."

Molly smiled.

"Don't you be grinnin'. You kissin' that mouth? The mechanic's?"

Molly blushed.

"I thought so." She elbowed Molly. "He any good at it?"

"If he was any better, I'd need a defibrillator."

After another half hour, the swing worked. When baby Jax took his first ride, his giggles were payment in full. He pumped his little legs and banged his rattle.

Sam tossed the cardboard and scraps into the back of his truck. "I'll stop at the dump's recycling and get rid of this."

"Appreciate that."

"One more thing." Molly hurried to Sam's truck and came back with a shopping bag. "Here you go. Use them."

Mystified, Brant peeked in the bag. "Baby monitors?"

"They're wireless. Put one by your bed and one by Jax's crib. You'll hear every noise he makes. You can sleep in your own room without worrying."

He wrapped an arm around her waist and drew her in for a kiss.

When she stepped back, she blinked, speechless.

Darlene chuckled. "I think you misrepresented certain things, Molly. Defibrillator, my butt. How about a fire hose?"

"I don't under—" Brant started.

Sam held up a hand. "Let it be. Some things we're better off not knowing."

Molly smiled, then gave Jax a big smooch. "You be good, okay?"

Brant curled his fingers around Molly's arm. "Why don't you stay for lunch? I've got stuff for sandwiches, and we'll run you into town later."

She made the mistake of glancing toward Darlene, who threw her a wink and a thumbs-up.

"What am I missing here?" Brant's gaze moved between the two.

"I'm telling you, don't ask," Sam warned again.

"I'd love to, Brant," Molly said. "I really would, but I have to open my shop. Can I take a rain check?"

"Sure. How about a movie here tonight? With popcorn."

"She'd love that," Darlene said. "She'll see you at six."

"Darlene!"

"Well, you *would* love it, so stop beating around the bush. The boy's offered to entertain you. Let him. For heaven's sakes, enjoy each other. Have some fun. Let the future take care of itself."

Sam started toward his truck. "You children have fun." He slapped a hand on his thigh and opened the passenger door. "Come on, Hobo. Hop in."

With a wave over his shoulder, Sam rounded the truck and slid into the driver's side. He tooted his horn and was gone.

When Darlene pulled up in front of That Little White Dress, Molly threw her arms around the older woman. "I can't thank you enough."

"Glad I could do it. And those monitors were a good

idea. The man could use some sleep." Darlene took Molly's hand in hers. "Enjoy tonight. Regardless of what happens, the sun will still come up tomorrow."

"You're right." Molly grabbed her purse and hopped out.

Moonshine and Mint Julep yapped from the back seat. Molly reached through the open window and gave each a head pat, careful not to muss their bows.

Unlocking her door, she sprinted up the stairs. Since Hobo, Moonshine, and Mint Julep had all contributed, she wore enough dog hair on her skirt to carpet the boutique. Stepping out of it, she promised to attack it with the lint brush later. Not now, though. Glancing at the clock, she slid into black cigarette pants and a long-sleeved pullover. She slicked her hair back into a ponytail and added a simple silver necklace. A touch of lipstick and she called it done.

"'Bye, Bubbles. I'm off to work. Again."

Downstairs, she hit the lights and flipped the sign to Open. In the back room, she dug a yogurt from her fridge and, leaning against the counter, made fast work of it. Not the same as sandwiches with Brant, but it would do.

Fortified, she headed to the front of the shop.

The door opened, and a woman in her late sixties breezed in.

"Good morning."

"Good morning to you, too, dear. I'm Lettie Dowmeyer."

"It's nice to meet you." Molly took her offered hand. "How can I help you?"

"By giving me a job."

"Excuse me?"

"Honey, I'm sittin' home bored silly while you're runnin' this place all by yourself. Last I heard, you've got a gal over in Rincon doin' your alterations."

"Yes, ma'am."

"It's Lettie, please. I'm a seamstress—an excellent seamstress, and that's the truth, not braggadocio. I worked at a bridal shop in Savannah, so I've dealt with my share of high-strung brides. Clerked there, too, so times you need to be gone—like this mornin'—I can keep the store open for you."

Molly opened her mouth, then closed it again. A steamroller had just barreled through her door.

"My kids are grown, my grandkids too busy for me, and my husband is drivin' me crazy. Now that he's retired, he's home all day doing nothin'. I love him, but I need some time away. My gettin' a job here's the perfect answer. For both you and me."

"I've considered hiring someone, but—"

"You don't know me, don't know if you can trust me to do right by your gowns and customers. Understood." She dug in her purse and came out with a handful of letters, which she thrust at Molly. "These are from people I've sewn for, people right here in Misty Bottoms."

Baffled, Molly took the references. Since she'd thought about hiring help only in an abstract way, she didn't even have an application form. But she liked Lettie. She might be exactly what the shop needed…if she could indeed sew.

"Tell you what," Lettie said. "I've caught you off guard. Why don't we agree on a trial? If, at the end of a week, I'm not what you need, I'm out of here. No questions and no hard feelings."

Molly studied the older woman. With her puff of white hair, electric-blue glasses, and conservative strand of pearls, she looked like somebody's favorite grandma, a grandma made for hugs. And her smile was absolutely contagious.

She should read the letters, then make a couple of calls. Be smart about this.

"When can you start?"

"Right now. Even brought my lunch." She patted an oversized purse, then pointed at Molly. "I can't do that, though."

"What?" She looked down at herself.

"Wear black. I've been by the shop a few times and noticed you're always in head-to-toe black. Me? I like color."

"Hmm. I wear black so I don't compete with the bride, with the quintessential bridal white." She chewed her lower lip. "No white, but I guess other colors would be okay. Pastels might be a problem, though."

Lettie laughed. "No pastels for me. I like bold."

Molly nodded. The fire-engine-red dress Lettie wore today packed a real punch. It might work. Besides, she'd spend most of her time in the back doing alterations rather than working the floor. "Let's give it a try."

Life dropped little gifts into your lap once in a while, and Molly believed Lettie Dowmeyer would prove to be one of those. She grinned.

She had an assistant.

⸻

By the end of the day, Lettie had sold a negligee set and hemmed a slip for one of their brides. Molly had planned to call the seamstress in Rincon and run the slip over tomorrow after closing. Now she wouldn't need to make the trip.

She waved goodbye to Lettie and locked the door. What a day. She'd treated herself to breakfast at Sweet Dreams, Brant had baby furniture, and she'd hired her first employee. On top of that, she'd enjoyed her time with Darlene and Sam. Moving here had been the right choice. So had hiring Lettie.

Since she had movie plans with two handsome guys, Molly hustled upstairs for a quick shower. Wrapped in a robe, she fed Bubbles and grabbed a sandwich for herself. Then she slid into jeans and a soft yellow blouse. Halfway out the door, she raced back upstairs and switched on a small lamp.

"I won't be gone long, baby. But if I am, you're to be in bed by ten, got it?"

The cat meowed and wandered off to find trouble.

Molly hoped she'd find a little of her own.

When she knocked on Brant's screen door, the scene was almost shockingly domestic.

Jax, safely ensconced in his playpen, banged on an old pan with a wooden spoon. The second he spotted her, he grinned and discarded his toys to crawl toward her.

"Come on in," Brant called. "I'm in the kitchen."

"I'll be right there. Just saying hello to Jax." She leaned in for a couple of noisy kisses.

"Yeah, the kid's always stealing the spotlight."

She started to laugh, but it stuck in her throat when she stepped into the next room. A tea towel slung over one shoulder, another tucked into the waist of his jeans, Brant stood at the sink washing baby bottles. Reaching for the doorjamb, she watched him. What was there about a man in the kitchen that kicked up the heat?

He turned and smiled, his dimples winking. "Hungry? I should've offered dinner tonight."

"No, I ate."

Laying the bottle brush in the drainer, he crossed to her. "Sorry, but I have to do this or die."

With that, his lips captured hers. Changing the angle slightly, he went deeper. Tongues dancing, bodies touching, he groaned, an inherently male sound. He pulled back and dropped his forehead to hers. "I've missed you."

"It's only been a few hours."

"Four very, very long hours."

"Did the baby give you trouble?"

"No. You did. The smell of you in the house, the echo of your voice, your laughter."

"Brant—"

"I know. Nothin' serious. But babe, you're messing with my head."

"Not on purpose."

"Somehow that makes it harder to deal with." He ran his hands down her arms, laced his fingers with hers. "How was your day?"

Tingles zipped from her fingers and sizzled through her entire body. "It started off great. I helped deliver baby furniture to a gorgeous hunk!"

"Oh yeah?" He grinned and ran the tip of one finger down the side of her face, along her jaw. "Did this grand specimen of a male thank you sufficiently?"

"Well, there were other people around, so he was kind of shy about that. I got the feeling, though, if I could catch him alone, he—"

The kiss, hot and searing, stole her breath. Where the first kiss had started slowly and built, this one was impatient, insistent. By the time he drew away, she wasn't sure which end was up.

"Okay." He exhaled.

"Might I second that emotion," she said. "And you're welcome. Very."

Molly toyed with the top button on his shirt. "I hired an assistant this afternoon." She frowned. "Maybe she hired me."

His forehead creased. "What?"

"I'm not sure exactly how it happened. I opened the door, and Lettie sort of blew in. Kind of like Mary Poppins. She had that same take-charge air about her."

"Did you check her references?"

She slid his button through the hole, then buttoned it again. "Not exactly."

His brow lifted.

"She gave me some letters of recommendation, but I hired her before I read them."

"Why?"

Molly lifted one shoulder. "I don't know. She felt right. Kind of like when you found the new spot for your business. We agreed on a one-week trial period."

"Okay, I—Shoot!" He ran toward the sink and turned off the water. "Good thing the water was just trickling. I forgot I put the stopper in."

"What's that crunching noise?"

Brant grimaced. "Macaroni."

She took a step back and heard another crunch. Sure enough, a crushed piece of macaroni was under her shoe.

"Jax grabbed a box this afternoon and chewed on it. I figured it kept him busy, so no harm, no foul. Until he managed to gnaw a hole in it. Even without teeth, the kid's like a beaver. Maybe the cardboard simply caved beneath all the slobber. Anyway, before I realized what he'd done, he was shaking the box, and macaroni flew all over."

She grinned.

"You think it's funny, huh?"

"The mental image?" She tapped her forehead, her grin growing. "Yeah, I do."

"You have a sick sense of humor." He scanned the floor. "I swept. Three times. Guess I missed a few pieces."

With a sad shake of her head, she said, "Finish up here. I'll go play with the beaver." Halfway out of the kitchen, she asked, "What are we watching?"

"You have to ask?"

She thought for a second. "Yeah, I guess I do."

"Only one movie to watch today. It's a Wylder family tradition." He hesitated. "You do know what day it is, don't you?"

"February second."

"And?"

"Movie day?"

"No! It's Groundhog Day."

She said nothing.

"Don't tell me you've never seen *Groundhog Day*. Bill Murray? Andie MacDowell?"

"Afraid not."

"Then you're in for a treat." He rubbed his hands together in glee. "Up for it?"

"Oh yeah."

"Yet another reason you're my kind of girl."

Brant flopped on the couch and put his feet on the coffee table, the remote in his hand. "My cable isn't on yet, but they promised it by tomorrow. Man was not meant to live without TV."

She tsked. "All those football games. Those NASCAR races."

"Thank heavens for the internet."

When she sank onto the sofa, Brant crooked his finger.

"Come closer. I'll keep you safe."

"Seriously? Safe from what? Bill Murray? A groundhog?"

"You never know."

"You're incorrigible." But she slid nearer, Jax perched on her lap, jabbering a mile a minute. "What do you think he's saying?"

"He's crowing because he's got the best seat in the house." Brant draped an arm around her and Jax popped his thumb in his mouth, his head resting against her and his face tipped up to watch her. They looked like any young American family.

It felt weird…and wonderful.

Brant hit Play, and she got caught up in the movie.

Ten minutes in, he nudged her. "Look at Jax. The kid's taking it all in."

Sure enough, Jax was fixated on the screen.

"My nephew's a genius."

Molly simply shook her head.

Half an hour later, the genius started fussing.

"How about I get Jax ready for bed while you fix

a bottle, then make that popcorn you promised me?" she asked.

"I think I'm getting the short end of the stick."

"Yeah, but it's your stick."

"True."

After drawing a couple of inches of water into the tub, she tested it to make sure it wasn't too warm. She scooped Jax from the playpen and carried him into the bathroom. "Let's take a bath, sweetheart. Won't that be fun?"

"Cut it out," Brant called from the kitchen.

"What?"

"You're teasing me. Setting off all kinds of pictures in my head. Not nice."

She laughed. "Uncle Brant can be kind of grumpy, can't he?"

The baby let out a stream of babble while she undressed him.

"Oh, I do wish I knew what you were saying, child."

"He said you should take a bath—or a shower—with Uncle Brant to sweeten him up."

"In your dreams, big boy."

"You got that right."

"We'll ignore Mr. Grump, Jax."

"I heard that."

"That was the point," she called back, lowering Jax into the water.

Happy splashing commenced immediately.

"Ah! I should have worn a raincoat. Guess you're a water baby, huh?"

He let out a squeal and kicked his feet, laughing.

"Oh, look, you have a rubber ducky."

"His name's Ebenezer."

"Get out of here. Ebenezer?" She knelt by the tub, soaping the baby down with his special soap.

"Every boy needs a pet."

"And Jax has Ebenezer," she finished.

"You got it."

With a lot of splashing and even more laughter, Molly managed to bathe Jax. She was afraid to hurry, because wet, he'd become a slippery little bugger. But she didn't want him to catch cold, either.

She looked up to find Brant leaning against the doorjamb watching, an odd expression on his face.

"What?"

"Nothing. It's just—nothing."

He walked back to the kitchen.

She stared after him. Strange.

Jax grabbed her hair.

"Yes, I know." She pat-a-caked his hands. "You want my attention, sweetie. But your uncle? A curious and complicated man."

Holding the sweet-smelling, hoodie-towel-wrapped baby close, she carried him into his room and dressed him in a clean diaper and pajamas.

Brant had a bottle ready, so she sat in the rocker and cuddled Jax while she fed him. His eyes fluttered shut, his breathing evened out, and his little hand dropped from the bottle. Her throat constricted as she held the warm, sleeping baby. Nothing else had ever come close to this feeling.

Very carefully, she carried him to his new crib, touching her lips lightly to his rosy cheek.

Brant stood behind her, his green eyes forest-dark. She raised a finger to her lips, and he nodded.

She stepped from the room, and he partially closed the door behind them.

The room smelled of fresh popcorn and butter. Brant had turned off the bright overhead light, and the remaining small lamp gave the room an intimate air. Even the worn furniture and faded rug looked less shabby.

"Ready to finish the movie?" She took a handful of popcorn and curled up on the lumpy sofa. Again, the normalcy of the scene struck her. The baby bathed, fed, and in bed, the lights low. The happy couple...

Brant dropped down beside her.

"You are going to let him sleep in his own room tonight, aren't you?"

He leaned in and nuzzled her neck. "Probably, since someone set me up with a baby monitor. Why don't you stay the night and keep me company?" he whispered against her ear. "Keep Uncle Brant from getting lonely."

She shivered as his breath caressed her skin. "So not going to happen, Wylder."

"Maybe I can convince you."

His lips moved along her neck, over her jaw, and up her face till she was desperate for them on her own lips. "Brant."

The kiss was heated, deep, and long, and arrowed to her core. She forgot all the reasons she shouldn't give in as her entire body became one huge erogenous zone. Her blouse dropped to the floor under his clever fingers. His lips slid along her throat again, trailed lower until they found her breasts. Through the lace of her bra, his mouth closed over her, and she bowed up to meet him.

Her own hands went to work on the buttons of his shirt, uncovering that fabulous, hidden six-pack.

Jax's cries finally forced their way through her sex fog. Placing her palms on his chest, she drew back.

"Brant…"

"I hear him." He drew her against him, bare skin to bare skin. "I swear, I'm gonna follow that kid when he takes his first date parking. Right when they get to the good part, I'm gonna turn on a flood light. Better, I'll borrow Sam's police car and hit both the lights and the siren."

"You do that." She patted his fabulous bare chest. "Right now, though, you need to change a dirty diaper, and I'm heading home. We can finish the movie another night."

He rolled off the sofa, muttering to himself.

Darlene was right. He definitely could stand to have that beautiful mouth washed out with soap.

Chapter 14

BRANT DASHED AROUND THE HOUSE, THROWING HIS AND Jax's dirty clothes into the hamper and the dirty dishes into the sink. His brothers were coming in today. True, they'd stay at Annabelle's, since he had only the one bed, but—He stopped. What the heck was he doing? Cleaning for his brothers? Oh geez, he'd turned into his mother. No way would either Tucker or Gaven expect Brant's house to be white-glove clean. Well, maybe OCD Tucker would, but too bad about that.

He wouldn't throw the clothes he'd already tossed in the hamper back on the sofa, but if anything else was lying around, it could stay right where it was. Lainey and the kid kept him far too busy to dust knickknacks.

Maybe he could talk one or both of his brothers into babysitting tonight, and he and Molly could take a breather over at her place. A breather, heck. He wanted to *steal* her breath.

Why? Because he couldn't have her? Because it had been a while since he'd been with a woman? The Tennessee–Georgia excuse didn't work anymore, since he was looking at moving here. If anything, proximity was a mark on the negative side of the list.

Speaking of lists, Molly's was an annoyance.

Molly, herself? Definitely *not*. Kind. Giving. Beautiful. Sexy. What wasn't to like? Yet, like a thorn, she'd worked her way under his skin, and it wasn't totally comfortable.

He grabbed his wallet from the counter and slid it into his back pocket, then picked up his keys.

"Ready, kid? If we leave right now, I'll have just enough time to grab a quick breakfast on the way."

―∾∾―

Rather than have his brothers catch a cab, Brant had decided to pick them up. He and Jax parked at the Savannah/Hilton Head International Airport and were waiting by the luggage carousel when Tucker and Gaven came down the escalator.

On the way to the hospital, Brant filled them in on Jason's visit.

"Good thing I wasn't there." Tucker's jaw tightened. "I'd have punched the jerk's lights out."

"That's the Marine talking," Brant said. "You think I didn't want to?"

"Why didn't you?"

"Because I had the kid and a nearly hysterical Lainey to deal with. A knock-down, drag-out fight in front of them didn't seem the way to go."

"You're right," Tucker grunted.

―∾∾―

As they strode through the hospital doors, Gaven carrying Jax, heads turned. Sandwiched in the middle, Brant was a year younger than Tucker and two years older than Gaven. His poor mother.

Although they all hovered right around six foot, give or take an inch, he and Gaven shared unruly brown hair and green eyes, while Tucker's eyes were hazel to go with his nearly black hair, cut in a modified Marine style. They all carried scruff on their faces, worked hard, and had the muscles to show for it.

Yet they hadn't managed to keep their baby sister safe, and that was a bitter pill to swallow.

Embarrassed, Lainey greeted Tucker and Gaven quietly, her gaze on her hospital wristband.

"Uh-uh." Gaven, the extroverted, easygoing one, moved to the bed and drew her into a hug. "No walls, Sis." His voice cracked. "We love you."

Tucker, not quite as easy with emotion, stepped in after him with a quick, hard hug and a pat on the back. "It'll be good. Things'll be okay, Lainey."

Then she reached for Jax, cradling him in her good arm. When tears rolled down her cheeks, the brothers cringed, furtive glances passing between them. Picking up on his mother's angst, Jax grew fussy.

"Can you feed him?" Brant nodded toward the cast on her arm.

"Yes."

Brant readied the bottle, then moved to a chair by the window to give his brothers time with Lainey. It was the first time they'd seen her since the accident.

They made small talk, then Tucker said, "Sis, you have a lot going for you. We got through this before, and we will again."

"We?" Gaven asked. "You weren't here."

"That's right. I was in the Middle East getting my ass shot at so you could play Romeo with the girls in Lake Delores."

"Hey, guys." Brant stood. "Not now."

"Gaven's right," Tucker owned. "I wasn't here, and I'm sorry about that. Doesn't mean I didn't care. Didn't worry. This time I am, and I'll do whatever it takes to pull you through."

"And you don't need Jason," Gaven insisted. "You and Jax are both better off without him. Brant told us he showed up here."

"I'm glad he did." Lainey handed Tucker the empty bottle, and he tossed it across the room to Brant.

Brant caught it one-handed. "You're glad he showed up? You can't be serious."

"Oh, but I am." She squared her shoulders. "You're right, Gaven. Jax and I don't need him. If I had the slightest doubt about that, it's gone. He did me a favor coming here. I don't know what I saw in him, but I sure am glad we made this baby." Her demeanor softened.

Before any of them could speak, a knock sounded at the door, and an aide peeked inside. "Lainey, it's time for your X-ray."

"And time for us to go." Tucker leaned down for a quick kiss. Gaven did the same.

"Brant, can you stay another minute?"

"Sure." He nodded at his brothers. "I'll meet you guys by the front door."

The hospital worker said, "I'll be in the hall, when you're ready."

When the door closed, Lainey asked, "Will I have to go to jail after rehab?"

"No, sweetie. Your lawyer and I have it covered. Since you're voluntarily entering rehab, there'll be no jail."

"I've forced you into the role of protector again, haven't I? I'm so sorry."

"I don't want apologies. I want your promise this will never happen again."

"It won't." Tears coursed silently down her cheeks, and she dropped a kiss on Jax's forehead. "I'll miss him so much."

"We'll take good care of him."

She nodded. "I swear I'll do my job while I'm in there. When I come out, I'll be a mother my son can be proud of."

"I know." He kissed her, gently took the baby from her, and left the room, the sound of her weeping shredding his heart.

As they crossed the parking lot, Gaven swiped at his eyes. "I'm not glad Mom had a stroke, but I'm relieved she and Dad aren't here today. That visit would have about killed them."

"She'll get it right this time. She's strong," Tucker said.

Brant listened to his brothers. Gaven's approach to life centered on emotion, while Tucker, a Marine at heart, took a more cerebral, hard-line approach. For him it was all about figuring out what had to be done, then doing it.

Gaven offered to sit in the back and entertain Jax.

They stopped at a fast-food place on the way out of town. While his brothers ordered, Brant changed Jax and sent Molly a message.

Miss you. Wish you were here with us.

Her reply was almost instantaneous. Miss you, too. Hope it went well.

It hadn't, but he wouldn't drop that on her.

Gaven and Tucker arrived with the food. Over

burgers, fries, and a jar of pureed garden vegetables and beef, he told them a little more about the location he'd found and what he thought they might do with it.

"You say it'll work, it'll work," Tucker said.

Brant looked at Gaven.

"I agree."

After they ate, Brant drove his brothers to the old service station.

Tucker rolled down the car window and whistled. "Why hasn't somebody else snapped this place up?"

"It's perfect." Gaven got out of the car with Jax. "Way to go, Bro."

Quinlyn pulled in. When her car door opened and she slid out, Gaven took one look at her long legs and jabbed Brant in the stomach. "This the one you're dating?"

"No, this is our real-estate agent, Quinlyn Deveraux, and you'll leave her alone. If we make this our base, you need to remember it's a small town. You start working your way through every single woman in Misty Bottoms, we'll end up tarred feathered and run out on a rail."

"What about you and your bridal-shop owner?"

"That's different."

"Of course it is." Gaven rolled his eyes. He held a squirming Jax at arm's length. "Uncle Brant's not playing fair, is he?"

Jax let out a squeal, his little legs pumping in midair.

"I couldn't agree more," Gaven said.

Quinlyn joined them and together, they poked into every nook and cranny and walked every inch of the property.

Tucker stood in the middle of the parking area, thumbs in his pockets. "It's exactly what we need."

Gaven agreed. "What do we do to get the ball rolling?"

"I've explained to the owner it'll be a cash deal," Quinlyn answered. "Kemper Dobson will have the paperwork wrapped up in a week or so. In the meantime, with the earnest money you've agreed to, Frank told him to give you the key so you can start renovations."

"Think that's smart?" Gaven shifted uneasily from foot to foot. "I mean, what if we dump money into it, then the deal goes south?"

"It won't," Brant said. "In Misty Bottoms, a man's word is golden. Heck, Jax and I are living rent-free in a house that belongs to somebody I've never even met."

"That's just weird," Gaven said.

"That's Misty Bottoms." Quinlyn laughed.

"You two want to sleep on this?" Brant asked.

"Heck, no," Tucker said. "I want to rip into the place. Make it ours."

Gaven nodded. "Let's write that check and get started."

———

Brant dropped his brothers off at Annabelle's, and his mind sailed straight to Molly. According to the dashboard clock, even though the day felt forty-eight hours long, it was only a few minutes past seven. Could he stop by? Call?

Before he could talk himself out of it, he pulled out his phone.

Thinking about you tonight, he texted and hit Send.

Then he and Jax, two lonely bachelors, headed home.

—⟋⟍⟍⟍—

Molly woke before her alarm the next morning with a smile on her face. Last night she'd been missing Brant, replaying her movie night with him and Jax, when her phone pinged. After reading his text, her mood had shifted for the better. She practically floated into the kitchen for her first coffee. A glance at the antique wall clock showed she had plenty of time, so she slipped outside to the deck. The temperature had fallen overnight. Dropping onto her chaise, her robe wrapped tightly around her, she savored the coffee, the morning, and her thoughts.

Could she and Brant continue this *thing* between them on a permanent basis? No. Could she enjoy the here and now with him? Absolutely. Darlene had been right about that.

She wondered if he was as confused by what was happening between them. Red light, green light, red light. Maybe yellow defined them best. *Caution*.

She hoped yesterday had gone well. More likely, though, it was a day of tears for Lainey, repressed ones for her brothers, and a whole lot of self-blame by all, deserved or not.

When her parents decided to divorce, had the situation been this fraught with emotion? She'd been a child, and she realized now she'd seen only what they wanted her to. What had gone on behind the scenes? Self-recrimination? Doubt? Sorrow and anxiety?

Had her dad walked away from them as easily as she'd assumed, or had he been more affected than he'd let on?

And why was she dwelling on this?

She forced herself to put it away and think about Cricket's wedding. Ten chilly minutes later, she headed inside for her shower. Time to start the day.

Halfway down the stairs, she heard a rap on the front door.

There stood Brant, a grinning Jax in his arms.

"Hi." She opened the door wide and reached for the baby. "Good morning, sweetheart."

Jax cooed back at her, and she dropped a kiss on his cheek. "Look at you. All dressed up in a tousle cap and sweater." Then she stepped aside "Brrr. Come on in, Brant. I didn't think I'd see you today."

"Don't I get a kiss?"

She rolled her eyes and dropped a chaste kiss on his cheek. "Ooh." She ran her fingers over his scruffy chin. "Somebody didn't shave this morning."

"Nope. Can't we do better than that little peck?"

"Well, I—"

He cut her off, his lips stealing hers. When he pulled away, he said, "My brothers love the old gas station."

"Fantastic."

Jax kept himself busy with a musical toy while Brant spilled their plans for the place. "We're gonna start ripping into it tomorrow."

"But you don't actually own it yet, do you?"

"Nope, but the owner gave us the green light."

"I'm happy for you."

"Since you were there the first time I saw the place, I thought you might want to come by when we take our first swings, start the reno."

"Is that an invitation?"

"Ya-ya-ya!" Jax squealed.

———

Yesterday had flown by. The bell over the door had rung often enough to make Molly smile. Misty Bottomers and out-of-towners alike had stopped in to buy gifts and do some window shopping. She was busy restocking the accessories wall when Lettie stepped out of the back room. "All done altering that bridesmaid's dress and free to cover the shop this afternoon."

"You know, I'm not sure this is a good idea. Won't I be in the way?"

"No, you don't. No changing your mind. Run upstairs and freshen up. That man of yours will be here before you know it."

"He's not my man," she mumbled.

The sky had never been bluer, but the air held a nip. Since she doubted they'd have heat in the old station, she changed into jeans and a medium-weight white-and-black sweater.

She'd be comfortable and could toss it in the wash after Jax slobbered all over it.

———

Brant showed up at twelve on the dot.

"Bye, Lettie."

"Bye, Boss. Have a good time."

She sent a look over her shoulder at the older woman, who smiled innocently back at her.

Lettie followed her outside and waved at Brant, then leaned into the back seat to give Jax a kiss. "He seems in fine fettle today."

"We can only pray he stays that way." Brant planted a kiss on Lettie's weathered cheek, then turned to Molly. With a hand on either side of her face, he leaned in and kissed her soundly.

When Molly drew away, she was laughing. "You can't do that."

"Sure I can. Want me to do it again?"

"No." Grinning, she said, "I want to kiss this young man you brought with you."

Jax kicked wildly when Molly drew close. "Morning, baby. Has Uncle Brant been a good boy today?"

"Baaa!"

"Exactly what I thought." She turned to Lettie. "If you need anything, call me. I can come back."

"I'll be fine. Go."

Brant herded her inside the car and reached for her seat belt.

She smacked his hand. "I can do that."

"Yeah, but it gives me a chance to get close enough to smell your perfume."

"I'd say Jax isn't the only one in fine fettle today. What exactly is a fettle?"

"Don't have a clue."

She glanced sideways at Brant. In the long-sleeved green Henley, his eyes looked deeper, richer. "That color's perfect for you. You look great."

"May I say ditto." He eyed her jeans and sweater. "A good choice for demolition day."

"I'm not actually doing any demolition. I'm observing. Remember?"

"Yep."

Jax started to fuss, and Molly reached back, took his

hand, and rubbed his fingers. He settled right down, and she smiled. She could do this.

When they pulled in front of the shop, Gaven and Tucker strolled out to meet them.

"Thought we'd start with those two walls in the bay area. Take a sledgehammer to them." Gaven turned to Molly. "Want to give it a try?"

She shook her head. "I'll keep Jax company."

Before long, though, she found herself wearing goggles and whacking drywall.

Brant, who'd replaced her on baby duty, had cut a paper mask to fit Jax and slipped it over his nose and mouth to protect him from the dust. Then, holding Jax, he leaned against the wall that would eventually be the office and grinned.

"You look good holding that tool."

"You got that right," mumbled Gaven.

Brant nailed him with a look.

She brushed herself off, then made a muscle and patted it. "Not quite Rosie the Riveter yet, but getting there."

Brant shook his head, and Tucker and Gaven laughed.

After she washed up, she moved outside with the baby to sit in the warm sunshine. A few minutes later, Brant sat down beside her and took Jax. Holding him under the arms, Brant let him practice his faux walk. Molly couldn't help but smile.

"The guys are sending me dirty looks. Guess I'd better get back to it."

She and Jax moved into the shade. Sprawled beneath a tree, they watched the guys' progress. A wall went down, and Jax flinched at the noise.

"Time we headed home, isn't it?" When the guys

stopped for a water break, she sidled up to Brant. "How about I take Jax with me while you finish here?"

"You don't mind?"

"Not at all. Lettie's at the shop. Between the two of us, we should be good."

"Thanks, Mol." He cupped a hand beneath her chin and tipped her face up to his. "I'm glad you came today, helped us knock down these walls. Someday we'll look back at this and say, 'Remember when.'"

Molly blinked. This was his first mention of a future. How did she feel about it? Happy? Sad? She honestly didn't know.

"One small problem. I don't have a car."

"Take mine."

"Your Camaro?"

"Sure." He fished the keys from his pocket.

"You're sure?"

"Absolutely." He met her eyes. "I trust you."

She went brain-dead for all of three seconds. Breathlessly, she said, "I'll take good care of it. Of both your babies."

"Let me help with his car seat. It's a real bugger." After he strapped the baby in, he pulled her close, kissed her gently.

"Mmm." She opened her eyes and met his. Tugging on the neck of his T-shirt, she drew him to her. "One more."

This kiss was far from gentle. Its heat nearly melted the enamel off her teeth.

"Till later."

She nodded, unable to form words.

A sleepy baby in the back seat and a diaper bag beside her, Molly pulled Brant's Camaro onto the two-lane road. She didn't dare meet her own eyes in the rearview mirror for fear of what she might see there.

Traffic was light on the street outside her shop the next morning. Brant and his brothers had collected Jax and his car a little before six the previous night. They'd offered to include her in dinner, but she'd opted out. They needed time together—and she needed some time alone.

Still, Brant had sent another text just before bedtime. One that gave her some very pleasant dreams.

Molly lit several vanilla candles for both the scent and the ambience, then checked to make sure everything was in place and spotlessly clean. Lettie wouldn't be in today, so she had the shop to herself.

She'd barely turned the sign to Open when two women breezed through the door, talking and laughing. "Good morning. Welcome to That Little White Dress. How can I help you today?"

"Hi. I'm Dawn Brower, and this is Starr. Shelly Clark, one of our best friends, is getting married, and we need a phenomenal shower gift. Something that will make everyone else jealous they didn't buy it for her."

"Shelly found her dress here," Molly said. "She'll be a beautiful bride!"

Eyeing the gowns on the rack, Starr nodded. "She mentioned you have some really great lingerie. We thought maybe we'd buy a set for her."

"Wonderful idea. Let me show you what I have."

"You, uh, know her size, right?" Dawn asked.

"I do."

Half an hour later, the decision made, Molly gift-wrapped the red lace underwire bra and matching tap panties. The door had barely closed behind Dawn and Starr when the bell jingled again.

"Be right there," she called from the back room.

"No hurry."

She recognized that voice.

"Dad?" Dropping the empty box she'd been folding onto the counter, she hurried into her showroom. "I was thinking about you this morning."

"Oh yeah?" He flicked a glance at her, then turned his gaze to the store and its merchandise. "Came to check out my investment."

"Want me to get the books?"

"That would be great."

Heading for the back room, she stopped. "What NASCAR driver do you follow now? Since Rusty retired?"

He frowned. "Where'd that come from?"

She shrugged, not wanting to explain the need to know her own father better, to feel their old connection.

"I was following Junior, but the kid decided to retire."

"Junior? Rusty's son?"

Her father guffawed. "No, honey, not Rusty's kid. Dale Earnhardt Jr. You do know who he is, don't you?"

"Yes. He's done some commercials. Jeans, soda, insurance."

"Sure has. Earned himself some nice change with them, too. I kind of like Matt Kenseth. The kid's good, and he drives clean."

"Okay." She vowed to look up Kenseth to find out

what she could about him. It would give them something
to talk about. "Do you want something to drink, Dad?"

"No, I'm good. I'll have lunch later, then head back
to Savannah."

The day's happy bubble burst. He hadn't come to see
her, to tell her he'd missed her. He wanted to make sure
his money was safe, not his daughter.

Brant and his brothers worked their butts off, determined
to make as much headway as possible before Tucker
and Gaven returned to Lake Delores. They'd argued and
haggled and finally decided on the best layout for their
new space. Darlene's niece volunteered to babysit Jax
for a few days so he wouldn't be exposed to the dusty
construction zone.

From the second they dropped the baby off until it
was time to pick him up again, the brothers sweat buck-
ets at their new Wylder Rides shop.

But today they decided to take a lunch break rather
than eat while they worked. Tucker and Gaven headed
to the house, while Brant shook off the dust and washed
up, determined to sneak in a visit to a good-looking brunette. If he managed to grab a bite while he was in town,
so much the better.

The sign said Closed, but the door was unlocked.
"Molly?"

He found her in the back room, eyes red, tear tracks
down her cheeks.

"Sweetheart, what's wrong?" He wrapped his arms
around her, and she practically burrowed in. "Is someone sick? Hurt?"

She sniffed and swiped at her eyes. "No, I'm being a baby."

"I seriously doubt that. What happened?"

"I was sitting on my deck this morning, thinking about your sister and her situation. My mind travelled to my parents and their divorce, and I wondered if maybe it had been harder for my dad than I realized." Her bottom lip trembled.

"Okay." Brant tread carefully, not sure where this was headed.

"A little bit ago, my shop door opened and there he was. My dad. I thought he'd come for a visit, but he'd come to check the books." She swiped at her eyes again. "You'd think I'd learn."

Clutching his shirt, she whispered, "Somewhere, somehow, I let him down."

"No, Molly, *he* let *you* down." Brant hugged her tighter. "Honey, you got caught up in an adult situation. You became collateral damage. You have no ownership in what happened between your mother and father."

"That's what my mom said, but—"

"But nothing. What's your dad say?"

She shook her head. "We've never discussed it."

Brant snarled. His parents had always had his back, with love. Not much wonder, Molly wasn't in a hurry to commit to anyone. Yet here she was selling dreams to others.

The woman amazed him.

"Where's Lettie?"

"She has today off."

He nodded and held her for a while longer. "Listen, I'm running out for lunch. What would you like?"

"Nothing."

"*Bzzzz*. Wrong answer."

She smiled crookedly. "A grilled cheese on white."

"You got it."

Brant left Molly's shop with a grim determination to track down her father. The prick hadn't even asked her to join him for a sandwich. It seemed Jason had someone breathing down his neck for the "Worst Father of the Year" award.

Since Dee-Ann's was the closest lunch spot, Brant steamed toward it. The minute he walked in, he recognized Mr. Stiles, who was sitting by the window in his expensive shirt and well-creased pants, his shoes shined to within an inch of their lives. He resembled Molly. Or rather, Brant corrected, Molly resembled him. The hair, the color of the eyes. But while her eyes held kindness and passion, her father's conveyed indifference.

Dee-Ann waved to him. "Have a seat, Brant, and I'll be right with you."

He nodded and walked over to Stiles's table.

The man looked up, startled, when Brant slid into the chair across from him.

"Do I know you?"

"Not yet." Brant kept his voice level and folded his hands on the table.

Dee-Ann set a glass of sweet tea in front of him. "What'll you have?"

"Burger. Medium well and loaded. I'll need a grilled cheese on white, too. Both to go. I'm having lunch with Molly so she doesn't have to eat alone. She's a little rattled today."

Out of the corner of his eye, Brant saw Stiles go on alert.

Concern filled the older woman's eyes. "Anything I can do to help?"

"I'd say you could ask this guy, but I doubt you'd get an answer."

Mr. Stiles looked confused.

Dee-Ann glanced from one man to the other. "Everything okay here?"

A muscle twitched in Brant's jaw. "Yeah, we're good. Can't say I have too much respect, though, for a man who drives from Savannah to Misty Bottoms and then can't be bothered to invite his daughter to lunch."

Mr. Stiles tossed his half-eaten Reuben onto the plate and leaned toward Brant. "Who the hell are you?"

"Want me to call Sam?" Dee-Ann asked. "Deputy DeLuca left here not more than a few minutes ago."

"No. We're fine." Brant threw her a smile. "Why don't you get those sandwiches together? Molly's dad and I are gonna have a little talk."

"Molly's dad?" Dee-Ann squinted at him. "Thought you looked familiar." She looked back at Brant. "You let me know if you need anything—*anything*," she said.

"Got you. Thanks." Taking a quick look around the diner, he saw only two tables occupied on the other side of the room. Good. This talk was best done without an audience.

He turned back to Stiles. Keeping his voice low and controlled, he held up a finger. "First off, Molly doesn't know I'm here." He held up a second finger. "Second, I'll admit I'm probably crossing a line." Another finger popped up. "But third, you're a real jackass."

Red crept up from beneath the collar of that crisp shirt and spread over the older man's face. "I hate to repeat myself, but who are you?"

"Brant Wylder, a friend of your daughter."

Stiles said nothing for a few seconds. "That still doesn't explain why you come slamming in here, all but crawling up my butt."

"You hurt Molly. I don't know why, and I guess that's none of my business, but when you walked out on her and her mom, you owed her an explanation. You owed her your time and love, too. From what I've heard, you've been pretty stingy with both."

When Mr. Stiles started to interrupt, Brant shook his head. "Uh-uh. I'm talking, you're listening. You waltzed into her shop this morning, a shop she's poured herself into, a shop that's incredible, and didn't bother to ask about her or tell her how fantastic that shop is. Instead, you wanted to look at the books. Then"—Brant stopped for a breath—"you left her to eat alone instead of spending an hour with that amazing woman. You left her wondering yet again how she'd failed you."

This time Stiles's mouth dropped open. "Molly has never failed me."

"Have you ever told her that?"

Anger flashed in his eyes. "I don't need to. She knows it."

Brant shook his head slowly.

"The girl's never, ever let me down," Stiles spat out between gritted teeth.

"Molly thinks you left your marriage because of her." Brant recognized he was telling tales out of school, but without some outside interference, nothing would ever change between father and daughter. If she hated him for sticking his nose in, well, he'd have to learn to live with it—or change her mind.

Stiles raised his coffee for a drink, and the cup wobbled. "I had no idea."

"You do now, so the question becomes what are you going to do about it?" With that, he pushed back his chair and walked to the counter. "I'm starving, Dee-Ann. My burger ready?"

She hustled out of the kitchen, bag in hand. "Right here."

He threw her a wink and a very generous tip, knowing she'd given him extra time to finish his business. "Thanks. You're a special lady."

He walked past Molly's father without so much as a glance and headed out the door and down the street to another very special lady.

Chapter 15

WITHOUT EVEN OPENING HER EYES, MOLLY NUDGED Bubbles. "Let me sleep, baby."

She rolled over, her back to the cat.

"Meow." Bubbles tapped the side of Molly's face.

"Five more minutes. Please."

Bubbles head-butted her.

Molly pried open an eye. Morning light streamed through the window.

"Oh no!" Jumping out of bed, she hugged the cat. "Good girl. I forgot to set the alarm!"

Bubbles squirmed free and trailed in Molly's wake as she rushed into the bathroom.

Around her toothbrush, she muttered, "It's Brant's fault. He doesn't leave room in my head for anything else." When the cat meowed again, Molly said, "I know, and I really hate that he caught me during my meltdown. Then he offered a sympathetic ear—and brought me lunch."

She sighed and set down her toothbrush. Those darned texts he sent every night at bedtime didn't help, either. Without breaking a sweat, the man had worked his way into her life.

How did she fight it?

More important, did she want to?

"Maybe I'll take a ride after work, Bubbles. If I happen to drive past the new Wylder Rides shop and Brant happens to be there…"

A quick shower later, she put on mascara and lip gloss and arranged her hair into a loose, low bun. She tossed on sleek black slacks with a long-sleeved black top, low-heeled pumps, silver earrings, and a funky necklace. Good to go.

Coffee in hand, she practically flew down the steps. Lettie would be here any minute, and Molly could grab her go-to yogurt then.

Instead, she'd barely turned on the lights when a couple showed up.

"Good morning!" She held the door for them. "How are you today?"

"We're wonderful," the beaming woman said.

The large man beside her, a silly grin on his face, nodded. Molly sized him up. Six five and two eighty, maybe. Wow.

"I'm guessing you're not from Misty Bottoms, are you?"

"No, ma'am, we're from Atlanta." The giant, his voice deep and smooth, slid his hand over the woman's. "We stayed at Annabelle's last night."

"It's wonderful, isn't it? A friend of mine has two brothers staying there."

"The Wylders?"

That stopped her. "Yes."

"Told you that was them!" The guy elbowed his companion. "I recognized them from TV. Man, they do some kind of work. They've got magic hands when it comes to cars."

Heat crept up Molly's chest and neck. At least one of them had magic hands when it came to other things, too.

"Do you know why they're here?"

Molly hesitated, then decided what the heck. Since most of the town already knew their plans, it wouldn't be long before word spread. "They're renovating an old service station for a new shop here in Misty Bottoms. I think, though, Tucker and Gaven left late last night or early this morning."

"That's why we didn't see them at breakfast." He hugged the woman beside him. "Baby, I've got to have them do my ride for me."

"Why don't we talk about today first, sweetie?"

"You bet." He turned to Molly. "This is a little unconventional, but we'd like to get married."

Molly couldn't help it. She laughed. "Most of the people who walk through my door want exactly that."

"Today."

She choked on the laugh. "Today?"

The outside door opened and closed. Lettie stood a step inside, purse in hand. From her wide-eyed expression, it was clear she'd overheard the conversation.

"Do you think Mrs. Bryson can fit us in?"

"You want to get married at Magnolia House. Today."

"Yes, ma'am."

She studied the pair. "You're serious?"

They grinned at each other. The bride-to-be said, "Very. It might be impromptu, but we want it all. The dress, the cake, the flowers." She sighed. "A beautiful venue."

"Today." Molly knew she was repeating herself, but holy Toledo. *Today?*

"Today." Looking slightly embarrassed, the groom shuffled his feet. "Guess you don't recognize me." He held up a hand. "Not that you should, and that's exactly why we're here."

Molly turned to Lettie. "Do you know him?"

"Nope." Lettie shook her head. "I'm sorry, but I don't think we've met."

"This beautiful woman is DeVonne Maxwell."

The ladies nodded to each other, then he held out a hand the size of a turkey platter. "Tyrone Sterling. I play for the Atlanta Falcons."

"Football," Molly murmured as they shook.

"Yeah. DeVonne and I planned to do this next spring, but the whole thing has gotten totally out of hand. We want this to be *our* wedding. We want it to be about *us*. Instead, it's turned into a three-ring circus."

"So we're running away," DeVonne said. "That being said, I still want a wedding to remember. Today's the day we start our life together as husband and wife." She drew a breath. "We'd like you to help us."

"Have you made arrangements with Jenni Beth at Magnolia House?"

"No."

Oh boy. Molly's mind raced. She had no appointments, so Lettie could cover the shop. What about Tansy, Cricket, and Jenni Beth, though? They could already be up to their elbows in obligations. And Magnolia House might be booked.

"Let me make a couple calls. Lettie, why don't you get our bride and groom some coffee? I have some wonderful cranberry-orange muffins in the kitchen from Sweet Dreams."

"Absolutely. Right on it, Boss."

Boss? Again? She and Lettie were going to have a conversation about that. Later.

"Do you mind if I peek at your dresses?" DeVonne

asked. "I've got a monstrosity of a gown back home that my mom insisted was perfect. I can't lie. The thing is gorgeous and, yes, perfect. For somebody. But it's not me."

"You didn't tell her?" Molly stopped in her office doorway.

"I tried."

"Yeah, like we *tried* to keep the guest list down to a couple hundred. Family and *real* friends," Tyrone added. "Last time I checked, the list was bumping six hundred! Then our moms and the wedding planner got together again this week."

"The list grew by another sixty-four people," DeVonne said. "Everything from the dress to the flowers to the menu and cake, the limousine…it's crazy."

"Now DeVonne's mom is making noises about a Cinderella coach. We're done." He spread his hands in front of him. "Today's gonna be about the two of us. Period." Lifting his fiancée's hand to his lips, he kissed the back of it.

And Molly hoisted the white flag. She knew right then and there, one way or another she'd make this happen.

"Take your time, DeVonne. Let's see if we can find *you* here." She studied the bride. "Lettie's needle is absolute magic, so fitting you won't be a problem."

Molly pulled her phone from a pocket and stepped into the office. Behind a closed door, she called the other three on a conference call. They checked schedules, shifted tasks, then shifted some more. In under ten minutes, they had a plan.

With a smile on her face, Molly walked back into the display area. "Looks like we can make this work."

The bride squealed and threw herself into her fiancé's arms just as the door opened.

"Hey, Molly, Jax and I wondered if we might take the most beautiful gal in Misty Bottoms to lunch a little later." Brant stopped midstride. "Sorry. I didn't realize you had customers."

Still cradled in her future husband's arms, DeVonne announced, "We're getting married!"

"Congratulations."

Molly's heart stuttered at his quick grin, those incredible dimples.

Jax let out a happy gurgle, and the bride wiggled out of Tyrone's arms. "A baby?"

Brant turned so the baby, in his backpack carrier, faced her. "Jax, meet—Sorry, ma'am. We haven't been introduced." He swung his gaze to Molly.

"Brant Wylder, this is DeVonne Maxwell and Tyrone Sterling."

Brant kissed the bride's cheek, then extended a hand to the groom. "Thought I recognized you."

Tyrone swallowed Brant's hand in his huge one. "One of the Wylder brothers."

"Guilty as charged."

"Dude, you guys do some out-of-this-world work."

"And you're football," Brant said. "Defensive end."

Tyrone nodded.

"And this good-looking guy is Jax." Molly made a face at him, and he gave her a sloppy grin.

"Yours?" Even as the bride dropped a kiss on Jax's cheek, her eyes met Molly's.

"No. Jax is Brant's nephew."

DeVonne narrowed her eyes.

"Uh-oh." Tyrone groaned. "I know that look. What's going on in that pretty head?"

"We have a ring bearer!"

"Jax?"

She nodded.

Brant pointed out the obvious. "Uh, he can't walk."

"But you can."

"And I happen to know you have a tux," Molly said.

"You do?" DeVonne's eyes widened.

Brant thought of the shoes that went with that tux. The pain. The promise he'd made to never again wear them. His smile slipped into oblivion.

"You don't need to get right back to the shop, do you?"

Mentally rescheduling his day, he said, "Nah. Gaven and Tuck flew home on a red-eye last night. We ripped out a ton of Sheetrock yesterday, so I figured I'd let the dust die down and give my muscles a rest." He arched his back and stretched. "Starting tomorrow, Jax goes to day care, so I thought we'd play today. I could have dropped him off this morning, but we had a late night. I'd hate for things not to go well. First day and all, you know?"

Molly grinned. "Nervous, Uncle Brant? Separation anxiety?"

"No, but first impressions are important."

"So you're free. Will you help? Take part in our wedding?" The bride-to-be held her hands together as if in prayer.

Imagining those shoes, his feet already hurt. "Why not?"

DeVonne kissed him smack on the lips. Brant met the eyes of the giant across the room and relaxed when Tyrone laughed.

"It's good, man. It's all good."

DeVonne snatched the baby from his carrier. "Think of the pictures. Oh my gosh, baby, you are so adorable."

Jax, on his very best behavior, babbled to her.

An expression of horror crossed DeVonne's face. "We don't have a photographer." She turned to her fiancé. "Tyrone."

The big man stared at her like a deer in the headlights.

"Mr. Beaumont, Jenni Beth's father, is an excellent amateur photographer," Molly said. "He'll be happy to pitch in if you'd like."

"We'd like," Tyrone said decisively.

While the two women fussed over ring pillows, Tyrone pulled Brant aside. "Is there a jewelry store in town? We've got our rings, but I'd like to buy DeVonne a little something. You know, a memento of our wedding day."

Brant remembered seeing a small jewelry shop, Cappy's, and told him where to find it.

"Great. Later, maybe you and I can talk about a vehicle I'd like to have Wylderized."

"Nothing I'd love more." Even as he said it, his gaze wandered to Molly.

"She's some looker, isn't she?" Tyrone asked.

"DeVonne? You bet."

"Yeah, she is, too, but I was talking about your lady."

Brant's mouth went dry. *His lady*. Was she? Despite her protests, had they somehow reached that point?

"She is," he murmured. "She really is."

"I can't make up my mind, Tyrone." DeVonne held up three lace and satin pillows.

"Let me throw something else in the mix." Molly

picked up a small, vintage jewel box. "It's different, and it would be a keepsake you could use."

"I love it!"

Tyrone grinned. "Molly, you're making my girl very happy today."

DeVonne gave him a smoldering kiss.

When Brant sent Molly a look every bit as hot, she locked her hands behind her back to keep from fanning herself.

"Tyrone, go away somewhere while I find a dress," DeVonne said. "Shoo, now."

With his hand on the doorknob, Tyrone shot her a look, then nodded at Brant. "I'll be back soon. I'm ready to get this done."

After the groom left, Brant tossed a blanket on the floor for Jax—not that he'd stay on it—then made himself at home on the little blue love seat. Lettie, Molly, and DeVonne each chose a gown for the bride, then disappeared into the dressing room.

"Why don't I get to pick one?" Brant complained.

"Because you don't," Molly answered.

While she helped DeVonne into her own selection, Molly's mind wandered. Brant continued to surprise her. The man was so easy, so comfortable in any situation. She thought of all the balls he juggled with his sister, his mom, Jax, and the renovation project. Not everyone, man or woman, could handle all that. Yet he made it look almost simple.

And now here he sat, pure male, in a very feminine boutique, helping a bride he'd just met select her gown.

After a few minutes, he asked, "You gonna let me see? I'm good, darned good, at critiquing ladies' clothing."

"She's not shopping for lingerie, Brant," Molly called out.

DeVonne and Lettie laughed.

"Ha, ha. Come on. Jax and I are waiting with bated breath."

Jax, hearing his name, started chattering and scooted off toward the dressing area. Brant scooped him up, held him high, and flew him airplane-style back to the love seat.

Molly, peeking around the corner, shook her head. "You're sprawled there like you're waiting for the Super Bowl to start."

He held out his hands. "So where're the chicken wings and beer?"

She nailed him with a raised-brow expression, and he laughed.

"Bring it on. We haven't got all day, you know. We have a wedding to go to."

He heard DeVonne's delighted sigh and a rustling of silk.

When she stepped around the corner, he nodded. "Now there's a bride to take your breath away."

The cocktail-length dress had a fitted bodice with a full tulle skirt. Its champagne color burnished her smooth caffe-latte skin.

"I like it." DeVonne twirled in front of the three-way mirror.

"But do you love it?" Molly asked.

"I don't know."

"Then let's give another one a spin."

When she stepped out again, she wore a short ivory dress.

"I don't like that one quite as much," Brant said.

"Why?"

"I don't know." His brow furrowed. "I could see that at some little tea party or something, but it doesn't shout 'Bride.'"

DeVonne squinted at the mirror. "I think he's right."

"Okay, consider it gone." Molly started to follow her, then turned back. "Why so comfy with this, Brant?"

"Why not?" He shrugged. "I have a sister. And a mother."

"And no doubt a string of girlfriends."

He met her eyes. "Only one girl in my life right now."

She couldn't speak.

He threw her a smug grin. "This is my first go at bridal-dress shopping, and I have to admit, I'm glad it's Tyrone tying the knot today and not me."

"There's a surprise." Molly disappeared, and Lettie handed him a fresh coffee before greeting a woman who'd come in to find a negligee for her tenth-anniversary cruise.

"Lucky husband," Brant commented.

When the woman held up two for his opinion, he said, "The red one. It'll drive your husband wild."

Bouncing up and down on Brant's lap, Jax agreed with flapping arms and a mile-wide grin.

She bought it.

Three more choices, one a trumpet gown Brant vetoed, a mermaid gown he was lukewarm about, and a sheath that knocked his socks off, and DeVonne had her wedding dress.

"Beyond gorgeous." Brant gave DeVonne a cheek smooch. "Tyrone won't know what hit him. He's one lucky son of a gun."

"He is, isn't he?" She ran her hands over the off-white, sleeveless dress, then glanced over her shoulder to catch the reflection of the low back in the mirror. "This is the one I've dreamed about."

Molly, all business, said, "Let's get it off before Tyrone comes back. We don't want him seeing it before the ceremony."

"No problem. I've got you covered," Brant said. "I told Tyrone I'd give him a buzz when it was safe to return." He popped a Tootsie Roll into his mouth, a small piece of banana into Jax's, and slid out his phone to make the call. "Mol, before she takes that off, why don't you have her try that second pair of shoes there with it?"

Molly considered them. "I think you're right."

"Of course I am."

When she bent to pick up the shoes, Brant's grin deepened. Darned if Molly didn't have a tattoo playing peekaboo.

Five minutes later, the door opened and two men walked in—Tyrone and Molly's father. Even though she willed herself to stay loose, her spine stiffened.

"Dad. You've come at a bad time."

"That's okay. I was close by and thought I'd stop in." He startled when he saw Brant.

"I'm busy, Dad. If you want to check this month's books, you'll have to come back later. Tomorrow would actually be better."

His face deflated, his expression sad.

Molly frowned. "What's wrong?"

"Me." He glanced at Brant, then back to his daughter. "It seems I have been for too long."

"I don't understand."

"Don't worry. I'm in no hurry. Take care of your customers."

Molly blinked. "Okay."

Tyrone spotted Brant on the love seat and dropped down beside him.

Her dad took a good look at the guy he'd come in with. "Tyrone Sterling?"

"That's me."

"Honey, do you know who this is?"

"He told me, yes."

"But…" He stuck out a hand. "Preston Stiles. My daughter, Molly."

"Molly and I have met." He shook her dad's hand.

"What are you doing here, Tyrone?"

"Dad—"

"No." Tyrone held up his huge hand. "It's okay. Actually, it would be nice to have a few guests. Got time for a wedding, Preston?"

Molly's head was spinning. Try as she might to maintain it, control was slowly slipping from her grasp. Brant, a tuckered-out baby asleep on his chest, football superstar Tyrone Sterling, and her generally absentee father talked cars, although there was something going on between Brant and her dad she couldn't quite figure out. DeVonne and Lettie chatted about how best to fix collard greens.

And at least a dozen details still needed to be dealt with.

"Okay, everybody," she said. "This is nice, but we have a wedding to finish up."

DeVonne clapped and gave another of her little squeals.

"Tyrone, you have your tux, correct?"

"Yes, ma'am. I brought it with me. Didn't figure I'd be likely to find an off-the-rack suit to fit me."

"Good thinking." Molly took a deep breath. "Here's the drill. DeVonne, Helen at Frenchie's beauty shop will do your hair and makeup. Brant, you need to run home and pick up your tux and shoes."

His face fell. "Do I have to?"

"Afraid so. Jax is the ring bearer, and since you're his transportation, you need to look good, too."

"Oh, for…"

"I'll get tickets on the fifty-yard line for a couple of games next season for you and your brothers," Tyrone offered.

Brant sprang up from the love seat. "Let me go get that tux."

"You're that easy?" Molly teased.

"I can be." He threw her a heated look. "With the right incentive."

"Oowee!" DeVonne waved her hand back and forth in front of her face. "Seems to me you ought to jump on that, Molly." Then she remembered Mr. Stiles was in the room. Aghast, she turned to him. "I didn't mean—"

Preston shook his head. "My daughter's old enough to do what she wants."

Molly valiantly fought the five-alarm fire Brant had started in her belly and pushed on. "Since the dress needs no alterations, Lettie will run down to Sue Ellen's

and find an outfit for our ring bearer. By the time y'all
are back, the rest of the details will be taken care of."

"Brant," Tyrone said, "how 'bout you be my best
man? Mr. Wylder Rides. The guys'll be so jealous."

"If you get him, I get her." DeVonne pointed at Molly.

Brant and Molly looked at each other and threw in the
towel. "Sure," they both replied.

Keys in hand and thankful he'd had his tux dry-
cleaned after Jax peed on it, Brant asked, "Is there time
for me to take Tyrone and your dad to see the shop—or
what there is of it?"

"Say yes, Molly." Tyrone rubbed his hands together.
"Please."

"Okay, but you boys remember we're on a schedule.
Look and leave. No playing."

"Got it." Brant hugged the still-sleeping Jax to his
chest.

"Brant promised me he and his brothers will trick out
my Denali, DeVonne."

"Give us a little time to get the new place up and
running, then we're on it. That Denali's right up Wylder
Rides' alley."

They agreed to take two cars. Brant and Jax headed
for the Camaro. When Molly's dad made to get into
Tyrone's vehicle, Brant stopped him. "Why don't you
ride with me?"

Molly, watching from the doorway, swore she read
unease on her father's face. Despite that, he nodded.
What was Brant up to?

Well, no time to worry about that now. The guys
were gone, DeVonne was on her way to Frenchie's, and
Lettie had headed off to outfit Jax. Molly shut the door

and leaned against it. What a morning! And this was the eye of the storm. The calm wouldn't last for long.

She grabbed her phone and hit Cricket's number.

"Are the flowers ready?"

"They are, and if I do say so myself, they're outstanding. DeVonne wanted a cascade bouquet in Atlanta Falcons red and black, so I used red roses and black feathers. Very dramatic. It'll be gorgeous in the photos. I have a red rose boutonniere for Tyrone and Brant and a single red rose tied with a black ribbon for you."

"Thanks, Cricket. Talk to you later." Molly hung up and tossed her phone on the counter. She and Brant would walk down the aisle together again. This had to stop.

Would it be three strikes and you're out—or a home run? Her stomach fluttered. *Not now. Set it aside, Molly.*

She made her second call. "Is the cake finished?"

"It is. I used a couple layers I already had baked. And before you jump all over the 'couple' part, I know they said small. It's a *small* two-tiered cake."

"Tansy, Tansy."

"It's their wedding! Both layers are frosted in black buttercream. I did rose scrolls on the bottom layer and a smooth finish on the top, then added a wide band of red ribbon at the base of the second layer, along with a gorgeous red rose and some baby's breath Cricket sent over. The topper's a tower of fresh roses."

"Sounds perfect."

"It is perfect, and it'll taste great, too."

"You need to work on that poor self-image, friend."

She laughed. "Yeah, that's what they all tell me. You want me to run it over?"

"I'll pick it up. Thanks, Tanz. I know you have a thousand other things to do."

"Business was a little on the slow side today, so it worked out."

Molly hung up and phoned Jenni Beth with the song list.

"I'll queue them up on my stereo system," Jenni Beth said. "What's your ETA?"

"Brant took the guys by his shop, and DeVonne is at Frenchie's. If nobody gets hung up, my guess is another hour and a half."

"We'll be ready."

The wedding went off without a hitch, and Mr. Beaumont seemed to be everywhere, snapping picture after picture of the happy bride and groom. Jenni Beth, her mother, their housekeeper Charlotte, and Preston Stiles made up the guest list, a far cry from the six or seven hundred DeVonne's and Tyrone's families wanted.

The minister Jenni Beth had enlisted pronounced the couple husband and wife, and Molly released the breath she'd been holding. This might have been put together quickly, but it was another picture-perfect wedding for a Magnolia House bride.

Molly fingered her lovely red dress, simple in design with a sweetheart neckline and tulle skirt. After Tyrone heard about her fledgling prom-dress program, he'd insisted on buying and donating the gown for some young girl who'd adore it.

Brant sidled up to Molly, the ring bearer on his hip. "What's the moral of today's story? That everything in life doesn't have to be planned? That sometimes spontaneity works best?"

"It could be, but then again, sometimes quick decisions make long sorrows."

He jerked his head to where the bride and groom chatted with Jenni Beth's mother and Charlotte. "You think that's what they're looking at? A bad marriage? Heartbreak and sorrow?"

"No. They're the real deal." She grimaced. "I wouldn't want to be them, though, when they tell their parents they're married—that the wedding extravaganza they've planned for months is off."

She looked around the room. "Speaking of parents, I don't see my dad."

"He left. He said he'd call later."

"Oh."

"You pretty much ignored him."

She stiffened. "I had a lot to do. He should have called instead of barging in like that. I didn't have time to go over the books with him again."

"Maybe that's not what he wanted."

"It's the only reason he ever shows up. Tyrone derailed him, but this whole situation with my dad is a disaster. I never should have accepted his loan."

"I'm not so sure he came to talk business today." Brant toyed with a curl that had escaped her updo. "He doesn't know what to do with you, Mol."

"That's because he's never tried." She swore she wouldn't cry, wouldn't care.

"Maybe he'd like to change that. We all do things we regret. Some matter more than others, and the more they matter, the harder they are to fix."

She studied him. "What exactly did the two of you discuss on your ride to the shop?"

The guilty expression, quickly masked, told her everything she needed to know. "Me. You talked about me."

"Molly—"

She cut him off. "It doesn't matter."

When she turned away, he laid a hand on her arm. "I think it does."

She shook loose. "I need to get back to work. There's still a lot to tie up."

"I don't think I've ever met anyone like you. You don't trust yourself or anybody else."

"You're starting to make me mad."

"Yeah, I probably am. It hurts sometimes to take a good look at ourselves." Jax started to squirm. "This guy's getting restless. Time for me to say goodbye to the bride and groom, then run for the hills before the sweet baby in Tyrone and DeVonne's wedding photos morphs into the beast."

With that, he left her standing alone in the center of the room.

Chapter 16

BRANT MANAGED TO STAY AWAY THREE ENTIRE DAYS, THREE of the longest of his life. When he finally gave in and stopped by the shop, Molly wasn't there.

"She's at Magnolia House," Lettie said. "They're putting the final touches on Cricket's wedding."

He thanked her and drove off, regretting the way they'd left things at Tyrone and DeVonne's wedding. But he'd brought his secret weapon: Jax. Molly couldn't resist him.

When he knocked at the front door, Charlotte welcomed him, a big smile on her face. He'd expected the cold shoulder from Molly, and she didn't disappoint. Without so much as a word, she walked to the window and faced out, arms crossed over her chest.

"Oh, for—" Brant stalked after her, ignoring the others. "The silent treatment? Seriously? You can do better than that."

Swiveling on her heel, she asked, "What are you doing here?"

"I thought we should talk."

"Now, after three days without a single word, you want to talk?"

"Well, I—Ouch! Holy Hannah, what's wrong with you?" He jerked away, rubbing his ear.

She turned to her friends. "It's probably best if Neanderthal and I take this discussion outside."

As haughty as any queen, she marched out to the porch.

He stared after her, then turned to Cricket. "Before I go out there—and assuming I survive—how are you getting to the airport after the wedding?"

"I don't know. I haven't thought about that." She pulled a face. "Maybe Sam has."

"We have a car hauler coming this week. There'll be a vintage Rolls-Royce Silver Cloud and a '55 Chevy on it. Either would make a sweet ride, and I'd be more than happy to play chauffeur. Let me know."

Cricket stared at him. "Are you serious?"

"Yes."

"Even if Molly's still not talking to you?"

"Even if."

"I ought to feel like a traitor, but—" She threw herself at him and gave both him and Jax a kiss. Then she caught sight of Molly on the front porch and pulled away.

"I know," Brant said. "Problematic, isn't it? Talk it over with Sam, see what he thinks."

"I will. Thank you!"

"I'd better get out there." Brant nodded toward them. These friends of Molly's were all so different. Tansy, her red hair curling wildly, Cricket with all her eccentricities and that chopped, nearly white hair, and Jenni Beth, the "lady of the manor."

"Do you want to leave Jax with us?" Tansy asked anxiously.

"No, ma'am. I figure she won't hurt me if I'm holding the baby."

"Make sure you don't hurt her, either," Jenni Beth warned.

"I'll do my best." With that, he left to face Molly's wrath.

With her jaw set, Molly tapped the toe of another killer pair of stilettos on the porch's refinished wood floor. "I'm busy."

"Then I won't take much of your time."

She stabbed a finger at him. "You're making judgment calls without all the facts."

"And you're being stubborn."

She stamped her foot. "It's *my* business."

"I agree one hundred percent. I actually came to apologize."

Incredulous, she stared at him, the wind momentarily taken out of her sails.

"Look, I, of all people, should know how complicated family can be. I don't condone what your father did. I hate that he hurt you. That said, people do change. I think—"

"Hold that thought." She nodded toward the drive. "You have company."

His head swiveled at the sound of tires crunching on gravel. His brothers.

With a grin on his face, he hurried off the porch, holding Jax tightly.

Molly opened the screen door and whispered, "Girls, come out here. You have to see this."

Tansy, Jenni Beth, and Cricket crowded around her on the porch.

"Whew," Molly breathed. "Can anything top that for a view?"

"I sincerely doubt it," Cricket said. "And I'm speaking as a very happily engaged woman."

Molly sank onto the swing and slid over, making room for Jenni Beth. *I'm not interested*, she reminded herself. The man had stuck his foot in where it didn't belong. Besides, she didn't have time for a tall, handsome guy right now.

Still, a girl could look, couldn't she?

A few minutes later, the guys walked up the steps, crowding the front porch.

"Y'all remember my brothers, right?" Brant pointed to his dark-haired sibling. "Tucker's the old man."

"Hey! Watch who you're calling old."

Brant laughed and pointed at his younger brother. "And this is Gaven. How'd you two find me?"

"When you weren't home, we stopped by Molly's. Lettie told us you'd come here."

"I didn't expect you till tomorrow."

"We finished the '55 T-Bird early, and might I take a moment to say she's a thing of beauty." Gaven plucked Jax from Brant and hiked him overhead. "How's my favorite nephew, huh?"

"Tired. He needs a nap."

"Ooh, Daddy, you sound grumpy," Gaven teased, swiping at the drool collecting on Jax's chin.

"Tell you what." Brant smiled. "Since he's your favorite nephew and all, and seeing as how you don't get to spend much time with him, I'll lend him to you one of these nights."

Gaven paled. "Nah, that's okay. Probably best not to screw up his routine."

"I insist."

"Come look what we've brought you," Tucker interjected.

Brant followed his older brother off the porch.

"We trailered your motorcycle." He folded back the tarp. "Thought you might want it. Although…" His gaze landed on Jax.

"Big boy Jax goes to day care now, so I can ride this beauty during the day." Brant ran a hand over his Harley. "I've missed this."

After a few more minutes of small talk with the women, the brothers piled back into their vehicles. Brant stuck his hand out the window and pointed at Molly. "You and me? Not finished."

As he started down Magnolia House's oak-lined drive, Brant checked his rearview mirror. Three of the women on the front porch waved goodbye. One did not. Seemed he still had a way to go in the apology department.

Tucker and Gaven followed him to his house while Brant tried to figure out how to make the small place work for the four of them. Annabelle's would be okay, but it didn't make sense for his brothers to spend the week there.

One of them could bunk on his couch. The other, though, would end up on the floor, because darned if Brant would share his bed. Been there, done that, growing up, and he'd promised himself never to do it again.

While he was hauling Jax from the car, he heard Gaven's truck door slam. Tucker took the baby.

"Mom said you'd probably appreciate some clothes," Gaven said, "so we tossed a bunch of your things into a couple empty storage tubs we found in your basement."

"Bring my boots?"

"Sure did."

Carting a tub into the house, Gaven spotted a picture and picked it up. "Tyrone Sterling?"

"Yep."

He whistled.

"Molly helped with their wedding a few days ago."

"So why are you wearing a tux?"

"One of those domino kind of things. Their families hijacked their wedding plans, so they ran away to tie the knot. Jax and I walked in during the preparations, and the bride took one look at the kid here and insisted he be her ring bearer. Since short stuff can't walk yet, I provided his transportation down the aisle." Brant paused. "This is where the two of you say thanks."

"Why?"

"Because it netted the three of us fifty-yard-line tickets for a couple of the Falcons games next season."

"No kidding?"

"No kidding."

Tucker and Gaven gave him a thumbs-up.

"Molly didn't look too happy this morning."

Brant made a dismissive sound. "We had a little tiff."

"Ah, trouble in paradise. The reason he's out of sorts," Tucker said to Gaven.

"I'm not out of sorts," Brant grumbled.

"Good. Glad to hear it." Gaven nudged the tub toward the wall. "Let's go see what you've done at the shop while we busted our butts on that T-Bird."

Too tired to cook after three days of back-breaking work at their new shop, the brothers pulled into the dirt parking lot of Fat Baby's Barbecue.

Gaven grinned. "Look at that. They made pink pigs out of old propane tanks." He pulled his cell from his pocket. "Let's take a picture of us and send it to Mom and Dad. You can take one to Lainey this weekend. The four Wylder guys gone to the pigs."

Brant and Tucker both groaned, but Gaven refused to go inside till they got the shot.

"I thought you were starving," Brant reminded him.

"I am, so quit bellyaching and let's get this done." He made a "come here" motion to a young woman who was stepping out of the door. "Would you take our picture?"

"Sure."

Gaven straddled the pig and held out his hands for Jax. With Brant and Tucker crouching on either side, they immortalized their first family trip to Fat Baby's.

He hit Send. "The folks will get a kick out of that."

Brant made a face, but Gaven was right. The picture would mean a lot to their mom and dad.

Tucker stepped inside the door and breathed deeply. "If the food tastes half as good as it smells, we're in for a treat."

"Tastes better." Brant juggled the baby while he spoke to Lulu, their sparkly-eyed, gray-haired hostess.

"Look at that." Gaven pointed to a winged pig that hung from the ceiling. White lights outlined it, and a fancy white fur hat perched on its head. "When pigs fly."

With a pained look at Tucker, Brant asked, "How old is he?"

Halfway to their table, he stopped in his tracks, and Tucker bumped into him.

"What—"

"Molly, I didn't expect to see you here," Brant said. "Tansy. Gracie Bella. How are you?"

"I'm good," four-year-old Gracie Bella chirped.

"Mama let me get a soda. I ask for them all the time, but she always says tomorrow." She threw her arms around Tansy. "But tonight I got one. Do you like soda?"

Tansy opened her mouth to shush her daughter, but Brant shook his head.

"I love soda, Gracie, but it's best to only have it once in a while. That way it's special."

"Daddy Beck says that, too."

"Your daddy Beck is a smart man."

"He is, and he kisses my mama all the time." She twisted a dark curl around her finger. "They don't think I see."

Tansy blushed, and Brant figured the pink crept clear to her toes. Laughing, his eyes met Molly's. "Kissing can be fun."

"That's what Daddy Beck says."

"Yep. Daddy Beck's definitely a smart man." Again he met Molly's gaze. "And a man after my own heart."

"Brant." Molly shook her head in warning.

"Just sayin'."

When Lulu tried to seat them a few tables away, he stopped her. "Could we have this table?" He pointed to the one beside Molly and Tansy. "The scenery here's pretty spectacular."

Their hostess grinned. "Sure." Laying their menus in front of them, she said, "Since we're short-handed tonight, what with Krystal off to a high school dance, I'm your waitress, too. What'll you have to drink?"

The brothers glanced toward Gracie Bella and grinned.

"We'll have what she's having," Tucker said.

Lulu raised a brow. "Clever."

The women made a fuss over Jax, who ate it up. As

he was passed from one to the other, Brant swore Jax sent him a smug "Don't you wish you were me?" look. Brant's eyes narrowed as Molly covered Jax with kisses. Maybe the kid was on to something.

When Gaven cleared his throat, Brant jerked his attention back to their table. "What?"

"Exactly my question," he whispered. "You've got it bad, BT."

"Do not."

"Afraid I have to agree with Gaven on this one," Tucker said.

———

Holy smackers! Molly wished she'd dressed in layers so she could peel off a few. Her stomach had started doing strange little dance moves when she caught sight of Brant with Lulu, and her temperature had risen to steamy.

She might still be a tiny bit perturbed with Brant, but when he and his brothers showed up en masse, the sexometer, handsome gauge, and testosterone level all went through the roof.

Molly had returned Jax to Brant earlier, but when he held out his arms to her again, she threw in the towel. The heart she'd fought to barricade broke free.

"May I?" She held out her hands.

"Absolutely." He leaned toward her.."You want to hold Jax—or me?"

She shook her head. "You're impossible."

"Impossible to resist?"

Raising her hands to her throat, she mimed choking herself.

Straight-faced and ignoring her antics, Brant handed the baby to her.

Between eating, talking, and sneaking little bites of mashed baked potato to Jax, she relaxed. Tucker and Gaven were every bit as outgoing as Brant, and the conversation flowed easily.

When the checks came, Brant nabbed them from both tables.

"Brant, we've got it covered." Molly tried to stare him down.

"So do I."

As they collected their things, he leaned toward Molly. "Have any plans for the rest of the evening?"

"No. I'm headed home."

"Did you drive?"

"I did."

"Want to go to Duffy's for some music and a beer?"

Despite the warning bells in her head, she heard herself say, "I'd love that, but that doesn't mean you're forgiven for interfering. Or for sticking up for my dad."

"I didn't stick up for him. I told you—"

"Uh-uh," Tansy said. "Not here. Little ears." She tipped her head toward Gracie Bella.

"Sorry," Molly said.

"Me too." Brant stuffed his hands in his worn-jeans pockets. "You'll go?"

"Against my better judgment."

"Since when did judgment have anything to do with it?" Tansy murmured.

Molly scowled. "Whose side are you on?"

Tansy flashed a wide-eyed, innocent look. "Me? Go on. Have fun."

"You'll have to drive," Brant said. "I came with those knuckleheads."

"Who are you calling a knucklehead?" Tucker challenged, strapping the baby into his seat.

"What about Jax?" Molly asked.

"Uncle Gaven will take him home and put him to bed."

"Me? I never said—"

Molly didn't miss a beat. "How nice of your brothers to give you a few hours off, considering you've had him for, what, two or three weeks by yourself?" She gave Tansy a hug. "We need to do this more often. Gracie Bella…" She opened her arms and the young girl threw herself into them.

After a hug and a kiss, Molly said, "Next time, it's Dairy Queen for that strawberry sundae."

"Hear that, Mama? Molly's gonna buy me a sundae!" Gracie Bella clapped her hands.

"Wonderful! We'd better get home. Daddy Beck's going to wonder what happened to us."

Gracie Bella's smile disappeared, and she placed her little hands on either side of her mother's face. "Nothing happened to us, Mama. We're right here."

Tansy laughed. "Yes, we are, oh literal one. Don't forget your sweater." Molly's friend winked at her. "Have a good time. And Molly, listen to your heart. Let it talk to you."

Chapter 17

IN THE PARKING LOT, MOLLY WAITED WHILE BRANT planted another kiss on Jax and issued an admonition to be good for his uncles, along with an apology for the fumbles they'd make. "They mean well, Jax. Be kind to them."

"Maybe you should take him home, BT." Gaven threw an arm around Molly and winked. "I'll take our girl out for a drink, and you'd better believe I won't fumble that."

"She's not *our* girl, sonny boy." Brant smacked him playfully upside the head. "Hands off."

"She your girl?" Gaven asked.

Molly held her breath.

Instead of answering, Brant said, "You've got my number if you need me."

"Get out of here," Tucker said. "We'll be fine."

"Oh, if they only knew," Brant said as he and Molly walked toward her car. The night was soft and the only sounds were the ones drifting from the restaurant. He took her hand in his and pointed up at the stars. "The Big Dipper. I love the night."

"Me too. I spend a lot of them on the deck, wrapped up in an afghan, enjoying hot cocoa. Bubbles usually keeps my feet warm."

They reached her car, and he opened the door. As she made to get in, he bent down and sent a shiver through her as his lips touched her cheek. Oh boy. She needed to breathe or she'd pass out and miss whatever tonight might bring.

She filled her lungs with cool air.

When Brant slid into the passenger seat, Molly's palms grew damp. Tucked inside her Mini together, darned if first-date jitters didn't set in. Except it wasn't actually a date, she reminded herself. He'd asked her out for a beer—and only because they'd run into each other. It wasn't as if he'd planned it.

Still, she wished she'd worn something more exciting. Prettier. Sexier.

Duffy's was packed.

Brant closed the door behind him and whistled low. "They givin' away free drinks or something?"

"It's the only place in town for music."

He eyed her. "Sweetheart, it's not really music. It's a jukebox."

Sweetheart. Whew. Her belly did a little flip. He'd called her that before. Heck, he called everybody that. Well, some people. A few people. And she was rattled. Somehow, tonight, with only the two of them, that *sweetheart* sounded different, felt different, and she'd kill for a drink. Her mouth had gone Sahara dry.

There was no baby, no Jax, as a buffer.

"Molly?" One finger beneath her chin, he tipped her face up. "You okay?"

"I'm fine. And you're right, it is only a jukebox, but it gives Duff's customers a chance to dance."

His hand at the small of her back, Brant led Molly to a corner table.

Binnie threaded her way through the crowd and handed them a menu. "What'll you have to drink?"

They both ordered beers, and Brant slid the menus back to her. "We ate at one of your competitors."

Binnie tsked. "Sorry you had to put up with subpar food."

Brant flashed a grin.

After their drinks arrived, he strolled to the jukebox and fed a few dollars into it.

He came back to the table and held out a hand rough from the construction work he'd been doing. "What do you say we hit the floor and snuggle up a bit?"

Breathless, she nodded.

Holding her hand, he led her onto the little square reserved for dancing. When he pulled her into his arms, she felt his heat, the beat of his heart. She closed her eyes and breathed in his fresh Irish Spring scent.

One dance became two, then turned into three. The songs Brant had picked wrapped around them. "Wonderful Tonight," "Just the Way You Are," and the Righteous Brothers' "Unchained Melody." Their bodies melded perfectly, and Molly couldn't remember why she'd been mad at him. Might have to forgive him this time. Maybe.

With Brant holding her close, nothing else seemed to matter.

By the time they returned to their seats, their beer was warm. Molly sipped at hers to wet her parched throat. Brant, with those muscles rippling beneath his T-shirt, did crazy things to her, sent her pulse racing like a wild-fire, hot and out of control.

He pushed his drink away and asked Binnie for a cold Coke.

"I'm going to visit the little girl's room," Molly said.

Coming back to the table a few minutes later, she caught Brant on the phone. He hung up when he saw her.

"You called to check on Jax, didn't you? Is he sleeping?"

Brant took a swig of soda. "Want to dance?"

"Uh-uh. I want the truth." She grinned. "You look so guilty."

"Okay, I checked on him." He rubbed the back of his neck. "Neither of my brothers has done any babysitting."

"Had you? Before that police officer placed Jax in your arms?"

"No, but..."

"It's that control thing, Brant. Loosen your hold on those reins. There's no reason your brothers shouldn't help out."

"I know. Jax isn't crying, but he's not sleeping, either. They asked how soon I could get home."

"I say buy the kid a new teething ring for a job well done."

A quick burst of laughter erupted from him. "That's one of the things I enjoy about you, Molly. Your smart-ass sense of humor."

He pushed out of his chair and caught her by the hand. "Come on. One more dance."

It started slow with an added dip, then he swung her out with a quick twirl. When he added a touch of dirty to it, Molly almost swooned. The man was good.

When the song ended, he simply held her close, his strong arms wrapped around her, his clean scent surrounding her.

She wanted him.

It wouldn't be a forever thing, but why not enjoy it

short-term? Short was good. In some things, anyway. Her lips turned up in a grin.

"What?" Watching her, he drew back.

"Nothing." Heat raced over her face.

His eyes crinkled in a slow grin. "Okay, we're all entitled to our secrets. I hope, though, that heat has something to do with me…and you."

She simply mimed turning a key over her lips.

Brant dropped a quick kiss on the top of her head. "Understood."

Molly sighed. "As much as I hate to say this, it's late, and I have to work tomorrow."

"You're right, Cinderella. Time to get you home." Then he frowned. "Technically, I guess it's time you get *me* home, since you're driving, and how bizarre is that?"

On the way, she asked, "Just curious here, but why does Gaven call you BT sometimes?"

"To remind me what a sorry middle name Mom and Dad saddled me with."

"And that name would be…?"

"Truman, after our thirty-third president."

"Brant Truman Wylder. I kind of like it."

"'Cause it's not yours. Although my brothers didn't get off any easier. Tucker Kennedy and Gaven Roosevelt."

"Mom's or Dad's idea?"

"Dad's."

When she pulled up in front of his house, the moon was riding high in the sky.

Brant faced her, one long arm stretched over the back of the seat. He leaned into her, unfastened her seat belt, and turned off the ignition. Wrapping his hand around the back of her neck, he drew her as close as the car's gearshift and console allowed. This time, their lips met in a feverish kiss. One followed another until Molly became lost in them.

Nuzzling her neck, Brant asked, "Can we go to your place, Molly?"

"Yes."

When he drew away, she felt chilled. Was she making a huge mistake? She finger-combed her tangled mass of hair.

Brant reached over and stilled her hand. "Leave it. It looks all bed-mussed. Sexy. Like you and I already had a really great time."

"Whew. You've got me all flustered." She closed her eyes. "And I probably shouldn't have admitted that."

He chuckled. "We should get goin', darlin', before one of my brothers hauls me inside to watch the kid."

With shaky fingers, she started the car and pulled back onto the road.

By the time they reached her door, Brant was kissing the back of her neck, whispering in her ear, and making it darned near impossible to fit the key in the lock.

Halfway up the stairs, he pinned her against the wall, the full length of his body against hers. He claimed her lips in a frenzied kiss as his fingers made fast work of her buttons. As her blouse fell open, his gaze blazed a hot trail from her eyes to her lips to her silk-covered breasts.

He groaned, and she sent up a thankful prayer that beneath her practical jeans and soft cotton long-sleeved blouse, she'd worn lacy pale-yellow lingerie.

Within seconds, both the jeans and the top were

history. His followed, and she swallowed hard. The man was gorgeous and seriously ripped.

Molly ran a hand over his abs, then followed with her mouth.

"I wanted to go slow this first time, Molly, but…"

"Take me, Brant."

And he did, right there in the stairway.

Afterward, he carried her to her bed. This time they made love leisurely, exploring every inch of each other's body.

When she had her breath back, Molly asked, "How'd you get this scar?"

"This?" He rubbed the spot on his thigh. "Stupidity. We had a car on the rack with rusted fenders. Lots of jagged metal." He met her eyes. "It was just Gaven and me then. Tucker was still away. Anyway, I stood too close when Gav brought it down, and a piece of metal caught me. Bled like a son of a gun. Ten stitches."

She made a face. "Ouch."

"My own fault. Roll over."

"What?"

"Roll over. I want a closer look at that tattoo riding your backside. I caught a glimpse of it when you bent over for DeVonne's shoes, and I've been fantasizin' about it ever since."

"I'm not rolling over so you can look at my butt." Hot color raced up her face.

"Sure you are. Besides, sweetheart, I've already seen your butt. First-class." He waggled his brows. "Now I want to check out your tattoo."

When she opened her mouth to protest, he simply flipped her onto her stomach.

She let out a little squeak. "Brant Wylder—"

She stopped and drew in a breath when his lips kissed the small bluebird.

Resting on an elbow, Brant traced it with a fingertip, and when she looked over her shoulder, he met her eyes in the moonlight that filtered through her curtains. "Nice." His voice was husky. "Very, very nice. I approve."

"I'm glad, since it's there to stay."

But she knew *he* couldn't, wouldn't stay.

Truth? She was scared spitless tonight would alter everything, and since she couldn't let that happen, she went on the offensive. "Brant, you understand tonight doesn't change anything."

"You trying to convince me or yourself?" He ran a finger lazily along her bare back, over her hip to the top of her leg, his green eyes darkening. Then he leaned closer and whispered, "Maybe we need to try harder."

Before she could answer, he rolled her onto her back. His lips captured hers, his hard body blanketing her. His mouth and hands roamed over her, leaving not an inch untouched, and by the time he finished, both were out of breath, drenched in sweat, and bone-meltingly satisfied.

"Everything's changed, darlin'. You said three years, right?"

Wide-eyed, her gaze flew to his.

"I'm a patient man, and I'm in no hurry. I can wait."

"Brant—"

"Molly."

———

He meant to go home, but the bed was warm and the woman beside him so tempting. Another few minutes of stolen time wouldn't hurt, would it? He drew Molly in and closed his eyes. When she snuggled closer, he draped a leg over hers. This felt right. He didn't want a one-night stand with this woman, her list be damned.

He drifted off to sleep.

———

An uneasy sensation of being watched woke him. Bubbles sprawled across the top of his pillow, her blue eyes staring unblinking into his.

"Go away. Shoo. Go."

Molly stirred. "What's wrong?"

"Your cat. She's giving me the heebie-jeebies."

"Bubbles, come here." The sheet slid down as Molly reached for her pet.

His breath caught, but he forced himself to say, "I should go home."

"Really?" She squinted when he turned on the bed-side lamp.

"The squirt will be up in a few hours, and I need to be there. To save *him* from my brothers, not the other way around."

"Okay." She closed her eyes, one hand stroking her cat, the other spread across his stomach. "Give me a second."

"Any appointments this morning?"

"No."

"How about I take your car? Stay in bed where it's nice and warm, and I'll deliver it before lunch."

"Sounds perfect. The keys are on the stairs some-where." She fingered the sheet. "Brant, I was serious before. Nothing's changed."

"So was I. We turned a corner last night, Mol. One that can't be unturned. *Everything's* different today." He leaned down and gave her a toe-curling kiss. "I'll lock up behind me."

He'd thrown down the gauntlet. Would she take it up?

━━∿∿∿━━

Brant stood motionless in the doorway of his rental, tempted to turn around and leave. The house was a disaster. Baby bottles and toys were strewn everywhere. A wadded-up, dirty diaper lay on the floor next to the couch, a half-eaten jar of baby food sat on the counter, and both his brothers were fast asleep, fully dressed. Tucker sprawled the length of the sofa, and the baby was tucked up beside Gaven on the roll-away he'd somehow talked Annabelle into lending him. Nobody had bothered to change Jax into pajamas.

He glanced at his watch—4:10 a.m. The mess would wait.

Stumbling over a pair of shoes, he made it to his room, closed the door, and dropped onto his bed, fully clothed. Might as well join the club.

━━∿∿∿━━

Jax didn't disappoint, rising with the sun.

"What the heck?"

Brant smiled sleepily. That would be Gaven.

A grunt came from the living room. Tucker. Good. They were both awake.

"Brant! Hey, Brant, get out here. This kid's crying. Again."

"Feed him and change his diaper. He'll be fine."

"No way," Tucker said. "We had duty last night."

"Yeah, and I've had it a heck of a lot longer. No relief. No downtime." He pulled a pillow over his head. "You'll do fine."

Ignoring the banging and cursing, he actually managed to get another five minutes of shut-eye before his door flew open.

"He reeks." Gaven held a crying Jax at arms' length.

"It's last night's dinner. It runs right through him, I swear." He sat up. "Give me five minutes in the bathroom, then I'll rescue you."

Brant knew as sure as he knew his own name that if he changed and fed the kid before he showered, he'd step out of the bathroom to find his brothers gone. They'd be sitting at Dee-Ann's counter, eating breakfast. Not gonna happen.

"And while I'm in there, clean up the place. It looks like a pigsty. Mom taught you better." At the bathroom door, he stopped and took another look at his brothers. "You both look like you have the mother of all hangovers. If I didn't know better, I'd think you'd hit the bars. Hard."

Tucker raised a hand to the back of his head. "There were two of us, and we couldn't keep it together. How do you do it?"

"Honestly? The first few days, I thought I'd died and gone to hell. There are still times I feel that way. But to be honest? I can't imagine life without the little guy, stinky diapers and all."

An hour later, Brant figured Molly would be up and around…and more than a little tired. He grinned, thinking about how they'd spent the night. Molly was so sweet and demure. But get her heated up, and she was more than he could have dreamed.

He wanted her again. And again and again. Instead of appeasing his appetite, last night had whet it, and he craved more.

When he dropped Jax off at day care, he gave him a dozen little kisses, then left without looking back. He'd learned really fast that if he took that last peek, both he and Jax had trouble separating.

Brant drove to Main Street and parked in front of Tansy's. Another couple of months and all those azalea bushes would be in bloom, and he'd be here to see them. Feeling good, he swung through the intricately carved front door.

Mouth-watering smells of fresh brewed coffee, blueberry blintzes, and warm cinnamon rolls welcomed him. Tempting, so tempting. How did Beck resist all this?

Tansy stood behind the counter, all that incredible red hair forming a halo around her striking face. And those vibrant blue-green eyes. Looking into them was like staring into the Caribbean. Beck Elliot was one lucky guy.

He didn't want red hair and turquoise eyes. He wanted dark-brown eyes and coffee-colored hair streaked with caramel tones.

Brant thought of Molly and the way she'd looked when he left this morning, all tousled and sleepy eyed. Oh yeah. He and Beck had both hit the lottery. Except Tansy and Beck were a couple. He and Molly? That might take some work, but he figured he was up to it.

And that she'd be worth the effort.

When had his wants, his expectations, changed? This new determination to have Molly in his life ought to scare the bejesus out of him. It didn't.

"I didn't expect to see you this morning," Tansy said, breaking into his thoughts. "You two have a good time last night?"

"We did." The understatement of all understatements.

"What'll you have?"

While he waited for his order, Sam DeLuca strolled in.

"Sam." Brant nodded at him, noting he was in his uniform of jeans and an MBSD shirt and ball cap. "Going on or off duty?"

"On. A few more days, and Cricket and I will be on our honeymoon. No callouts and no alarms."

"Wearing a wedding band," Brant added.

Sam gave him a goofy grin. "Yeah."

Out of the corner of his eye, Brant caught Tansy's slow smile.

"Glad I ran into you this morning," Sam said. "I wanted to run something by you. When I first came to town, my aunt's house was practically collapsing in on itself. It needed more work than I could handle on my own. A high-school kid named Jeremy Stuckey gave me a hand. He'd had a run-in with the law before I came."

Sam removed his hat, and after smoothing his dark hair, replaced it. "Thing is, Jeremy's daddy, not too long before all that happened, ran away with a girl not much older than Jeremy. Needless to say, there were some pretty hurt feelings and a whole lot of anger. The kid paid for what he did in blood, sweat, and—my guess—a few private tears."

"Gotcha."

"Jeremy's handy and could use the money, if you can see fit to hire him a few hours here and there. It's good for him to have some responsible male figures in his life."

"Responsible? You're talking about the Wylder brothers, Sam."

"I know." Sam didn't blink. "I heard you played taxi after your friends stayed too long at Duffy's Pub and that you're nephew-sitting while your sister gets help. Think about giving Jeremy a shot. The kid can do anything. Right now, he's helping Lem with a couple projects. Then he's all yours, if you'll take a chance on him."

"My brothers will be gone by then, so bring him by when he's ready."

"Thanks." Sam clapped him on the back. "Okay if I pour myself a cup, Tanz?"

"You bet." She handed Brant his bag along with a coffee and tea to go. "Jeremy's a good kid who caught a bad break. Tell Molly hi for me."

Brant walked out of the bakery, scratching his head. A baby, a teenager who might or might not be a juvenile delinquent, two brothers camped out at a house he wasn't paying rent on, a rundown service station, and a woman who turned him inside out without even trying.

Was it too late to cry uncle?

―◦◦◦―

Molly leaned into the bathroom counter and stared in the mirror. Shouldn't she look different? Last night had been totally unexpected, totally off the charts, and totally fantastic.

Her cat wandered into the room, and Molly gathered

her close. "Bubbles, I should be exhausted. I barely got any sleep." A sly smile crossed her lips. "And isn't that a wonderful thing?"

She moved to her bedroom and peered into her closet. Her wardrobe choice this morning gave her some trouble. A sunny yellow dress called to her, echoed her mood. After actually walking out of the closet with it, she'd forced herself to hang it back up. Today was a workday. Her concession? She fastened a happy daisy pin on the stark black A-line dress.

Spotting a pair of black heels with discreet white piping along the edge, she slid into them. The doorbell rang, and she glanced at her clock. Still early.

Halfway down the stairs, she faltered. Brant stood outside, wearing dark glasses, a sexy attitude, and carrying a Sweet Dreams bag. Flustered, she ran a hand over her hair.

"Brant. I didn't expect to see you this morning." Her heart pounded practically out of her chest.

Totally unruffled, he bussed her cheek casually as though they hadn't spent the entire night making love. "Your car's out front. Thought you might need this." He handed her the tea.

"I do. I planned to make a cup once I unlocked my doors."

"It's not time to hang the Open sign yet, is it?"

"No. I still have almost half an hour."

"Good. Let's go upstairs."

Her heart kicked into a higher gear, one she hadn't known existed. "Brant, I—"

"I'm thinking we should take these drinks and croissants and sit on your deck, sugar. It's a beautiful morning. You'll want a sweater."

She nodded and led the way upstairs. While she unlocked her patio doors, he brushed her hair aside and dropped small kisses on the back of her neck. She raised a hand to his head, ran her fingers through all that thick hair, and nearly purred.

"I needed a taste, Mol. You're a hell of a lot sweeter than anything Tansy creates."

When she turned, he set their breakfast on the small table and took her in his arms. Their lips met in a sweet morning kiss.

"I wanted to make sure last night wasn't a dream," he whispered.

Heat raced up Molly's neck and across her cheeks.

He laughed. "Come on. Let's feed you so you can get to work, then I need to do the same."

"Where's Jax?"

"Day care."

"You should have brought him along. How'd it go with your brothers last night?"

She chuckled when he told her about the mess he'd walked in on.

The croissants finished, he got to his feet. "Time for work."

Her mouth nearly got ahead of her brain. It was on the tip of her tongue to ask how he could be so easy-going this morning while she was one huge bundle of nerves. Every time she glanced at his mouth, his lips, she thought of the previous night. She watched him wrap his fingers around the coffee cup and remembered the delicious, magical things they'd done to her body in the wee hours of the morning.

"Molly?"

"I'll walk you down." Bubbles wove in and out of her legs when she stood.

But before she took even one step, he threaded his fingers through her hair and planted a kiss that nearly melted the soles of her white-piped shoes.

"I'll try to stop by tonight. Things might get a little crazy, though, with Tucker and Gaven here."

"It's okay. We agreed nothing—"

He laid a finger over her lips. "Shh. You agreed. I didn't. Then or now. By the way, happy Valentine's Day. Stay here and put your feet up another minute. I can show myself out."

That's exactly what she did, too befuddled to move. She'd started Valentine's Day off by having breakfast with Brant Wylder. No, not true. Even better, she'd started it out tangled up in the sheets with him.

Maybe it was time to read her list again, although she was having a hard time remembering why it mattered. He was here. She was here. Both planned to stay.

That didn't mean he'd stay with her, though.

Her father hadn't.

Keith hadn't.

Could she handle living here in this small town and running into Brant constantly after he moved on to someone else?

And no doubt he would. No man had ever stuck.

Why should he be any different?

Chapter 18

BRANT'S BROTHERS HAD DROPPED HIS CAR AT MOLLY'S.

By the time he got home, they sat at the kitchen table, eating cereal.

Tuck looked up. "You need a better place, Brant. If it was a week or two, maybe, but since you're planning to stay, this doesn't cut it."

His gaze traveled over the cracked linoleum, ancient wallpaper, and faded paint, the kitchen so outdated, it was nearly back in vogue. Before he could agree, though, his phone rang. Afraid it was day care, he answered quickly. "Brant Wylder."

"Morning. Kemper Dobson here. I heard your brothers are in town."

"They are. No problem with the property, is there?"

"Nope, we're good to go. The paperwork's done, so whenever you three can come in, we'll get it signed, and the place is yours."

"Thank you, Mr. Dobson. That's great news."

Not one for wasting time, Tucker said, "Let's get it done."

They were in and out of the lawyer's in half an hour.

"It's ours." Gaven rubbed his hands together in glee.

Brant slid behind the wheel. "Nice to have that finished before you head home."

On the way to the house, they agreed that until they saw how things went, they'd keep their Lake Delores office open. Rudy, their go-to guy, would run it for them and send any new clients to their Misty Bottoms shop.

"The timing's perfect," said Gaven. "Other than our barn-find Vette, we have nothing pressing. Once Tucker and I get home, we'll make arrangements to have our equipment moved."

"Tyrone's still making noises about us tricking out his Denali," Brant said. "That'll give us a start here."

"Chances are good we'll pick up a couple of his buddies, once they see his ride," Tucker added.

At Brant's, the three hunkered over sketches at the scarred kitchen table and argued over priorities.

"We need to get that fence up. Secure the place."

"And," Gaven pointed out, "hire a contractor to expand the building and set up the paint booth."

Brant nodded. "I have one coming in day after tomorrow."

"This is going to be so much better than the place we have now."

"Yeah, it is, and with the acreage, we'll have room to expand," said Tucker. "This was a real find."

Brant looked at him. "You do understand, not everyone is happy about us setting up shop in Misty Bottoms."

Tucker shrugged. "That's bound to be the case."

"And you'd better believe all our business will be discussed over morning coffee at Dee-Ann's."

"Already is," Gaven said.

"Oh?"

"I ran in for a couple to-go coffees after we dropped

your car off, and a few old codgers had the back booth."
He deepened his voice. "They bring all those motorcycles in here, and next thing you know, Hells Angels
will be pourin' into town."

Tucker hooted with laughter.

"First brides," Gaven intoned, "then motorcycle
gangs and hot-rodders. Misty Bottoms is changin'."

"Well, we can't stop the talk."

"But wait." Gaven held up his index finger. "The best
one. Rich folks comin' to town thinkin' we'll bow to
them and their highfalutin ways."

"You're making that up."

"Hand to God I'm not, Mr. Rich Folk." He grinned.
"You gonna share all that money, BT?"

"Sure. Just as soon as I see some." He hauled a pitcher
of sweet tea from the fridge. "Anybody?"

Sprawled around the table, Tucker and Gaven both
held up their glasses.

"Same plan as before?" Brant asked.

"Yep. If it ain't broke—"

While they'd all get their hands dirty and work on the
cars and motorcycles, it would be Gaven who'd actually
be in charge of the shop itself. He'd been blessed with
the golden touch when it came to restoration work. On
top of that, he was a whiz at anything and everything
mechanical. Brant had watched him start with a heap
of metal, and by the time he was done, the bodywork
and trim, the interior, and the engine made grown men
weep...and pay big bucks for that heap.

But Gaven hated the details of running a business.
Things like paying electric and water bills, ordering supplies, issuing paychecks—all jobs he passed on to his

oldest brother. Tucker had the head for business, and his borderline OCD made him perfect for the job.

Himself? He was their marketing guru and jack of all trades.

Somehow, it worked.

"So how serious are you and Molly?" Gaven poked.

"Where'd that come from?" Brant drew back. "We're..." *What?* he wondered. *Sure as hell not just friends with benefits. Lovers? Girlfriend, boyfriend?* That sounded pretty high school. "It's complicated."

"Yeah, I'd guess so," Tucker ribbed. "Listen, I have to run. Gonna borrow your truck, Gav. I shouldn't be more than a couple hours."

"Where're you goin'?" Brant frowned.

"You can drag your feet all you want, Bro, but I've got an appointment with Quinlyn. I plan to buy a house."

"Why?"

"Because I'll be living here in Misty Bottoms, too."

"Maybe I should go with you," Gaven said.

"To make time with my real-estate agent?"

"Nah. So I can pick out my room."

"No way, baby brother. I don't want a roommate."

"You're kidding."

"Nope. You're on your own."

—⁓—

Molly had been surprised when Tucker called to ask her to house-hunt with him. She was giving Lettie a few last-minute instructions when he pulled up out front in Gaven's pickup. "Got to go."

She grabbed her purse as the door opened and Tucker stuck his head inside. "Ready?"

"I am. Lettie, this is Brant's brother, Tucker."

"We've met." Lettie, never the shy one, asked, "Brant know you're here for his girl?"

"Lettie, I'm not Brant's—"

"Go on. You can feed that to somebody else, and they might buy it. Me? Tush!"

Tucker chuckled. "Brant has no idea I'm stealing her away this afternoon."

"Really? I was just joshin'."

"See? Fresh gossip. You'll be the belle of the ball at Dee-Ann's this afternoon."

Molly raised her brows. "You really are a trouble-maker, aren't you?"

"I can be."

"We're looking at houses with Quinlyn, Lettie."

"For who?" the older woman asked.

"For me. Brant's not the only one moving to Misty Bottoms." He held the door. "If you're ready, we should probably head out. I promised we'd be on time."

Once they were in the truck, Molly was amazed that just like Brant's, it could never be mistaken for a woman's. It was all male. It had that attitude, that scent—and that huge engine, she thought, when it roared to life.

Men and their vehicles.

"I only asked her to bring one set of keys." Tucker drove with efficiency and confidence.

"The old blacksmithy." He'd asked her about it at Fat Baby's the other night.

"Crazy, huh?"

"Not really." She tipped her head. "A little eccentric maybe."

He laughed. "The polite Southern difference."

By the time they pulled up in front of the house, Molly decided she liked Brant's older brother. He was serious, yes, but considering he'd done several tours of duty in the Middle East, that came as no surprise, although according to Brant, he'd pretty much been that way before. But the man also had a wicked sense of humor, and he wasn't afraid to poke fun at himself. Some woman would fall head over heels for this handsome guy.

Despite Lettie's poking, it wouldn't be Molly, because in spite of herself, she'd developed a real case for Tucker's brother.

Quinlyn waited in the yard for them, looking both feminine and professional in her tan-and-black long-sleeved sweater and black slacks. All that gorgeous blond hair was pulled up in a twist.

The agent swept a hand toward the building. "It's something else, isn't it?"

Brant and Gaven had just finished installing a new heavy-duty hot-water heater Beck had delivered, when Tucker strolled through the door.

Brant swiped the back of an arm over his brow, wiping off the sweat that beaded there. "How'd it go?"

"I made an offer."

"You did what?" Gaven laid the Crescent wrench on the shelf beside him.

"I bought the old blacksmith shop."

Brant stared at him. "The two-story stone building on Firefly Creek?"

"Yep." Tucker nodded.

Gaven looked from brother to brother. "Exactly how old is old?"

"Pre–Civil War. She's been kicking around since 1860."

Brant's hand shot out to feel his brother's forehead.

Tucker knocked it away. "Cut it out."

"You're crazier than me."

"Molly says I'm eccentric, not crazy."

"Molly?" An uneasy feeling, one he didn't like, slithered through Brant. "When did you talk to Molly?"

"She went house-hunting with me."

For an instant, a monster Brant hadn't known lived inside him reared its ugly head. Then he caught his brother's grin.

"Got you."

Brant relaxed. "I didn't think she'd go anywhere with a mug that ugly."

"Oh, she did go. As a friend. As my brother's girlfriend."

"She's not my girlfriend," Brant groused.

"Suit yourself." Tucker shrugged. "The lot's incredible. Tons of mature trees, and the yard runs right down to the creek."

"How big is the house?" Gaven asked.

"No." Tucker shook his head.

"No, what?"

"You're not moving in with me. We already had this conversation. I want my own place."

Brant understood. In Lake Delores, Tucker had rented a tiny apartment over the five-and-dime store when he'd mustered out of the Marines. That had worked, but this new place would suit him better. He'd have privacy and elbow room.

"Right now, the place is pretty much a shell—but a nice sturdy shell. Space for a media room and a pool table. Extra bedrooms, in case Mom and Dad want to come for a bit."

"But you won't let me stay," Gaven muttered.

"They'd be temporary. You'd sit your hide down permanently."

Gaven turned to Brant. "Looks like it'll be you and me then, pal."

He was tempted to say yes. The fixer, right? "Sorry, baby brother. Gonna have to find your own place."

"What?"

"Call Quinlyn, see what she can round up for you—temporary for now or something permanent. That's up to you. Tucker's right. It's time we stop living in each other's pockets."

"What the heck does that mean?"

"It means it's time this band of brothers has separate, as well as entwined, lives."

Gaven frowned. "Don't I get a vote?"

"No," Tucker and Brant said in unison.

"I'm getting a glass of water. For me. You two can get your own." Gaven sulked out of the room.

The second he left, Brant narrowed his eyes. "Everything else aside, I have to agree with Gaven about the property you're looking at. That place is pretty big for one person."

"I'm not looking at it, BT. I bought it. And I'm not having this discussion again. We both know I'm better off alone. Some people are born one half of a couple.

Not me. I'll do some gal a favor by *not* getting involved with her. You want to marry somebody off, look to Gaven for that."

Their younger brother stuck his head around the corner. "Marriage? Me? I tried it, remember?"

"Yeah," Tucker said. "For eight months."

"Eight and a half. Not for me."

The two turned as one toward Brant.

"Don't even go there," Brant said. "Hope you've got some raggedy jeans in the trunk of that car, Mr. New Homeowner." He handed Tucker a sledgehammer. "We've got another wall to take down."

With Cricket's wedding looming, the next couple of days flew. By the time Friday night rolled around and rehearsal had been dealt with, Molly was bushed…and confused. Although she'd talked to him and he'd sent her a beautiful bouquet for Valentine's Day, she hadn't seen Brant since they shared breakfast on her deck.

That was okay, she assured herself. Actually, it was better than okay. She'd asked for space, and he was giving it to her. Add in that he was caring for Jax, keeping tabs on Lainey, and working madly on the new building, and the man was slammed.

The rehearsal party moved to Sam's house. With a nip in the air and a roaring bonfire, the outdoor, casual venue made perfect sense. Molly, being an only child of divorced parents, was shocked when Cricket's and Sam's big families poured in. Happy chaos ruled the night.

They roasted hot dogs, made s'mores, and laughed.

As promised, the champagne flowed. Chubby Checker's "The Twist" streamed from Sam's stereo. Grabbing Cricket's niece, Molly joined the dancers on the lawn. The stars shone brightly, and the fire crackled and snapped. It was by far the best rehearsal dinner Molly had ever attended.

The only thing missing? Brant.

<hr />

The bonfire, as great as it had been, left her smelling smoky. Bubbles, after one sniff at the top of the stairs, deserted her with her tail in the air. Molly needed a shower and shampoo.

The water felt heavenly, and she stayed under it far longer than she'd meant. With her head back and leaning against the tile, she let the spray wash away the long day. Afterward, wearing her two-sizes-too-big Atlanta Braves T-shirt, she fell into bed with Bubbles curled up beside her.

As she reached to turn off the bedside lamp, the phone rang.

She didn't need to check caller ID. It would be Brant. She swore the man had psychic powers. Last night, just like tonight, she'd no sooner slipped into bed than her phone rang. He'd wanted to check on her, to wish her good night.

It rang a second time. Should she answer it? Rolling her eyes, she called herself all kinds of a fool. Of course she would.

"Hello, Brant."

"Hey, beautiful, how did rehearsal go?"

And she was lost. That deep, sexy voice seduced

her as he asked about her day and shared the highlights of his.

"I miss you, Molly."

"I miss you, too." After a heartbeat, she asked, "Where have you been?"

"Working like a dog."

"Where are you now?" She held her breath and wondered if he was standing outside, waiting for her light to go out. If only he were that close.

"Standing on my porch, staring at the stars. Where are you?" he asked.

"In bed with Bubbles."

He chuckled. "Good night, sweetheart. Sleep well." On an oath, she clicked off, wishing she had a landline so she could slam the receiver. The man was infuriating. After a call like that, she wouldn't sleep, well or otherwise, and he knew it. She hadn't lied, though. She missed him. Without thinking about it, she traded her pillow for his and caught just the faintest scent of him.

Tomorrow she'd strip the bed and shut off her phone…and get some sleep.

———

Cricket's wedding day broke gloriously sunny.

When the stunning bride walked down the aisle in her soft-ivory gown, there wasn't a dry eye in the house. The corset top with its off-white beading showed off Cricket's incredible figure, while the tiered tulle skirt increased her wide-eyed fairy look. For her "something blue" she'd chosen a gorgeous pair of pale-blue heels. The girl had taste.

During the recessional, though, it was the sexy-as-all-get-out man in the fourth row Molly couldn't keep her eyes off. Brant hadn't been sure he'd make it, but there he sat. Instead of his jeans and T-shirt or his tux, he wore dark trousers and a crisp white shirt.

She met his gaze, and he winked; she missed a step and nearly stumbled.

During the reception, Molly wandered from guest to guest, noting all the little details that made this wedding so special. A crystal chandelier decorated with gardenias and greenery hung above the table that held the five-tiered cake. All in all, the wedding fit the bride and groom to a T. Maybe best of all, they'd hired two food trucks to provide their guests' meal. From the bonfire to the food to the dance with Brant beneath the magnolia trees, the wedding hit all the right notes.

Then Brant gave her a whopper of a kiss and donned his chauffeur's cap to drive the happy couple to the airport in a gleaming Rolls-Royce Silver Cloud.

Chapter 19

Sunday morning, Jax woke early.

Brant groaned and rolled over.

"I've got him," Tucker called out. "You're going to have a big day. Catch another half hour."

"Thanks." Brant pulled the covers over his head and burrowed beneath them. He wished today were over... and knew that made him less of a man. Of a person.

Today, he and Jax were heading to Savannah to see Lainey. It would be their first visit since she entered rehab. The day could go really, really well—or really, really badly.

He tossed and turned for a few more minutes before giving it up. Once he was awake, he rarely went back to sleep, and today was no exception. That didn't mean he intended to deny Tucker his time with the little guy, though. With an evil grin, he headed to the shower while his brother fed Jax.

—◦◦◦—

Showered, shaved, and dressed, Brant stepped into an amazingly calm scene. Jax, still in his footie pajamas, scooted around the living room on all fours, chasing a ball Gaven rolled away from him.

"There're some scrambled eggs if you want them," Tucker said.

"I do. Thanks." He looked around. "Where'd my brothers go?"

"Funny." Tucker grabbed him in a headlock and gave him a noogie. "Go eat before they get cold."

"I made a fresh pot of coffee," Gaven called over his shoulder.

"Don't suppose you'd like to give the kid his bath?"

"We're off to the royal swimming pool as we speak," Gaven answered, slinging Jax under his arm.

"Okay," Brant said. "Wait a minute."

Gaven stopped as Jax jabbered away and drooled down his leg. "Hey, kid, this is my last clean pair."

Jax waved his hands.

"What's wrong?" Tucker asked.

"Something's up."

"What?"

"Something's up." Brant's eyes narrowed.

"Gav and I had a long talk yesterday. You're pulling a lot of extra weight. We both know that. We know, too, that today's gonna be one hell of a day. Visiting Lainey's not gonna be easy. Since the doc suggested we start slow, one of us at a time, you drew the short straw."

"It's only fair Tuck and I do more to help. So we're helping." Gaven flew Jax around the small room, making buzzing sounds.

"You might want to slow down," Brant warned, "or you're likely to be wearing the kid's last meal."

Gaven grimaced. "Right. Off to the baths with you, Caesar."

Brant watched him fly the baby toward the bathroom. "Think Gav will ever grow up?"

Tucker thought about that for a couple of seconds, then shook his head. "Nah."

"Agreed." Brant poured himself a mug of coffee, then filled a plate with the light, fluffy eggs. "I didn't know you could cook."

"I do a mean scrambled egg and an even better grilled cheese sandwich. After that? It's all amateur hour."

It felt good to eat in peace. He ignored the splashing, the vision of a water-covered floor, and the occasional groan or mutter from his younger brother. Half an hour later, Jax was returned to him bathed and dressed.

"He's barefoot."

"Yeah." Gaven dug socks from his back pocket. "Darned if I could manage these."

"Why?"

"The kid's sneaky."

Jax laughed.

"Yeah, see?" Gaven pointed at him. "Even now he laughs."

"Give them to me." Brant pulled the socks from Gav. Sitting down on the sofa, he placed Jax in his lap. "Uncle Gaven can't put your socks on. Should we show him how it's done?"

Jax leaned back to stare into Brant's face, and Brant fell in love all over again. The chubby little baby hand came to rest on Brant's cheek, and he turned his face into it and kissed it. Then he put the first sock on the baby…or tried to. Every time he got near Jax's foot, the baby curled his toes.

"What's this?" Brant tipped his head up to look at Gaven. "You teach him a new game?"

"Heck no."

After a good five minutes of struggling, Brant had both socks on. "Voilà." He spread his hands. "And that's how it's done."

"Oh yeah?" Tucker nodded at the baby, who was now chewing on the sock clutched in his fist and wiggling his bare toes.

Brant's shoulders sagged. Resigned, he turned to wage the battle again.

Looked like it was going to be one of those days after all.

The visitor's area fairly vibrated with positivity—simulated positivity, the smiles the same as the one worn by a doctor who welcomes you into his office right before he delivers crushing news. Then he spotted Lainey. The smile on her face wasn't feigned when she caught sight of him and Jax. It lit up the room.

"Jax!" Crossing to them, she took the happy baby into her arms and smothered him in kisses before leaning in to drop one on Brant's cheek. "Thanks. I know you hate this, but it means so much to me."

"I don't hate it," he lied.

"Yes, you do." She grinned, the old Lainey peeking through. "But you came because you love me."

"I do, and that's the God's honest truth." He hugged her and Jax tightly. "So." Brant tipped his head toward Jax. "How's he look? I'm doin' okay?"

"Oh my gosh, he's getting so big. You're doing a wonderful job, big brother." She all but buried her face in her son, kissing and touching and talking baby talk to him. "Where'd you get this little sailor suit, hmm?

Look at my big boy. You're so beautiful, and Mommy's missed you so much!"

"If you can bear to let go of him for a sec, put him down and watch him go."

Reluctantly, she set him on the floor. He dropped to all fours and then, with a mile-wide grin for his mother, took off across the room, heading to a bright-red chair.

"He's hell on wheels, Sis. Nothing safe anymore."

Blinking back tears, she put her fingers to her lips. "I've missed him so much. I really screwed up."

"But you're doing the right thing now."

"I am."

Strength threaded through her words.

"There's a courtyard in back of the building," Lainey said. "I think it should be warm enough today. Why don't we go out there?" She glanced around the room, indicating all of the others with their visitors. "We'll have more privacy."

He followed her outside into air untainted by that distinctive institutional smell and instantly felt better. Lainey was right. The temperature was mild, the sun shining.

"The dogwood's all budded out. It'll be beautiful in another week or so." Lainey pointed to a bed of annuals interspersed with white camellias. "We planted those this week. I loved digging in the soil, watching the color bring the area to life. I think when I get out of here, I'll apply at the garden center down the road from Mom and Dad's."

Brant marveled at the change in his sister. At her plans for the future. At her happiness. And best of all, the difference felt real. Deep. He allowed himself to hope.

"That sounds wonderful, Lain, and it'll give you a

chance to get out with people and spend time outside. Both will be good for you."

"It will. I'll have to put Jax in day care, though."

"I don't think you need to worry about that. Jax is thriving at Lucinda's center." He shared some of the stunts the baby had pulled in the past couple of weeks and the sock fiasco that morning. "Your kid's keeping me on my toes, Sis."

"I don't doubt that for a second. Speaking of Jax, I heard from his father."

Brant held his breath, then listened as she filled him in.

"I thought you should know, but now I don't want to talk about him anymore. How's the shop going?"

He allowed her the change of subject, deciding he'd mull over her news on the way home. "Better than any of us could have imagined. I can't wait for you to see it." He pulled up a few photos on his phone.

They talked about the changes they were making to the building, about the friends he'd made in Misty Bottoms, and how the town felt like home already. "I like it there."

"Speaking of liking"—Lainey grinned mischievously—"how's Molly doing?"

"She's good. She sends her love."

"Am I the only one she's giving love to?"

"That would come under TMI, little Miss Nosy."

She smiled smugly. "You just told me everything I need to know. Didn't he, baby?" She kissed Jax's round cheeks and smiled again when he giggled. "Soon, sweetheart, we can be together again. I can tuck you in at night and be with you in the morning.

Mommy's working hard—yes, she is. And I'm getting better every day."

She raised eyes that swam with unshed tears. "As hard as this is, I'm glad I'm here. I need to be here, to go through this. Thank you for taking care of my baby so I could. I know it hasn't been easy."

"We're doing okay, Lain." He slung an arm over her shoulder.

Her face turned to granite. "I'll make you a promise right here and now. I won't ever need to do this again." She gave Jax a smooch on the top of his head. "This little boy means too much to me. I won't let weakness take me away from him ever again."

She took Jax's hand in hers. "I'm making that promise to you, too, son of mine. I'll be the best mother ever, and I'll be a much better person when I come to pick you up."

"It's hard, isn't it, Lainey?"

"Truth? I've never hurt so much in my life. Emotionally and mentally. The counselors don't stop till they hit the sorest spot in your psyche. Then they make you work to heal it."

Brant nodded. He was thrilled that she was doing well. It was what he'd prayed for. Yet with her talk of release, his own heart hurt. She'd soon take her son back—and that was as it should be.

Conflicting emotions raced through him. It wouldn't be long till he'd have his life back...and watch a huge piece of his heart drive away. Not long ago, he hadn't been able to figure out what to do with Jax, and now he'd be darned if he could imagine life without him.

—◦◦◦—

Brant left the rehab center feeling like he'd been run through a meat grinder. He looked at Jax, freshly diapered and fed by his mother, then made the mistake of glancing at his own reflection in the mirror. Haggard. Helpless. Humbled.

Lainey was holding up her end and working hard to get better, but the cost was high. Beneath the smile, the bubbly behavior, and positive attitude, her eyes held weariness and hurt. The counselors were digging deep. They had to. Without facing her demons, his little sis would never get better, and nobody could do it for her. This was something she had to do alone.

And now? He'd face his own demon. Or was it Molly's? Should she be here instead of him? Whatever. He'd do some of the groundwork, and the rest would be up to her and her dad. And her mom.

Not for the first time, he wondered what he'd been thinking when he arranged to meet Preston Stiles for lunch. Too late to back out now. In for a dime, in for a dollar.

He hefted the baby carrier out of the back seat. "Jax, buddy, I'm gonna need your help."

"Ga-ga-ga-ga-ga."

"Yep, that's exactly what I'm talking about. Stiles is gonna be a tough audience."

The men had agreed to meet at Clary's, so at least he wouldn't leave hungry.

When he walked into the restaurant, he spotted Mr. Stiles sitting toward the back.

Carrying a babbling Jax, he asked the hostess for a

high chair. When he reached the table, Brant nodded. "Mr. Stiles."

"Brant. Why don't you call me Preston? Cut the formalities."

"Fine with me." The high chair arrived, but Jax didn't want anything to do with it. He clung onto Brant's neck and shirt, stiffened his legs, and made it clear this wasn't for him.

Preston stood. "Let me." He took the baby from a very surprised Brant and jiggled him a couple of times. "Don't want to go in there, huh? Sometimes, little man, we have to suck it up for the good of the cause. Uncle Brant and I have a few things to talk about, so let's get you settled."

While he talked, Jax stared at him, jabbering back and running a hand over Stiles's face. Preston nipped at his fingers, and the baby laughed. Before he knew it, he found himself strapped into the chair and gumming a cracker Preston had handed him.

"Good work." Brant eyed Molly's dad with a little more respect.

"Trick is to divert their attention. Their thought process is pretty scattered, so give a baby something else to think about, and they'll forget what they were originally fussing over. Always worked with Molly."

"Good to know. I'll keep that in mind." Picturing a baby girl with Molly's dark hair and those big eyes, he smiled. She must have been beautiful even then.

Their waitress showed up with coffee.

Brant's concern for that baby all grown up had him plowing right in. "I'm not gonna beat around the bush. Your daughter has some real issues, and a lot of them are wrapped around you and your wife, the way you ended things. You're probably wondering who I think I am, talking to you about this, but—"

Preston held up a hand. "Stop right there. I know who you are. You're a man who cares about my daughter. Cares enough to put yourself on the line for her. Quite frankly, I like that. I like you. I'm glad Molly has you in her life."

Caught off guard, Brant frowned. He'd expected to meet resistance, expected Mr. Stiles to tell him to take a hike. He opened his mouth to speak, but Stiles held up a finger.

"I'm not done. If you intend to spend much time with my daughter, there are a couple of things you should keep in mind. On the surface, the part of herself she shares with the world, Molly's all sugar and spice and all that garbage. Beneath? The girl's stubborn as all get-out."

Brant nodded. Hadn't he thought of her as a strange amalgam of whimsy and business? Hadn't he witnessed that stubborn streak, bumped heads with her temper?

"Molly's mom and I have both told her time and time again that nothing she did or didn't do caused our breakup. She won't accept that. I don't know what you want me to do."

"Did you tell her the real reason?"

"That's between her mother and me."

Brant fed Jax a bite of the mashed potatoes the waitress had delivered. The baby grinned and opened his mouth for more. Scooping up a little butter with the next bite, Brant airplaned it in.

Then he turned his attention back to Molly's father.

"See, that's where I disagree. There were three people in that family, in that breakup. You owe it to Molly to come clean, whatever you did."

"What makes you so certain I was the guilty party? That I'm the one who did wrong?"

For the first time since they'd sat down, Brant smiled. "The guy's always at fault. You don't know that yet?"

Her dad chuckled. "You got that right, boy. Guess I should keep that in the forefront, shouldn't I?"

"Yes, sir, you should." He handed Jax a bottle, one he could handle on his own now, and the two men tucked into their own food.

Brant breathed a little easier. Maybe the Stiles family could, after all this time, find closure.

And with that, new beginnings?

Despite telling herself she had no right to be, Molly was miffed. Brant had left the wedding to drive Sam and Cricket to the airport, and she hadn't seen or heard from him since. Fine—it didn't matter. She had more than enough to keep her busy: cleaning, restocking her fridge and pantry, laundry. All the typical Sunday stuff. Boring, but necessary. She didn't miss Brant at all. Not one bit.

Shouldn't he at least call?

The sun dipped below the horizon.

Molly poured a glass of zinfandel and decided to get comfortable. Dressed in a pair of baggy sweats and her old Atlanta Falcons sweatshirt, she sat on her deck watching the stars and remembering last night's dance with Brant and the one they'd shared right here.

"What do you say we watch some reruns of *Say Yes to the Dress*, Bubbles?"

In no time, she and her fluffy white friend were curled up in bed, watching brides try on dress after dress until they hit the jackpot and found that one creation in all the universe worthy of a walk down the aisle.

In the middle of their fifth segment, Molly couldn't stop yawning. "Time to call it a night, pal."

The cat yawned and stretched.

"You too, huh?"

She clicked off the TV and turned out the light. Her head had barely hit the pillow when she fell asleep. In her dream, she sat behind a desk the size of the *Titanic*. The phone rang and rang and rang, but she couldn't find it.

With a start, she woke. Her cell phone rang again. Blinking, she groped for it. She hadn't closed her drapes, and the light from a streetlamp at the end of the block cast the room in shadows.

"Hello?" she mumbled.

Bubbles, annoyed that her sleep had been interrupted, jumped from the bed.

"What are you doing, sweetheart?"

"Brant?" She cleared her throat. "I'm sleeping. Or I was. Is everything okay?"

"Absolutely."

"Where are you?"

"Look out your front window."

She did. He stood on the sidewalk, phone to his ear, devastatingly handsome in a bomber jacket and worn jeans. His Harley was parked at the curb, a helmet dangling from the handlebars.

"Mmm. There's a good-lookin' man outside my apartment."

He chuckled. "Everybody at my house, including Jax, is finally asleep. I missed you."

"I missed you, too."

"Will you come down, or can I come up?"

"Come up. I have ice cream, and I'm willing to share. I'd planned to have it for dessert but ended up with a glass of zin instead. Give me a sec, and I'll be down to unlock the door."

She rushed into the bathroom, brushed her teeth and hair and, looking down at the sweats she'd fallen asleep in, shrugged. This is what a man got when he came calling at—she glanced at the clock—1:22 in the morning.

They'd both pay for this tomorrow. Later today, rather.

And she didn't care.

A cat-that-ate-the-canary grin on her face, she hurried down the steps.

The second the door opened, he had her in his arms, his mouth devouring hers. He smelled of fresh air and the night. Then his lips left hers to travel down her neck to the shoulder exposed when her sweatshirt slid from it.

With a groan, he pulled away to rest his forehead on hers.

"This isn't what I came for, although it's a heck of a bonus. I wanted to see you. To talk to you. I just"—he shook his head—"I just needed to be with you."

Stepping back, he held her at arms' length. "Cute outfit."

She grimaced. "Bubbles and I weren't expecting company, so we went for comfy."

"Looks like you've got that covered. Falcons, huh? I'd suspect Tyrone gave you that, but from the looks of it, you've had it for a while."

"My dad bought it for me a few years ago, when we went to one of their games."

And that's why she went to it for comfort, Brant thought. That connection with her father.

"So where's the ice cream?" He tipped his head. "Or did you get me in here on false pretenses?" He'd second-guessed himself the whole way to town, but now he wondered why he hadn't come sooner. She made him happy.

"We actually have a choice of flavors."

"Oh yeah?"

In the kitchen, she opened the freezer door and held up two containers. "Chocolate marshmallow or salted caramel blondie."

"Ooh, tough decision."

"And…" Setting the ice cream on the counter, she pulled a jar of cherries, one of chocolate sauce, and a squirt bottle of whipped cream from the fridge.

"Somebody's ready for a party."

She swooped back a strand of hair that had fallen forward. "I am."

His libido shot through the roof, and he fought to keep his hands to himself. Ice cream, although good, took a distant second to what he really wanted. He needed badly to drag Molly into the bedroom and make wild, crazy love to her.

But that wasn't why he'd come. Not entirely, at least. He wanted that, but he needed more.

"Brant?" Ice cream containers back in hand, she looked at him. "These are cold. Which one?"

"A scoop of each."

"You're one of those."

Minutes later, they sat at her kitchen table with the dark outside her windows. Wrapped in the snug cocoon, he couldn't remember feeling more content. Right about now was when he usually cut bait and ran. He didn't want to this time.

It confused him.

"We visited Lainey today."

"How'd it go?"

"Far better than I hoped. She looked good and is making plans for the future. In fact, she's talking about going to work for a landscape business in Lake Delores. She really had it together. And Jax was a trooper. He's missed his mom."

Molly laid her hand over his. "That little guy will get her through this. She loves him."

Brant nodded. "So do I. Gonna be rough to let that little stinker go when the time comes." He hesitated. "Lain got a card from Jason yesterday, wishing her well. He apologized for his behavior at the hospital. Said he'd screwed up—both with her and the baby. Not quite sure what to make of that, but we'll see. He's moved back to Lake Delores."

"And that's where Lainey's going after rehab."

"Yep. I don't trust Jason, but Dad will keep an eye on things."

"Maybe his moving back is a good thing."

Brant sent her a look that said he disagreed.

"I can tell you from first-hand experience that a child needs his father." Her voice was velvet-edged, but strong. "Maybe you all need to give Jason a chance. Not for him, but for Jax."

A twinge of guilt nearly had Brant confessing to his lunch date with her dad. He resisted. "The guy's a jerk."

"I won't argue that, but he's Jax's father."

Brant popped a cherry into his mouth. "Enough about that."

When they'd scraped the last bite from their bowls, Brant gathered them up and loaded them into the dishwasher.

"I should go. Let you get some sleep."

Molly said nothing, an invitation in the smoldering depths of her big eyes. She crossed the kitchen, wrapped her arms around his waist, and laid her head on his chest.

"I can hear your heartbeat," she said.

"I'll bet you can. It's getting a power workout tonight." He raised his hands and ran them through all that gorgeous hair, then dropped them to the sides of her face. "You get to me, Molly. You make it hard to breathe, make my heart pound."

She smiled. "Want to come to bed?"

Okay. Yep. This has to be a dream. A five-star dream.

"I can't." He grimaced. Was that his lips and tongue forming those words?

"No?"

He scrubbed both hands over his face, certain the man-card cops would arrive any second to confiscate his, but it couldn't be helped. "Jax will be up soon, and my brothers and I have a thousand things to do today. I could use a couple more kisses, though, before I head into the dark."

Two turned to three, then four. She tasted like chocolate ice cream and Molly, and the need for her grew till he ached.

He lost the battle. She lost the ugly sweatshirt.

The sun was peeking through the trees when she walked him downstairs.

He laced his fingers with hers and pressed a kiss to her forehead. "Thanks for the ice cream."

"You're welcome—anytime."

All tousled and sexy, Molly stood in the doorway as he pulled out. He revved his bike, waved, and drove off into the early morning.

Maybe she'd think about him…and forget that list of hers. Those blasted three years.

It hit him like a brick. The problem between them had nothing to do with the list. Unfortunately, the problem was bigger than that. It was all about trust. Molly needed to learn to trust before she could accept love.

Chapter 20

BRANT'S BROTHERS GAVE MISTY BOTTOMS ALMOST TWO weeks, turning the interior of their new building on its head while simply sprucing up the outside, since the original exterior suited their business perfectly. They added the paint booth as a separate building and extended the original bays to fit their needs. A few changes to the front office left it vintage, yet efficient.

"We got a lot done," Tucker said.

They stood in the parking lot, studying their handiwork.

"Still a heck of a lot to do, though," Brant mumbled.

"It'll come."

"Not tonight." Gaven kicked at a pebble. "It's time we come up for air. Other than a trip to visit Lainey last weekend, we've been doggin' it."

"What do you have in mind?" Brant rubbed his jaw and realized he needed a shave. Badly.

"I thought we could get a poker game together."

"The three of us?" Tucker asked.

"No, let's invite Beck and Cole. Sam's back from his honeymoon, so he might be able to make it."

"I don't know." Tucker took another look at the shop. "If you ask me, I say we rip into that lift and get it running."

Gaven scowled. "You know what, Bro? You've turned into a stick-in-the-mud. What happened? Those Marines take all the fun out of you?"

Brant stepped in before things turned ugly. "Tell you what. A night off will do us all good, and another few hours won't make much difference. We'll have the game here, show off our shop."

"I don't know."

"Come on, Tucker. Lighten up."

The look Tucker sent his youngest brother reminded Brant that Tucker had seen things, done things in battle they could only guess at. Maybe the Marines and his tours of duty *had* taken the fun out of their older brother.

If so, they'd have to help him find it again.

Brant glanced at the clock. "I need to pick the kid up by five. By then, it'll be time to stop anyway, since you guys plan to hit the road tomorrow morning."

"See?" Gaven looked at Tucker. "Told you."

"Cut it out, brat. Nobody likes a bad winner." Before Gaven even saw it coming, Tucker had him in a head-lock and was giving him a Dutch rub.

Brant shook his head. "I'll give the guys a call. See if they're free to play with you kids tonight."

It turned out all three were not only free, but eager for a guys' night out.

Cole said he'd bring a couple of card tables and some chairs, and Sam offered to pick up the pizzas, since he had to drive right by Mama's on his way. Beck would furnish dessert, courtesy of his wife's bakery.

Gaven ran home to shower before running in to town for ice, beverages, cards, and chips.

That left Brant and Tucker to sweep up ten layers of dust and debris. Earlier, Brant had anchored temporary sheets of plywood over the pits so nobody would tumble into one accidentally. It would be safe tonight for both the guys and Jax.

Keeping Jax corralled, though, would be tough.

Brant leaned on his industrial-sized broom. "Everything okay, Tuck?"

"Yeah, but Gaven's right. I do need to lighten up. There's a lot going on. And with Mom and Lainey…" He shook his head. "I'm not telling you anything you don't know."

"I'm not gonna give you a pat answer, that everything will be okay," Brant said. "But I will tell you this. We'll get through it. We're Wylders, and that's what we do."

"You're right."

"Nothing else bothering you?"

Tucker looked him straight in the eye. "I won't lie, Bro. I'm workin' real hard to delete some footage from the last few years. If nothing else, maybe I can archive it." He tapped his watch. "Right now, you'd better get into town and spring the kid."

"Fine, but if I stop, so do you. The guys know this place is a work in progress. Why don't you run to the house and get cleaned up? Jax and I'll stop off on our way so I can catch a shower. Otherwise, nobody'll want to get near me."

"I was gonna mention that," Tucker said.

"Hah! You don't smell like a rose yourself."

Tucker sniffed. "Got you." He grabbed Brant's broom and carried it with his to the corner. "We're out of here."

Still in uniform, Sam strolled in, carrying two big boxes from Mama's Pizza and Wings. The rich smell of tomato sauce had everybody's mouth watering by the time he set them on the office counter.

"Maybe we should eat first," Gaven said, "before the pizza gets cold."

"I'll second that," Beck added quickly. "We were busy at the lumberyard. No lunch."

While they ate, Jax sat on Sam's lap, licking sauce from his finger. "You know, Brant, tonight might have been a mistake."

"Why?"

He nodded at Beck and Cole. "When I started dating Cricket, the guys invited me to a poker game at Cole's. I wasn't sure what was being served up that night, pizza or me."

"Hey," Beck said, "Cricket's my cousin. It's my job to watch out for her. Strange guy comes into town, messing with our girls…" His gaze swiveled to Brant.

"See? What'd I tell you?" Sam took another bite of pizza, then gave Jax a piece of crust to gum to death.

"Okay, I won't play dumb, but Molly and I aren't dating."

Sam simply raised a brow.

Gaven nudged Brant in the ribs. "If you're not dating her, can I ask her out?"

"What?"

"If you and Molly—"

"I heard you."

"Then why'd you ask? So, can I? She's hot."

"Only if you want that pretty face of yours rearranged, little brother."

Sam and Beck grinned at each other.

"Let's play cards." Tucker started shuffling the deck.

"Have a seat, gentlemen, and open those wallets. I'm ready to take your money."

They played quietly for a bit as everyone settled into the game. Brant had hauled Jax's swing to the shop, but instead of using it, the guys took turns holding him. He passed from one lap to another, enjoying the male attention and trying to eat the cards.

Finally, Gaven said, "Maybe I'll ask Lucinda out."

Brant smacked him upside the head. "Leave her alone. She takes care of Jax. Don't mess it up."

Jax, hearing his name, started babbling.

"You like Lucinda, don't you?" Gaven took the baby from Beck.

"So do I." Brant tossed a card onto the table. "That doesn't mean I have to date her."

"Quinlyn?" Gaven asked.

Tucker rolled his eyes. "I'll see your bet, Sam."

<hr>

Early the next morning in the fog-shrouded yard, Gaven and Tucker tossed their duffels into the pickup.

"That does it," Gaven said. "Ready to roll. Don't forget to call Quinlyn today about a house."

"I won't."

Gaven shot a glance at Brant. "That's what you said last week and the week before that."

"Been kind of busy."

"Me too, but I managed to buy a house," Tucker reminded him.

"Still can't believe you did that."

"When I see what I want, I grab it." Tucker sent him a loaded look. "You might keep that in mind."

Brant narrowed his eyes. "We still talkin' about houses?"

"Not necessarily."

Gaven grinned. "God, I love you two. Take care of my nephew, Brant."

"You know it."

The brothers slapped each other on the back in man hugs.

"Drive safe," Brant said.

"Will do."

With that, they hopped in and drove off.

Brant stood alone in the mist, thinking how much life had changed in a very short time. When Jax's cries carried through the open window, he headed inside. Once again, the full responsibility for both the baby and the new shop rested with him.

When he'd power-washed the concrete outside the station the other day, he'd noticed a handprint with "Little Billy" inscribed beneath it. Since then, he'd been playing with the idea of pouring a new pad for Jax's handprints.

Today seemed as good a time as any. Lucinda wouldn't mind if Jax was late.

The morning was beautiful, and Jax seemed to understand he'd earned a short reprieve. They stopped by Tansy's and had breakfast, everyone making a fuss over the smiling baby.

With a bag of concrete from Elliot's Lumberyard in the trunk, and fueled by great coffee and an even better cinnamon roll from Sweet Dreams, Brant pulled into the old station. Jax bounced and chatted in his seat while Brant framed up the pad and mixed and poured the concrete.

"Okay, brat, ready to do this?"

Jax blew bubbles and grinned.

"I'll take that for a yes."

He had to smooth the concrete three times before they got it right. Every time he spread the baby's hand in the mix, Jax curled his fingers and grabbed a fistful. Finally, though, they got the job done.

Brant wiped the worst of the goo off the little hand with an old grease rag, then rinsed the rest with a bottle of water. Crouched, the baby straddling one leg, Brant carefully wrote *Jax Wylder* in the still-wet mix, along with the date. "We'll send a picture of this to your mama, okay?"

Jax raised his chubby little hand and patted Brant's face.

He'd just started to stand when he heard the old truck coming up the road. Sam DeLuca. "Looks like we've got company."

Sam pulled up, his windows down and Hobo perched in the middle of the bench seat. A teenage boy sat on the passenger side, one arm resting on the doorframe.

Sam opened his door, and the dog followed him out.

"Sam, Hobo." Brant knelt and patted the old dog, while the baby ruffled his fur.

Sam nodded at Jax. "What are you up to, kid? Aren't you supposed to be in school?" Then he waved a hand at the gangly teen leaning on the truck's tailgate. "This is Jeremy Stuckey, the young man I mentioned earlier."

Brant held out a hand. "Nice to meet you, Jeremy."

The teenager shook his hand. "Sir."

"It's Brant. We don't stand on ceremony here."

The kid nodded.

"Jeremy's a senior this year." Sam tousled the boy's too-long hair. "Since he's got today off, too, thanks to a teacher planning day, I figured it would be a good time for you to meet."

"Hah! You wanted to get me out of bed on one of the few days I could sleep in," Jeremy groused. But the quick grin he threw Sam told Brant these two had a solid relationship.

Sam's gaze skimmed over the station. "Like I said before, if you need an extra hand, this guy's the one to lend it."

"I can sure as heck strip wallpaper faster than Deputy Dawg here."

"Ouch," Sam said. "Is this how you repay me?"

"You lost the bet, remember? Cost you one of Mama's pizzas!"

"You're hired," Brant said.

Jeremy's mouth dropped open. "Just like that?"

"Just like that, but"—he held up a finger—"I've got a couple stipulations."

"Should've figured that."

Brant laughed. "They're easy ones. Necessary ones. First, you've got to stay in school, and you have to keep up your grades."

"You sound like my mom," the boy grumbled.

"Maybe, but I'll bet she's prettier than me."

The corner of Jeremy's mouth kicked up. "She is. A whole lot."

"That's a relief," Brant said. "The other thing? If you get swamped, have a big project or a test, or start to fall behind, you tell me. Right away. We'll adjust your work schedule till you get things back together."

He met Sam's eyes over the kid, who'd leaned down to scratch Hobo's ears. The glance expressed gratitude on the deputy's part. Clearly, Sam thought the world of the kid, and that was enough for Brant.

After Sam and Jeremy left, Brant did a quick diaper change, then turned on the old CD player. Carrie Underwood's voice filled the room, and Jax danced in his seat. The kid loved her almost as much as he loved the Barrett-Jackson auctions.

"Tell you what, champ. Since you're happy, why don't I tackle these old shelves, get them off the wall and out of here?" He grabbed his tool belt from the car, moved Jax to the far corner of the room, and got busy.

Not ten minutes later, another car slowed and pulled in, and he glanced out the bay window. Molly.

Brant freed Jax from his seat and strolled outside. He opened her car door, stealing a quick kiss as she got out. The woman definitely revved his engine.

"Ooh, look at you." She placed a hand over her heart and made patting motions. "A sweaty man wearing a tool belt and holding a baby. I should grab my camera. This on a poster? I'd make a fortune."

He laughed and swiped at the sweat on his brow. "Right."

Jax started kicking and jabbering.

"Hi, baby. Come here, sweetheart." Molly held out her hands, and Jax squirmed his way into them. Rescuing her sunglasses from his busy fingers, she planted smacking kisses on his face and arms, making him laugh out loud. "Why aren't you in school, huh? Are you playing hooky, Jax Wylder?"

"I called him in late. We had an important project." Brant made a follow-me wave and walked her over to the new concrete pad. "What do you think?"

Molly stared down at the tiny handprint and blinked back tears. "Brant, this is…" She swallowed. "It's so perfect. What a guy."

"Perfect enough to earn me a kiss?"

"Totally." Holding the baby, she rose on tiptoe and met Brant's lips.

Jax wanted nothing to do with it and, arms flailing, smacked them both in the face.

Laughing, they pulled apart.

Molly reached into her pocket for her phone. "Kneel beside it with Jax."

Sighing, he did as she said. "I'd planned to do this, but hadn't got to it yet."

After a quick tickle, Jax rewarded him with a huge grin.

"Great," Molly said. "I'll share it with you, and you can send it to Lainey."

"Consider it done. Thanks." Brant rose.

"I passed Sam on my way here."

"Yeah, he brought Jeremy out to meet me. He's gonna give me a hand after school."

"That'll be good for both of you." She traced the toe of her shoe over a patch of grass. "Will you replant this area?"

"I don't know yet. I might pave the whole front."

"Seriously?"

"It's a business, Mol."

"I know, but it should still look pretty."

His brow arched, but he said nothing.

"Do what you need to do," she conceded. "I heard Tucker and Gaven were leaving this morning and wondered if you might want some company. I see, though, you've got some." Jax sucked his thumb industriously. She lifted the hem of his shirt and wiped drool from his chin. "He's got a tooth coming in. You ought to pick up a teething ring, one you can toss in the freezer. It'll make his sore gums feel better. And maybe get some gel to rub on them."

"I'll do that when I run him in to day care. How do you know all this?"

"Baby showers—a font of information."

"I was gonna call you a little later. You busy tonight?"

Unconsciously, she raised a hand to her heart. "No."

"Up for dinner, maybe a little necking?"

Heat raced across her face. "I think I can manage that."

"I've got a sitter for the kid, so we'll take my bike. Dress casually."

"Your motorcycle? Really?"

―⁓―

When Molly heard the deep rumble of the Harley, her heart gave a quick kick. She'd tried explaining her strong attraction to Brant Wylder on the situation he'd found himself in. Argued it was Jax. That it was Lainey.

It wasn't.

It was the man himself, and she had no clue what to do about it.

Her feelings for Keith were a faint shadow of the emotions this Wylder brother triggered.

Today at the station? What a picture he'd made standing there in his tool belt with Jax in his arms. Add in the scent of a man who'd been working hard, the heat, and fresh drywall studs and sawdust. Both kinds of studs. *Whew*.

Hurrying to the window with Bubbles scurrying behind her, Molly peeked out. Brant removed his helmet, and she watched him absently rake his fingers through his thick, disheveled hair. She envied those snug-fitting jeans and the leather jacket that wrapped itself around him.

Glancing down at her own outfit, she decided she'd chosen well. This time of the year evenings grew cool, and according to the weatherman, it would dip into the high forties tonight. She'd gone with jeans and a red cotton sweater with low boots. Since they'd be on the Harley, she'd pulled her hair back in a high ponytail.

The doorbell chimed, and Bubbles scrambled beneath the bed. Molly grabbed her leather jacket and hurried down the stairs, her heart thumping.

Brant leaned in for a kiss the second the door opened. "You sure do smell good." He nuzzled her neck.

She laughed. "The necking comes later. A motorcycle ride and dinner are the first items on tonight's agenda."

"You sure are bossy."

"Best you remember that." Then she grabbed the lapels of his jacket and drew him back to her, her lips brushing across his. "You smell very, very good yourself, Mr. Wylder. Very male. Very sexy."

"Keep that up, and dinner is gonna get bumped right off those plans."

"Uh-uh. I'm hungry, and you promised to feed me."

"Okay, then." He took her hand and led her to the bike. "I'm assuming you've ridden before."

"Not nearly enough."

He stared at her through hooded eyes. "You know, you keep gettin' closer and closer to my idea of the perfect woman."

She laughed. "I'm so far from perfect, the dart doesn't even hit the board."

"You play darts?"

"I've been known to."

"Like I said…" He handed her a helmet. "Will it fit over your hair?"

"You bet." She pulled it on and buckled the strap.

He straddled the bike and steadied it while she slid on behind him.

Wrapping her arms around him, she leaned forward and snuggled in for the ride. Oh, she could get used to this…and that was the problem, wasn't it?

Well, she'd think about that later.

"Ready?" He glanced in the rearview mirror.

"More than."

He started the machine and revved the engine, and they shot off into the night.

The sun had set, and as they headed out of town, Molly had the feeling she and Brant were the only two people on Earth. Cool air rushed past, and she wanted to throw her arms up and shout for joy. Instead, she simply smiled and snuggled closer.

She hadn't even asked where they were going.

It didn't matter.

—⁓—

Brant figured he could ride like this forever. The evening enveloped Molly and him, and he felt free and young again. He needed this far more than he'd realized.

Why hadn't he thought of a sitter before now?

Up ahead, he caught sight of the little Italian mom-and-pop restaurant he'd spotted on one of his trips to Savannah. As he pulled into the parking lot, he noticed it was nearly full. Since it almost always was, he took that for a sign the food would be worth the drive.

The minute he opened the door, his hand on Molly's back, he knew he'd been right. The rich tomato scent of good sauce, garlic, and warm bread teased him. Soft lighting and quiet music completed the picture.

"I already love it," Molly whispered.

A young blond bounced up to them, menus in hand. "Welcome to Grandma Annie's. Have you been here before?"

"Nope," Brant answered. "This is our first time."

"You're in for a treat," their greeter chirped.

"If the food tastes half as good as it smells, I'm sure we are."

Seating them, she said, "Brenda will be right with you."

"Thanks."

Brant passed on the wine, and so did Molly. That bit of understanding got to him. Molly Stiles, beautiful inside and out.

After they ordered, she dipped a slice of warm, crusty

bread into the herbed olive oil. "Mmm, taste." She held it toward Brant.

His eyes never leaving hers, he took a bite. "Oh yeah. Even if nothing else is edible, this makes the trip worthwhile."

"I never did ask who's babysitting tonight."

"Kitty. I stopped by Sweet Dreams the other day, and she offered to watch Jax if I needed a night out. I did. With you."

With a sly smile, she said, "You managed to sneak out a time or two while your brothers were in town."

"Yeah, I did." The memory sent his pulse racing. "Kitty's husband dropped her off on his way to a meeting, and I'll take her home. She offered to drive, but that's a dark, lonely stretch of road for a woman alone. What she really wants is a ride home on my bike. I warned her it's gonna be cold, but she insists she has a coat and not nearly enough adventure."

"Sounds like Kitty."

When their platter of fried zucchini arrived, they both dove in.

"My dad called this morning."

"Oh yeah?" Had her father mentioned their trip to Clary's? Uneasy, he asked, "What'd he want?"

"It was the strangest thing. He asked how things were going, and I told him the shop had been busy this week." Her brows knitted together. "He said that was nice, but how was *I* doing?"

"That's good, isn't it?"

A slow smile curved her lips. "Very."

His world righted, and he speared another zucchini slice, leaned across the table, and fed it to her.

Molly actually groaned when Brenda returned, placing an overflowing plate of spaghetti in front of her. "I'll hate myself in the morning."

"Eat what you want and leave the rest," Brant said.

That's exactly what she did.

Over coffee and a shared tiramisu, Brant grew serious. "Mol, we need to talk about us."

"Us?"

"Yeah." He circled his hand. "When this whole thing between you and me started, my time in Misty Bottoms was limited to a couple days, in and out, although I'd be lying if I didn't admit to wanting you the first time I saw you." His lips quirked in a half grin at her surprised expression. "And yes, that would be the night of the infamous bouquet toss."

Molly simply stared at him with those huge eyes.

He sipped his coffee, then set it down again. "Then I found myself back in town—and thinking I might be staying. When I saw you again, I thought I'd steal a dance, maybe a couple kisses. I'd hoped for more but didn't figure that would be very smart."

Tapping his fingers on the table, he said, "Now? Here we are, both of us living in Misty Bottoms and, if I'm not reading things wrong, enjoying each other. Very much. So, yeah. It might be a good idea to talk about us."

Brant read the nerves in Molly. Her easy expression faded, and her mouth opened as though she wanted to speak but didn't know what to say.

He reached for her hand, but she pulled it away and dropped it in her lap.

"Brant, I'm sorry. I'm confused."

He regretted bringing up the subject. Still he said,

"You had to have known we'd get to this talk sooner or later."

In a quiet voice, she said, "Let's not spoil tonight."

"Fair enough. You ready to hit the road?"

"I am."

He signaled for the check.

Halfway across the parking lot, Brant hesitated. "The logistics of getting everyone home's a little more complicated than I'd originally thought. I'd planned to drop you off, then go back to the house and pick up Kitty and Jax. If I take her home on my motorcycle, though—"

"I've already had my ride, so I'll stay with Jax, then you and he can deliver me home in your car." She looked at him sideways. "And you can pray Jax falls back asleep after all that."

"Being a single parent is tough. Puts a big dent in my love life."

She chuckled, and he figured they were back on steady footing. Nothing had been gained, but nothing had been lost, either.

Right there in the parking lot, he pulled her in and kissed her till he ached. "I can't begin to tell you how much I love that mouth of yours."

He kissed the tip of her nose, then dropped another on the top of her head. "I want you, Molly."

What scared him to his very soul was the niggling suspicion that having her physically, no matter how many times, wouldn't be enough. Somehow or other she'd worked herself under his skin. Inside his head. Into his heart?

Molly stood in the open doorway as Brant drove away with a bundled-up Kitty, her arms wrapped tightly around him, hooting and hollering in glee. Good thing Brant had no close neighbors.

"Kitty's on her way home, Jax, and you need to go nighty-night."

Even though Brant had pulled in quietly, the baby had heard them and woke. They'd caught Kitty on her way to the makeshift nursery when they crept in.

"How about some nice, warm milk?" Molly asked.

"Bababa."

"Great." She yawned. It had been a long day, and tomorrow would be another.

Bottle prepared, she carried both it and Jax to the rocker. It didn't take long to realize he was more interested in playing than sleeping, though. She glanced toward the bedroom. Maybe if they lay down, he'd fall asleep more easily. She didn't want Brant to come home to a fussy baby, although right now, Jax seemed perfectly content. They'd have to take him back out, but since he slept well in cars, it might be okay.

She toed off her boots and settled on the bed with Jax cuddled against her. Within minutes he was asleep. Soft moonlight played around the curtain's edges. That, mixed with the baby's quiet breathing, soothed her. It had been a nice evening—until Brant turned serious. About them. She didn't want to go there, didn't want to think about the future.

Things were good between them, easy and unassuming. Why analyze their relationship or try to make it more? He took care of his family, yes. They all counted on him. But could she? What if he lost interest in her and walked away?

She refused to live an echo of her mother's life.

———∿∿∿———

Brant let himself into the nearly dark house. Darned if he hadn't enjoyed his trip into town with Kitty. The woman must have given her husband one heck of a ride all these years, and Brant wouldn't be the least bit surprised if Harvey found himself in the market for another motorcycle. According to Kitty, it had been almost fifteen years since he sold his last one.

He whacked his knee on the corner of an end table and swore.

"Molly?"

No answer.

Taking off his shoes, he peeked into the baby's room. Empty. That left his bedroom.

Standing in the doorway, he rested a hand against the jamb. Sleeping Beauty was right there in his bed, her incredible hair spread over his pillow and his nephew tucked in the crook of her arm, his little head resting on her breast.

For the first time in his life, Brant found himself thinking of forever, and the lady wasn't interested. The irony didn't escape him.

For all of two seconds, he considered waking her. He eyed the couch, then turned back to Molly. Too tempting to resist. He pulled a blanket from the linen closet and covered her and Jax. Giving up the fight, he lay down on the other side of the baby.

In that moment, all was right in his world.

~~~

Molly woke slowly as a ray of early-morning sunshine kissed her cheek with its gentle warmth.

As her mind engaged, she recognized the sound beside her: a baby's happy gurgling. Smiling, she opened her eyes and found herself face-to-face with a babbling baby and a very sexy, heavy-eyed, five-o'clock-shadowed Brant.

"Good morning, beautiful." His voice, husky with sleep, touched her heart.

She was hip-deep in quicksand and sinking deeper by the minute.

"Good morning, Brant. You should have woken me last night." She grimaced. "I didn't mean to steal your bed."

"You didn't. We all fit just fine. And for the record?" His beautiful green eyes penetrated her soul. "You're welcome in my bed anytime."

"Brant—"

"Just puttin' it out there."

She sighed, her emotions too scattered to speak. Peering at the clock on his nightstand, she blinked in surprise. She still had several hours before she opened her shop.

Brant's gaze followed hers, then returned to her face.

He reached out to play with her hair, and her stomach fluttered.

"With you here in my bed, I can think of so many ways to start the day." He tipped his chin at the squirmy baby. "He negates every single one."

"A shame, isn't it?"

"Oh yeah." His hand roamed down her neck, over

her shoulder. "Let me at least feed you before I take you home. This one needs a diaper change and some food, too. Not quite as easy to hop out of bed and go as it used to be."

"No, I don't suppose it is. Why don't you let me change Jax while you make coffee?"

"An offer I can't refuse." Propping himself up on an elbow, he leaned over the baby to drop an easy kiss on her lips, then rolled out of bed.

By the time she'd given Jax a quick bath and dressed him, Brant had her coffee poured and breakfast started.

She picked up her cup and breathed in the rich aroma before taking a drink. "Do you mind if I take a quick shower?"

"Not at all. Want company?"

"Not this time."

Brant's spatula clattered onto the counter. "Does that imply you will the next time?"

She sent him a saucy grin. Coffee in hand, she left the room.

———

Her freshly shampooed hair slicked back in another ponytail, she moved into the kitchen. "Smells good."

Brant had set the table and placed a jelly jar full of wildflowers in the center.

"Breakfast *and* flowers. Wow."

"That's me. Mr. Romantic."

She snorted.

"Did you hear that, Jax?" He held up the baby. "We braved the cold and hunted high and low for those flowers, but does she appreciate them?" He shook his head in mock disdain. "Women. You can never make them happy. Remember that."

Molly gasped. "You can't tell him things like that."

"Sure I can. I just did." He belted the baby into his high chair and bent down to his eye level. "You want the truth, right?"

Jax let out a delighted shriek and banged a rattle on the tray.

Brant met Molly's eyes. "See?"

She simply shook her head.

"I think Molly's upset with us."

The baby giggled.

Molly pulled out a chair and sat down. "I'll forgive you if I can have another cup of coffee and a couple slices of that bacon."

As she ate, she prayed no one would be peeking out of their store windows to witness her walk of shame this morning. Even if she told the truth, who'd believe it?

Yeah, she and Brant spent the night together. In the same bed. But there'd been no sex. Not even a good-night kiss.

How pathetic was that?

Chapter 21

BRANT DROVE MOLLY HOME AND LEFT HER AT THE DOOR with a less-than-chaste kiss.

It had been unbelievable to wake up beside her, to share breakfast and a few morning kisses. He'd do it again tomorrow morning if she would let him, but she'd made her feelings pretty clear on that.

Jax had been dropped at day care, Lainey was doing well and had loved yesterday's picture, and Tucker called to say their mother was making amazing improvement with the new physical therapist. With the help of a cane, she was walking, and her speech was close to normal.

Brant's family was healing.

Which meant he had no excuses for putting off work. He made a quick stop at Elliot's to pick up a few supplies, then at Tommy's for gas and another coffee.

The smell of the ham biscuits Tommy's wife made was impossible to resist. "I'll take two, Tommy. They'll be lunch. Save me a trip into town later." He added a couple of bottles of cold water.

The train that ran through town sounded its lonely whistle. At one time, it would have been invaluable to Misty Bottoms, connecting it to the rest of the world. Now it had become nearly irrelevant.

Kind of sad, but things changed. So did feelings.

He thought of Molly.

Yep. Feelings changed. By leaps and bounds.

And sometimes a fellow wrestled with what he was supposed to do about that.

——◄◊◊►——

Tucker had drawn up a schematic showing exactly where he wanted the bay area's shelves and precisely what size went where. Brant decided to tackle them.

Up to his armpits in sawdust and brackets, he heard, over the sound of his drill, the front door open and close.

Spitting out the screw he held between his lips, he called out, "Not open yet."

"I know that."

Brant recognized the voice of the station's former owner. "Hey, glad you stopped by."

"Got coffee?"

"Give me time, old man."

"That's right. Respect your elders." Frank chuckled.

"I do. Nice business you ran here, and my brothers and I thank you for taking such good care of the building."

"I like you, son," the guy mumbled.

"See you're still wearing your old service-station shirt."

"Why not? I've got a closetful, and my wife keeps them cleaned and pressed. Speaking of my wife, I almost forgot. She'd have had my hide."

Holding up a finger, he moseyed out to his old Buick, then came back carrying a plate. "Lettie baked you some oatmeal raisin cookies."

"What a minute. Lettie's your wife?"

"Sure is."

"Is she a seamstress?"

"Yep. None better. Works at the new bridal shop in town."

"Molly's shop."

"That's it. I told her she didn't need to work, but she claimed she wanted to get out of the house a bit."

Brant grinned. Yeah, she probably did.

Frank held up the plate. "Figured you wouldn't mind sharin' these. Gotta have coffee to go with cookies, though." Turning in a circle, he looked around the office. "Where's Rosie?"

"Who?"

"Rosie. Our coffeepot. That old gal kept us happy and in coffee three hundred sixty-five days a year." He tipped his head. "Well, guess I closed for Christmas and a few other days. Still…I don't see Rosie."

"She retired. Same day you did, Frank."

"Sorry to hear that. Don't see no replacement. What kind of a place you runnin', without coffee?"

Brant rubbed his chin. "See, that's the thing. We're not actually running anything yet. We're not open for business."

"But you're gonna have coffee, aren't ya?"

"We are. The next time you stop by, there'll be coffee. For now, how about a cold water?"

"Guess it'll have to do, won't it?"

Amusement flickered in Brant's eyes. "Guess so."

Frank spent the next little while poking around the garage and inspecting the changes. He pointed at the building out back. "What's that?"

"Our downdraft paint booth."

"Hmph. Why do you need it?"

"The cars we work on are pretty high-end, and our

customers expect—and get—as close to perfection as is humanly possible. That booth provides both dust and fume protection."

"Gotcha. Can I take a peek?"

"Sure." Brant thought about the shelves that wouldn't get hung today.

After Frank checked out their paint booth, he nodded toward Brant's Camaro. "Nice shape."

"Thanks."

"You take care of them, they'll take care of you. Kept Furlon Jennings's old Chevy runnin' way past its time. Thing threw fan belts like Sandy Koufax threw strikes, so I always kept one or two in stock." Frank rubbed his whiskered jaw. "I can lend a hand, if you need it. Show you boys how to install a muffler quicker than you can whistle 'Dixie.'"

"I'll give you a call if we run into something we can't handle." Brant managed to keep his expression neutral.

"Heard you're dating Molly Stiles. You be good to her."

"That's my plan."

With a nod, Frank sauntered toward his car. "You promised to have coffee next time I stop. We'll see how good you are at keepin' your word."

A loaded statement, if Brant had ever heard one.

Frank opened the Buick's door. "Don't work too hard."

Brant laughed. "Too late for me. Save yourself!"

"Think I will."

As Frank drove away, Brant realized that under all the good-old-boy stuff, he'd been warned. Old Frank cared more about Molly than her own father did. Maybe.

Instead of being pissed, Brant found himself pleased the old guy had decided to play protector.

He headed back to the bay and the pile of lumber, and despite the interruption, managed to finish the job. When he'd pounded in the last nail and tightened the last screw, he stood back to study the new shelves.

Tucker had done a darned good job with the design.

Brant needed a shower, but a glance at the clock told him it would have to wait. Locking the bays and front door, he wiped away the worst of the dust and headed into town to rescue Lucinda. Halfway there, he decided he'd make a quick stop to pick up a coffeepot. In case Frank came back with more cookies. In case he had to prove he was a man of his word.

He had the new Keurig unpacked and ready to go when Frank pulled in the next morning.

"See you kept your promise. On this, at least."

Brant hid his smile, then listened while Frank complained about all the new-fangled, fancy gadgets. It didn't stop him from accepting a coffee from the machine, though. After his first few sips, Brant handed him a tape measure.

"How about you run the dumb end for me? I need to figure my layout for the bottom cabinets in our storage area."

When they finished, Frank helped himself to a second coffee, then announced he had to make a post office run. Brant saw him off, then went back inside to hang a peg-board for their small tools.

Not two minutes later, another car pulled in. Brant

tossed his screwdriver on top of a banged-up filing cabinet. How was he expected to get anything done if Frank and half of Misty Bottoms stopped by for coffee and a chat every day?

Ready to bite off the intruder's head, he stopped, mouth half-open, as Molly slipped out of her car, looking fresh and tempting in a swingy black skirt and a long-sleeved lacy top that jump-started his engine.

He wiped his hands on an old oil-cloth and strolled out to meet her. "Hey, good-lookin'. What brings you here?"

She reached into the car and came out with two Sweet Dreams cups. "I thought you might be ready for a break."

All thoughts of work fled. "You bet I am." Ignoring the fact he'd already had enough caffeine, he took one of Tansy's specialty coffees. "Not working today?"

"I'm taking a breather while Lettie watches the shop for half an hour."

The day flirted with cool but had stayed just shy of uncomfortable. He held up a finger. "Hold on."

He ducked inside and came out with two raggedy stools. Plopping them into a small patch of sunshine, he wiped off the thin layer of dust with his hand and covered the seat with an old flannel shirt he kept at the station. "These aren't the greatest, but they're all I've got."

Then he swiped his dusty hand on the side of his worn jeans. He'd caught them on a nail and ripped a big hole in the right leg.

Giving Molly a sideways glance, he asked, "You bake?"

She looked affronted. "Of course."

"Frank, the guy I bought this place from? His wife is your Lettie."

"You're kidding. She never said a word."

"The woman makes a mean oatmeal raisin cookie."

"Lettie does everything well." Molly grinned. "You know why she wants to work?"

Brant laughed. "I do. To get away from Frank. I—" Frowning, he tipped his head to the side. "Hear that?"

"What?"

"Listen."

She grew quiet. A small, distressed sound broke the silence. "An animal."

"Yeah, one that's in trouble." He hopped off his stool and set down his coffee, then walked cautiously toward a stand of trees close to the two-lane road.

Molly was right behind him.

The yelps grew louder.

A yellow Labrador retriever pup was caught in a snarl of briars.

With a cry, Molly raced around Brant. "Oh, you poor, poor baby." She knelt beside the pup. "Help me get him loose."

Brant dropped to his knees and, with the help of a pocket knife, managed to free the pup. He lifted him, holding him one-handed.

Tears sparkled in Molly's eyes. "He's half-starved. His little ribs are showing. Oh, Brant, you have to keep him."

"I don't want a dog, Molly."

"But…"

"If I wanted a dog, it would be a hot dog, preferably a Sabrett's."

Her mouth dropped open. "You're awful!"

"No, I'm not. I love animals, but I've already got more than I can handle." He swung his free hand wide, indicating the shop, the land. "I have to get this place in shape. That's my business, my bread and butter. I'm living in a house that isn't mine and could use a little work, and I'm being *very* kind there. On top of that, I've got a baby who doesn't like to sleep, a sister in rehab for alcoholism, and a mother recovering from a stroke. And none of that's whining. It's fact. Period."

"Are you done?"

"Probably. You want a home for this pup?" He held it out. "Take him. He's yours."

Molly backed up a step. "I can't."

"Why not?"

She tapped his totally out-of-proportion paws. "He'll grow into those feet. I have a small apartment and no yard."

He simply stared at her.

"Come on, Brant. Bubbles wouldn't survive a puppy."

"I don't have a house."

"Yes, you do. Lem won't care." She laid a hand on the puppy's head and stared at Brant with sad eyes.

"I'm already cleaning up baby poo. Why would I want something else that's not housebroken?"

"I actually know the answer to that," Molly said.

"Oh, you do, do you?"

"Yes. Research shows a pet nurtures a child's EQ."

"His EQ?"

"Emotional quotient, how well he's developing. Kids need pets."

"Lainey won't take it when she comes for the runt."

"Probably not, but by then I don't think you'll want her to."

"You're wrong. Molly, I can't." His gut ached. "I lost Henry, my collie, a few months ago. He kept me company for fifteen years, first at the house, then as our shop dog. I can't go through that again."

With a sigh, he set the puppy down in the grass.

He tripped over Brant's foot, skidded, and fell, whimpering.

Molly cried out.

Brant stood, head back. What difference would it make to take in one more stray? He plucked it up and got a quick swipe of stinky dog tongue in thanks.

Molly wrapped an arm around his waist and buried her head in his shoulder. "Thank you. I knew you wouldn't let him die."

"You're being melodramatic."

"No, I'm not. He'd have starved or been hit by the first car to come along."

"We'll make him the new shop dog. What do you say to that, Lug Nut?"

"Lug Nut? What kind of a name is that?"

"It's spot-on. If he's gonna work at the shop, he needs a name that fits. Unless you want to take him with you." He held out the dog again. "In that case, you can name him anything you want. If he stays here, it's my call."

"Fine. I'm sure the name will make sense to somebody."

"It absolutely will." He frowned. "Do you think he'll get along with Jax?"

"You'll have to watch them, but Labs are great with kids."

"I must be insane." Closing in on the shop, he placed the dog at his feet again. Two steps, and Lug Nut somehow managed to step on his own ear, tumbling head over heels. Brant jammed his hands in his pockets. "Guess this means another trip to town, for dog supplies. Between the pup and the baby, I'm gonna be penniless."

"I'll buy what you need. I'm the one who talked you into keeping him."

"Nah. I'll pick it up on my way to day care, but he needs a bath before Jax starts chewing on him." The pup's needle-sharp teeth caught the hem of Brant's jeans, and he backed up, growling and shaking his head.

Reaching down, Brant pulled him loose. "This should be fun. Which of you will win the chewing game? Of course, Jax has no teeth yet, so he'll probably just pull your ears off."

"What?"

"I'm kidding, Molly! Have you no sense of humor?"

She met his gaze. "No."

"What am I going to do with you?"

"I ask myself that all the time."

He chuckled. "Come by tonight. With a kid and a new pup, I can't leave. Take pity on me."

"I'll bring dinner."

―⁓―

When Molly got back to the store, she sent Lettie off to have lunch and run some errands. Almost instantly, she regretted it. A group of five friends had driven up from the city, and they came ready to shop. She sold them lingerie, jewelry, and shoes.

They'd barely left when the door opened again to

a newly engaged woman and her mother. The bride and her fiancé had booked Magnolia House for their upcoming wedding, and Amy hoped to buy her dress in Misty Bottoms.

She rejected the first one before Molly even had it zipped. Five dresses later, the bride fell in love with an ivory tulle mermaid gown with a court train, appliqués, and pearl beading. Lettie returned in time to discuss the necessary alterations.

When five o'clock finally rolled around, Molly was for once happy to lock up.

A woman on a mission, she stopped at the store and bought a teething ring in case Brant had forgotten. She also grabbed a small rawhide bone to give Lug Nut something to chew on besides Brant's jeans.

Then she ran into Dee-Ann's to pick up dinner. She'd hoped to sneak upstairs to put something together, but since that didn't happen, she'd called in an order.

"Hi, Dee-Ann."

"Had a busy day, did you?"

"And how."

"Well, your dinner's all ready. There's meat loaf and mashed potatoes, with an extra scoop for Jax. I put the gravy in a separate container, so you can add it yourself."

"Thank you!"

"Everything will travel well, and you can heat it up in the microwave," Dee-Ann said. "There're two big slices of coconut cake, too. Tell that man of yours I said hello."

"Oh, but—"

The bell in the kitchen rang.

"Gotta go. That's the pastor's order, and he's in a hurry tonight."

Bags in hand, Molly stepped outside. Her man? Brant wasn't her man. He couldn't be.

She headed to his house, her mind moving faster than the car.

He'd been right today. His plate was heaped until she didn't know how he kept it all from tumbling off.

But he wasn't the only one with a lot going on.

After the busy afternoon, she'd run upstairs to change and found the message light blinking. Her dad. Guilt nagged over not returning his call.

She would tomorrow and give him a run-down on the business and do what she could to ease his mind about her ability to repay the loan on time.

This thing with Brant was even more unsettling.

Now that he was living and working here, things had changed. They no longer had a preset expiration date. And when they did finally call it quits—and didn't the idea of that make her want to hop into bed and pull the covers over her head—it would suck big time.

In a town the size of Misty Bottoms, they'd run into each other constantly. Brant would eventually find someone else and settle down. Make babies.

Taking a turn too fast, she watched their food bag slide across the seat. She slowed and willed it not to tip over.

It didn't, and she let out a big breath.

Her mind churned out another thought. Maybe, after his stint with Jax, he'd decide on a life of chastity, unwilling to risk a baby.

She groaned. What a waste that would be, like locking away a national treasure. Maybe she'd experience a little of that national treasure after the baby went down for the night.

Ugh! She slapped herself on the forehead. That was exactly the problem.

How could she ever walk away from Brant Wylder?

All the turmoil in her mind settled when she pulled up in front of Brant's and caught sight of him on the front porch. He sat in the old rocker, reading. Lug Nut was asleep at his feet, a teddy bear in his mouth, and Jax banged a rattle on his new swing.

She opened her car door, and Lug Nut woke with a start, tearing off the porch to greet her. Kneeling, she rubbed his ears, which Jax hadn't pulled off. "You look and smell a whole lot better than the last time I saw you, puppy."

Reaching inside the car, she pulled out the small bone and held it out to him. He dropped the bear and nipped the bone between his teeth. Then he wrestled with the bear, trying to get it in his mouth, too. Finally, he dropped to the ground where he was, paws on the bear, bone in his mouth.

"What's with Teddy?"

"Jax tossed it at him, and the scrawny little thing adopted it. I don't have the heart to take it from him." Brant stood. "Need help?"

"Nope, I've got this." She gathered the bags and held them up. "Not quite home-cooked, but…" She shrugged. "The shop got crazy busy. I sold a wedding gown."

"That's great, Mol."

"It is."

The pup abandoned the bear and scrambled up the steps ahead of her. Dropping his bone, he put his paws on the side of the swing and licked the baby's face. Jax leaned toward the dog and licked him back.

"That can't be hygienic," Brant grumbled.

"When you were a kid, I'll bet you had a dog lick your face," she said.

"That was different, and I darned well didn't lick the thing back."

Different. Yeah. So was her world a few weeks ago. What would it look like a few weeks, a few months, from now?

Lonely.

Chapter 22

Brant felt restless.

Last night's dinner with Molly had been fun. Their stolen kisses were excellent, but not enough to slake his hunger.

The rest of the evening? Frustrating. Jax hadn't wanted to sleep, and Molly'd gone home before things got serious, leaving him to a cold and solitary midnight shower. Not quite what he'd hoped for.

While Brant was practically inhaling his morning caffeine, Kemper Dobson called. He'd spoken with Jason and laid out how and when his child-support payments needed to be made. Afterward, Jason's father called their attorney, who confirmed that everything Dobson had outlined was correct.

At this point, Jason was straddling the fence. While he didn't want to give up his parental rights, neither did he want to assume the financial responsibilities of a father. He'd agreed Jax was where he needed to be right now and promised there'd be no more surprise visits, no more threats.

While Jason wasn't even close to what Brant wanted for his sister, he hoped they could work something out. He'd hate to have Jax find out someday that his own father wanted nothing to do with him.

Since he'd spent the whole day spinning his wheels, Brant hung it up early, picked up an ecstatic Jax from day care, and drove home. The temperature mild, Brant moved the playpen outside so he could keep an eye on the kid while he pruned a bush to let in more light.

Accepting that he really did need to find another house, he looked up when a vehicle rounded the corner.

Lem Gilmore swerved into the drive in a new Cadillac Escalade.

Lug Nut had been snoring, sprawled in the grass beside Jax's playpen. When Lem, dressed in bib overalls and a ragged Atlanta Braves cap over wispy gray hair, got out of the vehicle, the pup fell all over himself in his rush to greet this new person.

Lem crouched, his knees creaking. "Come here, little guy."

The puppy dropped onto his side and wriggled to work himself closer. Lem scowled at Brant. "This animal's nothing but skin and bones."

"You should have seen him yesterday. Molly and I found him alongside the road, tangled in some briars. I've put out some feelers, but nobody's claimed him." He laid the clippers on the porch and pulled off the leather gloves he'd bought at Beck's store. "Listen, if I've overstepped my bounds and you don't want a dog in your house…"

Lem raised his hand. "I've got no problem with that." He ruffled the dog's ears. "I'd love to have one myself."

"Want me to tie a bow around this one's neck?"

"Nope. Lyda Mae'd kick him and me both out to the garage. She's a good woman in every other way, but she's not a dog person."

Brant made an assenting sound. "Feel free to come visit him anytime you want."

"What's his name?"

"Lug Nut."

Lem smiled. "I like it." He stood and walked, more than a little bowlegged, toward the baby. "And look at you, young man."

Jax started jabbering. His ball cap was twisted to one side, and he wore a snazzy pair of red sunglasses.

Lem took one of the baby's tiny hands in his own gnarled one. "Lyda Mae'd eat you right up. Yes, she would." When the baby babbled back at him, Lem put a hand to one ear. "What's that? You want a cookie? Grow some teeth, boy." He chucked the baby under the chin. Stuffing his hands in the pockets of his overalls, he scuffed a foot through the grass. "Heard you were good with cars."

"You could say that." Here it came. The price of this *free* rental.

"Sam, the new cop in town, bought my truck."

"He used it to deliver some baby furniture to me."

Lem dropped onto the porch's edge and nodded toward the Cadillac. "That's our go-to-town car. Don't like to drive it much. Gives everybody the wrong idea."

Brant smothered his hoot of laughter. From everything he'd heard, Lem Gilmore, who enjoyed playing the down-on-his-luck card, could buy and sell the whole darned town. Sam had paid dearly for his rust-bucket truck with coffee, meals at Dee-Ann's, and trips to the dump with Lem. Still, Sam really liked the old guy.

And he'd put a roof over his and Jax's heads.

Time to pay the piper. "What do you need, Lem?"

"Bought myself a new truck." Lug Nut practically crawled into Lem's lap and earned himself another good rub. "Sam, now that he's working and he and Cricket got themselves hitched, doesn't have much time to haul me and my stuff around."

"Hmm." Brant remained noncommittal.

"Anyway, this truck's a beaut. You ought to see her. She's a '66 El Camino."

Brant whistled, genuinely impressed.

Lem grinned. "My friend Sid bought the thing new. Since he can't drive anymore, I bought it."

"Tell me you're not thinking about using it as a beater."

"Kind of."

"There are people who'd give their eyeteeth for that truck."

"That's what I hear." He swiped a hand over his day's growth of gray beard.

Brant dropped onto the front-porch steps, the puppy tugging at his shoe laces. "I'll provide the labor gratis. I owe you that for putting Jax and me up, but you'll need to pay for the parts."

Lem nodded. "Fair enough."

"Here's the thing, though. Right now, I don't have the tools to pull it off...or the space. The old garage isn't ready yet."

"I'm in no hurry."

"Then you've got yourself a deal." Brant stuck out a hand, and they shook.

He heard another car. Recognizing the Mini's engine, he smiled. *She'd* come to *him*. Again.

A hand on the railing, Lem slowly stood as Molly pulled behind his Cadillac. "Time for this old man to skedaddle. What with that wedding business of Jenni Beth's and all you young'uns moving into town, sure is a lot of romance in the air." He winked. "Might be time to steal my sweetheart away for a weekend in Savannah."

"Enjoy, and I'll let you know when we can start on your truck."

Lem walked to Molly's car, leaned in, and spoke to her. Then he straightened, waved to Brant, and left.

"Hello, beautiful," Brant called out.

Molly crossed the small yard, stopping to rub Lug Nut's belly. She plucked Jax from the playpen, kissed him, and sat down on the step beside Brant. "Thought I'd watch the sunset with you tonight."

———

Hard at work the next day, Molly heard a motorcycle. She peeked out the shop window, and there was Brant leaning against his Harley. He crooked a finger, and her pulse kicked into overdrive.

She opened the door.

"If you can take time for a quick picnic lunch, I've got one. Stopped at Schatzie's." He patted his saddlebag.

"Pastrami on rye?"

"You got it."

"Lettie—"

"Go on," Lettie said from behind her. She dropped her voice. "Get out of here. You don't want to resist that, even if you could." Louder, voice stern, she said, "Have her back by two thirty. She has an appointment."

"Yes, ma'am."

Instead of driving out of town, they picnicked in the town square. The Ladies' Garden Club had been busy, and the park was picture-perfect pretty. So was the day.

They sat side by side on the park bench and shared the deli sandwiches. "I need a couple of days off, Mol. I'm tired."

She shifted to face him.

"I thought I'd go home to Lake Delores for two or three days."

"You should."

"But?"

She laced their fingers. "I'll miss you."

"Come with me."

"What?"

"I know it's asking a lot, but is there any way you can clear your calendar for a few days? Lettie can take care of the shop, right? I want you to meet my mom and dad."

She blanched. "Meet your parents? Brant—"

"No, no. Not like that." He shook his head. "I haven't forgotten that blasted timeline of yours."

"It's not—"

He held up a hand. "That came out wrong. Sorry. You're important to me, Molly. They're important to me. I'd like you to meet each other. No strings, no obligations or expectations attached."

She shouldn't. She really shouldn't. "When are you leaving?"

"Tuesday. Since you're closed on Thursdays, you'd only need coverage for two days. It's about an eight-hour drive, although with Jax it might take longer. Cole offered to keep Lug Nut for me. They've already got animals, so it won't put them out too much. If we leave by seven, we can be there by midafternoon. That'll give us Tuesday evening and all day Wednesday with my folks. I'll pack some of the things I need from my house Thursday morning, then we can head back."

"I'll talk to Lettie this afternoon and check my appointments, see what I have coming up." She raised a hand to her lips. Whose mouth had those words spilled from?

Before she could take them back, Brant said, "Thank you." Packing up the remains of their lunch, he hustled her back to the bike. "Hop on. We still have some time, and I want to show you something."

Half a mile from town, he pulled up in front of an empty house.

On the back of the Harley, Molly sighed. "I love the wrap-around porch and those live oaks. Think of the shade they'll provide on a lazy summer afternoon. Perfect spot for a hammock."

"There's a gazebo out back and, the icing on the cake, a two-car garage."

"You're showing me this because…?" Molly asked.

"I rented it this morning, with an option to buy."

"You're kidding."

"Nope. It's in pristine shape, with hardwood floors and a great kitchen. Three bedrooms and two baths upstairs. And downstairs, there's a living, dining, and family room with a large fireplace and half bath. Plenty of space for Jax's things and for my parents, when they visit. But not a scrap of furniture."

"Ouch."

He shrugged. "While I'm in Lake Delores, I'll make arrangements with a moving company. I'm renting there, so no problem."

Molly felt the vise tighten.

Love and the vulnerability it created scared her. Her list had been her protective umbrella—until Brant poked it full of holes and made her see it for what it was: a faulty shield at best.

Chapter 23

A HARRIED-LOOKING BRANT KNOCKED AT MOLLY'S DOOR nearly half an hour late.

"You okay?" she asked, stepping out to meet him.

"I can't believe how much stress the idea of this eight-hour road trip is causing me."

"How bad can it be?"

"Oh, sugar, you have no idea. Both the back seat and trunk are packed with Jax's stuff. A stroller, a spray bottle—"

"Wait." Confused, she spread her hands. "A spray bottle?"

"In case his pacifier drops to the ground or even to the floor of the car. Or his bottle or teething ring. His hands might get sticky. I can use it to rinse them off."

She studied him with new respect. "Way to go, Daddy. I'd never have thought of that."

"Oh yeah, you would have. Given enough time around this guy, you'd have one of your own. A spray bottle, not a baby," he added quickly.

They'd reached the car and she leaned in to give Jax a kiss. "Good morning, sweetie."

He giggled and slapped his hands on the infant seat.

"So what other goodies has Unkie crammed in here with you?" She turned from the baby to Brant.

"Tons of plastic bags for dirty diapers, soiled outfits, used baby wipes. Some backup bottles ready to go, changes of clothes. Extra shoes and blankets. Toys, baby food, and juice. Crackers. Jax's clip-on white-noise-and-lullaby-music thingy." He leaned in and gave it a tap, then closed his eyes. "I have a veritable baby aisle packed in my Camaro."

"What's in the wide-mouth thermos?"

"I'd like to say something adult like tequila or even coffee." He grabbed the container and shook it. "But it's a couple of teething rings."

Her eyes widened. "Seriously? Smart man."

Sheepishly, he tossed the thermos on the seat. "I can't take credit for that. One of Dee-Ann's customers suggested it." Hands stuffed in his pockets, he sighed. "A few weeks ago, I'd have thrown an extra pair of jeans into a duffel along with a couple clean T-shirts, some skivvies, my toothbrush, and razor, and I'd have been good to go. Now? I spent half the night packing…and I still probably don't have everything I need."

"It'll be okay."

He met her eyes. "I sure as heck hope so. Lainey insists she's getting better, but what if she can't ever take him back?"

"She will."

Silently, he opened the car door for her, then moved around to the driver's seat.

Molly let the topic drop.

∼∿∼

Forty-some miles down the road, Jax grew fussy.

Half-turned in her seat, Molly talked to him, wound up his lullabies, and gave him a baby biscuit, which he ground to pulp. Nothing worked. He remained inconsolable.

"You need to stop, Brant."

"Yeah, I know. There's a roadside rest in a mile and a half."

After he parked, Molly volunteered to take the baby into the ladies' room with her. "He's wet. Maybe that's his problem."

A clean diaper didn't help, but as long as she held him, he was fine.

When she stepped out into the cool Southern day, Brant leaned against the car, feet crossed, waiting for her. The sight stopped her in her tracks. Dressed in jeans and a pale-green, long-sleeved T-shirt, dark glasses covering his incredible eyes, the man stole her breath.

She had it bad.

"Jax, I've got a hunch I'm never going to get your uncle out of my head…or my heart. And I'll bet you'll grow up to be every bit as handsome. Whose heart will you break?"

Reaching up, the baby laid a hand on her cheek. His little face serious, he babbled nonstop to the car.

"Sounds like you two are having quite the conversation." Brant straightened and moved to open the back door. "You talkin' about me?"

Molly's eyes widened. Did the man have ESP or had he bugged Jax's seat?

"Food. We were talking about food," she blurted. "Should we feed him before we go?"

"Yeah." Brant checked his watch. "We're on that proverbial slow boat to China."

"I know, but—"

"Yeah. But." He slid the diaper bag from her shoulder. "There're a couple of jars in here. You think it's warm enough to feed him outside?"

"I do. He's dressed for it." She zipped her own hoodie. "Are you okay?"

"Me?" Brant sent her a wicked grin. "I'm hot."

Molly decided it was best not to comment on that.

He laughed.

They moved to one of the picnic tables, looking like the other young families. But they weren't. Brant was a temporary, substitute daddy. Herself? Molly honestly didn't know what her role was.

And she wouldn't think about it now.

While Brant, with Jax on his lap, attempted to get more of the spinach, zucchini, and quinoa mixture into the baby than on him, Molly picked at some grapes.

"You're not gonna share?" Brant asked. He held out a spoon covered in green goo. "I'll give you a taste of mine."

She chuckled. "I'll feed you a grape if you *don't* give me any of that."

His eyes on hers, Brant didn't see the small hand slap out. The spoon shot up, and green slime dripped down the side of his face.

Jax laughed out loud and reached for the jar in Brant's other hand.

"*Argh*. No you don't." One arm around the wiggly baby, Brant swiped the back of the hand holding the jar across his cheek.

Molly made a choked sound, and he glared at her.

"Don't."

She tried, really tried, to hold back the laughter.

"I'm warning you, Molly."

The laugh burst out of her, and Jax joined in.

Before she could get away, Brant swiped spinach down her nose. A drop plopped onto the table in front of her.

"I can't believe you did that."

"I did warn you."

"Yes, you did." Without thinking, she grabbed Jax's bottle, aimed it, and squeezed. Formula hit Brant square between the eyes.

Some of it splashed onto Jax, who squealed in delight, slapping his hands on the table.

"You want to play dirty, do you, Ms. Molly?"

The air changed, charged with heat and adult longings.

"I think we'd better get cleaned up and hit the road."

"Yes, Mom."

The second Brant strapped Jax in his seat, he started crying again.

"What's wrong, bud?"

"He doesn't want to be back there alone." Molly slid from the front seat and hopped into the back.

"What are you doing?" Brant stood, the car door hanging open.

"I'll ride back here for a while."

"And I'm what? The chauffeur?"

"Get in and drive."

He did.

As she played pat-a-cake with Jax, Brant met her eyes in the rearview mirror. "This is ridiculous."

"This is having a kid."

"I don't like it. I want you up here. With me."

Her heart smiled.

Twenty miles down the road, Jax's eyes fluttered shut and he gave in to sleep.

Molly, fretting about That Little White Dress, called Lettie.

"This is the fourth time you've called, Molly. How am I going to get my work done if you keep bothering me? The next time the phone rings, I'm not going to answer," she threatened.

"You can't do that! It might be a customer."

"Then get off the line," Lettie said, "so that customer can call!"

"Okay, okay." Molly hung up and brooded.

"Everything will be fine," Brant assured her.

"Easy for you to say."

When they turned onto the lane that led to Brant's family home, Molly stared in awe. It was like a Norman Rockwell scene. The two-story house sat at the end of a long, winding drive lined with pines. White fencing ran along the boundary. A large stone chimney dominated one end of the house, and behind it, Molly glimpsed the river.

Along with the beauty, though, or maybe because of it, nerves showed up.

A sideways glance at Brant did nothing to quell them.

Turning off the car, he looked at her, those oh-so-green eyes questioning.

"You okay?"

She placed a hand over her hammering heart. "I'm so nervous."

"Me too." He raised her hand to his lips. "I've brought a couple girls home before, but none that mattered." His gaze bored into hers. "You do."

"Brant—"

The front door opened, and an older version of the man beside her stepped out.

"What if he doesn't like me?"

"He will."

"Your mom?"

"She'll love you because…well, because how could anyone not?"

Her heart nearly stopped. He hadn't almost said—no, of course not. That would be a disaster. Love wasn't in the plans. For either of them.

"Come on, Mol. My dad doesn't bite."

"We'll see how you feel when I drag you to Savannah to meet mine."

Instantly, she wished she could bite off her tongue.

"I already met your dad, remember?"

"Oh. Yeah." She shrugged. "That was different."

"You're right. I was madder than a mosquito in a mannequin factory, and that didn't leave any room for nerves."

She didn't get a chance to fire back, because the second she stepped from the car, she found herself wrapped in a huge bear hug.

"You must be Molly."

Brant's father drew back and she inhaled, replacing most of the air he'd squeezed out of her. "Yes, sir."

"Sir? After all you've done for my family?" His eyes grew misty. "Call me Neal. Please."

"I don't know what Brant's told you, Neal, but I haven't done much."

"Nonsense. You stood by my boy here and helped him when he needed it most. Lainey told Penny and me about how you visited her at the hospital and listened, really listened, to her and how you stood up to that no-good jerk she got involved with. My wife and I thank you."

Brant hefted Jax from the back seat.

"Might as well just tell Dad he's welcome, Molly. You won't change his mind. Your reputation precedes you."

"You're welcome, Neal." She took Jax so Brant could round up the baby's things. "Believe me, spending time with this one was no hardship."

Jax raised his hands to her face, and Molly leaned in for a kiss. The baby giggled.

"He looks happy."

"He is, Dad, despite a pretty rocky detour. How's Mom?"

"Doing better, but I can't get her out of the house."

Penny Wylder was sitting in a recliner when they walked inside.

Brant's face lit up. "I've missed you, Mom." Dropping everything inside the door, he crossed the room in quick strides and leaned down to hug her.

She raised a shaky hand to pat his cheek. "Missed you, too." Her speech, slightly slurred, was slow but strong. She looked at Molly. "You must be the per... per...one who helped my son and daughter."

"If you mean the one lucky enough to enjoy this sweet baby, then that's me. I'm Molly."

Penny beamed at her. "Welcome, Molly."

"Want some help with your luggage, Son?" Neal asked.

"No. We'll bunk at my house."

Molly blinked. That was news. A myriad of emotions barreled through her.

The tips of Neal's ears reddened. "We don't, you

know, expect you to sleep in separate rooms. I mean, your mom and I understand—"

Now Molly blushed.

"I've got stuff to do there, Dad. I didn't expect to be gone more than a couple of days, so I need to take some things back with me."

"You're leaving." His mom spoke quietly.

"Not yet. We'll eat and catch up, then we'll be back in the morning."

"No. Not what I mean. You and your brothers..." Penny's hands moved restlessly in her lap. "Leaving Lake Delores."

Brant looked crestfallen. "Why don't you come, too, Mom? You and Dad."

"This is home," his father said.

"I understand that," Brant answered. "But this house is too big for you, and the boys and I need to do this."

"Understood, but we're not ready to take that step."

"Maybe," his mother said. "Maybe."

"Let's leave it for now," Neal said. "Look at our grandson, Penny."

The door flew open, and Tucker and Gaven bounded in. The brothers pounded each others' backs and exchanged greetings.

Tucker gave Molly a polite hello, but Gaven pulled her into a hug and gave her a welcoming kiss.

"Find your own lady, Bro," Brant growled.

"Maybe I have." He kept an arm around Molly.

"Behave yourself, or I'll take you out to the wood-shed," Neal warned.

Molly's eyes widened, and everyone laughed.

"Mol, this man can't hurt a fly. If one sneaks inside,

Mom has to deal with it," Brant explained. "There's no woodshed. Not because we didn't deserve one, but because Dad's a softie."

"Maybe I've changed," Neal said gruffly.

"And maybe those pigs in Misty Bottoms really can fly," Gaven said.

"Speaking of pigs, I'm hungry. What'd you bring?" Brant grabbed one of the bags Tucker had carried in.

"We stopped at Monk's Deli. Mom likes his soup, don't you, Mom?"

Penny smiled at her oldest son.

***

The evening flew by. Molly realized that even when her father had been with them, they'd never been as boisterous and free as Penny and Neal's family. She liked it, enjoyed the easy give-and-take, the teasing, the helping. This feeling of home.

Before she knew it, kisses and hugs had been doled out, and she, Jax, and Brant headed to his place. The night was dark, with barely a star in the sky. The moon, if it was up there, hid behind pillowed clouds. A whole new level of nerves set in, and a twitchy little dance started in her stomach. Yet she had to admit to curiosity about Brant's house. It would be interesting to see him in his own environment.

She'd chalked up the anxiety she felt all day to meeting his parents. That wasn't it. It was Brant himself. He'd become way too important and consumed far too much of her thoughts.

Even at work, he threw her off stride. He showed up every other day or so to take her to lunch, and by noon, she found herself watching the clock. Whenever he came, she argued that she should stay at the shop, but she never did. And when he didn't show, she dragged herself upstairs to eat a moody lunch.

She thought of her list, the one Brant seemed hell-bent on destroying. It had worked until now, because the items on it weren't arbitrary whims. When her dad left, her life had splintered, and she'd had absolutely no control over any of it. Neither had her mom.

Preston Stiles had called all the shots.

Molly had vowed she'd always have a plan, always be in control.

The plan had gotten her this far, but maybe it was time she set the list aside.

And didn't *that* open up possibilities.

Brant turned into a paved drive, and Molly fought to still her mind. It had been a long day, and she was tired. She stared through the windshield at the sprawling ranch home.

"Let me go in first and turn on some lights." Brant checked his rearview mirror. "The kid played pretty hard tonight. He's out cold. I'll set up his travel crib."

Molly watched him walk up the stairs and disappear inside. The man was irresistible, and she was in Lake Delores, Tennessee, spending the night alone with him.

Well, with him and Jax.

Why not set worries aside and simply enjoy?

Molly waited for the lights, then stepped inside, carrying the sleeping child. She couldn't hide the quick grin. The house's decor shouted man. Shouted Brant Wylder.

"I set Jax up in the front bedroom. Why don't you settle him in there?" Brant pointed.

She shook her head and held out the baby and carrier. "You do it. I'm busy."

"Doing what?"

She extended her arm, palm up. "Getting to know you through your house."

"Dust bunnies can't be held against me. I've been gone."

"Duly noted."

While he put the baby down, she wandered through his rooms. The walls were off-white, but everything else acknowledged his love of color. The sofa was a comfortable blue-and-green plaid, echoing the colors of a pedestal globe beside it. Black-and-white-striped drapes hung at the two windows. The coffee table had been made from hard-used salvage wood, and a side table consisted of two vintage suitcases propped one on top of the other.

Orange throw pillows had *Camaro* emblazoned on them, and, though Molly couldn't be positive, she suspected they'd been made from vintage car upholstery. A blue-and-yellow neon sign touting *OK Used Cars* hung on one wall.

The dining room was even better. A plank table rested on metal legs. And the chairs! One looked like a wooden throne, another was an office chair on casters, and a third a vinyl sixties style. All six were unique.

A battered metal desk hunkered down in one corner, with an interesting mix of items covering its top. A Corvette insignia, a bust of ET, and a framed and signed photo of Steve McQueen on a motorcycle hung out with souvenir cups holding paper clips and pens. A seriously weathered BankAmericard sign hung on the wall above it.

Again, Molly's mind went to the pickers on TV. Wouldn't they love to snoop around in here? The man liked things, his collection eclectic. She completely understood why the old service station had spoken to him. It was basically an extension of his house.

Now he had to pack up everything and move.

When Brant stepped into the room, Molly forgot everything else as he wrapped an arm around her waist and pulled her to him. When his lips touched hers, she couldn't remember a single reason why he wasn't the best thing that had ever happened to her.

Waking up with Brant was breathtaking. Warm and loose, they took a leisurely pleasure in each other's bodies, picking up where they'd left off in the early-morning hours. When she finally made it to the shower, Brant joined her beneath the warm spray, pulling her against his hard body to shampoo her hair with his big, gentle hands.

Jax, bless his little heart, slept just long enough for her rinse.

At his parents' house, Molly fixed breakfast, giving his dad a break and Brant time to chat with his folks. Scrambled eggs scattered the floor around Jax. Standing to clear the table, she said, "Why don't you and your dad take a field trip, check on things at the shop? See if your brothers are actually working or goofing off."

Brant met her eyes. "You sure?"

"Positive. Your mom and I can't wait to have the house to ourselves."

Penny, still in her nightgown and robe, smiled and nodded.

"How about I take Jax with Dad and me? About time he starts learning what guys really do."

Molly glanced sideways at Penny. "Do you believe that?"

Brant's mom laughed. "Three sons."

"Yeah, you'd be the expert."

While Brant packed up his diaper bag, Jax crawled around the room, pulling magazines off the coffee table and upending Penny's coffee cup.

"Good thing it's empty," she said.

Molly stacked the last plate in the dishwasher and made a shooing sound. "Go play."

"Okay, okay." Brant kissed his mom's forehead and grabbed Jax, stuffing his arms into his jacket.

Molly walked them to the door. "You boys have fun."

Brant leaned in to give her a kiss. "Thank you."

"You're welcome. Your dad needs some time away."

Gratitude filled Brant's eyes. "You're the best, Mol."

"I am, and don't you forget it."

The second they drove away, Penny said, "Don't need to stay. I'm okay."

Molly, who'd been watching out the window, took a couple of seconds before turning around. Brant's mom was a lot like him—that pride and fierce independence, mixed with the need to prove she had plenty of both.

She liked Penny. This stroke had brought her down, made her dependent, and scraped away quite a few layers of dignity.

Mentally, Molly rolled up her sleeves. Time to do what she could to restore some of that self-esteem.

Hands on her hips, she turned, shaking her head. "Men!"

Penny frowned. "What—?" She sighed, frustrated when the right words wouldn't come.

"They don't get it, do they? I can see Neal and the boys are taking care of you, of the essentials, but they're guys. They forget the important things." She crossed to Brant's mom and sat on the edge of her footstool. Taking Penny's hand, she smiled mischievously. "How about a spa day—just you and me?"

"Spa?"

"You'll have to help me, though."

"Can't." Penny held up a hand. "Too shaky."

"All I need from you is information. You have makeup?"

Penny nodded.

"Nail polish, files, hair brushes?"

Penny told her where everything was.

"Do you mind if I snoop around?"

"Help yourself," Penny said.

Before long, Molly had collected everything they needed. They started with mani-pedis and moved on to facials and makeovers. She fixed fancy little sandwiches for lunch and served tea from a set Penny told her was a wedding gift.

"Long time ago," she said.

"How many years have you and Neal been married?"

"Thirty-seven." She pointed at a framed photo. "Us."

Molly studied it. "You look so happy."

"Still are." The smile on the older woman's face transformed her. "Love. All you need."

Was it? Molly wondered.

Once lunch was finished, Molly said, "Let's get you out of that nightgown. What's your favorite outfit?"

Penny insisted on jewelry, too. "Might as well do it right," she managed.

Then they settled in to watch an old favorite, *Sleepless in Seattle*.

———

When Brant and his father walked in, a sleeping baby in tow, both stopped in their tracks.

"Penny?" Neal grinned ear to ear. "Look at you."

"Ready to go dancing?" she asked.

Instead of answering, he gathered her close, and the two swayed to music only they heard—the best kind of dance.

His eyes misty, he drew back to kiss her cheek. "You're beautiful."

She laughed like a young girl.

Molly felt Brant's arm around her waist. When she turned, he looked near tears.

"Brant?"

"I'm okay." His voice was gruff and deep. He drew her closer. The kiss was not the quick buss he'd given her earlier in front of his parents. This was a holy-cow, curl-her-toes kiss!

"Mom looks like Mom again."

"She's been in there all along," Molly whispered. Aloud, she said, "We've had a ball today."

"You picked a good one, Brant," Mom said. "Take care of her."

"She makes that pretty tough to do."

"That's why I like her." Penny grinned.

Neal sniffed the air. "What smells so good? Besides my pretty girl?"

"Scalloped potatoes. Ham," Penny answered.

"Really?" Neal's head whipped around to Molly. "She's been hungry for that, and I—" He trailed off.

"You had everything I needed, so in between our beauty sessions and a movie, I popped a casserole in the oven."

She thought Brant's dad really would cry this time. Instead, he hugged her. Hard. "Penny's right. You're a good one. A darned good one."

After dinner and playtime with Jax, Mrs. Wylder yawned and her eyes drooped.

"Think it's time for bed, honey. Why don't you tell the kids good night? We'll see them again in the morning."

Penny kissed Jax, then Molly and Brant both gave her a hug and a kiss in turn.

Neal walked them to the door. "Molly, I cannot thank you enough for today. You've made my sweetheart smile again."

"I enjoyed every single minute."

"Thanks for dinner, too. It was terrific." Then he turned to his son. "Brant, if you've got a lick of sense in that hard head of yours, you'll find a way to keep this one."

Brant looked toward Molly. "Gotcha, Dad."

The second they had Jax strapped in and their car doors closed, Molly said, "Take me shopping."

"What? Now?"

"Now."

"Oh, for the love of—"

"Your mother."

"Excuse me?"

"Your mom needs some things."

"Oh. Okay."

She read the doubt in his voice, but he drove her to the town's only mall.

"It's almost closing time, so you'll have to hurry."

"I can do that. Follow me and see to Jax. Oh, and keep your credit card handy," Molly said.

She scoured the stores and picked out some new nightgowns for Penny along with some easy-to-get-in-and-out-of clothes without buttons or zippers. "There's something about getting dressed that makes a person feel better, and your mom will appreciate being able to handle that on her own. On the days she wants to stay in bed or in her nightwear, she needs something feminine and pretty, something that reminds her she's a woman."

Brant stared at her so long, she grew uncomfortable.

"What?"

"We should have done this for Mom, yet none of us thought about it. I—I can't tell you how much I appreciate this."

"Your mother's a sweetheart."

"So are you." Shifting Jax to one side, Brant leaned in and kissed her, right there in the middle of the department store. And she let him, her knees going weak.

When his lips left hers, she played it light. "Then you won't mind if I add a bottle of perfume and some wicked smelling skin cream to her goodies."

"Not at all."

Thursday morning they arrived at his parents', loaded down with shopping bags, to find Tucker and Gaven there.

"What's all this?"

"A few things Molly—Ouch!" Brant glared at her. "You pinched me."

"Yes, I did." She smiled sweetly. "These are a few things *we* thought Penny might like."

"Right." Rubbing his arm, he moved to sit by his mother, still in her nightgown. He showed her a couple of the new outfits.

Penny cried and hugged her son. "Thank you. This will help so much." Over his head, she met Molly's gaze and mouthed another thank you.

Molly nodded, her throat too tight to speak.

"Let me at least pay for all this." Neal reached into his back pocket for his wallet.

She shook her head. "Brant got it. An early Mother's Day gift."

Molly whipped up some pancakes while Brant fried eggs. Tucker set the table, and Gaven started a pot of coffee and poured the orange juice.

"Too bad you can't stay longer, Molly," Gaven said. "I could get used to this."

"I can give you the recipe."

He laughed. "That's okay. How about one more day?"

"I need to get back to work. Lettie's covering for me, but I don't want to leave her too long."

"Go to work for us."

"That's not on her list," Brant muttered.

"List?" Tucker frowned. "What list?"

Molly smacked Brant on the back of his head.

He raised a hand to it. "Geez, you're violent today."

"Because you're a jerk."

Out of the corner of her eye, she caught the look that passed between Brant's brothers.

Neal and Penny chose that moment to come back into the room, Penny wearing a new outfit and with her hair neatly combed. A touch of lipstick added color to her face. Her smile said it all: she felt like a woman again.

While they ate, Penny said, "Too bad…" She stopped, then started over. "Too bad it's not warmer. You could take the boat out. Do a little motorboatin'."

Brant choked on his coffee. He pounded his chest, then swiped at the tears in his eyes. "What?"

His brothers laughed, and Molly turned red.

"Isn't that what you kids call it? Heard it in a country song."

"Yep." When Molly met his eyes, he winked. "That's what we call it."

Brant offered to do the dishes. He set the infant seat way back on the counter. "Okay, kid, let's show them how it's done."

Jax jabbered while Brant washed two dishes, then rinsed them. When he turned to put them in the drainer, the baby waved his arms. Brant leaned in and gave him a big, noisy kiss. Jax giggled. Two more dishes, more giggling and wiggling, and another kiss. Every time Brant turned, the baby, anticipating another kiss, grew louder, giggled harder, and had everyone laughing.

When he dropped the final fork in the drainer and the final kiss on Jax's cheek, Brant plucked him out of his seat, and together they bowed low.

"And that, family, is how you manage to wash dishes with a baby."

Penny smiled. "Lainey would be proud. I am."

"That means the world to me, Mom." He crossed the room with the baby in his arms and dropped a kiss on her cheek, not as loud as the ones he'd given Jax but with lots of heart.

Grabbing Molly's hand, he said, "Take a walk with me. Tucker and Gaven can keep an eye on the baby."

Jax, who'd been planted in the center of a spread blanket, banged a rattle on the floor and talked to himself. Drool dripped from his lower lip and soaked his bib, now a constant accessory.

"He won't sit there long, Tuck, so watch him."

"I will."

"Button up, Mol," Brant said as they stepped outside. "The temperature's dropped, and the breeze off the water's nasty."

Molly shivered, and he draped an arm around her.

In the backyard, he partially uncovered a boat. "My brothers and I practically grew up on this thing. We were either in the garage or on the water. Wish I could take you out today, but that's not going to happen." Even as he eyed the storm clouds, the first snowflake drifted down.

Molly squealed and held out a hand, then watched in wonder as the flakes melted on contact. "My first snow!" Sticking out her tongue, she caught a snowflake on the tip.

He laughed. "My Southern girl!"

He waited for her to call him out and did a mental fist pump when she didn't.

Chapter 24

"We should make it to Misty Bottoms just in time for Jax's doctor's appointment. You still up for going with me?"

The goodbyes had been difficult, and they'd been a little late leaving his folks' house.

She studied his face—those deep dimples, that sexy mouth, and those mind-blowing eyes. Maybe she should have *sucker* tattooed across her forehead, but she had indeed promised. "Absolutely."

"Great. While I've got you captive, there's another problem you might be able to help with."

"Oh?"

"I need to slap some paint on the shop walls, but I keep changing my mind about the office color. Since that's where we'll actually sit down with clients, it matters."

"Yes, it does." She chewed at her lip. "Do you have a special color, one that makes you happy?"

"Like your blue?"

"Actually, I had a tough time with that. I played with the idea of an all-white shop but worried that both the bride and my gowns would get lost. My next thought was pink, which seemed too shopworn."

"How'd you end up with that particular shade of blue?"

"I've always loved blue, but to be honest? When it came time to decide, all those little paint chips at Beck's made my head swim. I couldn't pull the trigger."

"Yet you did."

"With Beck's help. He asked if I had anything I really loved for its color. I said yes, the dress I had on, and that was that. He matched the paint to it."

"You picked your shop's color based on the dress you were wearing?"

She shrugged. "You asked."

"I did."

"So, Brant, what one thing do you love the color of?"

"Your eyes."

She raised a hand to her throat. "Brant—"

"You asked."

They reached the city limits and headed straight to the pediatrician's. Molly flipped down the sun visor and glanced at the happy baby. Poor little tyke had no idea what was in store.

Did Brant? Had he checked today's agenda? She'd Googled it, and it didn't look pretty.

After they signed in, Molly played with the baby while Brant sprawled in a chair, reading an article in *Sports Illustrated* about baseball's upcoming spring training.

Not five minutes later, the nurse called them back, and surprisingly, the doctor walked into the exam room right behind them.

"I'm Dr. Yancy." He held out a hand to Molly, then Brant. "You've got yourselves one cute baby, Mr. and Mrs. Wylder."

Brant cleared his throat. "We're not married."

This stopped the doctor for only a second. "The important thing is you're both here for your child."

"Jax isn't…" Brant glanced at Molly. "Help me."

Men. "Dr. Yancy, Brant's sister, the baby's mother, was injured in a car accident. She, uh, she—"

Brant nodded. "It's okay. Tell him."

"Why don't you?"

The doctor looked from one to the other.

"It's easier for you," Brant said.

"Oh, for—His sister's out of the hospital now, but she's in rehab for an alcohol problem. Brant's caring for his nephew while she's there. I'm just a friend who's helping out."

Brant frowned. What was with this "just a friend" thing? Of course she was a friend. Anybody could see that. But *just*? No, she wasn't *just* a friend. Nobody kissed her friend the way she kissed him! And he sure as heck had never kissed a friend the way he kissed *her*!

That conversation would wait till they were alone, though.

He compromised and slid a hand over hers, interlacing their fingers. Then, his eyes on hers, he raised her hand to his lips, kissed the palm.

The expression on her face was priceless.

Then those incomparable eyes darkened. *Oh yeah, there'll be hell to pay later.*

He grinned, actually looking forward to it.

The doctor broke into his thoughts. "That explains the situation very well, Miss…"

"Stiles. Molly Stiles. I own That Little White Dress."

"Ah, the wedding boutique. My sister's on the hunt for her perfect dress. I'll send her to see you."

"Please do. If the dress exists—and I'm certain it does—we'll find it."

"Wonderful. Now, let's see how this little fellow's doing." The doctor reached for Jax, who turned his head in to Molly's shoulder.

"It's okay, sweetie." She handed him to the doctor. "Geez, I feel like a Judas."

Dr. Yancy gave Jax a quick visual inspection, tapped his belly, and checked his soft spot and gums. "He's got a couple teeth ready to break through, but I guess you know that." He flicked the damp bib, and Jax, quick as any pickpocket, grabbed the doctor's stethoscope.

"Whoops." Yancy extricated it from the small fingers. "Sorry."

When Jax wrinkled his face, the first sign of coming tears, Molly whipped a rattle from the bag, handed it to him, and once again they had a smiling baby.

The doctor measured and weighed Jax. "He's on the upper end of the chart for his age. You're doing a great job."

"That's a relief." Brant ran a hand over his head. "Jax has had a lot of upheaval lately, and I've never taken care of a baby, so it's been touch and go. We started out at Annabelle's, then moved to a small rental. Now, well, we're moving again."

"Lem Gilmore's old place?"

Brant's mouth dropped open.

"Small town, Mr. Wylder."

Brant frowned. If Yancy knew that, why didn't he know he and Molly weren't married? Had the good doctor been fishing? Was he thinking about putting the moves on Molly? That teeny-tiny green monster raised its head and gave a not-so-quiet roar.

"Any problems at feeding time?"

"None," Brant said, "except that it seems to be a twenty-four-hour event."

The doctor grinned. "Give him more protein."

Handing the baby to Brant, Dr. Yancy said, "Time for the more unpleasant part of today's program. This one needs his DTP and PCV inoculations. The nurse will be in to take care of that and go over follow-up care."

"Inoculations?" Brant's eyes grew wild. "You mean shots?"

The doctor nodded, shook their hands, and walked out, his white lab coat swinging behind him.

The nurse, a big smile on her face and two syringes in hand, slipped in before the door had even closed.

"Who wants to hold him while we do this?"

Brant went paper-white.

―◦◦◦―

On the way home, Molly laced her fingers in her lap. Her chest hurt, and she couldn't breathe. Too close. She'd gotten too close, too emotionally invested.

She had to take a step back. Had to protect herself.

"Brant."

He glanced at her, then sent her a second, longer look. "What's wrong?"

She wet her lips.

"Molly?"

"I need to ask a favor."

"Anything."

"I need some time. To myself." She hesitated. "Time away from you."

"What?"

"I need—"

"I heard you. I thought you enjoyed yourself at my folks'."

"I love your family. This isn't about them."

"Then what is it about?"

He looked so hurt, so bewildered, she almost backed down. Almost. "I need to get my head straight."

"Have I done something? Are you mad?"

"No."

His jaw dropped. "Are you dumping me?"

"Am I—No!"

"Sure feels like it."

Her chest grew tighter, and she felt light-headed. "This isn't about you, Brant. It's about me. I need some time to think."

"To think."

"Yes."

"Will you ever be ready to take that next step, Molly? To trust a man? You need to stop thinking so much. You analyze everything, pick it to death. Stop peeking in corners for monsters that aren't there."

He pulled to the curb in front of her shop, walked to the back, and lifted her suitcase from the trunk. "There you go. While you're doing all that thinking, remember this. I'm not your father. Nor am I just another guy trying to sweet-talk you. I'm the guy who loves you."

Without another word, without giving her time to say anything, he got in his car and drove away.

He loves me? He loves me?

Earlier, she'd wondered why she should expect Brant to be any different from the other men in her life. Maybe this was that difference. He loved her.

She'd never been more confused in her life.

Chapter 25

BRANT TOSSED HIS PAPERBACK ONTO THE END TABLE. He couldn't concentrate. To say he was baffled was like saying the guy who'd led the race at Talladega Superspeedway and got knocked out ten feet from the checkered flag by some jerk he'd already lapped would be a little miffed.

He'd left work early. Not wanting to go home to an empty house, he'd swung by day care and picked up Jax.

His furniture had arrived two days ago, and he and the baby had moved into their new house. The living room and kitchen were pretty well put together, and both the crib and his bed were set up. The rest could wait.

He missed Molly.

He twisted the ring he'd inherited from his grandfather, the ring Grandma Wylder had given him on their wedding day. Like Grandpa, Brant never took it off. When he told Quinlyn he'd take the house, he'd imagined Molly helping him settle in. Staying over. Spending time here with him and Jax. The azaleas around the gazebo would bloom soon, and he wanted to share them with her. And there was the elephant in the room. He wanted to be with her; she obviously didn't want to be with him.

Maybe.

Then again, maybe the problem was that she wanted to be with him too much. Had she panicked? Felt threatened personally or professionally?

She had daddy issues, no doubt about that. He'd hoped her father would step up and take action after their lunch, and he still might. Preston had called her several times now just to chat, and that was a good sign. Was it her shop? Surely she understood he didn't expect her to give up her dreams for him?

He'd stayed away as she'd asked, but it was killing him.

He'd played by her rules, and he didn't like them. At all. Time to change the rules. He glanced at his John Wayne clock. Her shop would still be open.

Before he could even get up off the sofa, the phone rang. Molly!

He grabbed for it. "Hello?"

"Brant?"

"Lainey?"

"I'm going home tomorrow."

Jax crawled over to him and, using Brant's leg, pulled himself up, babbling a mile a minute.

"Is that my baby?"

Fighting the deepening depression, Brant held the phone by Jax. "Say hi to your mommy, kid."

He felt torn. He should be happy. He *was* happy. Hadn't he wanted his life back? Lainey had hinted during their last weekly visit that she'd be out soon. Even without that, he'd known his time with Jax was coming to an end. Mother and son belonged together, but the pain was so bad, he wondered if he was having a heart attack.

"Brant?"

"Yeah, I'm here."

"Tucker's picking me up. I'll have some last-minute

paperwork to take care of, so I'm not sure when we'll get there."

"You want to stay the night?"

"No. I want to go home. I want to see Mom and Dad."

"Understood. You've been in touch with Jason?"

"Yeah. I don't see that going anywhere, but we'll talk."

"I'll have Jax's things ready."

"Thanks. For everything." Her voice broke. "I can't even think about what would have happened without you. Once again, you pulled me through. I love you."

She hung up.

Without conscious thought, he hoisted Jax to his chest and held him tight. "I'm gonna miss you, champ."

He buried his face in the baby's soft hair and swore he actually heard his heart break when those soft little arms circled his neck.

"Let's get you packed, kid. Mommy's coming tomorrow."

Dinner and bath time were tough. Everything took on new meaning for Brant, knowing it was the last time — the last rubber-ducky play time, the last jar of ghastly green peas. Should he call Molly? No. She'd already said her goodbyes.

To both of them.

Normally he couldn't wait to put Jax to bed. Tonight he dreaded it. They played, rolling around the floor, chasing balls, and roughhousing with Lug Nut. Brant memorized every moment, tucking all of them away and taking way too many pictures.

His life, with Jax, had changed so much. Jax himself had changed. Two teeth had finally popped through, and he was crawling and pulling himself up on furniture.

Now everything would change again. Long after Jax fell asleep, Brant sat in the rocker, holding the baby close.

—∿∿—

Just after lunch the next day, a knock sounded on the door. Dread pooled in Brant's stomach, and he peeked out the window. Shoot, Jeremy! He'd forgotten all about him.

Throwing the door open, Brant said, "Hey, kid."

"I stopped by the shop, but you weren't there. I thought we were gonna paint the storage room today."

Brant was torn. He ought to send Jeremy home, but he really didn't want to be alone.

"You know what? I'm bushed. Why don't you grab a couple Cokes from the fridge, and we'll watch a game."

"Sure." Jeremy's gaze darted to the corner of the living room, where Brant had piled the bags and boxes holding Jax's things. Ebenezer, Jax's yellow rubber ducky, peeked out of a duffel.

Catching the speculative expression on the teen's face, Brant sighed. "Jax's mom is picking him up today."

"Today?"

"Yeah. I don't want to talk about it, okay?"

"Sure."

Brant dropped onto the sofa and powered on the TV. Scrolling through his saved list, he brought up an old football game. Jax squealed, and despite everything, Brant laughed.

"Hear that, Jeremy? The kid's got good taste."

While he and Jeremy yelled first encouragement, then sarcasm, at their teams, Jax scooted around maniacally in his walker, running into every single piece of furniture in the room. It was like watching a giant pinball machine as his new set of wheels bounced from sofa to coffee table to doorway and back to the sofa. With the hardwood floors, the kid could really move.

Lug Nut peeked out from his safe place beneath the dining-room table. Brant patted the sofa beside him, and the pup raced across the room, hurtling onto the sofa and plastering himself against Brant.

Jax squealed and headed toward them.

"You're a Wylder, Jax. You love your wheels, don't you? Won't be long before you'll be trading that in on a dirt bike or four-wheeler. We won't tell your mom, though, 'cause she'd worry herself silly."

As he watched the grinning baby, Brant remembered those first harrowing days and the desperation he'd felt. Hadn't he prayed for this day, looked forward to a return to his own life? To sleeping in…to uninterrupted sleepovers. Somewhere along the line, though, things had changed. He placed a hand over his heart. It hurt.

He should probably get cleaned up before his sister came.

"Will you keep an eye on the kid, Jeremy, while I catch a quick shower and shave?"

"Sure."

Halfway up the stairs, Brant heard his brother's Mustang pull in out front.

He retraced his steps and moved to the porch. The car door opened, and his stomach took a nosedive.

"Jeremy?"

"Yeah?"

"Think you'd better go, bud. See you tomorrow."

———

Kneeling on the floor, Molly was steaming an ivory lace train, her mind on Brant, when Jenni Beth swung through the door.

"Molly?"

"I'm back here. What brings you in?" Dressed in a black silk blouse, pencil skirt, and leather jacket with the cuffs turned up, Molly stepped from her office. Catching a glimpse of Jenni Beth's face, she stopped. "What's wrong?"

"Lainey's at Brant's."

"What? He didn't say anything about her being released."

"Could that be because you haven't spoken to him in days?" Jenni Beth sighed. "Jeremy called. He said he'd tried you, but you didn't answer. You didn't answer my calls, either."

Molly pulled out her cell. "Oh geez. I put it on mute." She felt sick.

"I know you're not seeing him right now, but my guess is that he could use a friend."

"Lettie's running an errand. I'll close up."

Jenni Beth laid a hand on Molly's arm. "I can handle this until she gets back."

"You sure?"

"Positive. Go!"

"Thank you!" Molly grabbed her keys and ran out the door.

———

When she pulled up in front of Brant's, Lainey was standing beside Tucker's Mustang with Jax on her hip.

Molly quietly got out of her car but stayed put, not wanting to interfere.

Brant opened the door for his sister. "Remember, you need to watch him close. He can cover the length of a football field in a minute-ten flat, I swear, and he's into everything. Aren't you, Jax?"

He held out his hand, and Jax grabbed a finger and pulled it into his mouth to gum it.

Jax met Brant's gaze, gabbing away in his baby gibberish.

"Oh, and I promised to make him a partner in a couple of years, so don't take him too far, okay? I figured that would be all right with you and Gaven, Tuck."

"You bet. Keep it in the family for another generation, at least."

Lainey threw herself into Brant's arms. "I love you!"

Jax squirmed in his mother's arms and, whimpering, reached out to Brant, whose face crumpled.

He pulled himself together quickly. "You're going home with Mommy and Uncle Tucker, big boy. You be good."

Molly stepped toward them. "Hey, I hear somebody's taking a trip." She kept her tone light.

"Yeah, and I'm driving the getaway car." Tucker looked at her. "Glad you came." He shot a look at his brother. "BT might need some company."

"I'll be fine," Brant muttered.

"I know that," Tucker said. "Hate to rush you, Lainey, but we'd better get going. It'll be dark before we're home."

Molly took Jax's face between her hands and kissed both his chubby cheeks.

He grinned at her and twined his fingers in her hair. "Babadada."

"I'll miss you, too, sweetheart," she whispered, her eyes filling with tears.

When she looked up from the baby, his uncle stood motionless, holding a yapping Lug Nut's collar.

Molly kissed Lainey's cheek. "Good luck, honey." Then she made the mistake of looking into Jax's innocent green eyes. "You be a good boy for Mama."

Sniffling and swiping away tears, she called herself every kind of a fool. Jax was one male she'd known from the start was temporary, yet she'd happily handed him her heart. "'Bye, Tuck. Lainey. Jax."

She started toward Brant. Behind her, the car door closed, and the Mustang's engine roared to life. As the car pulled onto the two-lane road, Molly reached Brant.

"I knew this day was coming, and Lainey gave me a heads-up last week, then called yesterday to let me know she'd be here today. Still, it hurts." He pulled her close and held her.

Neither spoke. There was nothing to say.

They sat on Brant's new front porch, both of them looking for all the world like survivors of some horrid disaster. Each held a rapidly warming Coke.

"I should mow the grass."

"It'll wait."

"Yeah." He twisted the soda can round and round. "Thanks for coming, Mol."

She patted his knee.

Those incredible green eyes, so much like Jax's, looked into hers. "Looks like I need to schedule another trip home soon."

"You're a good brother."

"Really? If I were a good brother, would she have been in this mess?"

Her voice sharp, Molly said, "Don't you dare."

"What?"

"Don't put her troubles on your back. You're not responsible for her actions or for her choices. We've talked about this."

On a deep sigh, he said, "We have. And I know my sister. She'll do right by Jax. But I sure am gonna miss that baby."

He chugged his Coke, then crushed the can. His gaze drifted over her. "You're all dressed up. Go back to work, Molly."

She wanted to stay, yet instinctively knew he needed some time alone.

"Go. Please."

She kissed his cheek. He turned his head and took it deeper, stoking it into a hot, fiery furnace.

Then he walked inside, the screen door slapping shut behind him.

Molly made all of a mile before she had to pull off the road to shed the tears she'd been holding back.

———

When the phone rang, Molly sat straight up in bed. According to her alarm clock, it was 1:31—*a.m.*

Heart pounding, she grabbed her cell. "Hello?"

"Molly?" His voice sounded husky, raw. "You sleeping?"

"No, I'm talking to you." It was a dark night, and she flicked on her bedside lamp.

"And I'm talking to the most beautiful woman I know."

"Ah. Have you been drinking, Brant?"

"No."

"Where are you?"

"Standing outside your door, hoping you'll let me in."

She threw back the covers and ran to the window. Bubbles leaped off the bed to scurry across the floor behind her. With shaky fingers, Molly drew back the curtain. Sure enough, Brant's Camaro was parked outside her building.

Tonight would be about sorrow and loss.

She grabbed a robe and slid into it. The mirror above her dresser threw her reflection back at her. *Ouch!* Talk about bedhead. "Give me a minute, and I'll be right down."

"Thank you. I don't want to be alone tonight."

Chapter 26

WORK HELPED MOLLY GET HER FEET UNDER HER. IT always did. Even though Brant had stayed the rest of the night, neither had broached the subject of them as a couple.

In fact, there'd been little talk…and that was okay.

They'd needed each other last night, and that was enough.

Her mind today, though, had been an absolute jumble, and she'd basically staggered through the day.

"Lettie, why don't you go home? Nobody's coming this late."

"You sure?"

"Absolutely. Thanks again for covering for me yesterday."

"Jenni Beth had everything under control."

"She always does."

After Lettie left, Molly straightened the last few things.

Five o'clock finally arrived. As she was turning the Open sign to Closed, Brant pulled up on his Harley.

Molly's mouth went dry.

He straddled the big motorcycle and removed his helmet. Dark glasses hid his fabulous eyes, but she knew they focused on her. Worn jeans and a black leather jacket completed the sexy, bad-boy look.

But Brant Wylder wasn't bad. Far from it. He was

good. Very, very good. And his life had been turned upside down—again.

He opened her door. "Can I come in?"

"Sure."

Brant took in her short, swingy, long-sleeved dress, the red-and-black print scarf, and the leather boots. He wandered over to a display case. Picking up a shoe, he ran a finger along it, then set it back down.

His silence had her on edge.

"I know the timing is off, with everything that's happened, and I know you asked for some space, but I need to know. Am I whistlin' up an empty riverbed?"

She frowned. "What are you talking about?"

"You and me, Mol. Is there a you and me?" He scrubbed a hand over his face. "Things have been pretty intense these last few weeks. I've been on overload, and you've been scrambling, too. Seems to me, though, we…"

Brant stopped pacing and leveled his gaze on her. "Guess what I'm trying to say is that I'll back off if that's what you want, but you need to tell me. Right out."

"You confuse me, Brant."

"Maybe that's a step in the right direction, sugar."

"You control. It's what you do."

"No, I don't."

"You do. Out of necessity. You're used to taking care of everyone—your sister, your mom and dad, even your brothers. To do that, you pick up the reins."

"I'm handing them over to you."

"What?"

"The reins. I'm settling you in the driver's seat. You're in control, sugar. You decide whether or not we take more time to see what this is between us."

"I—"

"It's not the list, Molly, not the timeline. So don't even hand me that."

She said nothing.

"You use that as your armor, but it's nothin' but smoke and mirrors. The truth? The reason you keep dragging out that list? You're afraid."

"What exactly am I afraid of, Mr. Know-it-all?"

"You're afraid of you. Me. Love."

She wanted to argue, but she couldn't. She had no ammunition.

Brant stood his ground. "Here's what I think. You don't trust me not to turn into your dad, not to cheat on you the way Keith did, so you've built a wall to defend yourself. To keep you safe. That list is your wall."

Eyes narrowing, he took a step closer. "Here's what I'm wondering." He leaned into her. "What are you gonna do when you hit thirty? Hmm? Make a new list? Think about it."

Without another word, he walked out, quietly closing the door behind him.

Molly stamped her foot. How dare he dump that on her, then walk away? She wanted to scream, to throw something.

Instead, she dropped onto her little blue love seat.

Bull's-eye.

He'd pierced her armor dead center.

Brant took a long ride to cool off. Molly had him so twisted up inside, he didn't know if he was coming or going. That visit to her shop? A dumb move.

But he couldn't get her out of his head, out of his system.

He had to know where they stood.

Except he still didn't, did he? He'd made that big speech, then stomped off. He'd had to. He'd been scared to death she'd tell him right out that they were over.

In the morning, he'd take the next step.

Now? Lug Nut was probably walking around cross-legged, waiting to be let out.

Time he headed home. To an empty house.

***

Brant was up early. Time for school.

Through Jeremy, he'd found out the high school had a career day planned for the following week and thought it might be interesting to do a session. Without Jax, he had a lot of hours to fill, and he could only spend so many of them at the shop.

While he shaved, his brain kicked into gear. He could show clips from the television programs featuring Wylder Rides along with shots of cars and bikes both during and after restoration. Heck, he might even take in some car parts for the kids to mess with.

The biggest incentive? According to Jeremy, Molly and her friends were on the agenda. He had another reason, one he wasn't sure the school would buy into, but he intended to put it out there and see if it would fly.

Nothing ventured…

Walking into the weathered brick building, Brant experienced an odd sense of nostalgia. He'd enjoyed high school. The three Wylder boys had all played football and basketball and worn the school colors. But by far, the best part of school was the girls.

The worst had been the time spent sweating it out in the principal's office. He and his brothers had usually managed to wriggle out of whatever they'd gotten into, but when they didn't and Mom was called, all hell had broken loose. That woman, as small as she was, could put a guy in his place with one hand tied behind her back, which made the situation with her now that much harder. But she was improving, and Molly had been good for her. She'd reminded his mom that life was still out there to be lived, had turned her from an invalid back into a woman…and however things went down between the two of them, he'd be forever thankful for that.

A quick stop at the office earned him a sticky pass to plaster to his T-shirt, directions to the guidance counselor's office, and more than one flirtatious glance.

Brant knocked at Mr. Woods's door.

"Come in." A fiftyish man stood behind his desk with his hand out. "Nice to meet you, Mr. Wylder. I've watched some of your programs and enjoyed them."

"Thanks. I'd have been in sooner, but I didn't know about your plans until Jeremy Stuckey mentioned them yesterday."

"Good boy, Jeremy."

"Yes, he is. He's been helping me and my brothers pull our new place together."

"He did the same for Deputy DeLuca," Woods said.

"Yeah. Sam's the one who recommended him. The kid's one heck of a hard worker."

"You mentioned on the phone you're interested in taking part in our career day. Let's talk about that."

Brant told him what he had in mind.

The counselor was ecstatic, both to have him participate and to include his message about the dangers of drinking and driving. "The kids can't hear that warning often enough. Someone like you has credibility. They'll listen to you."

"I hope so," Brant said. "You'll have a setup for video clips and a short slide show?"

"You bet." Woods rubbed his chin. "You bought Frank's old station."

"We did."

"Maybe you could include some of what you've had to do there, the building renovation. Some of our students will undoubtedly end up in that field."

"I'll be sure to touch on it."

Brant turned in his pass at the office and walked back to his car. He had some big plans and a lot to do. He wondered if his room would be close to Molly's. Maybe she'd be ready to talk to him by then. He grimaced. Shades of high school!

He hadn't given up on her yet.

He had one more phone call to make—and that might seal the deal, for better or worse.

Monday rolled around way too fast. Before Brant had his head wrapped around the ramifications of what he'd done, he found himself back at school.

The ladies of Magnolia Brides were there, too, and what a sight they were. He leaned against his open door and watched them walk down the hallway. The boys of Misty Bottoms High would never be the same.

It was Molly, though, who made *his* heart beat faster with that mass of dark curls, those big brown eyes, and a body that would put a Victoria's Secret model to shame. Today she wore a tailored black suit. Brant's fingers itched to undo those three buttons and unzip the pencil skirt, leaving her in nothing but those black stilettos and the simple strand of gold nestled in the jacket's V-neck.

A totally inappropriate thought. One that put a stupid grin on his face.

Reluctantly, he stepped back into his room.

After he finished setting up, he wandered over to help the women. They'd been assigned the Family and Consumer Science room. Geez, when and why had they stopped calling it Home Ec? Each of the gals had a station, and the kids would rotate through them.

Molly ignored him, while the other three welcomed him, because they really did need another set of hands, hands that could reach higher than theirs.

When they finished, Brant whistled. "Nice job, ladies."

And it was. They'd spent a lot of time preparing.

Tansy had brought some half-finished cakes to use during her decorating demonstrations. Cricket intended to do a show-and-tell on flower arranging, Jenni Beth would divulge some of the secrets to keeping a bride's special day organized, and Molly would not only explain the different types of wedding dresses but talk about the business side of her shop.

Brant worried that none of the guys would attend their session, but since they had to stay with their homeroom group for the day, they had no choice. Each time the bell rang, though, they poured out of the room, chatting a mile a minute.

Who knew? Some of these boys might very well follow in the ladies' footsteps. A baker, a florist, a boutique owner, and an events planner. Lots of talent there. And it didn't hurt one bit that it came in such exceptional packaging.

———∿∿∿———

The day went well, but it was a long one. Molly had forgotten the energy level of high-school students. As the last of them left the final presentation, her jaw dropped.

There, at the back of the room, sat her father.

Tansy, coming toward her, frowned. "What's wrong?" She turned, following Molly's gaze.

"I don't know." Her eyes met her father's. "Dad? Is everything okay?"

"Everything's perfect."

She tipped her head. "Why are you here?"

"I came to watch my favorite girl."

Tansy laid a hand on Molly's arm. "Do what you need to do. We'll come back in a few minutes and load our things—yours included, if you want. Go! Talk to him."

She was vaguely aware of Tansy, Cricket, and Jenni Beth slipping out a side door, but her feet felt leaden.

Her father moved to her, enveloping her in a bear hug. "You make me so proud, honey."

Molly's eyes filled. Wrapped in his familiar scent of mint and Old Spice, she couldn't remember how long it had been since he'd last hugged her, told her he was proud of her.

"I love you, little girl."

"What?"

"I love you, Molly, and I'm sorry I screwed up. Badly."

Her throat thick, she said, "I love you, too, Daddy."

Brant passed by the doorway with the quickest of glances, then disappeared around the corner.

Suspicion nagged at her. "Dad, how did you know I'd be here today?"

He hesitated.

"Brant?"

"He has your best interests at heart."

She made a noncommittal sound. "He keeps sticking his nose in my business."

"Maybe it's time someone did."

She shrugged.

"It's way past time we talked, past time for an honest, no-holds-barred discussion. I'd like to start by apologizing, sweetie, for all the missed moments, big and small." He gave her another quick squeeze. "You always seemed so independent. I didn't think you needed me."

"FYI? A girl always needs her dad."

"Understood. You done here, Molly?"

She nodded.

"Why don't I help you load your things into the car? Then maybe the two of us can go to Dairy Queen for a chocolate malt. Would you like that?"

That nearly broke the dam that held back her tears. He remembered her favorite treat.

"I'd like that very, very much."

―◆◆◆―

Over their malts, father and daughter had a heart-to-heart years in the making.

Molly swirled her straw through the thick malt. "Dad, I need to ask something I should have long ago."

"Why did I leave you and your mother?"

"Yes."

"I've been expecting that question for the last four-teen years." Leaning toward her, he reached across the table and took her hand. "Have you talked to your mother about this?"

"I tried. She gave vague nonanswers, so I quit asking. To be perfectly honest, I was afraid of what she might say…afraid I'd done or hadn't done something that drove you away."

"So Brant was right."

"He had no business telling you that."

"The man loves you."

"No, he doesn't. We—we had words."

She tried to pull her hand away, but her father held tight. "A big part of the reason for that fight was my fault, wasn't it?"

She couldn't answer, didn't know what to say.

"I'll take your silence for a *yes*. I can't tell you how sorry I am about that, little girl. Anything I can do?"

"No." The hurt rose. "I shut myself off, Dad. Refused to let him in."

"I wouldn't be too sure. If that were the case, you wouldn't be hurting now. I think Brant may have scaled those walls."

"Maybe."

"Well, I'll leave it for the two of you to deal with. I like Brant. He's not afraid to stand up for the people he loves." He paused, then said, "I left not because of anything you did or didn't do, but because your mother asked me to."

"Why?"

"Before I answer that, I want you to know we both agreed she'd do a better job raising you, that a girl needed her mother."

"I needed a father, too."

"Understood. And I let you down. That was unforgiveable."

"Didn't you want to spend time with me?"

He gave a mirthless laugh. "In the worst way. But your mother was pretty angry with me and thought it best I stay away for a while. Too much time passed, and by then you were angry with me, too. We drifted apart. My fault. I was the adult." He met her eyes. "I don't want any more lost years."

"Oh, Daddy." She blinked back tears. "I still don't understand, though, why Mom asked you to leave." Reading the hesitation in his eyes, she said, "I'm not thirteen anymore. I can handle whatever the answer is a lot better than I can deal with not knowing."

When he remained quiet, she prodded. "You promised honesty."

"I'd been married and divorced before I met your mother."

"You were married to somebody else?"

He nodded. "I didn't tell her. Not because I was ashamed of it or trying to hide it, but the timing never seemed right. Then things got rolling, and I decided to let sleeping dogs lie. That was a mistake. A big one."

Molly sat back in her chair, slipping her hand from her father's and breaking the connection. All these years, she'd assumed her dad had cheated or hadn't loved them enough or loved someone else more, or worse, she hadn't been the child he wanted.

But this? Never.

Her dad cleared his throat. "Your mother felt betrayed. I broke trust with her. When she asked me to leave, I did, figuring it would blow over and she'd let me come home. It didn't, and she didn't."

"Do I have any brothers or sisters?"

"No. Anne and I never had any children."

"Her name was Anne?"

"Anne Beacham."

Molly chewed her lower lip. "How long were you married?"

"Five years."

"More than just a weekend mistake."

"It was, and your mother couldn't forgive I'd kept it a secret, couldn't quit wondering what else I hid." He raised shattered eyes to hers.

Molly slid her hand into his.

"Your mom never remarried, and that breaks my heart. I want her to be happy."

"You never got married again, either."

He gave her a sad smile. "I still love your mother. Don't make the same mistake, sweetie. When you find the one you love, grab him and hang on."

Reverting to small talk, they finished their malts, then she kissed him goodbye and waved as he headed back to Savannah.

Brant had interfered again. Instead of being angry, though, she was grateful. Without him stepping in, she and her dad might never have gotten around to the truth.

Like a tongue plaguing a sore tooth, part of her brain refused to let go of her parents' strange, sad story. How could her mother have been so closed-minded? Why hadn't her dad told her about his ex-wife sooner?

It all came down to trust.

She had a lot to think about. Brant had accused her of not trusting. Maybe the apple hadn't fallen far from the tree.

Pulling behind her boutique to unload, Molly wrapped her arms around the wedding gowns she'd taken for display.

Hearing her, Lettie opened the back door. "How'd it go?"

"Wonderfully! Even the boys enjoyed it. The girls? Over the moon. My guess is there'll be lots of dreams about weddings tonight in Misty Bottoms."

"That's good, as long as they remember to head here for their dresses." Not one to beat around the bush, Lettie asked, "Brant there?"

"Across the hall from us, and he had those kids glued to his every word. Every boy there wanted to be him, and every girl there *wanted* him."

Lettie guffawed. "Something's put a little extra sparkle in those eyes of yours."

Molly hung two of the gowns, and then, a third bagged one in her hands, she dropped onto the love seat. "My dad came to our last presentation. Brant arranged it."

"I'm not surprised."

"No, me either." Molly sighed. "Dad took me for a malt afterward."

"Oh, honey." Lettie sat beside her and wrapped an arm around her shoulder. "I know how much that means to you."

"We had the talk we should have had years and years ago."

The huge weight she'd carried for so long slowly dissolved. Brant had walked out after their fight, but he hadn't quit caring. And wasn't that a wonderful thing?

She and Lettie sat quietly for a few minutes, then Molly asked, "How'd things go here?"

"Beautifully. I sold two nighties, a pair of shoes, one of those pretty little clips for the hair, and you have an appointment for a wedding gown."

"Not bad, Superwoman."

Chapter 27

BRANT HAD TOLD HER HE LOVED HER. TWICE.

Argh, and she'd been so stupid. So...so...closed-minded. Like her mother. She'd learned a lot from her talk with her dad: the value of being honest and up-front and the need for trust—that five-letter word Brant kept throwing out there.

Her parents hadn't been honest and open...nor had she. Not even with herself.

That would start today with a phone call to her mother, the hardest she'd ever made. Curled up on her sofa with Bubbles sprawled beside her, she picked up her cell.

Her mother answered on the first ring. "Hi, sweetie. I hadn't expected to hear from you tonight. How's my favorite daughter?"

"You mean your only daughter."

"Yes, that one."

"She's a little confused, Mom. Dad and I had a long talk today." Steeling herself, she shared the discussion with her mother.

Complete silence met her on the other end.

"Mom?"

"Everything he said was true. Will you hear my side of the story?"

"Please."

Her mother spilled it all, held nothing back. When she finished, she said, "I made two huge mistakes. The first was asking your father to leave. I compounded that by not telling you the truth, letting him shoulder the blame. The longer I waited, the more impossible it became to make things right—with him and with you. I made the same mistake he'd made, the one I destroyed our marriage over."

After a few quiet sniffles, her mother said, "I still love the man. I ruined three lives, didn't I?"

"You put a really big dent in mine, but the real damage was to you and Dad." She took a deep breath. "Have you ever thought about calling him, telling him how you feel?"

"Only every day, but it's too late."

"I don't think so. Promise me you'll call him."

"He won't talk to me, honey."

"You might be surprised. I have to go. There's something really important I need to do. And Mom, let me know what Dad says, okay?"

"I will. I love you, Molly."

"Love you, too."

Molly hung up more than a tad shaky. That had been rough.

She tossed her phone on the coffee table. Okay, so much for her parents' love life. Now for her own.

"He did say he loved me, Bubbles." She ran a hand over her cat's silky back. "But does he *still* love me? If he meant it, then yes. True love doesn't come and go that quickly."

Still, she bit her lip.

Molly drove to Wylder Rides.

The bay door was open, so she stuck her head inside. Brant stood in the middle of what looked like a giant metal jigsaw puzzle.

"What are those?"

"Some of our tools. I'm trying to organize them." Hands on his hips, he asked, "You want something?"

Oh, did she ever. Deciding not to tip her hand yet, she shrugged. "I was driving by and thought I'd stop."

"Why?"

Okay, this might be harder than she'd imagined. "Actually, I came to thank you."

"Thank me?"

"My dad and I had a long-postponed talk. I know you were behind that, so yes, thanks."

"No big deal."

"I disagree." She held up a U.S. Postal Service box. "This was outside."

"Toss it on the desk in my office."

"You don't want to open it now? See what it is?"

"It's probably the hardware for our rack. They forgot to send it with the other parts."

"Oh. See you later, then."

"Yeah."

She took one step into the office and faltered. There was no furniture yet, but he'd put up molding and a chair rail in a rich cream to match the top portion of the wall. And below the chair rail? Soft brown.

Tears welled in her eyes, eyes the same shade as the wall.

Brant came up behind her. His voice harsh, he said, "I followed your advice. Every morning, when I open that door, I'll see you here. Not sure that's such a good thing anymore."

She turned. "I don't know what to say."

"Don't say anything." He stared at her a long minute. "I need to get back to work."

She'd been dismissed.

Laying the box on the corner of the desk, she left.

Molly sat in her kitchen with a cup of tea, feeling sorry for herself. Outside, twilight deepened and streetlights came on. She'd done what she could.

Obviously, it hadn't been enough.

When she heard the pounding on her door, both she and Bubbles jumped. She raced down the stairs and opened the door to Brant. Since the evening had cooled, he'd worn his leather jacket. Something about it and those close-fitting jeans always made her heart hammer against her ribs.

Without invitation, he slid past her and headed upstairs. "My turn to stop by to say thanks. You'll never believe what was in that package today."

She held her breath.

"My tickets to the Falcons' games. Tyrone came through."

"How can that be?"

He laughed. "Gotcha."

Then he sobered. "Mol, when I opened that box and saw your list... You framed it and gave it to me."

"I did."

"Your last line of defense."

Molly breathed a sigh of relief. She'd known he would understand. By handing her list to him, she'd left herself totally vulnerable. It was the biggest risk she'd ever taken.

He took her hand in his. "Did I ever share my philosophy on marriage with you?"

"Marriage?" She could barely breathe. "No, you didn't."

"I'll do it now, then. As far as I'm concerned, marriage is a one-and-done deal. It's a forever commitment."

"I agree. Totally."

"Good. I've also discovered recently that the woman I marry must love babies."

"I do."

"I know." Staring into her eyes, he dropped to one knee right there in her hallway, her hand still in his. "I want you, Molly Stiles. I want us. I want to make a baby with you. Two or three or four babies. You decide. I love you, and I want to spend my life with you."

She stared at him, speechless.

"Come on, Molly. Tell me yes. Say you'll marry me. I'll never give you reason to doubt me, and I promise I'll stay with you forever…and then some."

"Oh, Brant, I love you."

"But will you marry me?"

"Yes. Absolutely, positively yes."

"Now, or do I have to wait three years?"

"Tonight, if that's what you want."

With a laugh, he stood, picked her up, and spun in a circle with her. "Every day won't be perfect."

"That would be pretty boring, wouldn't it?"

"I hadn't planned to do this tonight, Mol, so I don't have a ring for you." Removing his grandfather's, he held it up. "Grandma Wylder gave this to Grandpa on their wedding day. It was given and worn in love," he explained as he slipped it on her thumb, then folded her fingers around it. "Until I can get you another, this will have to do." As they kissed, Bubbles crept from around the corner to wind in and out of their legs.

"Even Bubbles approves," Molly murmured before pulling her soon-to-be-husband in for a long, hot kiss.

Chapter 28

THE ENTIRE TOWN OF MISTY BOTTOMS TURNED OUT FOR
Wylder Rides' grand opening. Sawyer Liddell, the sole
reporter for the local paper, snapped photos and inter-
viewed townspeople and visitors alike. The *Bottoms
Daily* would have a record sellout tomorrow.

Sawyer, who'd made his way to the Wylders for a
quick interview, said, "One more question."

A group had gathered to listen to the three as they
chatted with the reporter.

One of the girls in the crowd shouted, "Who are you
dating?"

"Yeah," another called out. "Tell us about your love
lives. Inquiring minds want to know."

"Not what I planned to ask," Sawyer said, "but apparently we have a lot of single females in Misty Bottoms
who'd like to know the answer to that question. Must be
hard fitting that in around your work."

Gaven shook his head. "The day I'm too busy for
a love life is the day I'm too busy!" He grinned at
the group and threw an arm around Brant. "This guy,
though? He's off the market, ladies."

"I am," Brant said, "and I couldn't be happier. That
makes it your turn, Tuck."

Tucker shook his head. "I'm happy for you, Bro, but
it's not for me. I'm a lone wolf, and I like it that way."

"Uh-oh. Them's fightin' words, big brother. You

just tossed a challenge in fate's face." Gaven pointed a finger at him. "She's out there now, rubbing her hands in glee, determined to prove you wrong." Turning back to the crowd, he said, "She's coming for him, isn't she?"

The women hooted and gave him the thumbs-up.

"Get real, Gav. You make your own fate," Tucker argued.

"We'll see, won't we?" Gaven grinned. "You've got the house, Tuck. Now all you need is a bride to carry over the threshold."

Sawyer laughed. "Thanks, guys."

"Be sure you include that part about Tuck in your article," Gaven prodded.

"You're so juvenile," Tucker said.

Molly smiled, then wandered through the crowd.

Frank was there, holding court, showing everyone around and pointing out the "new-fangled technology" the "boys" had added.

"You'd think he still owned the place," Lettie said.

"He'll always be welcome here," Molly said.

"We'll see. He's liable to wear out that welcome mat soon enough," Lettie predicted.

"I don't think so." She wrapped an arm around the older woman's waist, and together they strolled through the crowd. Tansy's beautiful cake, a replica of the shop, complete with the Mobil sign, the old-fashioned gas pumps, and Lug Nut, had been gushed over and was now being enjoyed by the townspeople.

Cricket and Jenni Beth had stuck with vintage for the decorations and used old oil and gas cans for vases. And the coup de grâce? A few of the Wylder Rides' celebrity clients had driven into town with motorcycles and cars the brothers had restored for them. They parked them around the lot, along with Lem Gilmore's partially restored El Camino and the as-yet-to-be-started barn-find Corvette.

Moonshine and Mint Julep, Darlene's dogs, wore black-and-white sweaters and looked like walking checkered flags. Dee-Ann and Kitty wandered around with huge smiles on their faces and refilled platters of sandwiches and appetizers from the diner.

Lainey, looking healthy and happy, had come with Jax and her parents. Penny barely needed her cane, and Neal never left her side. Molly spotted her mother and father, who'd started dating again, sitting on a bench outside the bay area.

Even Annabelle and Willow had come. Jeremy seemed to be having a tough time keeping his eyes off Annabelle's niece.

But the true stars of the day were the Wylder brothers themselves. An aura of sexy competence mixed with a take-charge attitude surrounded them. They were so much alike, yet little differences marked each as his own man.

Gaven was a flirt through and through. Molly felt sorry for the woman who fell for that one. He wore a cloak of carelessness, yet Molly knew how hard he worked and how deeply he cared for his family. She also knew he had magic hands when it came to cars. He wore his sun-streaked hair a tad longer than Brant's, and even though today was a big deal, he'd shown up in worn jeans, a Wylder Rides T-shirt, and black Converse sneakers. He played the bad-boy card to the hilt.

Tucker, the oldest, was an ex-Marine, and that about

said it all. His dark hair wasn't quite as high and tight as in the photos she'd seen of him when he'd been active, but it was a whole lot shorter than his brothers'. Unlike the others, he had his mother's brown eyes. The smartly creased khakis and black polo shirt showcased a hard body.

And then there was Brant. So responsible and steady, he'd put his heart and soul into making today happen. He took care of what was his, regardless of the cost. There was a toughness about him, but Molly had seen his vulnerable side, too, and knew it ran every bit as deep.

He looked so good today in his Sunday jeans and a long-sleeved white shirt. The cuffs were rolled up and showed a smattering of dark hair. She loved his hands and his strong arms. She loved even more that they'd hold her every night for the rest of her life as she fell asleep.

Feeling his gaze, Molly looked up into two pairs of green eyes.

With Jax riding his hip, Brant put an arm around Molly and drew her close.

Bachelors, babies, and forever love. Life didn't get any better.

About the Author

Lynnette Austin loves long rides with the top down and the country music cranked up, the Gulf of Mexico when a storm is brewing, and an iced coffee while she writes or reads in her local coffee shop. She divides her time between southwest Florida's beaches and Georgia's Blue Ridge Mountains. Having grown up in a small town, that's where her heart takes her, to those quirky small towns where everybody knows everybody...and all their business, for better or worse. Visit Lynnette at authorlynnetteaustin.com.

RESCUE ME

In this fresh, poignant series about rescue animals, every heart has a forever home.

By Debbie Burns, award-winning debut author

A New Leash on Love

Megan Anderson would do anything for the animals at her no-kill shelter—even go toe-to-toe with a handsome man who is in way over his head. Craig Williams didn't expect this fiery young woman to blaze into his life. But the more time they spend together, the more he realizes it's not just animals Megan is adept at saving—she could be the one to rescue his heart.

Sit, Stay, Love

For devoted no-kill shelter worker Kelsey Sutton, rehabbing a group of rescue dogs is a welcome challenge. Working with a sexy ex-military dog handler who needs some TLC himself? That's a whole different story…

For more Debbie Burns, visit:
sourcebooks.com

MAGNOLIA BRIDES

These women have marriage on their minds
and love in their hearts...and in this small
Georgia town, anything is possible.

By Lynnette Austin

The Best Laid Wedding Plans

When Jenni Beth Beaumont inherits
her family's beautiful antebellum home,
her dream of turning it into a wedding
destination feels closer than ever. But
former crush Cole Bryson plans to buy
and tear down the house. Good thing
Jenni will do whatever it takes to keep
her dream—and protect herself from
falling for Cole all over again.

Every Bride Has Her Day

Sam Montgomery thought he'd have
no trouble finding peace and quiet
in the small Georgia town where he
inherited a rundown house. Until his
effusively optimistic neighbor, Cricket
O'Malley, storms into his life—and
his heart.

Picture Perfect Wedding

Beck Elliot thought he'd never again see the woman who broke his heart. But when divorced single mom Tansy Calhoun moves back to Misty Bottoms to open a shop, she's impossible to avoid...and so are his old feelings.

"Lynnette Austin has made her mark on contemporary romance."

—Night Owl Reviews for Picture Perfect Wedding

For more Lynnette Austin, visit:
sourcebooks.com

ONE MORE MOMENT

Third in the Shaughnessy Brothers: Band on the Run series from *New York Times* and *USA Today* bestselling author Samantha Chase.

Charlotte Clark wants to save the world—one needy person at a time. When she meets a down-on-his-luck guy at her local coffee shop, she decides to help him get back on his feet. The only problem? He's Julian Grayson, drummer of the world-famous band Shaughnessy, and he isn't so much down on his luck as he is avoiding the spotlight.

It's obvious Charlotte has no idea who Julian is. He'll have to tell her…eventually. But things get complicated when Julian realizes Charlotte gives him what he hasn't felt in years: hope.

"Chase just gets better and better."

—Booklist for One More Promise

For more Samantha Chase, visit:
sourcebooks.com

UNTIL THERE WAS US

New York Times and USA Today bestselling author Samantha Chase continues her beloved Montgomery series.

Megan Montgomery has always been careful...except that one time she threw caution to the wind and hooked up with a sexy groomsman at her cousin's wedding. But that was two years ago. Why can't she stop thinking about Alex Rebat?

Alex has been living the good life. He loves his job, has a great circle of friends, and doesn't answer to anyone. But now that Megan's come back to town, Alex hopes he can convince her to take another chance on him...and on a future that can only be built together.

"A fun, flirty, sweet story filled with romance."

—Carly Phillips, New York Times bestselling author for I'll Be There

For more Samantha Chase, visit:
sourcebooks.com

Also by Lynnette Austin